DANGEROUS

(Secrets of a Closet Sleuth)

ADMISSIONS

By Jane O'Connor

Dangerous Admissions

DANGEROUS
(Secrets of a Closet Sleuth)
ADMISSIONS

JANE O'CONNOR

AVON

An Imprint of HarperCollinsPublishers

This is a work of fiction. Names, characters, places, and incidents are products of the author's imagination or are used fictitiously and are not to be construed as real. Any resemblance to actual events, locales, organizations, or persons, living or dead, is entirely coincidental.

HarperCollins books may be purchased for educational, business, or sales promotional use. For information please write: Special Markets Department, HarperCollins Publishers, 10 East 53rd Street, New York, NY 10022.

FIRST EDITION

Interior text designed by Diahann Sturge

Library of Congress Cataloging-in-Publication Data

O'Connor, Jane.
    Dangerous admissions : secrets of a closet sleuth / by Jane O'Connor.—1st. ed.
        p. cm.
    ISBN: 978-0-06-124086-7
    ISBN-10: 0-06-124086-9
    1. New York (N.Y.)—Fiction.   I. Title.

PS3615.C59D36 2007
813'.54—dc222   2006036991

07 08 09 10 11 JTC/RRD 10 9 8 7 6 5 4 3 2 1

For Jim,
my Irish guy

Acknowledgments

There were many people who suffered through the ridiculously long time it took me to write this manuscript. For their support and sharp criticism, I want to thank Penny Brandt, Nina Solomon, Sam Alfstad, and Gayle Dinerstein, as well as my agent, the Whack-a-Mole champ Doug Stewart, and his very perceptive assistant, Seth Fishman. Jim, Robby, and Teddy O'Connor not only were wonderful readers but also provided many of the best lines in the book, sometimes unwittingly.

Chapter 1

S.W.A.K. KILLER STRIKES AGAIN: PERV MURDERER STALKS UPPER WEST SIDE blared the headline of the *Post* lying on the front seat of the Jag.

Olivia Werner shuddered and fired up a Parliament. What a complete sicko, leaving lipstick kiss marks on his victims after slitting their throats. The only reason her parents had James chauffeuring her to school was because all the bodies had been found near Chaps. Olivia wasn't complaining: She got an extra half hour to sleep, and more importantly she could smoke. You could hardly do that anywhere in this city anymore.

Accelerating through a yellow light, the car shot across Fifth Avenue and into the transverse at 85th Street. She'd make it to school in time to catch Mr. Tut before some other senior having a panic attack got to him.

Last night her mother had barged into her room while Olivia was sewing. As soon as Olivia said, "No, Mom, I don't want to 'brainstorm' essay ideas now," her mother dropped her eager, helpful smile and went on a rant about the Princeton application being due in two weeks.

"Mom, please. Face it. I'm not going to get in."

Being a double legacy didn't mean squat, not with her SAT scores and not when four brainiacs in the class were applying early. One of them—William Van Voorhees III—was claiming to be African-American because his grandfather came from Capetown. But that was Chaps kids for you, working every angle.

Olivia wanted to go to the Fashion Institute of Technology. Mr. Tutwiler understood. In fact, he "applauded her sense of direction." Those were his exact words. "Fashion does matter," he agreed. "The way we dress is the face we present to the world. With the exception of clothes, so little about our appearance is of our own choosing."

If a man over eighty got it, how come her parents didn't? At Werner family conferences, her mom's standard reply was: "We didn't send Olivia to Chaps for thirteen years so she'd end up in the Garment District."

The car pulled to the curb at 103rd Street and Riverside Drive. Shouldering her backpack, Olivia hurried through the gates of Chapel School—Chaps—a glowering, turreted hulk the color of chewed gum. She banged on the front doors until the guard let her in.

It was eerily silent in the Great Hall, a massive space that soared thirty feet to a barrel-vaulted ceiling. But in another fifteen minutes black Town Cars would be lined up outside, two and three deep, and seven hundred Chapel School students would come swarming through the doors, Lower and Middle School kids in Chaps uniforms, Upper School kids in anything that marginally passed Dress Code.

Her dad had gone to Chaps, class of '76, and complained about how the school had "changed," which Olivia understood wasn't about Chaps being coed or the way kids dressed. It was some sort of nasty code word for the fact that now the high school was twenty-five percent minority kids on scholarship. It killed her parents that practically all of them were guaranteed a spot at the Ivy of their choice.

From the Great Hall she crossed over to a neighboring brownstone known as the Annex. No need to check the wall directory; Olivia knew exactly where to find A. Lawrence Tutwiler, Director of College Admissions.

He was a Chapel School institution, the college advisor since way before either Chaps or any of the Ivies had gone coed. In a cover story last spring, *New York Magazine* had crowned him King Tut because he carried so much weight with college admissions offices. A lot of kids hated him. He didn't care who your parents were or how much money they promised your first-choice college. He could spot an application essay written by a high-priced tutor from the opening sentence. Some shrink suddenly claimed you were ADD and needed to take the SATs untimed? Uh uh. Didn't fly with Tut. It was one of the reasons Olivia liked him so much: Tut cut through the bullshit, judged you fair and square for what you'd accomplished at Chaps, and he let colleges know it.

In the Annex reception area, the new headmaster was talking to a couple whose little girl was sitting on the sofa, a half-naked Barbie on her lap. Obviously here to tour the school. Kindergarten had been so great; it was senior year that sucked. Olivia had loved school when she was little, everything about it—the school bus, lunch in the cafeteria, class trips, even the heinous maroon uniform. Her teachers had loved every single one of her art projects. Some were still displayed in the Lower School hallways.

As Olivia took the stairs to Tut's office, she worked at a hangnail on her thumb until it started bleeding. The Princeton application was in her backpack, the only part still blank was the space for the personal essay. *Tell us about something meaningful to you,* it asked. *Surprise us. Pick a topic that only you can write about.*

"Your brother's in rehab," Lily G. had said. "Just say how you want to devote your life to crack babies or something."

"She's right," Lily B. agreed. "Calm down."

What the Lilys didn't know (and never would) was that lately the only way she could calm down and get to sleep was by masturbating. Coming always left her feeling peaceful, almost with a sense of well-being—it worked way better than the Ambien her mother was quick to offer. So how about "Teenage Girls Jerk Off, Too!" for her Princeton essay? Couldn't get more personal than that.

The door to Tut's office was shut, which probably meant he wasn't in. A floor below, she could hear the chirpy voice of the little girl, but on the other side of the office door, total silence like during an exam.

Sucking her bleeding cuticle, Olivia peeked through the little window in the door. Tut *was* there; she could make out the bulk of his head and shoulders through the wavy glass.

"Mr. Tut," she called tentatively. "It's Olivia. I hate to bother you, but I'm kind of desperate."

Tut was pretty deaf so Olivia rapped harder, then put her ear against the door. No, he wasn't on the phone. "Hey, Mr. Tut. You okay?" Olivia waited three beats before a tickle of concern made her turn the knob.

Mr. Tut, in a yellow bow tie and blazer, was sitting at his desk, facing her like some well-behaved first grader waiting for the teacher to say, "All right, class. Please open your books to page sixty-seven."

Olivia's eyes traveled from the mammoth pile of college brochures and course catalogues on his desk to an overturned glass. It lay next to a bunch of soggy pink message slips all wadded together, the ink running. It was then that Olivia's gaze shifted back to Mr. Tut himself.

Something was wrong. His body was slumped, and his head tilted back in a funny way. Olivia could see bristly white hairs on his neck, spots he'd missed shaving. His mouth was hanging open with dried spit caked in the corners. . . . And Tut's skin was waxy, a little blue. Like skim milk. Still, her brain didn't fully process what she was seeing until Olivia focused on Mr. Tut's eyes—cloudy and yellow and open way too wide.

It was then that Olivia started screaming.

KISS OF DEATH

The body of another woman was found early this morning, her throat slashed and her mouth covered with duct tape bearing a lipstick "kiss." A janitor discovered the fully clothed body in the alleyway at 133 West 111th Street. The victim appeared to be Hispanic, and the police estimate her age to be around thirty. There were no outward signs of sexual assault.

Detective Anthony Gemelli of the homicide division confirmed that the killing was linked to two other recent homicides in the neighborhood. He said, "There is no motive that we know of, nothing that we can piece together. We have no victim profile, nothing other than the way all three women were murdered."

On September 4th, just before midnight, Sharon Gates, 31, a film editor, was discovered dead in the basement laundry room of her apartment house at 100 West 109th Street.

Two weeks ago, the body of Ann Schwerdler, 22, a Barnard College senior, was found in the lobby at 188 West 101st Street.

Detective Gemelli said, "We urge all women, especially those living in the immediate vicinity, to take extra precautions and to be watchful."

The last time New York City was in the grip of a serial killer was 1976 when David "Son of Sam" Berkowitz began a thirteen-month reign of terror that left six people dead. Berkowitz, 54, is serving a life sentence at Sullivan Correctional Facility in Fallsburg, New York.

Chapter 2

A COP STOOD IN THE MIDDLE OF WEST END AVENUE, HIS ARM RAISED, blocking cars and taxis from turning onto the side street. As soon as Rannie Bookman rounded the corner, she saw why. An ambulance and two white-and-blue police cars were fanned out in front of Chaps.

A mental picture of Nate buried under a plaid comforter—"*Ma! Go away! I don't have class 'til ten!*"—stopped her from automatically switching into Frantic Mother Hyperdrive. Then the morning headlines made her suck in her breath. "What's going on?" she asked a throng of kids and teachers gathered on the sidewalk in spite of the drizzle.

A boy, with a wispy soul patch and a wool ski cap pulled low, shrugged. "Dunno. Just got here."

"If it's that S.W.A.K. pervert, I swear I'm transferring to Dalton," a blond girl announced to no one in particular.

Nate's English teacher, a large-boned, somewhat lugubrious woman, acknowledged Rannie with an anxious nod. "I keep asking, but the police won't tell us what's going on," Augusta Hollins said in her tremulous Southern drawl.

Lowering her umbrella, Rannie ("Rhymes with Annie," was her standard intro) took her place beside the much taller woman and attempted to peer over the crowd. Since losing her job at Simon and Schuster, she'd been working part-time at Chaps. In ten minutes she was due to conduct a tour.

Fired after ten years as Executive Managing Editor. A life-shattering experience made worse by the fact that the reason was an industry joke, gleefully reported in the pages of *Publishers Weekly*. Fifty thousand copies of a "pleather" collectors edition of the first Nancy Drew mystery, recalled and destroyed, all because of a single letter—one lower-case "l" missing from the last word in the gold-stamped title . . . a title that should have read *The Secret of the Old Clock*.

Heads had rolled, specifically the one belonging to the copyeditor responsible for the oversight as well as the one atop her much more highly paid shoulders. A perfectly timed excuse to downsize. Oh, she knew she was lucky—comparatively speaking. Money wasn't a pressing issue yet, not with decent severance, a rent-controlled apartment, no lavish tastes, and punctual child support payments. But she felt untethered, superfluous, a forty-three-year-old dangling participle.

Last night her ex-husband had called from San José, where he now lived, wondering why their daughter Alice, a junior at Yale, wasn't responding to any of his e-mails or phone calls. The short answer, of course, would have been, "Because you bolted nine years ago and she holds grudges." Instead, Rannie feigned ignorance and, in response to a casual inquiry about her day, said, "My day, Peter? First, I found out I didn't get a job at Random House, one that paid fifteen thousand dollars *less* than I was making before. Then, after seeing my pals on the unemployment line, a crazy on the subway got really shrill when I wouldn't share his baloney sandwich."

Peter laughed softly. "I hope that's not the best offer you've had lately."

Rannie made no reply.

"You need a break, Ran. . . . Come visit."

How many women, Rannie wondered, were propositioned by their former husband? Of course, she was as much to blame for the unresolved nature of their relationship, one which the New York State Courts had officially ended years ago.

During his last visit to New York, she'd wound up in Peter's hotel room. It wasn't the first time that what began as dinner between friendly enough exes left Rannie with a bad case of beard burn and, infinitely more humiliating, a hickey the size of Texas that she had to hide from her son and daughter. The simple fact was Rannie had no willpower when it came to sex. It had been the only problem-free area of her marriage. And, wouldn't you know it, post-divorce sex was even better—both comfortingly familiar as well as seductively forbidden.

Since their split, Rannie had indulged in a few flings . . . actually *many* flings. . . . Okay—*too* many flings. As for serious emotional entanglements, however, her policy was to lump them in the same category as reality TV shows, exercise machines, and butchered grammar . . . things to avoid at all cost.

A sudden stirring among the growing crowd pulled her back to the scene at hand.

"Oh, Lord!" Ms. Hollins's hand flew to her mouth.

"Holy fuck!" said the kid in the wool cap.

The Annex door had opened and a uniformed policeman emerged, followed by a stretcher maneuvered by a couple of Emergency Medical Technicians, beefy Hispanic guys who wheeled it to the waiting ambulance. Whoever was strapped onto the stretcher was under a white sheet.

"All right . . . move aside, everybody." The police officer by the squad car was cradling a cell phone under his neck while scribbling in a little steno pad.

The stretcher was hoisted into the back of the ambulance, something Rannie had seen often enough on cop shows, yet had never actually witnessed in real life. Then just as the back doors were about to shut, Rannie caught sight of an arm that fell from under the sheet, revealing a navy blazer sleeve, a stripe of Oxford-blue shirt cuff, and a hand with a gold signet ring on the pinkie finger.

Mr. Tutwiler, Rannie realized instantly.

Augusta Hollins did too and involuntarily clutched Rannie's arm. "Oh Lord, I was afraid of this!" There was a scolding, irritated edge to her words, as if she'd warned Mr. Tut many times about dying yet he'd gone ahead and done it anyway.

As the ambulance pulled away, Rannie felt tears suddenly spring to her eyes. She liked Mr. Tut enormously. So did both of her kids. Tut was elegant and courtly, a man of generous gestures who treated the Chaps tennis team to dinner after every game, win or lose. Just recently and most unexpectedly, she'd spent an hour in his office, looking at old photos and having her first taste of single malt scotch.

It was near the end of the school day. Rannie was shutting down her computer in her cube in the Annex. Tut passed by en route to his office and tipped an imaginary top hat Rannie's way. He was starting up the stairs then stopped.

"Didn't you tell me you'd gone to Yale?"

"I'm surprised you remember."

He tapped a manilla envelope under his other arm. "Care to see some photos of ancient Elis?"

Rannie followed Mr. Tutwiler as he proceeded slowly up the stairs, gripping the banister. There'd been whispering among the staff, *sotto voce* references to Tut "not being well," murmured with mournful shakes of the head—the implication, cancer. Some incurable kind.

But once Tut lowered his tall frame onto the cracked leather sofa in his office, the pinched, pained expression began to drain from his face, and as he handed over each photo to Rannie, he grew more animated, more relaxed. "The daughter of one of my college room-mates sent them. . . . Christ, I'm the only one still breathing."

There he was in an *a cappella* group, sitting in the grass on Old Campus, at the tables down at Mory's, and on the tennis team, "a lefty like Nate. I was a damned good player." He was damned good-looking too, she couldn't help noticing—lanky, dark-haired, and boyish, a little like a young Henry Fonda but with industrial strength eyebrows. Upon discovering that they'd both been in Davenport College and majored in English, Tut asked her to close the office door, then retrieved a whiskey bottle from the bottom drawer of his desk. Single malt scotch.

"Just 'a wee dram,' " Tut said, swiveling around in his chair to reach for a black lacquered tray on the window seat behind him. From a set of four glasses with the Chapel School crest in gold, he took two, poured a drink for each of them, and after clinking his glass against Rannie's, tilted back his whiskey.

"Dalwhinnie. Best there is. Don't let anyone tell you otherwise."

"I'm afraid it'll be wasted on me."

"It's very light, tastes almost as if there's a little honey in it. Try it."

Rannie did and smiled her approval, the warmth of the whiskey fanning out pleasantly inside her chest while she listened to Tut discourse on single malts; one distiller, he told her, was considered such a natural treasure, its stills were pictured on Scotland's ten-pound note. They chatted amiably for a while longer, Tut interested to learn about her work as a copy editor and pleased to share a mutual abhorrence of the overuse of "that."

Tut told her, "The first thing I used to write on the blackboard in Freshman English was: *That 'that' that that boy used wasn't neces-*

sary." Then he inquired how her daughter Alice was enjoying Yale, remarking that it was too bad Nathan wasn't interested in applying. "His tennis isn't good enough to get him recruited. But he's still a pretty strong candidate. . . . More important, Nathan's a *nice* boy." Tut pointed at Rannie's glass, which was still full, and obediently she took another sip. "I realize that may not sound like much of a compliment. But niceness is in short supply here, far too many entitled little shits at Chaps. There are some dangerous kids—I mean it. Get in their way and watch out." Tut took a healthy swallow of whiskey and looked over the rim of his glass to gauge her reaction.

Rannie couldn't have been more startled by the sudden turn in the conversation, startled both by Tut's outspokenness as well as his choice of words. Chaps kids. Obnoxious, entitled, selfish, thoughtless . . . okay, no argument. But "dangerous"? As in Columbine dangerous? Or maybe "dangerous," synonym for "reckless"—using drugs, driving drunk, having unprotected sex, that sort of thing? Or was Mr. Tut referring, however obliquely, to the notion that some grudge-carrying kid was out to get him? Both her kids said that Tut inspired "either/or" feelings: Kids were either die-hard fans or loathed him.

The scotch almost prompted her to ask which kids he meant, but before she could, Tut already appeared to be regretting his bluntness. With a curt nod of his head, read by Rannie as a clear signal that the subject was closed, he returned to lower-pitched emotional ground. He knew that Nate wanted to apply early to Stanford, and, although there were no obvious "flags" to wave, a Tut-ism meaning Nate wasn't ethnically desirable or a Westinghouse scholar, he concluded by saying, "Look, I'll put in a call. If Stanford is where he's set on going, well, we'll do what we can."

Rannie left Mr. Tutwiler's office eager to tell Nate that Tut had uttered the magic words, ones every Chaps senior hoped to hear. *We'll do what we can.* Translation: *I will personally talk to the powers that be at Stanford and, unless Nate gets a felony conviction between now and graduation, he may expect a nice, fat envelope in the mailbox.*

That had been no more than a week ago, and now Mr. Tutwiler was on his way to a hospital morgue. Rannie tried convincing herself it was only fitting that Mr. Tut died at Chaps. He'd spent most of his life at the school. Yet it bothered Rannie that his death was so public, such a spectacle.

Ms. Hollins looked stunned, one hand still pressed to her mouth, and remained standing in the rain, getting wetter. Rannie could feel Ms. Hollins trembling slightly, which Rannie interpreted as shock until she looked more closely at Ms. Hollins's face. She appeared angry, frightened, and, brusquely waving off Rannie's hand, hurried over to one of the cops.

A moment later the doors to the main building opened.

The scene greeting Rannie inside the Great Hall, as news spread, was pretty much what she expected. Weird crosscurrents of excitement, giddy shock, and even what appeared to be genuine sadness. There were typical high school histrionics with girls sobbing, "I can't believe he's gone!" while finding solace in the arms of the cuter boys. Other kids had an eye to the more immediate future, debating the odds of school closing.

"No way. If we're lucky, maybe no first period."

"You are so wrong. I'm heading to Mickey D's."

"Mickey D's? Whazzup?"

"Dude. You didn't hear?"

"Mr. Tut! He croaked! Right in his office!"

"No shit!" Then a pause. "Oh, man, I'm cooked . . . 'Good-bye, U. Penn. Hello, Penn State.'"

"Show some respect, man."

"The dude's not even cold."

Rannie listened to the boy catch more flack but he just shrugged it off, not bothering to work up a comeback.

When Rannie arrived in the Annex, Chaps's brand-new headmaster, Jem Marshall, was relocking the front door after the removal of Tut's body. He passed Rannie, shaking his head in grim bewilderment. Only a month on the job. . . . He certainly couldn't have expected that disposing of corpses would be among his responsibilities.

"Oh, Rannie, we knew this day would come! But still, it's so sad!" Mrs. MacSkellan approached. She was a shrunken arthritic lady with dyed jet-black hair, a gash of orange lipstick, and a tart tongue. Rannie was never quite sure exactly what Mrs. Mac's job was; but at Chaps, you name it, she took care of it.

From Mrs. MacSkellan Rannie learned the bare outlines of Mr. Tut's death. "He had on the same clothes he was wearing yesterday so it must have happened sometime last night. Olivia Werner found him about a half hour ago. . . . Poor man, cancer eating away at him. My sister—oh, I watched her suffer, too. Esophageal cancer. Not eighty pounds when she died." Mrs. Mac paused a moment as if mentally lingering on the image of her emaciated sister. "Yesterday was one of Mr. Tut's bad days. I could tell, not that he ever said anything. But he wasn't himself, he seemed so agitated and depressed. After his two-thirty with David Ross, his door was shut most of the day. . . ." Mrs. Mac dabbed at her eyes with a tissue held in painfully gnarled fingers, the nails painted the same lurid orange as her lips.

"Your tour's canceled, naturally," Mrs. Mac went on, "although the child's mother is still here and insists on talking to you."

They walked back to the Great Hall where Mrs. Mac gestured with a cock of her head to a tall blond, busy at a Blackberry. The woman looked both impatient and stylish in a black suit and stiletto sling-backs.

Last week alone, Rannie had taken twenty families on tours—soon she'd be able to make her way around Chaps blindfolded. Just the other day, she'd opened a letter of recommendation from the governor describing a four-year-old kindergarten candidate as "a fine young man of excellent character." The whole private school pressurefest . . . it was beyond nuts and, like so much else about living in Manhattan, both fascinated and repelled her.

Rannie found an umbrella stand and, ditching her freebie from the Clinique counter at Bloomingdales, she pushed thoughts of Mr. Tutwiler from her mind for the time being. Then she checked the name on the slip of paper in her purse.

"Mrs. Millstone, I'm Miranda Bookman." Rannie strode forward, extending a hand and a smile, and pretended not to notice the mascaraed eyes flick over her dismissively, registering everything—Rannie's dark, blunt-cut bob, minimal makeup and jewelry, just her father's wristwatch and a pair of silver stud earrings in the shape of commas, a fare-thee-well present from a colleague at S&S. For a moment Rannie considered opening her trench coat—no Burberry plaid lining but a size four, thank you very much—and twirling around so the woman could check out the brown ribbed turtleneck and corduroy trousers she was wearing. Rannie could practically hear the woman typecasting her, *Typical Upper West Sider.*

Though born and raised in the Midwest, Rannie supposed by now she did fit the stereotype. Never voted Republican; was a stalwart Zabar's shopper; and both her children would have been in public school if not for her ex-husband, a Chaps alum, and his mother, a moneyed Manhattan dowager who generously footed the bills.

"I'm so sorry your family happened to be here today."

"It was very upsetting for Phoebe. . . . Not that I didn't feel badly when I found out a teacher died."

Bad. You felt bad. If you have a defective sense of touch, then you feel badly. The copyeditor in Rannie held her tongue although the mistake hit her ear like a sour note.

"We heard this ungodly scream." From Mrs. Millstone's description, Rannie pieced together that the new headmaster had found Olivia in Tut's office.

"Phoebe—she's at Brick Church Nursery, fabulous place—well, we told Phoebe there'd just been a little accident. Our nanny came right away because my husband, he had to leave and..." The woman stopped herself. "I'm babbling. I know. But Chapel is our first choice. My husband and I are both committed to coeducation for our daughter."

Rannie nodded solemnly. It amused her how many times she'd heard these words from *uber*-Wasp parents, always uttered with fervor, the way other people might say that they were committed to gun control legislation or famine relief. It made Rannie secretly giggle, even though she knew that for Old Money New Yorkers, sending children to a coed school instead of Brearley or St. Bernard's was akin to wearing loud cufflinks or patent leather after Labor Day. Simply Not Done.

Promising to reschedule a tour and interview ASAP, she bade adieu to Mrs. Millstone, who departed, stilettos reverberating on the stone floor, leaving a contrail of perfume in her wake. Rannie shook her head in wonderment at the workings of the viciously competitive, only-in-Manhattan merry-go-round ... parents who were ready to kill to get their kid in to Chaps, Chaps kids who were ready to kill to get into Harvard.

➤ CHAPEL SCHOOL ◆

For more than one hundred and fifty years, Chapel School has followed its motto of Virtutis per Laborum *("Virtue through work"). The school first opened its doors as a charity institution for orphaned boys of "pious mien and keen intellect" whose fathers had died on the battlefields at Gettysburg, Chancellorsville, and Fredericksburg. By 1920 the school no longer boarded students and expanded enrollment to two hundred and fifty students. In 1980, the school ended its affiliation with the Episcopal Church and admitted girls.*

The first graduating class of five students all continued their education at Columbia College. From among last year's seniors, five again are attending Columbia. In addition, two-thirds of the class are enrolled at the following institutions: Amherst, Brown, Cornell, Dartmouth, Duke, Harvard, Haverford, Middlebury, Princeton, Stanford, University of Chicago, University of Michigan, University of Pennsylvania, Vassar, Wellesley, Wesleyan, Williams, and Yale.

As do all independent schools, Chapel School depends on tuition, income from its endowment, and annual giving for revenue. The four-acre campus is far larger than that of any other independent school in Manhattan. It is with the help of generous donors that Chapel School is able to maintain its exceptional facilities, attract and keep the finest teachers, and offer students an unparalleled education. For further information on donations, please contact:

Chapel School Development Office
349 West 103rd Street
New York, New York 10025

Chapter 3

Still Tuesday morning

RANNIE REMAINED IN THE GREAT HALL WHILE JEM MARSHALL BRISKLY
marched stragglers toward the staircase and classes. The headmaster's demeanor was stiff—ramrod-straight posture and blond
hair that looked parted by command—but perhaps he'd loosen
up given time, or perhaps the fact that he was barely past forty
made him mistake a certain stuffiness for gravitas. At an evening
assembly a week ago, he'd spoken about himself and his hopes for
the school.

Right after college he had come East, he told the audience, working his way up the ladder of school administration. "Growing up
in California, New York was always my dream," he stated, Rannie
mentally wincing. . . . New York hadn't "grown up" in California,
he had.

"I always hoped one day to head a school like Chaps, a place
with a long, illustrious history and living legends like Lawrence
Tutwiler." Jem Marshall had turned toward Mr. Tut who, sitting
onstage with the rest of the faculty, acknowledged the compliment
with a nod.

"So I ask you. How lucky can a man get? I am doing what I always wanted, exactly where I always wanted." Then he pinched himself to the amusement of the parents.

Watching him now, Rannie couldn't help thinking it was a shame his stewardship was starting off on such a depressing note. Then, just as she was retrieving her Clinique freebie from the umbrella stand, the double espresso drunk en route to school hit full force, and, no, she decided she couldn't wait till she got home.

A single stall unisex bathroom was tucked in the corner of the Great Hall. Rannie ducked in and as she locked the door, a wave of low-level depression rolled over her. She couldn't shake the vision of Mr. Tutwiler carried out so unceremoniously from Chaps. At the end of the day, did Mr. Tut consider the unswerving path he'd chosen satisfying, fulfilling? She hoped so.

The other night in the middle of dinner, Rannie surprised herself by announcing to Nate, "I think I peaked in high school."

"Ma, come on. What am I supposed to say ... 'Sucks to be you?' "

"You're right. Dumb remark."

"Only 127 days left 'til graduation," someone had written in marker on the stall door. *"Pray for snow days,"* was scribbled right below, and underneath that, someone else had scrawled, *"Or mono."*

High school—most people rated the experience somewhere below unanaesthetized dental work, something you survived, often just barely. But at Shaker Heights High School—simply Shaker to Clevelanders—she had been happy in an uncomplicated way that she'd taken completely for granted, where failing at anything or, at least, anything that mattered to her, seemed unthinkable. Senior year she scored an 800 on the SAT verbal *and* had a multiple orgasm. Yale wanted her; so did lots of cute shaggy-haired guys in flannel shirts who ended up at places like Oberlin or Bard and whom she never saw again. She was her father's pride and joy, his favorite of the three girls. Her future was full of nothing but great big, blinking-neon "yeses." The minute she graduated, she planned to live in New York, work at a publishing company—with a name like Bookman, surely that was destiny calling—and discover beautiful heart-breaking first novels.

Starting as a junior copyeditor at Farrar, Straus wasn't quite the same as landing an editorial position, but it was a bad economy and a way to get her foot in the door. Peter Lorimer, an aspiring writer, turned out to have no soul-shattering novel in him, although she met him at a book party for some other guy's brilliant publishing debut. . . . Four months later she was pregnant with Alice. My, how quickly reality had started sinking its teeth in.

Someone tugged on the locked door, jolting Rannie back to the business at hand.

"Oops, sorry," said a teenaged girl's voice. "Didn't know anyone was in there."

"I'll be out in a sec."

A moment later, she unbolted the bathroom door and found herself face-to-face with Olivia Werner. Actually more nose-to-chin. In platform-soled combat boots, Olivia, a tall girl to begin with, now loomed over her.

"Ms. Bookman!" Olivia clomped aside a step or two to let Rannie pass. Raccoon rings of smudged mascara were under her red eyes. Olivia's nose was red, too, and running.

"Oh, sweetie. I heard you found Mr. Tut. I'm so sorry."

She'd known Olivia since kindergarten and always had a soft spot for her. Olivia and Nate weren't close friends, yet unlike most of the "lifers," Olivia always smiled and waved whenever she passed Rannie in the halls at Chaps. Rannie opened her arms and Olivia wilted in them, sniffling and breathing raggedly. "It was awful." Olivia's voice was muffled, hunched as she was over Rannie, undoubtedly smearing blotches of eye makeup onto her trench coat. And just back from the cleaners. Oh well.

"Poor Mr. Tut." Olivia pulled back. "He—he was just sitting at his desk . . . staring. . . . It was like at first I didn't even realize he was dead." Olivia paused and shuddered. "I never saw anybody dead before."

Rannie stroked Olivia's bangs off her forehead. A heart attack could hit suddenly and fatally, of that Rannie was well aware after witnessing her own father seize up while reading the *Cleveland Plain Dealer* almost fifteen years ago. He'd flung himself half out of a Barcalounger as if trying to escape a tidal wave of pain. There had been no mistaking, not for an instant, the fact he was dead, and it had taken her a long time to push the memory of his contorted face and body into a recessed corner of her mind.

Rannie cupped Olivia's chin in her hand. "Why don't we sit for a minute? You look a little shaky." Rannie deposited Olivia on a bench and, fishing in her purse, handed her a Kleenex. Olivia blew her nose hard, the sound echoing in the empty hall.

"Mr. Marshall heard me screaming. He brought me downstairs and made me sit on the sofa with my head between my legs. . . ." Olivia let out a raspy sigh and stroked her skirt, a shaggy orange number that looked like a rug remnant from the 1970s.

From her report of events, the ambulance had arrived at Chaps quickly. So had the police. And while Mr. Marshall was letting the stretcher into the Annex, Olivia had fled to the boardroom. "I knew I'd freak if I saw them bringing Mr. T. down."

In the boardroom, a police officer had come to question her.

"She kept going, 'Are you sure you didn't disturb anything? How did you know he was dead? Did you feel his pulse?' I mean, no! I definitely did not feel his pulse."

"The police have to ask questions whenever somebody dies

alone." Rannie squeezed Olivia's hand. Her nails were bitten pain-fully low. "It doesn't mean anything," although it suddenly crossed Rannie's mind, recalling Mrs. Mac's comment about Tut's increas-ing pain and low spirits, to wonder whether the police suspected suicide.

Olivia nodded and shredded the Kleenex, blowing through her lips. "He was a cool old guy. He liked Stella McCartney."

"Who?"

"The dress designer. Paul McCartney's daughter. Mr. Tut knows I'm into fashion. . . . I showed him some of her stuff in *Vogue*."

That made Rannie smile, the picture of natty, bow-tied Mr. Tut-wiler and Olivia—in some cockamamie getup—sitting in his office, studying fashion magazines together. He *was* a cool old guy.

Olivia sat up a little straighter and attempted a soggy smile. Even with a runny nose and an unflattering choppy haircut, she was a beautiful girl, far more than just conventionally pretty, with full, pouty lips, a honey-toned complexion and wide-set eyes the color of amber. Rannie's hunch was Nate had a crush on her, not that he'd ever admitted as much.

"Lookit. Thanks for sitting with me. I feel better." She nodded, as if to convince herself, and rose. "I'm gonna go home now."

"Me too."

The rain had stopped although the slate-gray sky was still low and heavy. At West End Avenue, a cab saw Olivia's waving hand and was slowing to a stop when the girl turned uncertainly to Rannie. "Listen, would it be okay if we maybe stopped and got coffee? If you have time, that is. I mean, you probably don't. You probably have somewhere to go. So it's really okay if you can't."

"No, no. Sure I can. . . . I have plenty of time," Rannie said, oddly flattered.

Five minutes later, Olivia hobbling unsteadily atop her boots, they reached Rannie's neighborhood Starbucks. Over the past few months, she'd clocked a lot of hours here, bringing along freelance copyediting work. One manuscript had to be returned to the publisher with apologies, its pages neatly blue-penciled but stained cappuccino brown. They settled in armchairs on either side of a crumb-covered table, a latte for Rannie, some caramel-mocha concoction and sticky bun for Olivia. At the table next to them, a baby sat strapped in a stroller happily gumming biscotti while his mother was anxiously reading about the latest S.W.A.K. murder.

"Carlotta's not in 'til later. I guess I'm being a baby. But I don't want to be home alone."

Home, Rannie remembered from playdate pickups years ago, was a beautiful townhouse off Madison Avenue in the 70s.

Olivia peeled off a strip of sticky bun and began nibbling at it. "Mr. Tut'd always get up at Christmas Assembly in this dorky Santa hat and say the same thing every year, about how his hearing was bad so everybody had to sing extra loud. It was sweet." Olivia seemed to space out for a second, blinking. "You know, Tut was like the only one at Chaps who tried to stay in touch with my brother after—well, you know—after the whole mess. . . ." Olivia shrugged. "Tut wanted to be Grant's friend."

Rannie nodded. Olivia's brother had been in the same grade as Rannie's daughter, Alice. In fact, Alice had harbored a long-term crush on him, one that fortunately had gone unrequited. Though smart and handsome, Grant Werner was hot-headed, way too quick with his fists. There was a recklessness about him that seemed glamorous to other kids and worrisome to parents. He was the kind of boy who never turned down a dare. At some point in high school, he'd become seriously mixed up with drugs. And in the spring of Grant's senior year, Tut caught him selling cocaine to another boy. Tut ended up with three broken ribs courtesy of Grant. Both kids were expelled. No graduation for Grant, no Princeton. Still, he was lucky: He'd avoided jail solely because Tut refused to press charges.

"I hope Grant's doing well," was all Rannie said.

Olivia nodded and tore off another strip of her bun.

"He is. He's been living at this place, Windward, for over a year. It's in New Haven, and he's got a job at Barnes and Noble. He looks great—I saw him last weekend." Olivia's hand suddenly flew to her mouth. "Forget I said that. *Please.* My parents don't know he came in. Grant'll kill me if they find out." Then she pointed to the rest of her bun and gave Rannie a questioning look, but Rannie shook her head. Instead, she raised her coffee cup and touched Olivia's.

"To Mr. Tutwiler," Rannie said. "A gentleman, a friend . . ."

". . . And a cool guy," Olivia added before draining the last of her drink.

After they gathered their belongings Rannie put Olivia in a cab. Just before it took off down Broadway, Olivia rolled down the window and thanked Rannie "for playing mom. You made me feel like a gazillion times better."

Rannie smiled and waved. Funny how being a good parent was so easy when you were dealing with someone else's child.

Voice messages on Olivia's cell while at Starbucks

Olivia, Omigod! Where are you? Pick up!!! It's me, Lily. Lily's here too. Omigod, you found Tut. Was it gross? Is it like on tv? Call toute suite!!

Sweetie. School called. How awful for you. Wish I could get home but tied up in meetings all day. Call my cell if you need me. Also maybe try and schedule a double session with Dr. Ehrenburg . . . Ambien in my night table if you need it. Kisses.

Me again! You are famous! Everybody is talking about you. That cherry eleventh grader, Henry B., just came up and goes, "So is Olivia okay? Is she around?" Oh, is he ripe for the picking! He is loving you . . . Call! Call! Call! Lily and me are thinking of hitting Takashimaya after school. You in?

Olivia, Daddy just called from Quito. Told him what happened he sends love and also mentioned you should consider using this experience for your Princeton essay. . . . Your first brush with death. Think about it.

Chapter 4

NATE TOOK ANOTHER BITE OF CEREAL AND STARED AT OLIVIA, TWO ROWS in front of him in the photo in the *Chapel Courier.* The first issue of the school paper always ran a photo of the lifers on the playing field in their new lifer jackets. There were twenty-five lifers this year, a lot considering there were only a little over a hundred kids in the whole grade. *You're Looking at a Total of 325 Years at Chaps*, the caption said. Scary thought.

Lifer jackets were nothing more than standard issue navy blue windbreakers, the school name and crest planted right over your heart. Fairly cheesy looking but everybody—at least, guys—wore them because at parties it impressed girls from Brearley and Chapin and Spence who were harder up than girls at a coed school like Chaps.

In the picture, Olivia's hand partly covered her face, brushing away a strand of wind-blown hair. She haunted him. There was no other way to describe it.

Olivia was the only girl he ever thought about when he jerked off, a Kleenex still floating in the toilet bowl was smeared with the sticky evidence of his obsession. He'd thrown away all his porn magazines; he never logged on to *HotPussy.com* anymore. At a school clothes swap, he'd taken one of her tee shirts, now stashed in the bottom drawer of his dresser. He made some lame excuse how it was for his sister when Lily B. caught him with it and said, "Hell-o? That's a girl's tee shirt." The tee shirt had a V-neck and when Olivia had worn it, he could see the valley between her tits where a gold Elvis lightning bolt hung from a thin chain. *TCB* it said. *Taking care of business.* If he could touch that place between her tits, he'd give back a hundred points on his SAT scores. Maybe a hundred and fifty.

Nate had hoped a summer away would loosen her hold on him.

At Outward Bound, he'd hooked up for the whole three weeks with a cool girl from Colorado. But then the week before school started, there Olivia was at a party, and it was like being zapped by lightning from that lightning bolt of hers. Her hair was chopped off, and her nails were bitten down so low the tips of her fingers looked like raw meat. Didn't matter, all she had to do was give him a hug and say, "Hey, Nate." Her voice had a crack in it, like she had permanent laryngitis or something. He loved the sound of it. And her smile was a little off-center. Her smile—it drove him nuts. . . . Shit, he was getting hard again.

While the stereo in the living room played The Clash, Nate finished his second bowl of Fruit Loops and glanced at the article in the school paper. His mom had stuck on a Post-it saying, "*Read this.*"

CHAPSCHATTER BY BEN GORDON, 12TH GRADE

Your roving reporter took advantage of a chance run-in at the cafeteria to speak to our new headmaster. (Sorry, Mr. Marshall. Let me know if the ketchup stains don't come out!)

Nate skimmed the interview written by his friend Ben. Typical stuff about where Mr. Marshall grew up, what schools he'd worked at before. It was only when he got to the end that he understood why his mom had flagged it.

> CC: Thank you for your time, Mr. Marshall. Just one last question. I'm a senior, so I have to ask. Where did you go to college?
>
> JEM: I graduated from Stanford. And thank you for choosing to interview me.

Okay, the Stanford connection, although it was depressing to think Marshall had gone there. Nate rarely noticed the way people moved. They walked. They sat. They did whatever. But this guy Marshall. . . . It was like he had never quite gotten the hang of how his arms and legs worked. . . . Or maybe he was scared they had a life of their own and might break out in some weird spazzy dance like Steve Martin on old reruns of "Saturday Night Live."

Nonetheless, Stanford had seemed cool when he visited. He liked how it looked, with lots of palm trees and absolutely no ivy anywhere and kids playing tennis outdoors in February. He sat in on a class called Politics of Rock Music. Awesome that you could take stuff like that for credit. Stanford was his first choice, and he was applying early decision. Still, he'd pick fucking Olivia over getting into Stanford.

Chapter 5

Tuesday morning, 9:45 A.M.

IT WAS ONLY A FEW BLOCKS NORTH ON BROADWAY TO RANNIE'S APART-
ment house, a cream-colored brick building circa 1920. In summer,
a blanket of furry ivy ran rampant to the top floor, obliterating
cracks in the brickwork, turning the whole building into a ten-
story Chia pet. There was neither a doorman nor a canopy, but the
building bore a name—Dolores Court—incised in Gothic letters
over the arched entrance on the side street. Rannie liked to imagine
Dolores was the builder's daughter and that she might even be alive
today, one of the old ladies who, in nice weather, sat with their
Gristedes grocery bags, gabbing on the benches in the traffic islands
on Broadway.

She pulled out her keys and glanced over both shoulders before letting herself into the lobby. Even at ten in the morning, the
S.W.A.K. murders had her on her guard, a purse-size can of Mace
always in her handbag. All three women had been murdered within
blocks of her building.

Though the neighborhood (uncharitably dubbed Loco—for
Lower Columbia—by Alice) was practically the only patch of the

Upper West Side still awaiting gentrification, Rannie had a three-bedroom, rent-controlled apartment. Yes, the walls were peeling, the heat intermittent, and the kitchen appliances almost old enough to count as museum pieces; nonetheless, the sun-filled space was a terrific family apartment . . . the only problem being that, as of next September, there was going to be exactly one person living in it. It had been wrenching enough when Alice left for college. Now, as she entered to the sound of rock music blasting, a pathetic image of herself flashed before her, eating dinner with only National Public Radio and the roaches for company.

Nate was in the dining room at the long pine table hunched over a bowl of cereal, in a pair of plaid boxers and a bad case of bed head. An open copy of the school paper was doing double duty as a place mat.

"God, whoever invented Fruit Loops was a genius." Nate scrunched his shoulders in a sleepy stretch, wriggled the comically bony toes on his size twelve feet, and smiled. Such a great smile. It melted her to the core every time.

"Nate. Why are you still here?"

"You wouldn't deny me a wholesome hearty breakfast."

Rannie swatted him. "My problem is I deny you nothing." Then she turned off the stereo in the living room.

"*Ma,* come on. 'I Fought the Law' is the next track."

Rannie tossed her raincoat on the couch and came and sat cater-corner to Nate at the table. "Mr. Tut died."

"No way." Then Nate put down his spoon. "Oh wow," he said softly, shaking his head. He scratched absently at the patch of hair on his chest. *He has hair on his chest;* it still stunned her every time she saw it. Rannie repeated what little she knew about Mr. Tut's death from Mrs. MacSkellan and from Olivia.

"Olivia! You were with Olivia?"

Nate never revealed a word about his social life. She'd found out about his last girlfriend by accident, from a casual remark made by the mother of the girl, a junior at Chaps. "You didn't know!" the woman then exclaimed. "It's been going on for months." Nonetheless, the look on Nate's face now pretty much confirmed what Rannie already suspected—he liked Olivia.

Just then the phone, "land line" in Nate-speak, started ringing.

"I'd like to speak to Nathan Lorimer," a woman's voice told Rannie. She identified herself as Officer Noreen Heffernan from the Twenty-fourth Precinct. "I'm here at the Chapel School and trying to locate Nathan. Is he home?"

"Nate? Y-yes, he is." She handed over the phone and, frowning, listened to Nate's yups, uh-huhs, concluding with, "No problem, yeah. I can be there in fifteen minutes."

After he hung up, he looked at her, puzzled but unconcerned. "Weird. They want to talk to me. I was the last person to see Tut alive."

Rannie frowned. She didn't like the sound of those words one bit.

10:30 A.M. *Tuesday*
Text Messages during Prayers in Chapel School
auditorium between Lily Grey and Lily Black

Pls shoot me have killer hangover!
Me 2 can't listen 2 1 more teacher talk about tut
u know tut was losing his marbles, don't u?
?
Yesterday tut walks up 2 marshall and says Who r u?
    in this loud voice
Get out
swear like he never saw Marshall b4
glad he's dead he hated me
UR so bad!
can u read my essay? it's on tutoring in prisons
leave out part about hooking up with the guy who got
    paroled
duh i think dartmouth will like
when did u decide 2 apply? u know i am. We said u
    go 2 brown.
changed my mind
SO unfair T wanted me 2 go 2 dartmouth more than
    anybody said i'd fit perfect
cuz u r alcoholic?
bitch. go 2 takashimaya by yrself p.s. yr pants give u
    an ape butt & plaid is so over.

Chapter 6

Tuesday morning, 10:20 A.M.

AS HE WALKED DOWN BROADWAY, HIS MOTHER STRUGGLING TO KEEP UP with his much longer strides, Nate kept thinking, Mr. Tutwiler—his favorite person at Chaps—dead?

In kindergarten, Tut would come and read to their class. Right before leaving, he'd always pass around a little tin of lemon balls that were kept in his blazer pocket. Had Tut looked any different back then, any younger? You expected Tut to just keep on getting older; you didn't expect him to *die*.

At 103rd Street they cut over one more block to West End, his mom babbling about how all this questioning by the police seemed strange . . . first Olivia . . . now him. Didn't it strike him as a little strange?

"Ma. How should I know? You sound like you *want* there to be something strange. I wish you'd go home. I'm gonna look like a dick coming in with my mother."

They proceeded the rest of the way to Chaps in stony silence.

Chaps. On cruddy days it looked even uglier than usual, old and creepy, like a prison. Thirteen years at a place where everybody knew your fucking business. His mom thought he was so fired up about Stanford because he'd get to see more of his dad. And sure, that'd be nice although Nate knew by now that plans with his dad—already there was talk of taking Nate to Hawaii over Thanksgiving—had a way of falling through.

Stanford's biggest attraction was that nobody else was applying this year. Nate would get there and be the only one who knew that he used to get carsick on every Lower School class trip or that he was practically a midget until eighth grade. He could buy a bad-ass leather jacket and wear black jeans all the time, and people would figure he'd always dressed that way. Kids would say, "Nate Lorimer? Yeah, you know him. . . . He plays drums. A real tall kid, always in black."

Mr. Tut understood. He once told Nate that college was the perfect place to reinvent yourself; in fact, his freshman year at Yale, the first thing Tut did was drop his name—Angus or Augustus, something like that—and go by his middle name.

Nate followed his mother through the black iron gates just as a bunch of seniors were heading out. Olivia wasn't among them.

He couldn't get over his mom spending a whole half-hour in Starbucks with her. Nate pictured himself there, leaning over the table and gently wiping a tear from her eye. "Death sucks," he would have said in a comforting voice. No, no, not something retarded like "Death sucks," but something wise and insightful that would cause Olivia to press her lips together and nod slowly. Afterward, they'd take a walk in Riverside Park. Then all of a sudden Olivia would stop and look up at him with those amazing eyes, the exact same color as Sam Adams beer. "Nate, want to blow off school and come over my house and—"

Elliot Ross muscled by him, his piggy eyes narrowing, arms mashed across the chest of his lifer jacket, thumbs hooked under his armpits.

Okay, Elliot, we all see the brand-new biceps. But guess what. You still got man-breasts.

The first week of school Nate caught Elliot showing off for the Lilys by stuffing some sorry-ass little freshman into the equipment bin on the playing field. Nate grabbed Elliot from behind, told the freshman kid to beat it, and pushed Elliot in, sliding the bolt across the door. It took twenty minutes before a phys ed teacher finally heard Elliot and let him out. So now it was official: They were enemies, Elliot vowing to get him back.

In the Great Hall, a short chunky woman who looked like Rosie O'Donnell in a police uniform spotted them and walked over.

"Officer Noreen Heffernan." She flipped open her I.D., then shook hands with his mother and him. "I know you've got classes, Nate, so I'll try to make this quick." She motioned towards one of the benches and opened a spiral notepad. "So Nate—okay to call you Nate?—Mr. Tutwiler's calendar had you down for five-thirty."

"Yes, but I was a little late. I had practice."

"Football?"

"No. I'm in a band. I got over to the Annex, maybe," Nate paused. "Maybe ten minutes later."

"And Mr. Tutwiler was waiting for you?"

"No. Another kid in my class was still with Tut."

She licked her finger and flicked back a few pages in her notepad. "Elliot Ross? David Ross's son?"

"Yeah, that's right." Typical of Elliot to let her know right away who his father was. The Ross name was plunked on hotels and high-rises all over the city. According to Elliot, his dad was going to get him into Harvard, no *problemo*, just by handing over a wad of money for a new gym or something. Yesterday, Nate heard Elliot telling Tut, "I told you before what my father's gonna do." Tut had been unimpressed, saying only, "Let him do whatever he wants. You still don't have the record for Harvard."

"So anyway, when Elliot left, I told Mr. Tut about my interview yesterday at Columbia. . . . That was basically it." Nate shrugged. "I was out of there in . . . like five minutes tops." What Nate hadn't bothered mentioning to Tut was spotting Grant Werner, Olivia's brother, coming out of the West End by the Columbia campus. Supposedly Grant had cleaned up his act. If so, a bar didn't seem the smartest place to be hanging out.

"And Mr. Tutwiler, did he appear all right to you?" the cop asked. It bothered him that she kept pronouncing Tut's name wrong, Tut-*will*-er instead of Tut-*while*-er. Somehow it made Tut being dead seem realer.

Nate stretched out his legs and thought for a moment. "He seemed, I don't know, a little distracted." A couple of times Tut had glanced at the door as if expecting someone. Often Nate would stay, talking to Tut about tennis or whatever, but yesterday he could tell Tut didn't want him hanging around.

"Do you remember what time you left?"

"Mmm. Maybe a little before six, right after one of the teachers stuck her head in to say good night."

"What teacher?"

"Ms. Hollins, my English teacher."

The cop nodded. "Thanks, Nate. Tell me. Would you mind taking a look at Mr. Tutwiler's office?"

"You okay with that, honey?" his mom asked in a concerned voice. "I'll come too."

"Ma! It's okay! Really!" The words came spitting out too loud. But he hated how she acted like he was some hyper-sensitive nerd who needed his mommy.

"Nate, no need to get upset. It's all right if your mother comes."

Great, now the cop thought he was a mental case too.

"We just need to check a few things out. Purely routine," she said as they went to the Annex. Nate caught his mother's look. It was clear she wasn't buying what the cop said. But that was her. He could tell that already she was worrying he'd be leaving school in handcuffs.

On the second floor, the cop pointed with her pen to the only other office on the floor besides Tut's. It belonged to Mr. Marshall.

"Anybody in there when you were waiting around yesterday?"

"No. Mr. Marshall was locking up while I was out here in the hall."

"And nobody was upstairs, that you know of?"

Nate shook his head, explaining Ms. Hollins had left already and Mrs. Lewis was on maternity leave. They had the only two offices on the third floor.

"Because of the S.W.A.K. murders, everybody's usually gone by six when the guard goes off duty," his mother chimed in. "I work here part-time. That's how I know."

"The school's locked after that?"

His mother nodded. "Security cameras go on. They were just installed. One's inside the main entrance; we passed the other one coming from the other building."

The cop stood, the hand with the notepad resting on her holster, and said, "So Nate. Look around. Take your time."

Everything looked pretty much the same to Nate. A mess. A frayed Oriental rug with most of the fringes gone covered the floor. Against one wall was a mustard-colored couch, and in the middle of the office was Tut's desk, strewn with college brochures and folders. Behind the desk was a curvy window and window seat with a flattened-out cushion and more piles of stuff. Tut's diplomas from Chaps and from Yale hung on either side of the big window, along with photos of old Chaps tennis teams from when Tut was the coach. Another lefty with a dynamite serve.

Nate moved closer to the desk, the cop warning him not to touch anything. He let his eyes travel, more slowly this time, over the surface of the desk—besides the videos, catalogues, and mail, a glass lay on its side. Something must have spilled from it because ink on the message slips next to it had run. "I don't remember any glass being on the desk. But if there was, it wasn't knocked over."

"Um, maybe it's nothing. But one of those glasses is gone. There should be four." His mother was motioning to a round tray on the window seat. Two other glasses with the Chaps crest stood upside down on it. "I happened to be here about a week ago, chatting with Mr. Tut and he offered me a drink. The tray had four glasses."

What? Nate chewed at his lower lip, permanently chapped from the Accutane he was taking. Everyone knew Tut kept a bottle of booze stashed in his desk. But his mom said they talked about him and college, nothing about having a drink with Tut.

The detective nodded. "Before we go, anything else, Nate?"

Nate's glance returned to the desktop. His folder was still out. Elliot's too. Yesterday, Elliot had come out of Tut's office steaming mad, all red in the face, like some pumped-up Porky Pig. As he stormed by Nate, he said, loud enough for Tut to hear, "That sorry old shit better hurry up and die."

"Did you remember something else just now?"

Nate shook his head. It was a crappy remark some asshole made. It didn't mean anything.

The cop waited a beat. "Well, if that's it, we're done." She handed him a card. One to his mom, too. "Thanks for your time. You think of anything else, give a call."

The cop remained in Tut's office and Nate took off. On the stairs, his mom tried to grab the back of his jacket. Without turning he said, "Lookit, Ma. I don't want to discuss what *you* think that cop *maybe* meant with her questions."

Tut was dead. Nate felt really bad about it. But for now, all he wanted was to spend the rest of the day at school doing stupid normal stuff.

Chapter 7

A minute later

RANNIE STAYED ROOTED IN THE RECEPTION AREA, SHAMEFACED. NATE was right. Despite her fondness for Mr. Tut, part of her *was* hoping for something sinister—something to take her mind off the depressing state of her jobless, manless, loose-ends life. Her son was a better person than she was, more mature. There really had been no reason, other than prurient interest, for her to come traipsing back to school. She should have stayed home and worked on her current freelance job, copyediting a book about Josef Mengele. Or called the business textbook company that had advertised a duller-than-dishwater managing ed. job . . . It was embarrassing to recall the giddy little thrill—Nate had seen it too—that shot through her when she spotted the tray and glasses. The obvious reason for a missing glass was that Mr. Tut had broken one. Period.

Then, while she was tightening the belt of her raincoat, the women in Chaps Admissions all began to emerge from their offices, as if on cue, purses and totebags in hand, jackets slung over their arms, anxious expressions on their faces. "Talk about surreal!" Dotty Greenhouse, the admissions director, said to Rannie.

Mrs. Mac was shutting down her computer and reaching for a Duane Reade shopping bag under her desk.

"What's going on?" Rannie inquired.

"Rannie, I don't understand it!" The elderly woman's voice shook as she leaned closer, overpowering Rannie with a blast of acidic breath. "The police! They're bringing in forensic experts! They're closing off the Annex and searching Mr. Tut's office! We all have to leave."

No sooner did Rannie's brain absorb the words "forensic experts" than the good mother in her grew alarmed, worried for Nate's sake. If the police considered Tut's death suspicious, then the next step was to find a suspect, the noun that went with that particular adjective. Yet at the same time, the bad mother in her immediately felt like running out of the Annex and storming into whatever classroom Nate was in, shouting, "See! I'm not so paranoid. I'm not the nut job we both think I am. Something mighty strange is going on here." And damn it, she wanted to find out what.

Tuesday noontime phone call between classes

*Lily B: Omigod. I'm in the Great Hall. It's like CSI. What if
      they find out? I'm scared.*
Lily G: Don't be stupid. If they ask you anything, just
      act normal.
Lily B: Yeah but what about—?
Lily G: I'll take care of that. Look, I'm late for physics.
      Remember: Act normal!
Lily B: We're fucked! I won't even get into my safety school.
Lily G: Stop being such a drama queen. I'm hanging up.

Chapter 8

HER BROTHER PICKED UP AFTER THE THIRD RING, SOUNDING ANNOYED.

"Olivia, I'm at the bookstore. You know I can't get calls here."

"Mr. Tut died."

There was a nano-second of silence at Grant's end followed by a long exhalation of breath that whistled through the phone line.

"Dead? Holy shit."

She was on her bed, her head propped against a bank of pillows that matched the upholstered headboard. "It was me who found him. It was awful—listen, Grant? Yesterday, did you see him?"

"No. I never got to."

Olivia spotted a nice juicy hangnail on her left pinkie. She ripped it off with her teeth, spat out the tail of skin, and watched a dot of blood turn into a trickle and slide down her finger. "I had to talk to a cop, Grant."

"What? Why?"

Was there a ring of alarm in his voice?

"Look, Olivia, you didn't say anything to the cop about me *wanting* to see him, did you?"

"No."

"If Mom and Dad find out I was in, the shit'll hit the fan and—" He stopped mid-sentence and Olivia could hear him explain to a customer, "No, ma'am, paperback *New York Times* best sellers aren't discounted, only hardcovers." Then he said to Olivia, "Lemme call you from the stockroom," and hung up.

She remained on her bed, eyes closed, both tired and wired at the same time. This past weekend her father had been in Quito on business, her mother at some spa where all you ate was seaweed. Grant knew Carlotta would squeal to their parents if he stayed home "unsupervised," something strictly against rehab rules. So he spent the weekend up at Columbia with an old Chaps friend. Columbia—a neighborhood full of bars and dealers. Olivia didn't understand why Grant couldn't just wait for a weekend when one of their parents was home. But that was Grant for you; when he got something in his head, "later" was simply not a word in his vocabulary.

After years of bad-mouthing Tut, suddenly Grant had wanted to make amends. Making amends meant telling someone to their face every crummy thing you'd ever done to them, even stuff you only thought about doing, just like Carlotta at confession. Grant had already made amends to Olivia for what had happened last Thanksgiving. Grant on cocaine was scary, violent, somebody you wanted to stay far, far away from.

When she was little, he had been the best big brother. He made her feel protected. He laughed at all her dumb jokes. He'd take her to the movies or ice skating. And now he was almost exactly like the old Grant.

After getting expelled, Grant had been shipped off to some boarding school in Switzerland. That had been a total disaster. Yes, he got his high school diploma but he also came home with a heroin habit. But since living at Windward for the past sixteen months, he'd only had that one slip last Thanksgiving. Eleven months and two days ago. Now he was coming up on his one-year anniversary. An AA milestone, just like the first ninety days had been, only in Olivia's mind, this one was a much bigger deal. If Grant could stay clean and sober for a whole year, then Olivia could stop worrying . . . or at least worry less. Her brother had no idea she marked off each day of his sobriety in her school planner. Nor did he know she'd stopped drinking—not even a sip of beer—or smoking dope.

At Al-Anon meetings, everyone kept telling her stuff like that was just a game she was playing with herself.

"Okay, you don't drink or do drugs. Good. But it doesn't mean your brother's gonna stay clean," a boy told her.

"It's like moral support," Olivia defended herself. "Grant doesn't even know."

The woman who ran the meetings was more understanding. "I know how you feel, Olivia. It's like being on a plane and thinking that if you just concentrate hard enough on it staying in the air, the plane won't crash. . . . It's a false sense of control."

The photo of her and Grant, the first time she'd gone roller blading, stared at her on the night table. She was seven, Grant ten. He was holding onto her hand while her free arm was outstretched, to steady herself. Grant had a great big "you can do it" smile on his face.

The phone rang, making her startle.

"Okay. I can talk now." Grant went on to explain that he had spoken to Tut on Sunday and the plan was to meet on Monday. "Tut said to be at his apartment at one, but he wasn't there. I hung around in Riverside Park, called him at home and at school, but Mrs. Mac answered so I hung up. I don't know . . . I guess he forgot. I caught a seven o'clock train."

"Seven? Why so late?" Immediately Olivia imagined Grant at a bar or in Riverside Park buying a joint, scoring cocaine.

"I—I meant I got back here at seven. I just missed the three-thirty train so I took the next one and grabbed dinner before signing in." Then Grant said he had to get back to work and hung up, leaving Olivia, sitting cross-legged on her bed, sucking up the blood that kept pooling at the bottom of her pinkie nail.

Chapter 9

RANNIE WAS WALKING OUT OF CHAPS AS A PANEL TRUCK PULLED UP TO the curb; two forensics guys carrying giant-sized doctor bags and cameras jumped out and disappeared behind the front doors, NEW YORK CITY POLICE DEPARTMENT printed on the backs of their white medical coats. As Nate would say, "Un-fucking-believable."

Her brain felt scrambled from the surreal morning, her mind on overdrive. She had to get back to Dr. Mengele, but right now trying to sort out the unsettling events took priority. A little fresh air would clear her head, lower her anxiety level.

The nearest entrance into Riverside Park was a block away, down a path of stone steps. She headed south along the promenade, little kids on tricycles beeping horns as they pedaled by, people walking dogs or jogging. The rain had stopped and every once in a while the clouds parted just long enough to let weak sunlight spangle the surface of the Hudson.

Rannie loved Riverside Park.

Central Park with a zoo, two skating rinks, carousel, boating pond, and outdoor theater belonged to the whole city, a three-star destination in travel guides. Riverside Park, also designed by Frederic Law Olmstead, was a humbler neighborhood park, a narrow ribbon of green that ran alongside the Hudson River from 156th Street down to 72nd Street where a statue of Eleanor Roosevelt stood leaning against a large rock, lost in thought, one hand held to her chin.

Rannie's nerves began to settle as she walked alongside the community flower garden with its tough little Upper West Side rosebushes still in bloom. An attractive man jogged past her. He had silver hair, good legs, and when he stopped to retie a sneaker, she noticed that he was wearing a Chaps tee shirt. Suddenly she made the connection. A father who showed up at school functions alone, no wife in tow. He rolled his shoulders back and forth a couple of times, then resumed running, picking up his pace, growing smaller and smaller as he moved along the promenade.

For Rannie, the satisfaction of being proven right had already given way to uneasiness. Three things were certain. Mr. Tut was dead; something looked fishy to the police; and Nate, unfortunately, was on the cops' radar screen. But why whisk Mr. Tut's body to the morgue and *then* call in forensics?

Could it be that to the trained eye Tut's death appeared a suicide? The overturned glass flashed before her. After all, he was an eighty-something man in the throes of terminal cancer. But did you need forensics guys dusting and bagging stuff if that was the case? And anyway Rannie's gut told her that Tut was a fighter who'd tough out cancer, not someone who'd slug down one last glass of single malt with a fistful of sleeping pills as a chaser. And certainly not at school. . . . So where did that leave her? If it wasn't A) a nice and normal, run-of-the-mill natural death or B) suicide, then the only other choice on the menu was C) murder. But Mr. Tut a murder victim? Chaps a crime scene? No, it was too screwy. Rannie could picture herself cheerily reassuring families on the tour, "The yellow tape over there? Oh, don't worry about that. Just a little homicide investigation going on. . . . Why, yes, I do have a child at Chaps, only he's presently down at the precinct being interrogated."

At 91st Street Rannie exited the park and turned north, heading home. Time to sharpen her Col-Erase blue pencils and attack the Mengele manuscript. Time to act like a responsible adult and earn some money.

Forty bucks an hour was top dollar for freelance copyediting. But Rannie caught what other copy editors overlooked. In her own life she might miss something big and obvious—like the year-long affair Peter had carried on with his doubles partner, who accompanied him to California. But no book she worked on had ever needed an errata slip. It was just a knack she had—mistakes leaped out from the page.

Hotshot editors with fat Rolodexes and expense accounts might dismiss proofreaders as punctuation-obsessed fussbudgets, gnashing their teeth over split infinitives. But reading was such a crazy process when you thought about it. At some point you stopped being aware that you were decoding squiggles printed in black ink on white paper. Suddenly you entered another world. It was all an illusion, and misspellings, inconsistencies, anachronisms, wrong dates—whatever—wrecked the illusion.

Without even realizing it, Rannie's feet had taken her all the way to 102nd Street. She was about to cross Riverside Drive when she noticed the large, lumpish figure of Ms. Hollins huddled on a bench. She was holding a cigarette low to the ground, as if someone might catch her smoking and report her.

"Ms. Hollins."

Ms. Hollins looked up. Her eyes were red from crying, and strands of hair had come loose from the long dark braid she wore down her back.

Instantly, Rannie regretted intruding. "Oh, I'm so sorry!" she said. "I can see you need to be by yourself." Somehow the sight of Ms. Hollins weeping outright was more distressing than coming upon someone with a naturally sunnier demeanor in tears.

Ms. Hollins took a furtive puff of her cigarette. Student essays lay paper-clipped next to her. "No. No. It's all right. Really. I have to go in a minute anyway. I have a class—the one Nate's in." She attempted a smile.

"I feel awful, too," Rannie said. "And you were obviously much closer to Mr. Tut than I was."

Ms. Hollins suddenly stiffened and her drawl rose an octave. "Just what do you mean by that?"

"Excuse me?"

"What you just said, how I was '*obviously* much closer.'" She fixed Rannie with an accusatory glare. "Don't tell me you've been listening to those crazy rumors! Just because kids' hormones are raging, they think so are everybody else's!"

Rannie was stupified. "Ms. Hollins! I promise you, I've never heard any rumors. I wasn't implying anything! I used to see the two of you having lunch together in the cafeteria. I could tell you were friends."

Ms. Hollins's expression softened immediately, and she sagged back against the park bench. "Forgive me, please. I'm just upset. . . . Yes, Larry and I were friends. But close? . . . No, I would never say that. We'd trade books, have dinner occasionally, that sort of thing. . . . He was a terribly private person. You didn't dare step over certain boundaries with Larry."

Rannie nodded, noticing Ms. Hollins even seemed uncomfortable calling Mr. Tut by his first name.

"Since school started, he seemed to be going downhill fast. He looked awful yesterday." She dragged on her cigarette again. Her hands were as large as a man's. "I thought of calling him last night, just to check in, see how he was. But I got home too late." Fresh tears spilled as she told Rannie that Mr. Tut had asked whether she was free for an early dinner. "I already had plans. If only I'd said yes, he wouldn't have been alone. I could've called 911."

Rannie nodded. She understood. Her mother felt guilty to this day for having been shopping at Loehmann's when Rannie's father died. She'd say, "And I was so thrilled! I'd just found a Calvin Klein suit for eighty-nine dollars! I couldn't wait to get home and model it for him!"

"Is there any family?" Rannie inquired.

Ms. Hollins's face clouded over again. "No. None that I know of. He had an older brother who died in a boating accident when Larry was a boy. Chaps was his family." Ms. Hollins paused and managed a nervous smile, her hand fiddling with a large silver brooch pinned to the faded cotton turtleneck she was wearing. "You know, I've been meaning to mention how glad I am that Nate's taking poetry this year. . . . He's a good kid. You did something right."

"Screaming and bribery. I guess they worked."

Ms. Hollins smiled, acknowledging the feeble joke, then said, "Some of the kids at Chaps, honestly, they scare me." She paused. "This business of college, it's like a blood sport. One of the seniors—I won't say who—hinted that if I wrote a glowing recommendation, her family's place in Caneel Bay could be mine over Christmas."

Talk about déjà vu all over again. "Just recently Mr. Tut said something similar. He said he thought some of the kids were—well, 'dangerous' was the word he used."

Ms. Hollins arched an eyebrow. "I know exactly why he said that." She paused a moment, evidently considering whether to divulge more.

Go on, go on, Rannie mentally telegraphed to her.

"Larry got a letter at home, the week school started. All it said was 'Watch out. Your days are numbered.' It was typed but the lettering was made to look like a ransom note. In various fonts, with upper and lower case letters in different sizes."

"Are you kidding!"

"Didn't I see it with my own eyes? It shocked Larry and not much did after all his years at Chaps. Oh, he pretended to dismiss it, just shrugged it off and acted as though it wasn't any worse than a prank phone call." Ms. Hollins tossed her cigarette on the ground and stubbed it out with the heel of her shoe. "But to send something like that to a man who's *dying*? It was vicious. Purely vicious. And then seeing poor Larry on that stretcher—" Ms. Hollins choked up again and emitted, not a sob exactly but something more gutteral, a violent gulping noise. Then she added, "Well, I went right up to the police and told them."

There was Rannie's answer for why forensics arrived when they did. Still, how much credence would the police actually give to something like that? Serious killers didn't usually give their victim a heads-up.

"Did he have any idea who sent the letter?"

"He had his hunches."

"But you don't honestly believe it was a serious threat, do you? Or—or that it has anything to do with his death?"

Ms. Hollins seemed to weigh the possibility in her mind as she continued to fiddle with the pin on her collar. It was unusual, perhaps Celtic in style, in the shape of a monster with a curling tail and open jaws that appeared ready to take a bite out of her neck. "Honestly, I don't know. I didn't take it seriously, not at first. And part of me still doesn't, I guess. But the past few days Larry seemed preoccupied. I asked him if any more letters had come. He said no although I'm not sure he was telling me the truth. Something was bothering him, that I know." Ms. Hollins stood and sighed. "I have a class I'm going to be late for," she said, flicking ashes off the skirt of her sacklike jumper. She picked up the stack of papers, the top one marked A-minus in deep purple marker.

Rannie watched her proceed in the direction of school, head bent down, shoulders hunched, her long braid swishing mournfully. If Rannie hadn't known, she might have pegged Ms. Hollins for a potter, a weaver, a quiltmaker, someone you'd see plying their wares at weekend crafts fairs. Undoubtedly she'd been one of those large gawky girls who by fifth grade towered over all the boys and who'd remained self-conscious about her height forever after. "Stand up straight. Don't shlump!" Rannie felt like calling after Ms. Hollins, with the self-conscious midget inside her adding, "I've wanted to be tall all my life!"

GOODBYE, MR. CHAPS

At eight o'clock this morning a Chapel School student found the body of A. Lawrence Tutwiler, a longtime faculty member and director of college admissions, in his office at the exclusive K–12 private school on West 103rd Street. The cause of death is unknown at this time.

"The entire school is in mourning," said Jonathan E. Marshall, the headmaster.

Asked if he knew Lawrence Tutwiler, a freshman boy responded, "Of course. He's the dude who gets you into college. Well, I guess not anymore."

A Chapel School parent, who did not wish to be named, went on at greater length. "Mr. Tutwiler was famous for his connections at all the best colleges. And at the end of the day, a private school lives or dies by who goes where to college. We didn't all fight like lunatics to get our kids into Chaps so they could wind up at East Podunk U. No, college is the payback. I'll have forked over a fortune in tuition by the time my kid graduates. So, after Chaps, there better be a lot of ivy growing wherever he goes."

Chapter 10

MAYBE HIS MOTHER WASN'T COMPLETELY CRAZY. COPS WERE CRAWLING all over school; according to his friend Ben, a forensics team was in Tut's office right this minute.

"Don't anybody believe this bullshit about a heart attack. This is homicide, son." Chris Butler slid into a desk beside Nate and, opening a bottle of water, turned to him. "Looks like there'll be one less senior page in the yearbook."

"Huh?" Ben, sitting on the other side of Nate, said.

"You murder someone, you don't graduate."

"I'm innocent!" Ben held up both hands. "I told Tut I could be happy at Babson."

Chris laughed. "When I first saw cops, I figured, 'S.W.A.K. guy strikes again.'" Chris ran his finger along his neck and made a raspy, gurgling noise from the back of his throat.

"You wouldn't joke if you were a girl," Lily G. said.

They were in a fourth-floor classroom, all the desks in a semicircle, waiting for Hollins to show up.

"Poor Ms. Hollins." Katie Spielkopf, sighing, looked up from the notebook she was doodling in and said in that spacey, singsong-y voice of hers, "She must be devastated about Tut."

"I think she did it," Lily B. said matter-of-factly. She was sitting and playing with a strand of hair cut short like Olivia's.

"No way! Ms. Hollins was in love with Tut!" Then Katie paused, tapping her marker against her lip. ". . . Unless it was like, you know, an 'Angel of Mercy' thing."

Ben thought Katie was hot, but Nate couldn't see it. She was one of those annoying girls who thought being ditsy was cute.

"Uh-uh. Tut dumped her," Lily B. continued.

"Why? Cause Mrs. Mac swallows and she wouldn't?" Ben deadpanned.

Chris Butler choked, spraying water on the front of his shirt.

Lily B. ignored them. "Olivia heard her in his office yesterday. Around five-thirty. Hollins was crying." Lily B. started imitating Hollins's Southern drawl. " 'I'm not listenin'. Don't say that!' . . . Classic breakup scene. Ask Olivia if you don't believe me." Lily's thumb and index finger were cocked like a gun. "If she couldn't have him, then nobody could. Kapow."

"Except he wasn't shot," Lily G. said. "I texted Olivia. There was no blood." Then she leaned across the desktop attached to her chair, her eyes glittery. "Here's what I think. I think maybe she was trying to win him back, and they were doing it in his office Monday night."

This whole conversation was idiotic. "Cut it out," Nate said. "The dude was over eighty."

"Please. Grampy and his new wife had a baby last year," Lily G. said. "I mean have you ever taken a look at the stains on that couch? I would never sit on it. Maybe she was blowing him and he had a heart attack. So Hollins panics, zips him up, and tries to make it look like he was all alone when he croaked. But the cops aren't fooled."

"Except that Hollins left before Tut. I saw her," Nate said.

"Maybe it only *looked* like she was leaving," Lily G. said. She paused, eyebrows raised, waiting for Nate's comeback.

But he didn't have one.

Satisfied her point was made, Lily G. stretched her arms behind her back, like her shoulders were stiff, something she did a lot to show off her tits.

Chris took another swig of water and attempted to look solemn. "For all we know, forensics guys are down at the morgue right now dusting Tut's dick."

"Why? Do blow jobs leave lip prints?" Katie wanted to know.

Nate turned to Ben. *And you like her?* his look said.

"From what I hear, Lorimer was the last one to see Tut alive," Elliot chimed in, fake-smiling at Nate. "We all thought you were one of his pets. Maybe you've got some grudge we don't know about."

"*Me!* You were the one saying you wished he'd hurry up and die."

Elliot turned to the Lilys. "I never said that! That's what I heard *him* say."

"You're such a fucking liar. I didn't see you leave the building either."

"Maybe not," Elliot looked smug now. "But they did."

Both Lilys nodded. Lily G. said, "He's solid. We were waiting in the Rolls for a ride home."

Oro Johnston looked up from the portable video game he was playing. "If anybody was in school after six, it'll be on camera. Right, Chris?"

"You better believe that picture's going on my senior page."

One evening the first week of school, Chris had mooned one of the new security cameras, figuring it wasn't hooked up yet. He got hauled into Marshall's office the next morning.

"You think it counts as manslaughter if you blow somebody to death?" Ben said.

"No idea but it's not a bad way to go!" Chris slapped palms with Ben. "Tut was a lucky man."

Then the door opened. It was Ms. Hollins, clutching their papers on "Tintern Abbey" in her hand. The laughing stopped. So did the ping-ping gunshots of Oro's video game.

"Everything's just a big joke to all of you, isn't it? A wonderful man just died. And if anybody here had *anything* to—" A choking, almost gagging, sound stopped her from saying anything further. Her face crumpled and, after staring hard at each of them, as if it was some police lineup, she turned on her heel and was gone, leaving the door wide open behind her.

Chapter 11

Tuesday, 6:00 P.M.

OLIVIA SHIFTED IN THE BLACK LEATHER RECLINER OPPOSITE DR. EHREN-burg and idly wondered how many hours she'd racked up in this office. Her mom made her start coming when she was—what? Maybe four?—after she started insisting on calling Carlotta "Mommy" and her mother "Mrs. Wair-nair."

Olivia had told Dr. E. about finding Mr. Tut.

"That must have been awful."

Olivia was positive Dr. E. had had some work done. The lines that looked like giant parentheses on either side of her mouth were gone; so were the puffy bags under her eyes, which Olivia missed. They made Dr. E. look kindly. Dr. E.'s wedding band had also disappeared, and all Olivia's mother's friends went straight to a plastic surgeon the minute their marriage tanked.

"Everybody thinks Tut was murdered," Olivia blurted out.

"Why is that?" Dr. E.'s tone remained calm like always.

"My friends say cops are questioning everybody. Forensics guys were all over Tut's office—there's yellow tape across the door. I mean, that's not like—normal. . . . Grant wanted to see him yesterday, to make amends." Olivia noticed a tiny tag of cuticle on her left index finger, ripe for picking. She tried to ignore it and bit the inside of her cheek instead. "My parents don't know Grant was in—I'm worried he had a slip."

"He shouldn't be breaking rehab rules, Olivia, but that doesn't mean he got high."

"I know. It's just that he got nervous telling me what time he went back to New Haven. I'm scared he stayed late. . . ."

"We've talked about this before. You don't trust your brother, not yet. . . . So sometimes jumping to the worst possible conclusion is almost like a defense, like preventive medicine. If you think the worst—for instance, Grant getting high—then it can't have happened. Does what I'm saying make sense?"

"Yeah, totally!" Olivia relaxed in the chair. Dr. E. always made her feel better, like she wasn't crazy. . . . Or that she *was* crazy but her fears were irrational. Once she'd asked Dr. E. what all the numbers at the bottom of each bill meant. It was some kind of diagnosis code for insurance purposes, Dr. E. had explained. "Your number means 'anxiety disorder.' It's very common. Don't let it upset you."

Just the opposite. Olivia *liked* knowing there was a name other than "pyscho" for the way she acted . . . and that other people acted the same way too.

TO: alice.lorimer@yale.edu
FROM: bookperson43@aol.com

Alice, honey,
You may have already heard from Nate but Mr. Tut died and I thought you'd want to know. So sad and very hard to think of Chaps without him.

No news except that I miss you which is, of course, no news!

xxxxxMom

Dad called last night wanting to know what in particular he's done lately to tick you off. Told him I didn't have a clue.

TO: bookperson43@aol.com
FROM: alice.lorimer@yale.edu

Yes, Mom. I heard and feel very sad. Let me know when the funeral is and I'll try to come down. I loved Tut.

As for your former husband, no, there's no new offense. I think you and Nate have never come to grips with your anger and that's NOT just the pysch major in me talking.

Memo

SAFETY MEASURES AT SCHOOL
FROM: Jonathan Edwards Marshall, Headmaster

Because of the three so-called S.W.A.K. murders, many parents have asked what steps Chapel School is taking to ensure a safe environment. We have taken several important measures, but I do want to remind the community:

- The victims have all been adult women in their twenties or thirties—not children or teenagers.
- The attacks have all occurred late at night, long after school is closed.
- Although the victims were discovered in the general vicinity of the campus, Chapel School is further west of where any attacks took place. Streets east of Broadway have always had a higher incidence of crime than those west of Broadway.

We are being proactive:
- Security cameras at two locations in school go on automatically at six o'clock after the guard leaves.
- We now have two teams of parent patrols every afternoon. We have extended patrol hours to six o'clock. The patrol route now spans a mile-wide area. Parents are equipped with new walkie-talkies.
- The Twenty-fourth Precinct is adding an extra nighttime patrol car and an extra officer on foot in the immediate neighborhood.

I urge parents of students in the upper grades who sometimes remain at school in the evening to make sure children exercise proper caution. Children should leave in a group and have arranged transportation home.

There is no reason for panic. We are confident that your children are safe at Chapel School.

Message on Rannie's answering machine

Rannie, this is Celina Grey, your Parent Rep. This is a reminder about the safety meeting at school tonight. It's at six o'clock. I hope you'll be able to attend. Jem will also address false rumors surrounding Mr. Tut's death.

Chapter 12

MORE THAN TEN YEARS AGO, IN DEFERENCE TO A STUDENT POPULATION that was half-Jewish, the massive crucifix on the back wall of the auditorium had been taken down; however, the paler, pinker bricks behind it—in the telltale shape of a cross—continued to provide a constant reminder of the school's Episcopal underpinnings. There was no Chapel School chaplain anymore; the last headmaster had officially changed Daily Prayers to the more ecumenical-sounding Morning Meeting; and on the school calendar, Christmas Assembly was now listed as the Festival of Lights.

But as far as Rannie was concerned, Chaps was and would always remain a *goyishe*, male bastion, a place that still most truly belonged to boys with Roman numerals after their names, to her former husband and his father before him. And although Jem Marshall did not bear the title of Right Reverend as had past headmasters, he was definitely trying to look the part, standing stiffly behind the lectern like some nervous new minister about to preach a sermon to an unruly, demanding congregation.

Rannie's eyes skimmed the crowd of well-dressed parents mill-ing in the aisles, air-kissing, waving to other well-dressed parents already in their seats. So far Ben's mom, her only close friend from Chaps, was nowhere in sight. Joan Gordon, formerly a principal at a high school in Queens, was on the Chaps Board of Trustees. If anyone had the inside scoop on Tut, it would be Joan.

A moment earlier she'd run into Arthur Black, a divorced orthodontist she'd seen a few times over the summer. He was fairly attractive and said she reminded him of Natalie Wood with an overbite. But besides the fact that Nate referred to his daughter Lily as "spawn of Satan," Arthur Black had "commitment" splashed all over him like heavy cologne. Rannie ended it after a weekend at a bed-and-breakfast in Connecticut. The sex had been awful, Arthur constantly inquiring what to do next to "make it good for her," which was precisely the reason the sex had been so awful. "I don't come with an instructions manual," she'd almost blurted out at one point. After nodding a cordial hello, Rannie deliberately veered toward the opposite aisle of the auditorium.

Why did she always arrive at these gatherings early? They never failed to make her feel like a total loser, a loser whose shoes, now that she looked down, could have used a polishing. There were two distinct camps at Chaps—the haves and have-mores on one side with their multiple homes and power professions and the scholarship families on the other, almost all minorities working two jobs, almost none from Manhattan, almost never free to show up at meetings like this. Rannie, squarely in the middle class, belonged to neither camp and as she found herself a seat, she tried hard to remember she was a grown-up, a forty-three-year-old mother of two, and not back in junior high.

Ms. Hollins walked by, pausing to inform Rannie that Mr. Tut's obituary would be in tomorrow's *Times* with a photo. "He'd be so pleased," she said and then continued toward the stage where the faculty was assembling.

Rannie took a vacant aisle seat.

"Pretty amazing. Mr. Tut spent practically his whole life at this place."

Rannie turned to her right. A man in the seat one in from hers had obviously overheard Ms. Hollins. It was the jogger, the dad she'd seen in Riverside Park. Up close, he was even better looking, still boyish, despite a shock of gray hair.

"I couldn't wait to get out of high school. They weren't sad to see me go either." He smiled. Nice smile. He was more casually dressed than most of the other men, wearing a blue button-down shirt, no tie, sleeves rolled up. He had nice arms too. "I'm interested to hear how the head guy spins a dead body turning up at school. I'm getting an earful down at my place." From his broad vowels, Rannie pegged him for a Boston-area boy.

"Your place?" she cocked her head in a way that said, "Do tell."

"I own a bar near the Twenty-fourth Precinct. It's a cop hangout. The guys are saying get out your nose plugs 'cause this one smells."

Amen, thought Rannie. Nevertheless, hearing someone else voice the same suspicions she had been harboring sent a nasty tingle up her spine. She wished Nate had been miles away from Tut's office Monday evening. Rannie paused. "So the cops, are they treating this as if it's—" She left the end of her sentence dangling, unable to bring herself to utter the word "murder" here in the sanctity of the Chapel auditorium.

But the jogger was glancing around the auditorium and didn't answer. "A-list crowd, huh?"

Right now, squeezing into various rows, nodding thanks to people who stood to let them pass, were a network news anchor, a museum director, and a masthead editor at the *Times.* . . . The fathers in the class included some pretty heavy hitters, too.

The crowd fell silent, latecomers quickly finding seats, as Mr.

Marshall, clearing his throat, began speaking into the microphone. "Good evening, everyone. Thank you for coming. It's been a very sad day, a day we all knew would come eventually though that doesn't lessen our sadness."

Rannie felt a nudge on her shoulder. Her seatmate handed a little notepad to her. On blue-lined paper was written, all in neat caps: *I'm Tim Butler. Chris's dad. Who do you belong to?*

He proffered a ballpoint pen and waited for a reply.

Aren't we a little old to be passing notes in class? Rannie wrote back while finding herself smiling.

An hour later, Rannie decided flirtatious note-passing would have been much more fun and just as productive as listening to Jem Marshall. He never got to the subject of the S.W.A.K. murders. He spent the whole time bobbing and weaving questions from parents which were all on the same theme: Why are the boys in blue swarming all over Chaps?

With Kennedyesque conviction, he declared, "There is no reason to believe Mr. Tut died under suspicious circumstances."

With dismay, he sputtered, "No! His death is no way connected to the S.W.A.K. murders!"

And with stalwart constancy, he kept repeating, "No, I would not categorize the presence of police at school as an ongoing investigation."

The headmaster's evasions only served to fuel her own misgivings, and evidently Rannie's seatmate was of like mind. He stood and said, "I don't think he convinced anybody, do you? Tough crowd, but I don't see any flop sweat on him. He's a stiff, but a smart stiff."

Rannie stood too. "He'd better be. He makes more than three hundred thousand dollars a year. And—see over there?" She pointed to a man whose arm was clapped tightly around Jem Marshall's shoulder, their heads bent in private conversation near the podium.

"David Ross?"

"The new headmaster is getting an apartment at the River's End, rent-free."

"Nice perk." Tim Butler picked up his trench coat but made no move toward the aisle. "So? Want to grab a cup of coffee? Trade war stories about having teenagers?"

Rannie bit her lower lip, mentally torn. She was supposed to pick up more reference books on Mengele from the editor at S&S. But this man was very attractive. And he might have some concrete info about Tut.

"Sure." As they moved with the flow of exiting parents, she added, "I'm Rannie—rhymes with Annie—Bookman, by the way."

She suggested the Acropolis, a Greek coffee shop nearby that was like a second home to Nate. On the way there she learned Tim Butler was from Plymouth, Massachusetts, a widower, and owned the building his bar was in. "Living above the store isn't great." He shrugged in a whaddaya-gonna-do way. "It works, though, if you're raising a kid alone."

Just as they settled into a booth and Rannie was shrugging off her coat, Tim's cell phone rang.

Don't answer it, she silently requested. She abhorred people who were slaves to their phones. Victims of cellulitis. Nevertheless, after he glanced at the number and said, "Got to take this," she watched his face grow more serious as he listened, nodding, not uttering anything other than "okay" during the brief conversation.

Their own conversation was just as brief.

"Rannie, sorry, but I have to go. This is real important."

And that was that. He was gone before the waiter arrived to take their order. No offer to drop her home. No excuse given or rain check extended. A moment later Rannie stood, attempting to convince herself he wasn't *that* attractive and taking note of his use of "real" instead of "really," although from his mouth it had sounded natural and sincere.

Considering the hour and the neighborhood, she grabbed a taxi.
The S.W.A.K. murders had her blowing a small fortune on cabfare,
but a running meter sure beat winding up in a morgue drawer on
ice with a toe tag. The editor of the Mengele book lived at 94th
Street and Broadway. An hour later, Rannie emerged from the
apartment, fortified with coffee, industry gossip, more books on
Mengele, and—best of all—a lead on a job. Croyden and Woolf,
publishers of many Newbery- and Caldecott-Award-winning children's books, needed a head copy editor.

Under the building canopy, arm outstretched for yet another
taxi, Rannie noticed a tall woman coming down the steps of a
brownstone next door, a garment bag slung over one arm, a suitcase
on wheels bumping behind her. Quickly Rannie stepped into the
street, establishing her primacy for the next cab. Then something
made her turn to catch another glimpse of the woman.

It was Ms. Hollins. At the bottom of the stairs, Ms. Hollins
readjusted the garment bag on her arm and began walking down
the street, suitcase rolling alongside her. At Broadway, she turned
left.

Rannie had seen her in the throng of parents and teachers leaving
Chaps after the meeting. Where on earth was she going at this hour?
Then—for no reason that made any sense whatsoever—instead of
flagging the empty cab at the stoplight, Rannie followed her.

Eavesdropping. It was a minor vice she'd inherited from her
mother whose idea of a good time in New York was sitting on
buses overhearing other peoples' conversations. But what she was
doing now went beyond eavesdropping, she chided herself, all the
while continuing south on Broadway and over to West End, careful to maintain a reasonable distance between Ms. Hollins and
herself.

Except for a few dog walkers, West End Avenue was deserted.
However, uniformed doormen, two to a block, kept fears of lunatic

killers at bay. Only once, at 90th Street, did Ms. Hollins spin around to look carefully behind her. Rannie, half a block behind and momentarily caught under the light from a canopy, ducked into the shadowy recess of a doctor's entrance. Had Ms. Hollins spotted her? She was probably only making sure of her own safety. Another pang of guilt. This was not right, what she was doing, behaving like some long-in-the-tooth Nancy Drew in a stained trenchcoat. She waited for her heart to slow down. I'm skulking, she realized with some amazement. "Skulking," a verb that she never once imagined would describe her own actions.

At a squat four-story red-brick building on the south corner of 86th Street, a poor relation to the stately apartment houses lining either side of the avenue, Ms. Hollins stopped, took out keys from her pocket and disappeared through the front door.

A moment later Rannie hailed a cab. The minute she was in her apartment, the Manhattan directory confirmed that an A. Hollins lived on West End Avenue and 86th Street. So, if the squat red-brick building was home, the next question was: Who lived in the brownstone on 94th Street?

Quickly, Rannie flipped to the T's and felt the hairs on her arms stand up when her eyes landed on the listing she was looking for. Yup... hunch confirmed. *Tutwiler, A. Lawrence... 278 West 94th Street.*

What had Ms. Hollins been doing at Mr. Tut's? Obviously, she had a key. What was in the suitcase and bag ... stuff of his? ... stuff of hers? If so, that suggested sleepovers at Mr. Tut's and a relationship far more intimate than the one described to Rannie. Had they been lovers despite her demurral? Not out of the question despite the thirty or forty years' difference in their ages. Until recently Mr. Tut had been vigorous and attractive in a way that certain men never lost. But the plain truth was: Tut had sex appeal; Ms. Hollins didn't.

As Rannie thought about it over a late-night peanut butter and jelly sandwich, whether Jem Marshall owned up to it or not, there *was* a police investigation going on. Mr. Tut's apartment was bound to be searched. It was a big no-no for Ms. Hollins to clear out belongings, no matter whose they were.

A. Lawrence Tutwiler, a teacher and college advisor at Chapel School for more than fifty years, died in his office on Monday evening. He was 83 years old.

Mr. Tutwiler entered Chapel School in the eighth grade, beginning an association with the Manhattan private school that was to last almost six decades. "Mr. Tut, as everyone affectionately called him, was a true gentleman scholar," said Headmaster Jonathan E. Marshall.

A tall man with Mephistophelean eyebrows and the well-groomed look of someone fresh from the barber shop, Mr. Tutwiler was born in the Riverdale section of the Bronx. He graduated from Yale College; received a Masters in Education from Columbia Teachers College; and then returned to Chapel School to begin his career. He is the author of <u>Rebellious Heart: The Poems of George Gordon, Lord Byron</u> (Columbia University Press).

Mr. Tutwiler lived on the Upper West Side, only a few blocks from the school. He leaves no survivors.

Chapter 13

ARMED WITH HER WEAPON OF CHOICE, A LETHALLY SHARPENED Col-Erase blue pencil with a yellow eraser "helmet," Rannie had spent the past two hours making headway on the Mengele manuscript.

Freelance—what a thrillingly medieval word it was. Her sole allegiance was to the job at hand. She'd sally forth and ultimately four hundred and forty pages of misplaced modifiers, typos, dangling clauses, garbled phrases would surrender before her.

Like Starbucks, the second floor of the Barnes & Noble store at Broadway and 82nd Street had become a post-layoff workplace of choice, specifically a table farthest from the escalators and children's book area which, as colder weather approached, turned into an impromptu playgroup for Upper West Side toddlers and their mommies and nannies.

Fifty more pages of the manuscript were now neatly blue-penciled, she was pleased to see. And no use denying the morbid lure of Josef Mengele, chief physician at Auschwitz. Mengele had managed to flee Nazi Germany at war's end and live out his days in Uruguay, his death unverified until 1978 when DNA testing revealed that a body interred for ten years was indeed that of Mengele.

The page she'd just finished proofing was in a chapter tracing the history of genetic altering.

People assume that the notion of a master race was an exclusively Germanic obsession. Not so!

~~In the united States~~ in the early 1900's, the promise of eugenics — better people through selective breeding — swept across the U. S. (United States) *as part of the progressive movement. One noted biologist, who later became president of Stanford University, David Starr Jordan, hoped to discover how best to weed out genetic riff-raff.*

Germany took the lead from the United States in eugenic research when Count Otmar Von Verschuer at Frankfrut's Institute of Heredity, began an inventory of genetic defects in the German population. He also became the most famous researcher of twins of his time. It was through twin research that he hoped to unlock the secrets of heredity in order to create a master race. Verscheur hired a brilliant young assistant who'd graduated with highest honors from the university of Munich, earning both a medical degree and a doctorate in physical anthropology. The assistant was Josef Mengele.

The author, a professor of medical ethics at a Midwestern university, seemed a thorough-enough researcher—pages and pages of footnotes accompanied the manuscript. But in Rannie's opinion he went overboard in an attempt to avoid sounding overly scholarly. Her guess was that he underestimated what a lay reader could absorb or would find interesting, which might explain his addiction to exclamation points. Rannie queried ones to delete and attached a Post-it that read: *For me, the abundance of exclams unintentionally trivializes the info. I'd let the facts speak for themselves. Period.*

She heard the shuffle of footsteps near her. An elderly lady with an armload of books was circling the tables with an eye out for an empty chair.

"Take my seat. I'm leaving," Rannie offered. She scooped up her red barn jacket, brushed eraser lint off her trousers, and stashed her pencils in her jacket pocket. She was due at Chaps for a noontime staff meeting in the Annex.

"Nothing said here leaves this room," Dottie Greenhouse, the director of Chapel School admissions, instructed her troops—the heads of Lower School, Middle School, and Upper School admissions as well as various secretaries. Everyone was carefully balancing paper plates with sandwiches on their laps and looking grave. "Mr. Tut's death looked suspicious enough for an autopsy."

"Autopsy!" Rannie practically gagged on her chicken salad. Until now that was a word she had only heard on TV or in movies.

"Come on, Rannie. Are you really that surprised?" said one of the secretaries.

Well, no, actually. And as she continued to think about it, there was a possible bright side to an autopsy: A coroner could pinpoint the time of death, which in turn might cross off Nate's name from any list of suspects. He'd been home Monday evening by six-thirty, quarter to seven the latest.

"Mr. Marshall is waiting for the coroner's report and, of course, keeping fingers crossed. As we all are." Dottie held up hers, dutifully entwined, as if to prove the point. "The police are going over the tape from the new security cameras. It's all most alarming. To the outside world, however, we must be on the same page. Simply tell people who call to ignore rumors. This is Chapel School! Murders don't happen here! They're considering withdrawing their application? So be it. Currently we have ten applicants for every spot in kindergarten, and a record number of kids are applying for ninth grade. . . . If a few drop out, it doesn't matter."

Sooner than expected, Rannie had her chance to play loyal foot soldier when a call came in from her downstairs neighbor, Melinda Lowe, whose son was scheduled for a tour at one o'clock.

"Um, Rannie, I hate to cancel last minute, but Noah called from school, complaining of a sore throat. Is it possible to reschedule?"

"Absolutely. Just let me get the book," said Rannie, wondering whether Noah's sudden ailment was a convenient excuse. "It'll be better if Noah comes once things get back to normal."

"Rannie—I hear there's a police investigation. What's the deal?"

"Please, Melinda, don't tell me you're listening to silly park bench gossip?" Rannie said in a chipper voice that sounded rehearsed even to her own ear. She reached for the appointment calendar, penciling in a new date for a tour and interview.

"Chaps is still our first choice, Rannie." Melinda's son was in eighth grade, his final year at City Prep, the school where Jem Marshall had been headmaster before coming to Chaps. According to Rannie's neighbor, Jem walked on water—chlorinated H_2O, to be exact—spearheading a capital drive that had provided an Olympic-size pool and a state-of-the-art arts center.

As Rannie returned the appointment book to her drawer, she noticed two large hands gripping the edge of her desk.

"Just what do you think you were doing last night?" the woman attached to the hands demanded in a quavering alto. Augusta Hollins stood glowering down at her, eyes dark as thunder clouds.

"You were following me! Why?" she said, her voice atremble.

"What?" Rannie blinked. She could feel a moronic smile pasted on her face, and her eyes were open way too wide, shades of Lucy once again caught in the act by Desi.

"Don't bother denying it. I saw you sneaking down the street! There's a serial killer in the neighborhood. Are you crazy? You scared me half to death!" Her hand slapped Rannie's desk. Ms.

Hollins appeared startled, as if her hand had acted with a will all its own.

Mrs. Mac was staring at them, her eyes magnified to huge proportion behind bifocal glasses. The fracas caused Dotty to pop her head out of her office door and Jem Marshall to turn and pause on the staircase, a police officer directly behind him. Everyone appeared to be waiting for Rannie's answer.

"You must be mistaken," was the feeble best Rannie could come up with.

Ms. Hollins clearly wasn't buying it. She leaned in closer. "Just stay out of my business. You hear?"

Rannie nodded, eyes lowered, and nearly murmured, "Yes, ma'am." How was it that all teachers learned to perfect the art of intimidation?

Ms. Hollins turned and strode up the stairs to her office, her long braid twitching angrily down the back of another shapeless jumper. Mrs. Mac pretended to be engrossed in her phone message book; Dotty had ducked back in her office. Neither Jem Marshall nor the cop were in sight any longer. Shamefaced—the public dressing-down was deserved! she couldn't deny it—Rannie scooped up her belongings and fled.

Halfway home, it hit her. The Mengele manuscript. Her tote was under her desk. She had to go back.

Thankfully, no one remained in the reception area. The only people she saw were two cops coming downstairs carrying open cartons stuffed with files. Tut's, no doubt. Tote in hand, Rannie had every intention of making a quick exit until the telephone log on Mrs. Mac's desk caught her eye and beckoned. She waited until the Annex entryway door closed behind the cops. Then, furtively, she sidled over to Mrs. Mac's desk, wondering what demon had taken possession of her and how long it intended to stay in residence. *I'm not really doing anything wrong,* she rationalized, flipping back pages to check Tut's messages on Monday.

At two o'clock, there'd been a call from Eyesavers; his glasses were ready. Above that were earlier messages—David Ross's secretary confirming a two-thirty appointment, a message from somebody at Williams, another from somebody at Stanford. Also one from a Dr. George Ginandes. That sent up a tiny flare. Dire news perhaps? Tests that had come back with unwelcome results?

"Excuse me."

Rannie jumped.

Jem Marshall was standing beside her. Several typed letters were in his hand.

"I—I was checking about uh—tours. Mrs. Mac wasn't here."

"Yes, of course." Jem Marshall had the grace to act as if he believed her. "Excuse me. I need to leave these for Mrs. Mac."

Rannie moved aside. *Leave this instant! March!* her brain commanded. But her feet weren't responding to the signal. Frozen, she watched Jem set down the letters for Mrs. Mac.

"Uh-oh, left off a signature," he said. A ballpoint pen clicked open, and he bent over, his hand printing out his name in the same cramped, almost paralytic way Nate did.

"My son's a lefty too!" Rannie said in a weirdly joyous tone as if this established some intense, special bond between them.

He turned and nodded, a puzzled smile on his face.

He thinks I'm insane. I am insane. At last whatever neurons needed to connect did. Rannie began walking toward the Great Hall. "Buh-bye!" she called behind her gaily.

Chapter 14

Wednesday afternoon

AS SOON AS MADAME BERNBAUM SAID *"À DEMAIN"* TO EVERYONE IN DUMMY French, Olivia skipped English and ducked into the little playground near Chaps. Turtle Park was nothing more than a sandbox filled with cigarette butts and a few giant cement turtles for kids to climb on. A sheet stretched across windows in the project building next door saying, "Drug Pushers, Get Out of Our Neighborhood!" and indeed the two dealers who always used to hang out here were nowhere in sight.

It was nuts at school—cops questioning everyone—and her conversation with Grant yesterday had started nagging at her again. But one quick call would put a stop to the worrying. Like Dr. E. said: There was no reason to think he'd had a slip. Olivia believed Grant ... well, she believed him ninety-seven percent. If only she could erase the memory of his last slip.

Home for the Thanksgiving weekend, Grant had gone to the Macy's parade on Central Park West with some old friends from Chaps. She and Carlotta were downstairs in the kitchen making turkey gravy. When he came back, he was coked up. Right away, he started in about Tut fucking up his life, how if it weren't for Tut, he'd be at Princeton, not in rehab.

When Olivia said, "Hell-o, Grant? You were dealing drugs—in school. Remember?" he slugged her. Carlotta knocked him out cold with a skillet. Gravy flew all over the walls.

"Don' you never touch Livvy again!" Carlotta had screamed.

Now Olivia dug in the pocket of her duffle coat and found her Parliaments. Then she flipped open her mom's cell phone. Windward didn't allow Grant to have one, but last weekend while he was in the city, she'd made him keep hers. "What ... so you can check up on me?" Grant had said, adding, "I swear you're worse than Mom."

On the inside of her wrist Olivia had printed Windward's number in marker. Once again she practiced what to say.

A cheerful woman's voice answered the phone at Windward.

"Hi. This is Carole Werner, Grant's mother," Olivia told the cheerful voice. "I know you like us to check in after a weekend pass. I should have called before ..."

Olivia listened to the woman say she understood that parents led busy lives.

"Grant left home on Monday, the four-something train." Olivia's voice sounded completely fake to her and trembly, but she guessed it must be true what everyone said about her and her mother sounding alike.

"Hold on while I check the sign-in book, Mrs. Werner."

All she wanted the Windward lady to say was, "Yes, it's right in the book, Mrs. Werner. Grant was back here by seven." Then before they hung up, the woman would mention how thrilled the whole staff was with Grant's progress, how great he was doing.

Olivia's cigarette was smoked halfway down by the time the lady came back on the line. Her voice had lost some of its cheerfulness. "That was Monday you said? Well, I'm looking at the Monday page, and Grant didn't sign in until nine-fifteen that night. . . . Mrs. Werner? Are you there?"

"Sorry. My mistake. Uh . . . lookit, while I was waiting, I suddenly remembered. Grant picked his sister up at school. . . . And they went shopping. He took a later train."

"You're sure? I don't need to tell you how import—"

"Absolutely sure. Nine-fifteen is exactly when he should've gotten back. *Really.*" A little kid on one of the cement turtles was staring at her, picking his nose. "I'm so sorry, but I have to get off . . . another call's coming in. Thanks."

Grant had lied. He didn't leave New York when he said. He had hours in the city to get himself in trouble. He told her he never got to see Tut. Was that a lie too? What if he'd done some coke and got into a fight with Tut. . . . Olivia ordered herself to stop it. She was projecting. And anyway, it wasn't for sure that Tut'd been murdered. But here she was, jumping to the worst possible conclusion, just like Dr. E. said. And all that was doing was making her head spin, like when she used to get drunk and have the whirlies. Her cigarette fell out of her hand, and she frantically brushed an ember off her brand-new powder blue duffle coat.

Her brand-new duffle coat that now had a black scorch hole.

Chapter 15

"WILD IS THE ONLY WAY TO DESCRIBE GEORGE GORDON, LORD BYRON." Ms. Hollins was wrapping up Nate's last class of the day; there had been no mention of her bizarre exit the day before, no mention of Mr. Tut either.

"I love teaching Byron, because he was thoroughly reprehensible." She was leaning against a desk, her arms folded across her chest, one hand holding the poetry book. "He was a drunk, a drug addict. Incredibly handsome but a scoundrel and a tortured soul all his life. He had an affair with his half sister. Another woman who was in love with him described him as 'mad, bad, and dangerous to know.'"

The bell rang. Kids started gathering up stuff.

"Remember, read the first half of 'The Bride of Abydos' for tomorrow."

Nate grabbed his backpack and threw in his books. If he hurried, there was enough time to hit some tennis balls against the backboard before meeting his mother.

Who would have thought poetry written two hundred years ago was all about fucking? This guy Byron had a club foot and still was scoring all the time. *Mad, bad, and dangerous to know. . . .* That's what he wanted girls to say about him.

Outside the cafeteria, he saw Olivia talking to a junior guy. It was the first time Nate had seen her since Tut died. He went over and stood around until she realized he was waiting to speak to her. She stepped away from the kid and said, "Hey, Nate."

"You weren't in English."

"Yeah, well, I decided to blow it off."

"Listen . . . I just wanted to say I was sorry, I mean about what happened. You know, yesterday, finding Tut. . . . You doing okay?" *Was all this coming out sounding like R2D2?* He felt as if his lips weren't moving normally.

"Thanks. Yeah, I'm okay I guess," she said but she looked kind of nervous.

Nate shifted his weight from foot to foot and nodded, his lips pressed together. "Yeah, well good." *Boots, start walking.*

Forty-five minutes later, he was sweaty and his head felt pleasantly empty. He didn't think about Tut once or the fact that he seemed to be the only kid with no excuse. . . . Uh-uh, he told himself. An excuse was for gym or homework. He was the only kid with no alibi. Nate walked away from the backboard and, stashing his racket and can of balls in his locker, he peeled off his Chaps gym shorts and tee shirt. He left his sneakers by the pile of clothes and grabbed a towel from the shelf.

The shower room was completely empty, but he heard a door to one of the toilet stalls closing.

The hot water thrummed down on his back. He turned slightly to focus the hard spray on his left shoulder blade.

All of a sudden, the water turned scalding as a toilet flushed.

"Shit!" Nate jumped away from the steaming downpour. "Asshole, you're supposed to give a heads up!"

No answer.

When he returned to the locker room, a towel around his hips, his shoulder still stinging, he saw he had company. Elliot Ross. He was in black silk boxers, rolling on deodorant, facing his locker, zits the size of Everest on his back.

"Not funny, you prick."

Elliot didn't bother turning around. He finished getting dressed and exited the locker room in a rolling gorilla gait, arms held out from his sides. It was only after Nate went to put on his shoes that he realized Elliot hadn't even needed to flush the goddamn toilet.

He'd pissed in Nate's sneakers.

Swearing, Nate cleaned them off as best he could, got dressed, and texted Ben: "What's yr locker combo?" But after five minutes and no answer, Nate put on the sneakers. In the hallway the cop from yesterday, the Rosie O'Donnell lookalike, came up to him.

"Gotta minute, Nate?"

"Yeah, sure."

"Just a couple more questions." The notepad was out again. She wanted to know what he'd been wearing Monday. That was easy—a button-down shirt and decent khakis for his Columbia interview. And a sweatshirt under a lifer jacket.

"Monday, after you left Mr. Tutwiler's office where'd you go?"

"Home."

"Straight home?" She was multi-tasking, scribbling notes and eyeballing him at the same time. "What time did you arrive?"

"Well, uh, not *straight* home. I stopped at Circuit City." His voice came out shrill and girlish; she was making him nervous.

"Buy anything?"

He shook his head. *Was she into video games?* Then it clicked. *No, asshole, if you bought anything, you'd have a timed receipt.* "So anyway I got home around seven."

She flipped back pages in her notepad and was reading them. Her nose wrinkled and she sniffed. Fuck. His sneakers reeked.

"On Monday did you quarrel with Mr. Tutwiler?"

"No! Of course not. Why?"

She didn't reply, and all at once he remembered yesterday, before English, Elliot claiming Nate was the one hoping Tut croaked. Had Elliot told the cop that?

"I liked Mr. Tut! He liked me. Ask anybody." Except Elliot.

"So nothing else to add?"

Shit! Why hadn't he told her right away what Elliot had said? Now, if he did, it'd look like a lie.

"No. Nothing else."

Notepad flipped closed. "Well, thanks, Nate." Then right before she walked off, she glanced up and down the legs of his jeans. It took a second for it to dawn on him. The smell of his sneakers. She thought he was scared. She was checking to see if he'd pissed his pants. Fuck, fuck, fuck. Could this day get any worse?

Chapter 16

"COME ON, NATE. FINISH EATING OR BRING IT WITH YOU. WE'RE GOING to be late."

"This is so dumb, Ma," Nate said, stuffing more gyro in his mouth. "Eating *before* we go for dinner."

They were at the Acropolis in the last booth, one of the few that didn't have slashes of silver duct tape across the burgundy plastic seat coverings. Nate's news had killed Rannie's appetite; her souvlaki remained afloat in grease on her plate. She was always complaining how she wished Nate would open up more. Yet now he just had, and she wished he hadn't. Of course what Rannie wanted to hear was stuff about girls, his social life, his friends' social life. Not that the woman cop had come looking for him to ask scary follow-up questions. For Nate's sake, she had managed to put on a good front, insisting there was no reason to worry, all the while fighting to quell her own anxiety.

Fiddling with the scalloped corner of the paper menu place mat, she said, "You think maybe I should tell them their menu offers 'French fires' and 'dally specials'? They could make corrections before they print up any more."

"No, I don't. I think you should tell Grandma she never has enough food for dinner. Then we wouldn't have to come here first."

"I know, I know. But I can't. I'm a wimp. She really looks forward to seeing us. And I like going. It's just—there's yogurt sauce on your chin—it's just your grandmother is constitutionally incapable of serving normal-size portions of food. It's being a Wasp. Big drinks, yes. Big portions, no." Rannie sipped her Diet Coke. "Hey, what about this? I write a book and call it *Wednesdays with Mary*. Instead of sappy, Jewish-y, feel-good advice, it'll be full of chilly, Wasp, pop-philosophy. Like, 'No matter how hard the road you must travel, it's easier in sensible pumps from Bergdorf's'. . . . Or maybe, 'Crying in public is always unattractive—having a wet diaper is no excuse.'"

"Wha?" He swatted her hand away as she tried to daub away the yogurt on his face with a napkin. "Not a clue what you're talking about."

"You never heard of *Tuesdays with Morrie?*"

"No."

Rannie sighed as she left a twenty-dollar bill on the table. "My wit is wasted on you."

"Yeah, you're hilarious, Ma. There's open mike at the Comic Strip on Wednesdays. Think about it." Nate belched, wiped his chin with a greasy napkin which he left crumpled on his plate. "I'm done."

Earlier in the day, Rannie's brick-red barn jacket had been unnecessary. Now in the crisp October evening air, she was glad to be wearing it. She transferred pencils from the pocket to her bag—eventually the pockets of all her coats and jackets bore holes from the sharpened points of her Col-Erase blues.

They caught a cab that entered Central Park at 96th Street and rocketed through the tranverse. Rannie stared out the window, absently taking in the darkening sky and gloomy outlines of trees and bushes.

Nate had his eyes closed, his head resting against the back seat of the cab. Such long lashes. Rannie remembered the time he let Alice put mascara on him, a wand of Maybelline taken from Rannie's makeup drawer. "Don't get mad, Mommy," pleaded the four-year-old Nate, batting frightening, Carol Channing-like black eyelashes at her. "Al just wanted to make me pretty."

After the divorce, Rannie had worried that sweet-natured Nate was becoming too attached to her. He had been nine at the time, not a baby, but he seemed so much more vulnerable than Alice, who was a tough little cookie. Yet over the years Nate had indeed grown very self-reliant, and if it was disconcerting to be shut off from crucial things happening in his life, it was also reassuring. He was dealing just fine.

As a new mother, she would marvel to herself, "I am a parent now! This is what I'll be for the rest of my life." But the heavy-duty parenting was over before you knew it, and suddenly you were sitting in a cab beside a six-foot, two-inch person who once was your baby. Where had those years gone? Would anything even half as meaningful take their place?

Emerging from the park at Fifth Avenue, the cab headed east for two blocks before turning down Park Avenue. Mary Lorimer's building was a limestone monolith designed by Rosario Candela, the 1920s architect famous for grand-scale apartment houses. The building no longer barred Jews as residents; however, the coop board was still legendarily strict, recently turning down a Philharmonic conductor for fear of noise problems.

"Good evening," said the doorman, a dead ringer for Prince Charles, ushering Rannie and Nate into the lobby. "Mrs. Lorimer is expecting you." He pressed a button on a brass wall console, ensuring that the elevator automatically whisked Nate and Rannie to

the ninth floor. If you hit the button for another floor, forget it—
nothing happened. Her mother-in-law never had to worry about
homicidal maniacs lurking by the back stairs.

"My sweeties," Mary greeted them at the door of her apartment that had ten rooms, all decorated in faded chintz, mahogany
furniture, and needlepoint pillows with cute sayings. "Come on,
Nate. One kiss for an old lady. It won't kill you." Mary offered
her cheek. "Earla's made lamb chops. I know you love her lamb
chops."

Nate excused himself to do homework until dinner, and Mary
steered Rannie toward the den. Her tall thin frame was clad in a
periwinkle-blue sweater set that set off her silver pageboy, a hair-
style that had remained unchanged since Mary's post-war debutante
days. "Come. We have time for a cocktail. I read Larry Tutwiler's
obituary in the *Times* this morning, , , , I had no idea he was so old!"
Then Mary caught herself. "Honestly, will you listen to me? Don't I
have a nerve? As if he were generations older. He and Walter knew
each other, you know."

Rannie deposited herself in a silk blue-striped armchair in the
little den off the living room. There was another larger den, oak-
paneled and referred to as the library. This room was cozier, with
a small TV that Mary turned off before handing Rannie a glass of
white wine and settling into a matching chair beside her.

Rannie told Mary about being at Chaps when Tut had left via
ambulance.

"Lord. Please let me check out in the middle of the night, with
only the night doorman to witness my departure." Mary jiggled the
ice cubes in her tumbler of vodka.

"I'm with you. Although, it's silly, I suppose. Dead is dead. You're
not going to know who's there to watch. But I felt embarrassed for
Mr. Tut. He seemed so private." Rannie sipped her wine, which
tasted lovely and cold on her tongue, and then related what had

transpired since yesterday, a greatly abridged edition of events, all parts excised that would embarrass herself or upset Mary.

"Forensics? Lord, you don't mean to imply the police think Larry Tutwiler was *murdered*. The newspaper said he was eighty-three!"

"What does age have to do with it?"

"Nothing, I suppose." Mary crossed her legs, pondering. As usual, her 10 AAA feet were nestled in a pair of Ferragamo pumps with grosgrain bows. "But I guess when I think of murder, I think of a crime of passion. Real hatred. Old people don't arouse that kind of emotion usually."

Rannie chose not to reveal the possibility of Mr. Tut's late-in-life romance.

"Could they be looking to see if he might have killed himself?" Mary inquired. "I heard he had cancer."

"I wondered that too at first."

"Before he died, Walter once said to me—sitting right in the same chair you are—he said he wanted me to know that, if things got too bad, he had a big bottle of painkillers squirreled away. I nodded, told him I understood, and we never mentioned it again. When someone is in bad pain, it must be reassuring to know there's an escape hatch. Something quiet and unmessy."

"But, Mary, Tut would never have killed himself at Chaps. He wouldn't have risked some poor teenager stumbling in on his body. The girl who found him was a wreck."

"Well ... I see your point. Nevertheless, people I know simply don't get murdered."

So much for persuasive reasoning. . . . Rannie shook her head at the plate of withered celery stalks that Mary held out. Instead, she asked, "Remind me. How did Tut and Walter first meet?"

"From the club. He once gave Walter a great stock tip. I remember thinking at the time it must be a company that made toilet paper. It was Microsoft." Mary laughed. "After that, every year at Christmas-

time Walter always sent him a case of expensive scotch. . . . Dall—
something." Rannie smiled, remembering her own introduction to
single malt scotch.

"Larry was a very shrewd investor."

Rannie had always guessed Tut came from money; according
to Mary, no. His father had been a librarian at Columbia, and he'd
been on scholarship at Chaps. "The school will get most of his estate, I'd imagine. He had no family. Sad, isn't it?" Mary paused for
a long sip of vodka. "For a few years Larry was seeing a very lovely
woman with piles of money. She was from the South—Laura Scales.
A divorcée who also belonged to the club."

Divorcée, now there was a word you didn't hear very often. A
glamorous word from the fifties, conjuring up women in black,
elbow-length gloves, a martini glass in one hand, a cigarette holder
in the other. Rannie had been divorced for years, but she wasn't
remotely a divorcée. "When was this? How old was Tut?"

"I doubt Larry was even forty. Laura was about the same age.
They were quite a couple, both so attractive. We had dinner together several times. Walter used to tease me, said I had a sneaker
for Larry."

"A what?"

"Come on, you've never heard that expression? A sneaker is a
crush. And I'll admit Larry *was* terribly appealing, the kind of man
who made you feel whatever you said was perfectly fascinating. He
had lots of admirers."

Rannie nodded. She'd sensed that Tut genuinely liked women, not
simply sexually but in a way that appreciated their "otherness."

"I bet I have pictures somewhere. Wait."

From one of the wall cabinets Mary retrieved a photo album, its
maroon leather cover crumbling. Flipping quickly through pages,
she stopped and said, "Here." Then Mary placed the open album
in Rannie's lap.

The photo she pointed to showed a much younger Mary and Walter sitting at a poolside table, lifting cocktails to the camera. Standing behind them, also raising a glass was Tut, tall, tan and fit in khaki Bermuda shorts and a navy polo shirt. Next to him was a classic country club blond—gold shrimp earrings, velvet hairband, lime green and shocking pink shift.

"And here's another. Too bad. You can't really see Laura in the picture." Tut was in a tuxedo dancing cheek to cheek with his lady friend, her back to the camera, in a long dress with a slit up the side, her blond hair in a French twist.

"I remember watching them at club functions. Larry was a beautiful dancer. Gosh, look at Walter and me. I wasn't gray yet. This must be at least forty-five years ago. Ancient history."

Mary leaned over beside Rannie and flipped through a few more pages. "That's Laura. We were at some charity lunch." Both women wore tailored suits. From a round circle of gold wire around Laura's neck hung what looked to be an elaborately carved piece of jade.

"That's quite a hunk of jade."

"Laura loved jewelry. And Larry liked to buy her something on every trip. They took long wonderful trips in the summer—went to Hong Kong before anybody went there. India too. Laura had no children. So she was free as a bird."

Mary freshened her drink at the bar and went on. "At one point, I thought they might marry. But Laura despised the city in cold weather, spent all winter down in Hilton Head. And Larry wouldn't give up teaching. Anyway, it all ended very suddenly and unhappily. There were rumors flying—aren't there always?—that Larry was seeing someone else and Laura found out. The usual. I have no idea if any of it was true. I remember Laura looked awful. Puffy." Mary touched her eyelids and cheeks with her fingertips. "Bloated. I worried she was drinking, but Daisy said no—you remember my friend Daisy Satterthwaite. And Daisy would know. She and

Laura were very close. In any case, Laura left New York in a big hurry and went back home for good. I used to get a card from her at Christmastime."

Interesting . . . but then people's back stories almost always were. Nothing Mary said was hard to believe, and all of it was intriguing. "See if you can't find out more about what happened," Rannie asked.

"I'm having lunch with Daisy tomorrow at the Colony." Mary passed a silver scalloped dish with radishes to Rannie. "Join us. Daisy loves to gab."

"Yes. I'd like that." The wine was having its effect on her; she felt pleasantly tired and heavy-limbed. Mary asked after Rannie's mother—was she enjoying the cruise through the fjords?—and when Alice might be coming down to the city so Mary could take her on yet another shopping spree. Then Mary mentioned a recent call from Peter. "I think he spends most of his days playing tennis. He's never at that magazine he supposedly works for. I can't imagine why they're paying him." Mary sniffed and her face tightened slightly. Her other son was a Wall Street lawyer at the same firm where Walter had been managing partner. She looked straight at Rannie. "Peter's charming, and I love him. But he's a child. A forty-four-year-old child. Perfect for an affair. But not terrific husband material."

Rattled, Rannie found herself in the odd position of defending her ex-husband to his mother although Mary's assessment was clear-sighted. In one respect, Rannie appreciated Mary's frankness, knowing it was a mark of affection for Rannie. But who, if not your own mother, could you count on to always be on your side? Maybe that had been part of Peter's problem.

A moment later Earla's imposing, white-uniformed bosom preceded Earla herself, announcing that dinner was served. Nate met them in the dining room, beautifully laid out with a damask tablecloth, tall tapers in silver candlesticks, and *famille verte* plates. Rannie forced herself not to look Nate's way once they were seated, and Earla brought out a serving platter with three dessicated gray lamb chops, accompanied by a bowl of Green Giant Le Sueur peas floating in canned juice, and some boiled new potatoes, the size and color of testicles.

"Dig in!" Mary told them.

"Looks great, Grandma," Nate said, managing a straight face.

It was when they were ready to leave, Nate hoisting on his backpack, that Mary took Rannie aside and whispered, "I don't know if I should even mention this. But Nate. He reeks of garlic. Not just his breath but his skin too. It's as if it's coming out of his pores. I've noticed it before. It's not the food here. Earla *never* overspices the food. Do you suppose it's hormonal?"

"Possibly. I can ask the doctor about it."

Next week Rannie would have to remember to bring Certs to the Acropolis.

It was almost ten by the time Rannie and Nate returned to the apartment. She flicked on the kitchen light switch and opened the fridge for a Coke. A black waterbug the size of a Hot Wheels car skittered across the linoleum. Shuddering, Rannie grabbed the soda and installed herself in the living room on the rose toile-print sofa that was a hand-me-down from Mary. She composed a query letter about the copyediting position open at Croyden and Woolf and rejiggered her résumé to emphasize her experience in children's books.

The décor of her apartment was either "eclectic" or "haphazard" depending on a person's tolerance for mismatched furniture. Whatever, it suited Rannie—all comfortable, lived-in stuff acquired from different chapters in her life. In the living room, built-in bookshelves with scallop shell molding flanked the fireplace. More bookshelves, ones made by Peter early in their marriage, ran

underneath a row of three windows, and on the wallspace behind
the sofa was Rannie's collection of hand-painted plates. Her single
extravagance was cut flowers always placed in a green glass pitcher
on the mantle. Gorgeous stargazer lilies this week, almost overpow-
eringly fragrant. Cheaper than Prozac was her rationale.

Just as she was sharpening up some pencils, preparing to spend
another hour with Mengele, "Uncle Doctor" to his unsuspecting
young victims at Auschwitz, the doorbell rang. Odd at this hour.
Rannie left the couch. On the other side of the fish-eye in the front
door was the super.

"Rannie, somebody left this under the door in the lobby. I just
saw it."

Rannie undid the chain and opened the door. "Thanks, Frank."

Her name was written in purple marker on the envelope. *Miranda Bookman Lorimer*. How formal. Bidding the super good night,
Rannie refastened the chain and tore open the envelope.

There were only two words, printed in a font she was unfamiliar
with, a font that made each letter appear as if it had been cut out
from a newspaper headline: *STOP SNOOPING*.

A sickening little shudder traveled through her, and the sheet of
paper fluttered to the floor. She sank down on the couch. From Ms.
Hollins? Hard to believe and yet who else? If she meant to get back
at Rannie, unnerve her, well, she'd done the job. Rannie's hands
were shaking. On one level, Rannie guessed she deserved payback
for tailing Ms. Hollins although what she'd done had been spur of
the moment. This chilling warning was calculated, premeditated.
Exactly what was Ms. Hollins hiding? As Rannie ripped the paper
into tiny shreds over the kitchen garbage can, she tried to calm
herself with the notion that now the score was settled. Now they
were even.

Chapter 17

THE CRINGE-INDUCING THOUGHT OF SHOWING HER FACE AT CHAPS AND running into Ms. Hollins filled Rannie with dread ... well, maybe not "dread" exactly, but definitely trepidation. So she was overjoyed when a call came from Mrs. Mac saying her morning tour was canceled. She remained at home with Josef Mengele for company.

The beauty of copyediting was getting paid to read, to do something you'd do for free. In the process she acquired all sorts of interesting tidbits. Just a moment ago she'd learned that, contrary to what she'd always supposed, only fraternal twins ran in families. Identical twins were purely genetic odds.

After putting away the manuscript, she turned to some yearbook layouts that Nate had left out for her to proofread. The layouts were for the faculty section. First, using a school directory and last year's Chaps yearbook as reference, Rannie proofread the text, catching a couple of spelling errors in teachers' names and changing 1895 to 1995 as the year the head of athletics started at Chaps. Next, she checked "visuals." Each present-day portrait of a teacher was paired with the teacher's own senior year yearbook photo.

It was a clever idea, showing what authority figures looked like way back when, and she made a mental note to compliment Nate, the editor. One of the kindergarten teachers, smiling and pert now, had been a sullen Goth goddess; somebody who taught Middle School math already had a receding hairline at eighteen. Nate's physics teacher had been a drool-worthy hunk. Rannie felt conflicted emotions gazing at the photocopy of teenaged Ms. Hollins with the same long dark hair fanning around her shoulders like a cape.

On the coffee table, Nate had also left a stack of teachers' yearbooks and Rannie found the one from the exclusive all-girls boarding school Ms. Hollins had attended. There were photos of her on the staff of the literary magazine, in a madrigal singing group, and as head of something called "Saturday Salon" that sounded artsy/intellectual. In the few candid group photos that included her, she always seemed a little forlorn and on the periphery.

Mr. Tut's sixty-something-year-old Chaps yearbook was filled with photos of Gus Tutwiler as he'd been called back then. Senior Class president. Tennis team captain. Quintessential prep school wonder boy. In his senior picture, his fierce bushy eyebrows punctuated an oversized nose. It was a vulnerable, adolescent face still in transition and oddly endearing, a face whose features needed to solidify before Tut matured into the attractive man of later years.

Sadly, the photo of Tut from the most recent yearbook showed him already in diminished health though still spiffy in a school blazer and bow tie. Rannie inspected the photo more closely. There was something wrong. It took a moment before it clicked: The school crest on Tut's breast pocket was on the right, not the left. The photograph had been "flopped," accidentally printed in reverse. The only time flopped images stood out as glaring errors was in cases when visible lettering—on store signs or on theater marquees—showed up as mirror writing. Or, if a famous "lefty" like Babe Ruth was shown batting on the wrong side of the plate. Something small like the Chaps crest could easily escape notice. Still, copy editors worth their salt were always on the lookout for just such glitches, and Rannie felt a familiar little "gotcha!" thrill nailing this one. She stuck on a Post-it advising Nate to find the actual photo of Tut and to ask the printer to reproduce it correctly.

A glance at her father's wristwatch warned her that lunch at the Colony Club was fast approaching. But, Rannie lingered a moment longer, matching up the high school pictures of Ms. Hollins and Mr. Tut. Looking at them side by side, there was definitely something, an affinity between the two faces. Perhaps it was the depth and intelligence of the eyes that made their being drawn to each other understandable. Had it been an affair? The embossed numerals on the front cover of Ms. Hollins's yearbook revealed she was not many years older than Rannie. Of course, a strictly platonic friend of a terminally ill man might stay over in case of some night-time medical emergency. But then why lie? Why say they were merely casual friends? As Rannie closed the two yearbooks, debating what from her meager wardrobe to wear, she was left with a niggling sense that something more had gone on between this man and woman . . . although she was at a total loss as far as what the "something" might be or whether it had contributed in any way to Mr. Tut's death.

Chapter 18

Thursday morning

OLIVIA WAS IN THE BREAKFAST NOOK WITH CARLOTTA, BOTH DRINKING café con leche and eating English muffins dripping with butter. Carlotta was reading a story about "el maniaco S.W.A.K." in *El Diario*, muttering about what she'd do to that crazy man if she got her hands on him.

"Livvy, I hate you bein' in that neighborhood. Promise me you don' go wanderin' around with nobody. I worry." And when Carlotta kissed her, Olivia could feel the silkiness of the butter from Carlotta's lips on her cheek.

Olivia was going in to school late. At ten-thirty, she had to submit the design assignment for her application to FIT, eight outfits all with a fruit theme. There was nothing her mother could do: Olivia had paid the application fee herself.

Carlotta, who had taught Olivia to sew, thought her designs were gorgeous. "You gonna be a famous fashion designer someday! I'm tellin' you!"

She took a cab to Ninth Avenue and 28th Street. After dropping off the application, she stood around, watching kids hurrying to classes, portfolios and sketchbooks under their arms, and thought, "I'll be happy here. I'll make interesting friends." Since tenth grade when her only close friend transferred to boarding school, all she had were the Lilys, who were okay for shopping sprees but not much else.

To put off going to Chaps a little longer, Olivia crossed Seventh Avenue and started walking uptown. At 33rd Street, she saw two guys hanging out on the wide steps that led to Madison Square Garden. She recognized them right away. Her eyes trained downward on her New Balances, Olivia kept walking, hoping to hurry past unnoticed. No such . . .

"Hey Chiquita," the thinner of the two shouted to her while the other made lip-smacking sounds like he was beckoning a dog. "Come on! You remember us, I know you do."

It was Grant and his friends who first started calling them Arm and Hammer because the coke they sold was half baking soda. The names stuck. For years Chaps kids had been buying drugs from them in Turtle Park. This year they'd been around when school first started, but then it was as if they vanished into thin air. Right away the rumors started. "Arm got arrested and snitched out Hammer." "Hammer got shot and Arm left town." "Arm and Hammer? They're gay for each other. They moved to Vermont to get married." But some kids said they heard that Mr. Marshall had gone over to the playground and told them to beat it or there'd be trouble with the cops.

"Come on. Say hello," Arm called out teasingly. His neck was covered with so many tattoos that it looked like he was always wearing a blue turtleneck. Hammer was fat, with a blown-out Afro. Even when it was hot, he wore a puffy vest.

Olivia blinked in an imitation of surprise. "Oh, hey!"

"You saw us. Don't be pretending like you didn't," Hammer said. His eyes swept over her. "You looking fine!"

"So—anybody asks, you tell them this is where to find us," Arm said. "You got that? The business cards ain't printed up yet."

Hammer chuckled, shaking his head.

"We under new management. Moved to nicer digs. You like?" He gestured to a small building on the side street. "I can get my girl to get you an ex-spresso if you want it."

"A Frapa-fuckin'-chino," Hammer giggled.

"Got a new deal. Man upstairs. The man asked us to re-lo-cate." Arm was talking fast, but he accentuated each syllable of the word. "You know him, Chiquita. Man upstairs."

"Who?" Olivia said.

"He your man upstairs too."

"Blond nigga with the stick up his ass," Hammer said.

Arm stood up and took a few steps, feet pointing outward, shoulders stiff, head tucked in slightly; it actually wasn't a half-bad imitation of the way the new headmaster walked, a little like a waddle.

"Mr. Marshall?"

"That his name? We don't be looking for no trouble. We tell him that. Whatever he wants, here we are . . . happy to oblige. That right, son?" Arm turned for confirmation, but Hammer's eyes were glassy and blank. "That right, son?" Arm repeated. "Any time he wants to party. Here we are."

"Shit, nigga," Hammer said. "I'm fuckin' baked." They both started laughing, a sly, stoned laugh.

A cab pulled up in front of the entrance to Penn Station.

"Yeah, okay—well, see ya!" Olivia said and ran over, rapping her knuckles on the glass to get the driver's attention. Next stop Chaps. Just as she was slamming the door, Arm shouted to her, "Say hi to your bro. . . . Tell him there's always a discount."

Thursday morning
Invitation in Rannie Bookman's mail

Please join the Chapel School Community
Monday
at eleven o'clock in the morning
at the Cathedral Church of St. John the Divine
for a celebration of the life of
A. Lawrence Tutwiler

Following the service, there will be refreshments in the
basement of the Cathedral. Please note that school will be
closed that day.

Chapter 19

Thursday lunch

CUSTOM DICTATED THAT NONMEMBERS OF THE COLONY CLUB USE THE side entrance on 62nd Street just west of Park Avenue.

"Daisy's meeting us up in 'Strangers,'" Mary said while Rannie held out a hand to help her mother-in-law from the cab.

Strangers' Dining Room. Ah yes. Such a welcoming name.

Mary swiveled her legs around and hoisted herself up, wincing slightly as she did. Then slipping her arm through Rannie's, she proceeded gingerly to the building in the cautious way of elderly ladies who had yet to break a hip and intended to keep it that way. "Don't you look darling. I love that suit on you."

They were both in red, Mary in a short-sleeved dress, Rannie in a faux-Chanel braid-trim jacket and kick-pleat skirt—her interview outfit.

"Good. We're right on time." Mary checked the clock by the elevator. "Twelve-thirty on the dot. I hope you're hungry."

Behind its dignified four-story Georgian facade, the Colony offered its twenty-five hundred or so members, all ladies with a capital "L," a well-stocked library, sitting parlors, a card room, a sweeping ballroom for weddings and coming-out parties, a pool and gymnasium that put Chaps's vaunted facilities to shame, beautiful rooms for overnight guests, and a rarefied, Republican atmosphere.

Daisy Satterthwaite, at a table by a large window set in an arch, acknowledged their presence by lifting an empty martini glass and waggling the fingers of her other hand, which held an unlit cigarette. "Over here!" she called in a husky smoker's voice.

As they made their way to the table, Mary stopped more than once to greet friends—"girls," she still called them—many from her days at Chapin and Smith. Like Mary, these women came from families so blue-blooded that many of their last names had once been Manhattan telephone exchanges. Rhinelanders. Schuylers. Lehighs. "A forest of family trees" was the way Edith Wharton, a founding member, had described the club's membership.

"Forgive me for getting a little head start. I've already ordered martinis for you." Daisy was dressed in a double-breasted linen coat dress in a strange color that called to mind infant diarrhea. There was a stain on the collar.

As Mary and Rannie sat down in two Chippendale-style chairs, three more martini glasses arrived.

"Rannie, Mims told me you suspect murder! Now wouldn't that beat everything! So unattractive and grisly!" Daisy said with unconcealed glee followed by a wheezy, deep-lung cough and a generous sip from her martini glass.

"Mims, I remember necking with Larry when we were teenagers on Fisher's Island. He was damn cute."

Daisy Satterthwaite had short, coarse, dyed-blond hair; a deeply lined face; and a perpetual tan because, she once told Rannie, "Tan fat looks so much better than pasty white fat." The gold buttons on her dress strained across her bustline and were nearly identical to the gold earrings she was wearing.

"So? You want all the dirt about Larry and Laura Scales."

Rannie laughed. "So much for chitchat."

"Don't be embarrassed, Rannie dear. Daisy adores to dish."

"I won't deny it. I always remember Alice Roosevelt's motto—she was a member here. 'If you can't say something nice about somebody, then come sit next to me.'" Daisy coughed again, then continued. "I was crazy about Laura Scales. Simply crazy. Only woman I knew whose luck with men was almost as bad as mine. I've been divorced three times. Laura only twice."

Rannie found herself sitting up straighter while she and Mary listened to Daisy. One thing about Wasps, they had terrific posture.

"We met at Foxcroft. She was a year older, from the South, and took me under her wing. Foxcroft back then belonged to the Southern girls, it was *their* school; they were the most popular and tended to look down at us Yankees. But Laura was a smoker and so was I. We used to sneak out to the stables, nearly burned them to the ground once. We became best friends."

The trip to a buffet table laden with silver chafing dishes interrupted conversation, which continued to remain on hiatus while everyone ate, Daisy with gusto, Mary only nibbling. The Colony chicken with vegetables that Rannie selected, while unexceptional, was far tastier than the grim fare served *chez* Lorimer.

From where she sat, Rannie could see the beautiful loggia that adjoined the dining room. She wished it was warm enough to eat out there surrounded by frescos of birds—cormorants, flamingos, parrots, all painted in a vaguely Chinese style and in intoxicating shades of blues, yellows, greens, scarlets. So unlike the understated decor of the rest of the club, so giddy and beguiling.

Daisy reclaimed her unlit cigarette, which she'd placed beside her dessert fork as if it were another piece of flatware. "Christ! These idiotic laws! I tell a much better story when I'm smoking. . . . Anyway, I was in Laura's first wedding, to a boy from Richmond, Virginia. Henry Shackelford. Lovely but light on his feet. A fairy. Laura claimed they had sex twice the whole time they were married and I have no reason to doubt her word. The most well-moisturized man I ever saw. Not a wrinkle. Not one!" Daisy laughed raucously. "Finally ran off to Palm Springs with someone in the same eating club at Princeton. Cap and Gown, I think." Daisy stamped out her cigarette on an empty butter plate as if she'd actually smoked it and had barely raised her arm before the waiter nodded and appeared with another martini along with Rannie and Mary's order of coffee. "After that, Laura became involved with a married man—Ted Scales. *Plenty* of sex with him, puh-lenty, and after eons of carrying on, he finally leaves his wife to marry Laura. And what does she do? Divorces him within a year! No fun anymore for either of them! Can you stand it?" Daisy looked around the table, clearly delighted. "So she moved here and met Larry. That's what I loved about Laura. She was a little crazy. She really was.

"I brought some things to show you, keepsakes Laura left me." From a scuffed navy leather purse with a bamboo handle and knob closing, Daisy produced a velvet jeweler's bag with drawstrings. She handed it to Rannie who was surprised by its heaviness.

Loosening the drawstrings, Rannie let a disk of jade, the size of a blini pancake, fall into her palm. The shade of green was so pale that it approached white. A Chinese dragon was etched deeply into the surface, its eyes almost comically fierce, a small globe held in its mouth. "She was wearing this in one of the photos you showed me," Rannie said to Mary.

Sipping her coffee, Mary lifted her shoulders in a gesture that implied she didn't recall.

"Larry gave it to her. She loved dragons. He used to call her his Dragon Lady." Daisy rummaged around in her purse and found a red leather box with gold edging that she flipped open. Inside was a gold ring of a dragon's head with tiny ruby eyes. "Also from Larry," she said. "These, too." There were several stick pins ornamented with dragons. They lay on a bed of cotton in a box from a London antiques shop.

Daisy sighed and replaced everything in her purse. "He was a thoughtful man, and they loved each other. Larry got a kick out of Laura. She was good fun. If Larry wanted to go rafting down some river in South America, Laura was game. It was Laura's only grown-up—" Daisy interrupted herself. "—oh, I despise the word 'relationship,' but that's what it was."

"Why did it end?" Rannie asked.

Daisy fell silent.

"I always assumed it was Larry," Mary put in, as if providing her friend with an opening. "There were a lot of ladies who liked him."

"Well, Larry did end it. But not for the reason you think."

Both Mary and Rannie set down their cups of coffee and waited.

"Daisy, is that all you're going to say?" Mary was clearly exasperated. "After Rannie raced down from *Harlem* to have lunch? When did you suddenly become so tactful?"

"Laura hadn't been feeling well," Daisy offered.

Mary nodded. "I remember she was looking awful. Puffy. I thought maybe after he called it off, she was drinking."

Daisy laughed. "No, Mims. That's my cure for a broken heart. . . . My cure for just about anything, come to think of it!" Daisy drained her glass as if to prove the point. "Laura was gaining weight but not from booze. One day we were in a dressing room at Saks, and I remember saying to her that her boobs looked so much bigger."

"Daisy, please. Stick to Larry. Nobody's interested in Laura's bra size."

Rannie touched her mother-in-law's arm gently to silence her. Rannie was beginning to see where Daisy Satterthwaite was heading.

"Larry wanted Laura to remain in New York with everything exactly as it had been." Daisy stressed those last few words. "Just the two of them, spending lots of time with each other but keeping separate apartments. Laura didn't want that anymore. Things had changed. So she moved back South, to Asheville, North Carolina."

"She was pregnant, wasn't she?" Rannie said.

Daisy nodded. "Yup. Preggers." She paused. "I know they're both dead and buried ... well, that's not exactly true, Larry's *dead* and eventually he'll be buried. ... But I've never told a soul about this before. And I have a big mouth; you needn't pretend otherwise, Mims."

"That's absolutely true, dear. I'm amazed by your silence all these years." Mary lifted her coffee cup in salute to her friend.

Half an hour later, on the Madison Avenue bus, heading uptown from the Colony, Rannie mulled over the rest of what Daisy had divulged. Actually, to be more accurate, she hadn't divulged anything else; instead, Daisy simply continued to nod whenever the answer was "yes" to one of Rannie's questions. All Rannie could piece together was that Mr. Tutwiler wasn't enthusiastic about becoming a husband or father. Laura, on the other hand, considered the pregnancy something that was meant to be. She returned home to have her baby and that's where she'd remained.

Tut's indifference to having a family of his own disappointed Rannie. By her calculation, he was nowhere near codger-dom, so for him was it a matter of, "Yes, I like kids but only from nine to five"? To be so selfishly set in his ways lessened Tut in her eyes.

Chapter 20

"SO GLAD YOU COULD MAKE IT, RANDY! COULD WE HAVE ORDERED MORE perfect weather?"

Rannie smiled, not bothering to correct Olivia's mother and at the same time thinking it was typical that she not only knew Carole Werner's first name but that it was spelled with an extraneous "e." The Werners were hosting tonight's Senior Parents cocktail party. Tut's death did not warrant postponing the event, not when money needed to be raised for Chaps.

Olivia's mother, slim as a fiddlehead fern in sleeveless green silk, stood in the front hall of the Werner townhouse. On her left hand sat a diamond that wasn't as big as the Ritz perhaps but still very sizable.

"As soon as Olivia comes back down in the elevator, she'll take you up to the roof."

"How is Olivia? I was concerned."

Carole Werner either didn't understand the thrust of the question or chose not to acknowledge it. "Oh, fine, fine. Trying to figure out about college, of course." Her voice had the same appealing huskiness as her daughter's. "We told my in-laws that she might take a gap year in order to be a stronger candidate next fall. They looked at me as if I'd gone mad and said, 'Why on earth would selling jeans make her more desirable to colleges?' Isn't that hilarious?" Carole Werner continued chattering about Sophie Roper from last year's senior class—did Randy know the Ropers? Super people!—and how Sophie was off ice-fishing in Alaska, living with an Inuit family. "We considered that for Olivia, but frankly it's, well, it's not special enough anymore. And it's so hard to fly tutors up there."

No response was required as another mother had arrived and, while she was air-kissing Olivia's mother, the elevator door opened.

"Ms. Bookman, hey," Olivia said as the small mahogany car filled up with two more parents and slowly climbed three floors. Rannie took in Olivia's outfit. Despite the season, she was in a tummy-baring spaghetti-strap top, capri pants, and sequined flip-flops. Rannie wondered if Olivia knew how close she'd come to acquiring a new wardrobe of fur-hooded parkas and muk-luks.

"Make sure to have the baby lamb chops," Olivia advised. Then, with one practiced sweep of her hand, she pulled across the retractable gate and pushed open the elevator door.

It truly was a spectacular night, Cole Porter-glamorous. A cloudless and transparent navy blue sky, peculiar to Manhattan in the fall, hung overhead. And the evening was mild enough for the camisole Rannie was wearing with gray silk pants and Mandarin-style jacket, items filched from her daughter's abundantly stocked closet. She breathed in the balmy air and surveyed the Werners' rooftop. Under a striped awning a cloth-covered table served as a bar. Black wrought iron furniture was pushed against the opposite wall where waiters appeared through a door bearing trays laden with sushi, caviar on toast points, bite-sized quesadillas, and the vaunted baby lamb chops.

A moment later, armed with a glass of wine and a quesadilla, Rannie zigzagged through the crowd to the far side of the roof, avoiding both Ms. Hollins and Arthur Black. Eager parents clustered around Tut's newly-named interim replacement, a woman in a chic wrap dress who'd made a name as a private college counselor. Rannie sipped her wine and waved to her friend Joan who was busy chatting up David Ross, the real estate mogul. He remained in his trenchcoat as if only dropping by before heading off to a more important social engagement. Not far away Jem Marshall stood off by himself, looking like the "new kid" with nobody to talk to; Rannie decided to help him out.

"Hi there! Is this your first Chaps cocktail party?"

He nodded and smiled.

"Cheers, then." Rannie tapped her glass to his. "May you have many long and happy years at the school."

"Thanks. That's very kind. You're the mother of a lifer, if I'm not mistaken."

"Yes. My name is—"

"Oh, I know your name. Rannie Bookman. I see you at school. You're Nate's mother." His face grew solemn. "It must be very sad for you."

What? Being Nate's mother?

He saw the utter confusion on her face and sputtered, "Oh! You thought I was referring to Nate! No, no! I meant about Mr. Tutwiler passing. . . . He looked particularly ill Monday, don't you think?"

So he was still clinging to the "natural death" party line. God willing, maybe he'd be proven right.

"It's my loss I never got the chance to know him better," Mr. Marshall added. An uncomfortable smile, half mournful, half "hailfellow" jolly, sat uneasily on his face. Then, seeming to have reached the end of his remarks, he blinked a couple of times.

"Well, lovely seeing you," Rannie said to his evident relief, and, to avoid any awkwardness, she moved toward the door. She always checked out bathrooms at Chaps parties, as often they were the most dazzling feature of the apartment. One in a penthouse aerie had an entire wall of windows so you could bathe while enjoying a panoramic view of Central Park. Another was a Turkish-tiled fantasy the size of Rannie's living room.

The nearest bathroom *chez* Werner was down a flight of stairs. It was utterly simple and utterly luxurious in soft apricot matte marble. There was an orchid plant with blooms in the exact same shade of apricot and a Matisse print . . . nothing more than four or five black lines but—God!—what perfect lines.

Then returning to the rooftop, Rannie remained stationed near the door, snagging a baby lamb chop at every opportunity while she eavesdropped on bits of conversation. Some typical alpha-male chest-pounding, some "any word on Tut" inquiries, and one mother-to-mother exchange she wished her own mother could hear.

"He was all set to apply to Chapel Hill until we drove in from the airport. Churches everywhere. Not that I have anything against religion, mind you. But the signs out front! 'Forget e-mail, try knee-mail' . . . 'This church is prayer-conditioned.' One had a gigantic billboard saying, 'Apply SON-screen now to prevent burning later.' We turned right around and took the next plane home."

"Hello again."

Rannie, mid-bite into another baby lamb chop, looked up. The gray-haired, cute dad.

"Can I ask you something?"

She nodded and attempted to smile around the lamb chop.

"What are you doing with them? The bones, I mean." He had on a sportscoat and tie tonight.

Rannie swallowed. "I beg your pardon?"

He stepped closer. "I'm pretty sure that's your fourth lamb chop, but you don't seem to have the other bones. I'm curious. Where'd they go?"

"You're watching me eat?" Stuffing her face was more accurate.

"Look. Don't get offended. It's great food. And I'm strategically positioned just like you. Personally I like the chicken kebabs best, but they have those sticks." He pulled a few out of his jacket pocket. "So I just want to know. How did you make those bones disappear?"

Right then a waiter walked by with an empty silver platter. Rannie delicately placed the latest bone, carefully blanketed in her napkin, on it.

"I don't think that was so hard to figure out."

"I guess not. But what's that?" He pointed to a ficus tree in a brass planter right behind her. "An elephant graveyard?"

Rannie had no choice but to face the evidence—three gnawed bones poking out from among the white pebbles in the planter. She could feel her cheeks reddening. "I have no idea how those got there." She strove for a haughtily aggrieved tone, then, not thinking, added, "But if you knew, why ask?"

"Conversation starter?"

"You ditch me in a coffee shop, and now I'm getting grief about my manners?"

Although she remembered his name perfectly well, Rannie asked, "Remind me. Who at Chaps gets to call you Dad?"

He smiled. A great smile, with a front tooth overlapping the other just a little. "Tim Butler. And I'm sorry for the other night, but it was unavoidable." He scanned the rooftop which, in the growing darkness, was lit by hurricane lamps and waylaid a waiter. He presented Rannie with the last remaining lamb chop.

Rannie shooed away his hand although she couldn't help smiling. "Oh, no, you don't. . . . Absolutely not."

"Come on. Consider it a peace offering." He winked. Beautiful, curly eyelashes. So Rannie relented, allowing Tim to bury the remains in the planter along with the others.

"I don't know a soul here," he told her. His son had transferred to Chaps junior year. "All Chris's doing. I never heard of Chaps before. He was at Saint Eustace up in the Bronx, playing basketball, mouthing off to the priests. Normal kid." *Nah-mil* as pronounced by a man from Kennedy country. "Then spring vacation his sophmore year, he takes a trip to the Basketball Hall of Fame in Springfield with one of his buddies on the team. Sunday, the family goes for a drive in the country and stops for lunch in Amherst—'Ammersed' not 'Am-Herst,' he informs me is how you pronounce it. Anyway, he comes home and tells me Father Slattery can just forget about him applying to B.C. because this is where he's going to college. Next thing he's talking about switching high schools and ends up getting practically a free ride here. I'm paying no more than I was for Catholic School with eight hundred kids in a graduating class. And he's doing fine . . . has to take eleventh grade math and gets extra help in physics. But Latin? Honors class."

Rannie laughed and even found it endearing that Tim Butler looked so pleased to see that she wasn't annoyed. His expression, with its slight gleam of triumph, reminded her of Nate when he was a small boy who, after misbehaving, would quickly worm his way back in her good graces.

"Tell you what. Let me treat you to a meal at my place some time." He told her it was called The Offbeat. "I pour a good drink and the pastrami sandwiches are nice and thick."

So, a bartender, but one who was drinking nothing but club soda, she noticed.

"And you? What do you do? I'm guessing lawyer. Not corporate, nothing near Wall Street. More like public service."

Rannie shook her head. "Forget the 'no cigar.' You're not even close. I'm unemployed now. I used to work in publishing. . . . until Nancy Drew got me fired." It was a pretty good line, one she'd used before.

He smiled. "What happened?"

"There was a typographical error in a book—a doozy. And"— Rannie shrugged—"I was the managing editor in charge and the fall guy. They hired someone else with less experience at half the salary."

"Managing editor . . . sounds important."

"It's not. Believe me. I'm a copy editor, not a *real* editor. I was just part of the cleanup squad, checking grammar, making sure that the red car on page forty-seven isn't blue a chapter later. Or that a character isn't using a telephone in a book that takes place before 1870."

"A language cop."

"I never thought of it that way, but yeah." The term appealed to her. "It was the kind of work I could do from home when my kids were little. Then I went back fulltime."

"I read all of them as a kid."

"What? The Nancy Drews?" Rannie cocked a skeptical eye.

"I'm not putting you on. One of my older sisters had the whole series. *Witch Tree Symbol*, that was a good one. And *Something . . . Larkspur Lane*. But what was with the boyfriend? Ned? Strictly arm candy."

"*Password*. It was *Password to Larkspur Lane*." As for Ned Nickerson, Rannie chose not to share the classic comment of one editor— *"Yes, Nancy Drew has a boyfriend. But no, she does not have a vagina."*

A tinkling of silver against glass cut short their conversation. Carole Werner was tapping a wine goblet with a spoon, Jem Marshall at her side. She waited, toothy grin in place, while the crowd quieted down. Then after thanking everyone for coming, she turned to the headmaster, giving him a "take-it-away" wave of her hand. There was lipstick smeared on her front teeth, Rannie noticed.

Jem Marshall launched into a polished pitch for a new chem lab in the science complex that, with the generosity of the Senior Class parents, would bear Larry Tutwiler's name on a plaque. While Jem Marshall unfurled an architectural rendering of the space, his cell phone started bleeping inside his jacket pocket. He turned it off, barely missing a beat, and continued. It was only when Olivia appeared on the roof a moment later and started frantically signaling her mother at the same time pointing at the headmaster that Rannie began to sense something was amiss. Carole Werner squeezed past parents and after hearing whatever Olivia whispered in her ear, scurried over to Jem and in turn murmured something in his.

Making a hasty apology and promising to be right back, Jem left the gathering, the architectural scroll curling in on itself on the bar table, and despite Olivia's mother's urging for everyone to have another drink, the crowd stood stock still, as if playing a game of "Statue," with lots of raised, "what's-going-on?" eyebrows.

Everyone found out soon enough.

When Marshall returned, he marched solemnly to the same spot he'd been standing at before and faced the parents and teachers with possibly the queerest expression Rannie had ever seen. It was as if he had commanded his face to remain composed, but none of his features was completely cooperating. Finally he spoke. "You will all find out soon enough, so you might as well hear it from me. That was a call from the police. They have the results of the medical examiner's report, and—and this is awful news, just awful." His lips, now in open revolt, suddenly contorted into a grimace. "It appears—it appears Mr. Tut died from something called GHB."

"What!" and "Is that some drug?" and "Tut?" erupted from the crowd.

GHB? Rannie turned to Tim whose gaze remained trained on Jem Marshall. Rannie's first reaction was that GHB sounded like an industrial decontaminant or something an exterminator would carry.

"What are you talking about?" . . . "Tut took an overdose?" . . . "So it was a suicide?" The rapid-fire questions came to a halt when Jem Marshall thrust up his hand. "I don't know much; I'll tell you what I was told: GHB is a date-rape drug, and Mr. Tut did not take an overdose on purpose."

Rannie's hand clamped over her mouth. The spilled glass of Dalwhinnie . . .

"The police are certain now that Mr. Tut was murdered."

There was a loud thud, several feet away, as if the proverbial "other shoe" had dropped. It was Ms. Hollins. She'd fainted.

Thursday night, 11:00P.M.
Phone call Lily B. and Lily G.

Lily B: Omigod! Did you hear?
Lily G: Yeah, I heard. Calm down. I can hear you
       hyperventilating through the phone.
Lily B: The cops are gonna find out!
Lily G: Not unless you or Elliot blabs.
Lily B: It was just a prank. Maybe we should tell them.
Lily G: Are you crazy! NO!
Lily B: We can say it was all Elliot's idea.
Lily G: Just keep your mouth shut. Trust me on this.

Chapter 21

AFTER JEM'S BOMBSHELL, THE PARTY CLEARED OUT FAST. AS RANNIE EX-
ited the rooftop, a teacher was fanning Ms. Hollins, now revived
and slumped in one of the wrought iron chairs, while Jem Marshall
brought a glass of water to her. Accepting a ride from Tim Butler,
Rannie arrived home to find a note from Nate Scotch-taped to the
hall mirror. He was staying over at Ben's. When she called, all he
said was, "Yeah, I already heard. It sucks."

After trying Alice and leaving a message, Rannie headed to
her laptop and Googled in GHB. Did Nate know what it was?
She learned that the drug was sold in powder and tablet form
and, like its more popular cousin Rohypnol, whose street name
was roofies, it was odorless and tasteless. An online article on date
rape drugs from *New York Magazine* quoted a girl from an un-
named Manhattan private school: "You can black out from these
raver drugs real easy, especially when you're drinking. Some
girls I know roofie themselves up at clubs or a party because the
next morning they can go, 'Whoa! I did that? With *him*?' and not
feel guilty." One of the clubs kept a private ambulance outside,

which was the reason another girl claimed she was unafraid of o.d.-ing on Ecstasy. "With the ambulance right there, you're like at the hospital in no time."

Scrolling through various sites, Rannie read that GHB had first been synthesized in the 1920s as an additive in muscle growth formulas. The Food and Drug Administration had banned it in 1990. Through a search for "steroids" and "steroid abuse," some more info on GHB popped up. A health food store in Milwaukee had recently been closed, its owner arrested for selling GHB under the counter to kids who wanted "to look huge" but were scared of injecting themselves with something called Deca 300.

After logging off, Rannie got ready for bed, then lay there, her mind aswirl. Okay, no more "maybes." It *was* murder. Did this mean another round of questions for Nate? Should she talk to a lawyer? If so, who? At some point, she must have fallen asleep because the next thing she knew her alarm jangled her awake ... only it wasn't her alarm clock.

Sirens were screaming in the street six floors below.

She went to the window. A fire? No. There were squad cars, blue rooftop lights spinning, and for an instant an insane thought crossed her mind: The police were coming to arrest Nate for Tut's murder.

It was one-thirty. She could see a cop climbing into a dumpster on a flat bed no more than ten feet from the entrance to her building.

No answer when she buzzed the super, so Rannie threw on shoes and grabbed a coat. By the time she got outside, a cop on the sidewalk was holding back people from the dumpster.

"Another S.W.A.K. murder," Frank, the super flatly announced, shaking his head, his mouth pursed in disgust. "Can you believe this guy?"

Rannie gasped, grabbing him by the arm. "It can't be! The last one was just a couple of days ago!"

The cop heard Rannie. "Unfortunately, lady, this sick piece of scum isn't following anybody's schedule but his own."

Rannie asked the super to go back up in the elevator with her and then made him wait until she was behind a locked door. . . . Mr. Tut, murdered for certain. And another S.W.A.K. killing practically at her doorstep. It was too much. She collapsed on the sofa in the den, formerly known as Alice's bedroom. Wrapped in a blanket with her can of Mace and a baseball bat by her side, she watched reruns of sitcoms until at some point during the episode of Rhoda's wedding she dozed off.

Chapter 22

THE MINUTE OLIVIA HEARD MARSHALL TELLING ALL THE PARENTS THAT Tut had been murdered, it hit—a massive diarrhea attack. She barely made it downstairs to the toilet.

Now, even with a blanket crocheted by Carlotta wrapped around her, she was freezing. Both her thumbs were bleeding from gnawing cuticles. Phoning Grant was pointless. Windward never let through calls after ten o'clock. Frightening "what-if's" kept hounding her. What if he'd gotten really stoned on Monday? What if he *had* gone to see Tut?

At one o'clock, she hauled herself out of bed and found the shopping bag from Fabrications, a tiny clothing store where she'd taken sewing classes. She picked out a swatch of heavy velvet. The color went from deep purple to pale lavender gray and reminded Olivia of a grape ice pop, one that had been in the freezer too long. She started stroking it, over and over, between her thumb and index finger, the same way she used to stroke the ears of her favorite plush bunny. After a while her body relaxed and she started feeling drowsy. That was when she started touching herself, but it was ages before she came. And ages more before she fell asleep.

DATE RAPE DRUG TURNS DEADLY

New York: The crime most often associated with a group of stimulants and depressants collectively known as club drugs is rape, not murder. But this past Tuesday an 83-year-old teacher and guidance counselor at a Manhattan private school was found dead from an overdose of the sedative Gamma hydroxybutyrate (GHB).

An average dose of GHB (one gram or about a teaspoonful) attacks the central nervous system producing euphoria, drowsiness, and unconsciousness. Doses of five grams or more can induce coma and heart failure. According to the NYPD Homicide Division, an autopsy revealed extremely high levels of the drug in the body of A. Lawrence Tutwiler, a long-time teacher as well as director of college admissions at the Chapel School on the Upper West Side.

In a young person's system, GHB remains detectable for only a short period of time. Urinalysis tests must be administered soon after intake to establish its presence. However, the system of an elderly person retains the drug for a longer period of time.

"Sometimes you get lucky and stumble on something," said Dr. John O'Grady who conducted the autopsy. "This death looked for all the world like cardiac arrest. Pure and simple. I mean, what coroner sees an octogenarian on the table and suspects a date rape drug?"

Chapter 23

THERE WAS NO WAY THE JAG COULD TURN FROM WEST END INTO 103RD Street. It was insane, the traffic on the side street, the crowd in front of Chaps. "I'll get out here," Olivia told James, but no sooner did she step on the sidewalk than a reporter came barreling toward her, frantically motioning for a camera guy with him to keep up. "Did you know the victim? Can you tell us about the drug scene at Chaps? What about date rape drugs?"

She ignored the questions and pushed her way toward school where more reporters were shoving mikes in everyone's faces. Lots of little kids in Chaps uniforms were outside the gates, crying and telling their parents they wanted to go home. Her feelings exactly.

In the Great Hall, Lily B. spotted her and came charging over. "Everybody has to go to the auditorium," she said breathlessly. "Listen. The cops already know who did it!"

Olivia stopped in her tracks. "How? How do they know?"

"They have the guy on tape."

"What?"

"The *cameras,* Olivia. The security cameras. Hey, cool pants. Miu Miu?"

"For sure it's a *guy?*" She tried to sound offhand as they walked to the auditorium. "Has anybody actually *seen* the photo?"

But Lily B. had turned her attention to Lily G., who was waving wildly and pointing to two vacant seats beside her. "You guys!" she screeched as Olivia and Lily B. slid into them, "I may be on TV tonight. On 'Crime Blotter'! That's if they don't do the whole show on the new S.W.A.K. victim. . . . They want someone who knows the private school party scene."

Lily B. immediately started in about what a cheesy show "Crime Blotter" was. "You know who goes on that show? Hookers and trailer trash."

"Oh, right, like you wouldn't go on if they asked. They're gonna block out my face. But I'm going to wear that gangsta chain, the one with my name in rhinestones so everybody'll know it's me."

Olivia, sitting in between them, started mutilating her thumb nail. She noticed that Oro Williams, sitting two seats over, was reading an article in the *Post*. The headline read: THE SUBJECT IS MURDER . . . *at Swank Manhattan Prep School*. She leaned over Lily G.

"Oro, can I see that when you're done?" Olivia asked.

Lily G.'s lips were pursed. She was turning her head in the mirror and shaking out her hair. "Fuck, I need new highlights . . . I'll never get into Fekkai's before the show."

Oro handed Olivia the paper. The front pages were S.W.A.K., S.W.A.K., and more S.W.A.K. Inside there was an article with a photo of Tut. But most of the stuff was about celebrities whose kids went to Chaps. Nothing about a photo from the security cameras.

As Mr. Marshall was adjusting the microphone on the podium, Lily G. angled herself so she was facing both Olivia and Lily B. and whispered, "Listen, you guys. I'll TIVO the show, but in case I fuck it up, can you, too?"

"Could I please have everyone's attention."

Mr. Marshall said that in the coming days he expected school to stay open with students and teachers going about their business as normally as circumstances allowed. However, it was necessary to turn over the day's Morning Meeting to—Mr. Marshall glanced over his shoulder to a hefty middle-aged guy sitting behind him onstage—Sergeant Prada, or at least that's what the name sounded like to Olivia.

Sergeant Prada replaced Mr. Marshall at the podium. "I'm a homicide detective with the Twenty-fourth Precinct, and I'm in charge of the investigation." He went on to say how sorry he was about Mr. Tutwiler. "From everything I've heard, he was a terrific man. But somebody murdered him, right here at your school. Now you may not think you know anything. But search your mind. Even if you don't think it's important . . . I'll be handing out my card."

Afterwards, as Olivia climbed the stairs to math class, she persuaded herself that she truly didn't know anything worth mentioning. All she had were wacko suspicions because her brother had taken a later train to New Haven on Monday. If she went to the cops, they'd just think she was mental.

Messages on Rannie's Chaps voice mail

Hello. Susan Woo here. A sudden change in my schedule makes it impossible for us to bring May for her interview today. We'll—uh—we'll call back—uh—sometime.

This is Reese Courtland's secretary calling to cancel Maynard's appointment for the kindergarten tour this afternoon. The Courtlands apologize for the short notice.

This is Taylor Millstone. We have decided to withdraw Phoebe's application. We won't be coming for the tour and interview next Monday. Thank you.

Chapter 24

Friday morning

IN THE STANDING-ROOM-ONLY AUDITORIUM, RANNIE FOUND IT DIFFICULT
to stay focused on the homicide cop's words. Her mind's eye kept
returning to the horrific scene last night near her building. According to the news radio channel, the latest S.W.A.K. victim had
been a single mother with two kids . . . that hit way too close to
home.

Nevertheless, the sergeant's message came through, loud and
clear. He wanted information. Yet sideways glances across the aisle
at Ms. Hollins, who appeared genuinely stricken, fueled Rannie's
qualms about going to the police. As she joined the flow of people
exiting the auditorium, she asked herself if some residual taboo
from adolescence was at work, some deep-seated aversion to rat-
ting out *anyone*? Or did her reluctance have more to do with 'fessing
up to her own nosy-parker behavior? Whatever, it didn't matter, she
concluded: Her allegiance, first and last, was to Nate and information that she had might redirect the arrow pointing at him toward
someone else.

In the Annex, Dottie Greenhouse, Mrs. Mac, and other staffers were standing around, murmuring in solemn tones, doing a post-mortem on the meeting.

"I suppose we should be thankful. The S.W.A.K. murder kept Tut off the front page."

"Dottie! You're terrible," said the head of upper school admissions.

Rannie was about to join the confab when she saw her desktop and stopped cold. Someone had opened the can of Diet Coke she'd brought in earlier. Next to it now was a highball glass, one with the Chaps crest in gold. It was filled with Coke and ice. An index card that said "Cheers!" in purple block letters was propped against it.

Rannie inched over to it warily. "Did anybody do this?" she inquired in a wobbly falsetto and pointed to the glass. The women turned briefly, their response a communal head-shake no, and resumed chatting. Rannie sank into her chair. There were no carbonation bubbles rising in the glass, a sign that the soda had been poured a while ago. Could Ms. Hollins have done this? Rannie hadn't seen her before Morning Meeting, but she could've been upstairs in her office and waited to do this 'til everyone else had already left for the auditorium. It was a possibility . . . and even if Ms. Hollins wasn't spooking her, *somebody* was. Enough with the scary pranks, Rannie thought, and grabbed her stuff.

Outside, she called Officer Heffernan. She tried not to babble. "There's a glass of soda on my desk at school. Someone opened a can I brought in and poured it in a Chaps glass."

"You just saw it?"

"Yes. A little sign said, 'Cheers!' It was next to the glass."

"Have you touched anything?"

"No. I'm outside school now."

"Okay, look. I'll have it checked out. You—"

"There's more," Rannie interrupted and began jabbering away

about meeting Ms. Hollins in the park, running into her Tuesday night.

"Whoa, whoa, whoa. Slow down. . . . Look, Ms. Bookman, I think you better come down to the precinct and speak to the sergeant directly. Be here at one. I'll let him know to expect you."

Chapter 25

Friday lunchtime

HER FIRST FREE TIME WAS AT LUNCHTIME, WHIPPING OUT NEW AVIA-tor sunglasses from Bendel's, Olivia hurried to Turtle Park. Her eyeballs ached, almost as if she had a hangover, and the yogurt she'd just eaten in the cafeteria stuck like phlegm in the back of her throat. Olivia took out her cell and tried the bookstore. Whoever answered said Grant wasn't there yet.

Pacing, she decided to wait and try again. She bent down against the wind and, cupping her hand around a Parliament, lit up. When she straightened up, the chubby police sergeant was standing no more than ten feet away by a cement turtle. It was like he had materialized out of nowhere.

"Olivia, right?", he asked it in a way that didn't expect a reply and walked over. His jacket was way too tight and the shirt button by his waist was open, revealing a triangle of undershirt above his belt.

She nodded and tossed her cigarette.

"We're checking phone records on the day Mr. Tutwiler died. You called him on Monday."

The statement caught her completely off guard. "I did?"

He nodded. The gold wedding band he was playing with on his ring finger was tight too.

Olivia bit the inside of her lip, hoping her sunglasses masked how nervous she felt. Answering stuff like this was when it paid to be smart, 800s on your SATs smart.

Just then the cell phone in her bag started ringing, the first bars to "Hello, Hello" by the Beatles. . . . All of a sudden it hit her. Her cell phone. Grant had it with him on Monday. It had come back in the mail yesterday. Quickly she tried to reconstruct exactly what Grant had told her about trying to reach Tut. And what was she going to tell the cop? Was it going to be the truth? Olivia wet her lips and made up her mind. "Yeah, yeah. Now I remember. I called Mr. Tut's office."

"You weren't at school?"

"No, I was here."

"Why phone him?"

"His office is in another building." She patted her bag. "I've got a cell." Did this count as perjury? Could she go to jail? "I needed to talk to him about college . . . my essay for college." Grant's words were coming back to her now. "I also tried Mr. Tut at home."

"You call your teachers at home a lot?"

"No." As in never. "But I was feeling desperate. I'm kind of freaking about college. My parents are forcing me—well, not *forcing* me exactly—to apply to Princeton."

"That's a switch. I thought everybody at this place"—the cop gestured with his chin in the direction of Chaps—"was dying to get into the Ivy League."

"Well, not everybody. Anyway, I never got to speak to him. I didn't leave any messages. I figured I'd just come in early Tuesday morning . . . which is what I did."

Did he believe her? Hard to tell. Lying, Olivia realized, was not something she was accustomed to doing. And she didn't like it. There was a ton of stuff she never told her parents, like the fact that she had a tattoo on her ass of a lightning bolt. That was different, although Carlotta would still consider it a sin, a sin of omission. Yet here she was, not only lying but lying to a cop. Olivia half-expected her pants to burst into flames.

"So nothing more?" he asked and after Olivia shook her head, he repeated back everything she'd just said, writing it down in a notebook. Then he thanked her and walked out of the playground, stopping once to light a cigarette. He smoked Parliaments, too.

Olivia tried Grant again.

"Look, he's not here. Don't call again!" the same person at the bookstore said.

On the walk back to school, Chris Butler called her name.

"Wait up," he shouted. A copy of the *Daily News* was rolled up in his hand.

"Hey, Chris." Olivia felt bad; she could tell he was still hung up on her. All last year, his first at Chaps, she'd thought he was incredibly hot. The way he moved on the basketball court, staying completely focused, was a turn-on. He also didn't give a crap about how he dressed or impressing anybody. She liked that about him.

At a party at the end of junior year, she and Chris had been kidding around and while he was carrying her around piggyback, he went into a bedroom, slid her off his back, then stood facing her with a dead serious expression before locking the door.

Making out was fantastic. When he pulled off her tee shirt and pulled her to him by the chain on her TCB bolt, she thought she'd die. Sex with Chris was going to be amazing. Only it wasn't. Just like with other guys, it hurt. All during June, before she left for Greece, whenever she was with Chris, she'd find herself thinking about the most random stuff while they fucked . . . what she'd eaten for dinner or if she had keys with her. Dr. Ehrenburg kept bringing up

Olivia's "trust issues" and telling her that enjoying sex had a lot to do with trust. Maybe, or else she was just frigid.

"Guess I'm glad I'm not a lifer," Chris said.

"Huh?"

"No jacket."

"What?"

"You haven't seen the paper? There's a photo of a guy in a lifer jacket and a hoodie."

Olivia practically ripped the paper out of his hands. Hers were shaking as she stared at the grainy black-and-white photo of someone in a hoodie under a lifer jacket. You couldn't make out who it was for sure, especially with the hood pulled up and the person's head tilted down, although judging strictly from body type it definitely could have been Grant. Nevertheless, she found herself smiling dopily while Chris went on about how the rumor was that the security guard got canned for selling the photo to the *News*.

Grant didn't own a lifer jacket, not anymore. The night he got expelled, Grant set all his textbooks on fire with the lifer jacket blazing at the top of the pile, its rubbery smell wafting off the rooftop of their townhouse.

It didn't matter that she had just lied to the police; it didn't matter about Grant lying. All that mattered was that the picture in the *Daily News* had to be somebody else. Which meant Grant had nothing to do with Tut's murder.

Chapter 26

Friday, 1:30 P.M.

RANNIE WALKED FROM DOLORES COURT TO THE STATION HOUSE, A WHITE brick, three-story affair in the West 80s. White-and-blue cruisers were packed in a small parking lot next to it and double-parked on the street. None of the women who lived on this block had to worry about a psycho stalking them home.

Sergeant Thomas Peratta was ditching a can of Sprite and a greasy wrapper from a Subway sandwich when she entered the large office he shared with other cops. He stood behind a metal desk and shook hands.

"Please," he said, pointing to a gray metal folding chair.

Rannie sat, the chair scraping unpleasantly on the linoleum. On his desk was a framed prom-type photo of a girl with his same broad, friendly features, her hair done up in elaborate curls.

"She's a senior at Bronx Science . . . got 770 on her math board." He looked embarrassed. "She'd kill me if she heard me bragging. Your son, where's he want to go?"

"Stanford."

Eyebrows lifted. "Very nice. She's got her heart set on Johns Hopkins so we're keeping our fingers crossed."

The brief moment of "just between us parents" camaraderie made Rannie relax a little although it seemed odd sitting in a police station discussing college with a homicide detective.

He leaned back, settling his hands on his ample belly. "Officer Heffernan told me about the glass. It's already been tested . . . nothing but Coke in it. But we didn't find any sign."

"Index card," Rannie corrected.

"You have any idea why somebody went to the trouble of scaring you like that?"

"I'm not sure. . . . I think so." She grasped one of the pencils in the pocket of her barn jacket. Funny how holding one always gave her a sense of empowerment. "I'm sorry. I'm very nervous. The S.W.A.K. victim last night. The woman was found on my block."

"Take your time. That's why I'm here, to gather information."

Mentally she took a deep gulp. She began with an account of running into Ms. Hollins the morning that Tut's body was discovered, hearing about the note sent to Tut's home. He nodded, giving no indication of whether or not this was news to him. Maybe a poker face was like the badge—something that came with the job.

She recrossed her legs. "Then late that night, Tuesday night, I was coming out of a friend's building, and I saw Ms. Hollins leaving a brownstone next door with a suitcase and garment bag." Rannie supplied the street address for Peratta. "And—and then I started walking in the same direction she was."

"Did you speak to each other?"

"No, I was about a half a block behind her."

"You were on your way home?"

Rannie averted her eyes. Okay, no more dillydallying. "I know this is going to sound bizarre." She scrunched up her face. "I—I was sort of following her." She refused to glance up to calibrate his reaction.

"Why were you doing that?"

Unfortunately, there was no rational answer. Might as well say, "I'm a mother; all of us are raving paranoids when it comes to our kids," or "Being out of work is making me crazy," or "My life seems to have lost purpose," or even "The devil made me do it." But he was waiting.

"Um, I was curious to see where she was going." It sounded borderline nut job even to her own ears. "And, and then, when I got home, I looked in the phone book. Where I first saw her . . . well, it was where Mr. Tut lived."

He waited, still Buddha-like in his imperturbable calm, hands still clasped on his Buddha-like belly.

"She claimed they were casual friends. And—and then I see her carrying a suitcase out of his building?" The pitch and volume of her voice was starting to rise. "I mean, right away Tut's death looked suspicious, right? . . . and then here was Ms. Hollins—"

"Doing something that looked suspicious to you."

"Yes."

"This was Tuesday night, correct?"

Rannie nodded. "Ms. Hollins spotted me, uh tailing her. She confronted me the next day, furious. And then that night—"

"This is Wednesday night now?"

"Yes. That night around ten, the super rang my doorbell. Somebody left a letter for me in the lobby. It'd been shoved under the front door—like a menu. It was similar to the letter Ms. Hollins described, the one Tut received, in a typeface that looked like letters in a ransom note . . . only mine said, 'Stop snooping.' My name was written in purple marker. Ms. Hollins uses purple marker to grade papers."

"Did you bring the note?"

"No, I tore it up."

"Why?"

"Why would I keep something like that!" To put in a scrapbook along with the kids' baby teeth and first haircuts? "It was creepy, but I didn't consider it a real threat. It didn't say 'Stop snooping—or else.'"

His eyes stayed fastened on her; there was sleep sand in one of them.

"I thought of it as payback. I'd scared her by following her home. So she was scaring me ... and if it was comeuppance—I don't know, I guess I sort of felt like I deserved it. . . . But now knowing for certain that Mr. Tut was murdered . . . and seeing that glass on my desk . . ." If she gripped the pencil in her pocket any tighter, it would crack in two.

The sergeant remained silent for a moment longer, the corners of his lips curled down, at the same time staring at her in a way that became more unsettling the longer he held the gaze.

"Let me ask you something, Ms. Bookman. Where were you Monday evening?"

Talk about a curveball! She kept her voice as steady as possible and replied, "I had a five o'clock appointment at the Unemployment Office. I stopped for groceries at a Gristedes on Broadway and went home. I got there about six-thirty."

"So you were home before your son?"

"Yes." It suddenly struck her that the sergeant's last questions were not about establishing her own whereabouts but verifying Nate's.

"And what time was that?"

"Before seven." She remembered because she'd been making dinner and listening to National Public Radio. "Lieutenant, if you're thinking Nate is somehow involved—"

"Did you hear me say he was?" Then he asked if she'd told anyone what she'd just told him, and when she said no, he nodded. "Good. I don't want you discussing anything with anyone."

Right after that, he stood, so Rannie did too. The chair scraped again, the sound as grating as fingernails across a chalkboard. Fleetingly it crossed her mind that if Nate were indeed a suspect, the sergeant might not believe a word she'd said. The guy was a father. He understood to what lengths parents would go in order to protect a child. "I just want you to know I came here in good faith. I can't justify my own behavior but I can certainly vouch for Nate's. He and Mr. Tut were friends."

Then Rannie nodded curtly, a formal "good day, sir" nod as prelude to what she hoped was a dignified exit. On the way home Rannie passed several newsstands. All the front pages of the afternoon papers had grainy photos of a Chaps kid, head bent down, in a lifer windbreaker and a hoodie, a menacing hunched-over figure that looked like a grim reaper in training. Her mother's eye knew in a flash it wasn't Nate, but would the police be so discerning?

E-mail sent late Friday to all Chapel School families
FROM: jemarshall@chapelschool.org

This is a painful, shocking, and distressing time at Chapel School, whose mission is to educate children, to turn them into responsible, caring young adults. An unspeakable crime has been committed here, one that flies in the face of everything we hold dear. However, I have complete confidence that the New York Police Department will solve the murder of Lawrence Tutwiler. That's their job and they will do it.

Our job is to teach your children and we intend to do our job, too. In the coming weeks, our aim is to maintain daily routine and to keep school life as normal as circumstances allow.

Unfortunately, some parents are fueling hysteria in other parents. This is exactly the worst time for panic. For the sake of the students, I entreat you to remain calm and rational.

- School will not close.
- Only Mr. Tut's office on the second floor of the Annex is a crime scene and off limits. The rest of the campus and buildings are fully operational and open to students and faculty as usual.
- No drugs were found in the water fountains; there is no reason to believe they are a source of danger. Nevertheless, to alleviate the fears of some parents, the fountains will be turned off for the time being.
- Despite rumors, there have been no other cases of poisoning. A fourth grader passed out during snacks after he and some other children were seeing who could hold their breath the longest. The juice and crackers were not tainted.
- The cafeteria will remain in operation.

Chapel School has been educating children since 1867. With your help, we will get through this terrible time.

Jonathan Edwards Marshall

Friday night message on Rannie's phone

Hi. It's Tim Butler. I know this is kind of late, but are you free for dinner tomorrow at my bar? I'll call back.

Chapter 27

Saturday morning

OLIVIA FELT ALMOST LIGHTHEARTED AS THE JAG APPROACHED NEW Haven, a trip made in record time. "James is fucking allergic to traffic!" her brother always used to say. "It's like kryptonite to him."

The car drove past the sports arena at the edge of the city, buildings with boarded-up windows, and the tattoo parlor where she'd gotten the lightning bolt. In the front yard at Windward, a boy her age was playing Hackysack; a couple of other kids were drinking coffee on the porch.

The lady at the front desk recognized Olivia, smiled, and rang Grant's room.

Olivia flipped through an old issue of *People* magazine, debating whether to try and make it back to New York tonight for the dance at school. Nate Lorimer's band was playing. Yesterday afternoon, she'd stopped a moment to listen while they were practicing in the gym. She'd always liked Nate. He was funny but not especially cheerful. He scowled a lot, which was kind of hot. The way he looked pounding away on drums, very intense, his head barely moving, sweat pouring off him—that was kind of hot, too.

"Hey there!"

Olivia looked up. All of a sudden she had the weirdest sensation, as if her head had separated from the rest of her body and was drifting off, like a balloon.

"You okay?" Grant asked right before she fainted. He was standing in front of her, smiling, freshly showered and running a hand through his still-wet, blond hair.

He was wearing a Chaps lifer jacket and a hoodie.

Chapter 28

"NATE A SUSPECT? WHAT, RANNIE, WITH BEAVER CLEAVER IN THE GETAWAY car?" Joan Gordon said, glancing in the rearview mirror through Jackie O-sized sunglasses. They were heading east on the L.I.E. Destination: David and Danka Ross's weekend compound. Mission: For Joan to return with a hefty six-figure check for Chaps. The only time the Rosses could spare was brunch today, interpreted by Joan to mean, if she wanted the dough, she had to schlep out to the Hamptons to get it. Rannie was happy to tag along, eager to see the House That Ate the Hamptons and breathe some un-urban air.

"Look, there are twenty-five lifers in the senior class, seventeen of them boys. And of those seventeen, Rannie, I bet at least half could pass for the kid in the photo. . . . If I were you, I'd worry more about the S.W.A.K. maniac." Joan shook her head though not a hair of her blond coiffeur moved. "I think you and Nate should stay with us 'til they catch the guy."

"Thanks. I'll think about it." Alice had said essentially the same thing on the phone; only her suggestion was to camp out at Mary's.

Rannie passed a container of coffee with two packets of Equal to her friend's outstretched hand. Rannie had first met Joan when Ben and Nate were in kindergarten. They'd spent countless hours on playground benches together and had consoled each other through times of crisis—Rannie's divorce, Joan's bout with breast cancer.

"I still don't get it, why kill somebody who's already dying?" Rannie said.

"Poor impulse control?" Joan responded.

"Be serious."

"I am." Joan paused to change lanes. "I think some kid at Chaps did it. To me this murder screams 'pissed-off teenager.' Somebody got mad at Tut—I'm talking really, really mad—and couldn't stand to wait a few months and let Mother Nature do the job. And a date rape drug? Doesn't that say horny and under twenty-one to you?"

Rannie sipped her coffee. "Not necessarily."

"Why? It's a kid on the camera. Can't you picture some little shithead thinking, 'I hate Tut. He's not gonna get me into Yale. He's screwing me.' It's never '*I'm* not gonna get in, because I happen to be ninety-ninth in a class of one hundred. And for extracurricular activities, I like torturing small animals.' "

"But—"

"Wait. Hear me out. So we go from some kid blaming Tut for screwing them out of a good college and, to me, it's just a hop, skip, and a jump to, 'Tut deserves to die. Right this minute.' There are kids at Chaps with all the conscience of your average Venus flytrap."

The exact same thought Tut had expressed. "Yes, but what you said before—about impulse control. The way Tut was murdered wasn't impulsive. The opposite, in fact. This was planned . . . and planned to look as if it wasn't murder at all."

Joan tilted her head, quasi-acknowledging Rannie's logic. "Then maybe a parent of some kid who wound up at Stupid U? Someone who never forgave Tut for ruining their kid's bright and shining future?"

"Did you know that David Ross saw Tut Monday afternoon? Elliot is no brain trust, and I hear he's hell-bent on Harvard. Maybe David had gripes."

Joan's head swiveled in Rannie's direction for a second before pulling her gaze back on the road. "No, I didn't know he saw Tut that day. And, yes, I do know they didn't like each other."

"Why?"

"I never asked. Look, Rannie. I'm going out here to extract a lot of money from David Ross. I let you come because you said you wanted to see the house. So no pointed questions."

Rannie nibbled on a blueberry muffin that had an unpleasantly gummy texture. She returned it to the bag. Okay, she thought, no pointed questions, but maybe one or two with the rough edges polished down as smoothly as the pebbles on the Rosses' beachfront property.

Chapter 29

Saturday afternoon

WHEN SHE CAME TO, OLIVIA WAS LOOKING STRAIGHT THROUGH THE EAR-lobe of a Windward counselor, an older guy with ear spacers the size of nickels. He helped her into a chair and although she kept insisting that she'd passed out because she hadn't eaten, the counselor guy just nodded, at the same time checking her pupils and smelling her breath, probably thinking, "Like brother, like sister."

"Grant, you lied to me," she said when they were alone in his room. "You didn't leave New York when you said."

"What?"

"Monday. You told me you got back here at seven. You didn't. You didn't sign in 'til way later, like at nine-something. And what are you doing in a lifer jacket?"

"Fuck it, Olivia. Is that why you came up here? To cross-examine me?"

"You don't know about the photograph in the *Daily News*."

"What photo?"

"There's a photograph of somebody coming out of Chaps, somebody that looks like you, Grant." A cup of tea loaded with sugar, which Grant's counselor had brought for her, sat on a nightstand getting cold. "Someone wearing a lifer jacket leaving right when they think Tut was killed."

"Holy shit!"

Grant's expression morphed from pissed off to fearful. He'd been standing by the door that had a Coldplay poster stuck on with yellowing Scotch tape. Now he slumped into a chair and lowered his head in his hands.

"Shit, shit, shit," he muttered to himself. "How can there be a picture?"

"Grant! What did you do?"

"Nothing!" He took a deep breath, holding it in for such a long time she could almost swear there was a joint sticking out of his mouth. Finally he exhaled and said, "Okay, I lied. . . . I did go to Chaps. But it's not how you think." He told her that after Tut wasn't home at one o'clock on Monday, he wasn't sure what to do. So he'd gone back up to his friend Eric's apartment and borrowed his lifer jacket.

"I figured if I ended up going to Chaps, I'd blend in. Then I grabbed some lunch . . . at the West End."

"The West End! A *bar!*"

"I know it was stupid, okay? But I'd been there the night before with Eric and some of his friends from Columbia and it was like no big deal. I had Coke. Only on Monday, I don't know. . . . I think I was pissed that Tut forgot about seeing me." His eyes held hers in their unwavering blue gaze. "Olivia, I'm gonna level with you. I ordered a beer—"

"Grant! Fuck!" It was never "a" beer with him.

"Wait. I didn't drink it. I swear. I left and called AA. There was a meeting at four o'clock." He said it was in a little church on 108th Street. "It really got my head straight. When it was over, I went to Chaps."

According to Grant, by the time he got to school it was about quarter of six. The security guard hadn't stopped him; he looked like a student. "The ground floor of the Annex was empty. When I got to the second floor, I could hear Tut.

"His office door was open a little. Nate Lorimer was in there. I couldn't tell how long they were gonna be, so I went to the roof for a smoke. Neither of them saw me."

"Did anybody else?"

"No. On the third floor Hollins was at her desk. Her back was to me. She was gone by the time I went back down—that was maybe like five minutes later—but when I got to Tut's office, the door was closed."

"He'd left?"

"No. He was still in there talking to somebody."

"Nate?"

Grant shook his head. "I don't think so. The voice was different."

"Would you recognize Elliot Ross's voice?"

Grant shook his head again.

"Could you at least tell if it was a woman?" At five-thirty on Monday when Olivia had tried to see Tut, Ms. Hollins was in there, upset and arguing with him. Ms. Hollins could've gone up to her office and then back down again to Tut's.

"Tut was doing the talking. He sounded angry. I heard him say, 'You've got a lot of explaining to do.' Maybe not those exact words, but something like that."

"That sounds like what you'd say to a kid." Olivia shook out a cigarette from her pack.

"Maybe, yeah. I had the feeling whoever it was was going to be in there a long time. So I split. I made the seven-something train and was back before curfew. End of story."

"Except there are security cameras at school now because of the S.W.A.K. stuff. They go on at six. Grant, it's you in the photo."

Grant reached for her Parliaments. "You think anybody else recognized me? Anybody," he paused to light his cigarette from the end of hers, "anybody come up and say, 'Nice picture of your brother, Olivia. Rehab must be agreeing with him.'"

When Olivia answered no, Grant relaxed a little, leaned back in the chair, took a drag and scratched his unshaven cheek. He had a three-day Colin Farrell thing going. "But if I'm on the security camera, whoever was with Tut should be, too, leaving later than me."

Olivia could offer no explanation for that. She put out her cigarette in the teacup saucer. "The other day a cop—a homicide cop—asked me about the calls you made to Tut on my cell."

Grant waited.

"I lied. I said I made them."

"You're the best, Olivia! You think the cop believed you?"

"If they had any idea it was you, they would have already been up here, right?"

He looked relieved. "Come on. Let's go to the Doodle. My treat."

The Doodle was the best greasy spoon in world. You could get honey dip donuts, sliced, buttered and fried. Still, the visit was ruined. She left New Haven early. On the ride home she kept obsessing. The "almost slip" sounded like the truth. So did the rest of it. But what if "a" beer led to another and another and ended with Grant scoring coke? He'd beaten up Tut once before when he was high.

Still, Olivia's gut told her no: Her brother wasn't a cold-blooded killer. Slugging somebody . . . sure. But that was a lot different from spiking a drink. Dr. Ehrenburg had once told her she had a lot of "emotional intelligence" as if somehow that made up for not having the real kind. But as Olivia inserted the ear buds on her iPod, she worried that maybe her gut was actually no smarter than her brain.

Chapter 30

ROUTE 27 WAS BLISSFULLY FREE OF TRAFFIC. IN SUMMER THE ROAD WAS clogged end to end with high-ticket cars on their way to the resort towns along the south fork of Long Island. As far as Rannie was concerned, the Hamptons managed to distill all the frustrating, competitive, social-climbing worst of New York City living. Manhattan with sand and mosquitoes.

Rannie read aloud Mapquest directions once the car turned off Route 27. For several minutes they traveled down country lanes, passing ever higher privet hedges concealing ever grander homes, glimpses of which Rannie caught fleetingly through driveways. Shingle-style "cottages" with wraparound porches, grand colonials flying yacht club flags from tall poles, modern "starchitect" showplaces.

On Beach Road an inconspicuous wood sign planted low to the ground announced their arrival at "High Tide." The locals called it "Danka's Donut." And as the car turned into the property, Rannie decided that, yes, the glass and sandstone tubular structure did call to mind a gigantic donut, one with a big bite taken out of it. In the "hole" of the donut was the pool, surrounded by chocolate-brown chaises, all with a D. Ross insignia.

Mr. and Mrs. were seated at a table under an umbrella. They were dressed alike in beige linen pants and Ralph Lauren polo shirts, except no baseball cap covered Danka Ross's Lucille Ball–red hair, and David Ross wasn't wearing a hammered gold cuff bracelet, so wide and heavy looking, lifting a fork could count as exercise.

"Wonderful that you're here on such a beautiful day," Danka said pleasantly. Beside her was a doggy bed, a replica of the donut-shaped house. In the place of the pool was a chlorine-blue fleece pillow on which perched two small shih tzus.

David Ross wasted no time breaking the ice.

"Chaps is in deep shit. The last thing any private school needs is a dead body and homicide cops." From under his baseball cap, a pair of mistrustful eyes appraised Joan and Rannie. His other features sat bunched together in the middle of his pale face with too much forehead, cheeks, and chin surrounding them.

"Tutwiler." He practically spat out the name. "Could never shut up about how everything he did was 'for the good of the school.' So now he's gotten himself good and murdered." Ross looked around the table as if he'd said something clever.

"Oh, come on," Rannie said. "In fairness to Mr. Tut, isn't that game called Blaming the Victim?" She felt a little nudge from Joan under the table. "It's not as if Mr. Tutwiler was trying to get murdered."

Ross waited until a mountain of lobster salad had been served to reply. "What I'm saying is the man had plenty of enemies and he had a past. Oh, we all saw the obituary—how he went to Chaps and Yale and belonged to the right clubs, yadda yadda yadda." Ross paused to cross one leg over the other, exposing five elongated, exceptionally white toes. "But that wasn't the whole story, not by a long shot. Everybody has something to conceal."

"You sound like you know something," Rannie continued, ignoring the warning look from Joan.

"Look. Anybody crosses me or mine, I make it my business to find out what they *don't* want in their obituary. It's a useful bargaining chip."

Bargaining chip? To Rannie that sounded an awful lot like a euphemism for blackmail. Did David Ross know that Tut once fathered a child? But so what? Surely in this day and age, blackmail required something more damaging, unless there *was* something more damaging. "You saw Mr. Tut Monday afternoon, didn't you? Was he aware you had a—a bargaining chip?"

A tiny gasp burbled from Joan. Danka's expression remained implacable. David Ross leaned back in his chair. "That's a very nervy question. But it so happens I like nervy people." He pointed to Rannie's plate and ordered her to eat. "Sixty bucks a pound at Loaves and Fishes. Yes, I saw Tutwiler on Monday."

He snapped open his napkin so loudly, it almost sounded like a whip cracking. Joan tried to bait and switch. "Tut is gone, David. There's new leadership with Jem Marshall," she said in a mollifying tone.

"Yes, and he's a very reasonable man to deal with." Then he chuckled. "Irregardless of his crazy stock tips."

The non-word sent a Pavlovian shudder through Rannie. But all she said was, "What crazy stock tips?"

Joan looked uncomfortable and concentrated on her plate of food.

"You don't know? That's why you're here." David Ross took a bite of lobster salad and rolled his eyes heavenward to denote "delicious." "Marshall touts some bio med company and the board listens. Two weeks later, the company's under investigation for illegal stem cell research. The stock tanks. So the school needs a quarter-million-dollar check for an interest payment on the loan.

"Sure. I'll step up to the plate. But last Monday when I went to see Tutwiler about Harvard ..." David Ross began shaking his head in a Tut-like tremor and mimicked his nasal intonations. " 'Elliot doesn't have the record. He's not an attractive candidate,' he tells me. And when I say that I'm sure a sizable pledge to Harvard will make him more attractive, Tutwiler says I can give Harvard as much money as I choose, but that doesn't mean the school will support Elliot's application. *The school.* He meant *he* wouldn't."

"All right, darling, e-nough," Danka said, stressing both syllables equally.

Rannie felt like crying out, "No, no! I'm all ears!" So Tut had thrown up a roadblock on the route to Cambridge for Ross's heir apparent. Here was a vengeful adult for her vengeful adult theory.

"David, you promised you wouldn't discuss anything unpleasant today," Danka placed her gold-cuffed hand on his arm. Her voice was soft, the accent alluring. Now she stood and, cradling a bundle of shih tzu in either arm, said, "I will show Rannie around the house while you two discuss your business."

Ross lowered his head and looked up coyly, a gesture that had been fetching on Princess Di. "Okay, baby. Sorry." Then to Joan he said, almost contritely, "I have my issues. But I've always been generous to the school."

Danka slipped inside through a sliding glass door, Rannie following behind. For such a small person—Danka was even shorter than she was—Danka possessed stature. Yes, her face resembled one of those slutty-looking dolls that were so popular, the ones with inflated lips, no nose, and unnaturally large, cat-shaped eyes. But she carried herself regally. "The man is impossible. We come out here so he can relax." She shook her Lucy-red hair but the words were uttered with affection.

The décor was modern and severe. Letting the dogs run free,

Danka reeled off names of well-known Abstract painters whose artwork hung in different rooms.

"I grew up poor. And what can I say? I love being rich. David says that people who say, 'Less is more,' are liars . . . and I agree." Danka told Rannie that she'd been born in Budapest. "My sister and I went back a few years ago . . . She's my identical twin." Danka pointed to a photo on a lucite table of herself and another woman standing on either side of a man. "There we are with the President of Hungary."

The other woman looked nothing like Danka and appeared much older. The expression of puzzlement that registered on Rannie's face seemed to amuse Danka.

"Yes. Identical. But Maria does not believe in plastic surgery.

"When we were children, Maria loved piano, so often she would show up for my lesson, leave when it was over, and five minutes later return for her own lesson." Danka laughed. "Whenever I did come, the teacher was always wondering why I was suddenly so much worse, and why I was now favoring my right hand when I played. . . . Maria was a lefty."

"Oh, you're mirror-image twins." About twenty percent of identical twins were, a fact Rannie had picked up from reading about "Uncle Doctor" Mengele.

Danka nodded and called the dogs, who came running and yapping. "We'll return to the pool. I am quite confident Joan has her check."

On the way they passed an open area with Nautilus machines, a stationary bike, a treadmill, barbells, and a rack of free weights. David Ross was doughy and out of shape; it was hard to picture Danka bench-pressing. "Elliot's?" Rannie inquired.

"I suppose you haven't seen Ellie lately." Danka patted her own tummy, then squeezed her upper arm. "The six-pack. The biceps. I worry he is taking steroids. He has pimples on his back." Peemples

Jane O'Connor

was how she pronounced it. Danka placed her braceleted hand on Rannie's arm. "And his temper is worse than ever. Tell me. Have you heard of Chaps kids using steroids?"

"No. No, I haven't." However, the info she'd gleaned online the other night stated that uncontrollable anger was a sign of steroid use. 'Roid Rage.

Danka pursed her collagen-inflated lips. "Children ... Who is equipped to handle them? Animals are so much easier."

Forty-five minutes and many mini-eclairs later, Rannie and Joan were on the road again, Rannie in the driver's seat this time. Joan's head lay against the headrest, her eyes half-closed.

"Joanie, can I ask you something?"

An irritated sigh. "Rannie, I worked hard for this check." Joan patted her bag. "You think I like bowing and scraping to David Ross? And you were no help. Counterproductive, in fact."

"I *did* help. He enjoyed carrying on for an audience. . . . Just one question?"

Joan opened her eyes and looked warily at Rannie.

"Was Jem Marshall aware that Tut was rich?"

"Everyone on the board knew."

"So Jem expected Chaps to get a chunk of the estate?"

"Oh yes. He knew the school was going to get more than a collection of bow ties. . . . The best guess is in the neighborhood of five to six million dollars. . . . Wait a minute, Rannie! Now you think Jem Marshall killed Tut?"

"Jem lost a lot of money for the school at an inopportune time. That's all I'm saying."

Joan was shaking her head. "Think how long it takes to settle an estate. Jem would know that bumping off Tut was no quick fix for the endowment."

Joan was right. Rannie pulled a face. "Okay, then I'm back to Ross."

"I don't think you're right about David either. But if you are," Joan said, clutching her purse to her chest, "he better not get arrested 'til this check clears!"

Rannie returned the rental car. If she was quick about it, there was enough time to stop at Barnes & Noble before getting ready to meet Tim Butler.

The book was shelved in the Business and Money section. *David Ross: Deal Breaker*. Unauthorized and unflattering, the book had been published several years ago. There'd been lots of noise, Rannie remembered, from David Ross, cries of "Smear campaign!" and "Libel suit!" all of which had come to naught.

Thumbing to the index—bingo! The listing she was hoping for.

As she read the cited page, the event described came back to her. In a tax write-off scheme about fifteen years ago, David Ross had pulled down several tenements near school and built an apartment tower with a pocket-size playground. Chaps kids called it Turtle Park. It was publicized to great fanfare for offering attractive, affordable housing to low-income families. Code violations, however, caused persistent flooding in apartments and, far worse, a near-fatal elevator accident. The victim, left paralyzed, had been a maintenance worker at Chaps.

Who arranged for a top-notch lawyer who won a multi-million dollar settlement for the victim? Who found the family a new apartment? Who paid the victim's medical expenses?

Tutwiler, A. Lawrence, p. 214.

"David Ross left me in a wheelchair," the maintenance worker was quoted as saying. "Lawrence Tutwiler saved my family."

Oh, yes. David Ross definitely had issues with Tut, ones dating back from before Elliot had even enrolled in Chapel School kindergarten.

Chapter 31

"YOU GREW!" TIM BUTLER STOOD WHEN RANNIE ARRIVED, BRUSHING back his silvery hair with one hand.

Rannie smiled and sat down. So far she had managed to remain upright from the cab, through the front door, past the bar, and over to a corner table where Tim was nursing a club soda. But she wasn't about to push her luck.

Her daughter's shoes were sensational. Gorgeously vampy red peep-toe stilettos. For the first time in her life, Rannie had toe cleavage. She knew she looked pretty damned terrific in the sleeveless black turtleneck, black skirt, and wide red belt, yet again all items Alice hadn't bothered taking back to school. No longer was Rannie someone for whom the operative adjective was "cute." Tonight she was a woman to be reckoned with, capable of inflicting serious damage just with her footwear. Of course, one misstep and the whole effect would be shot to hell.

"So, this is your place," Rannie said, taking in the dark wood walls and hexagonal tiled floor. "I like it." She hung Alice's adorable silk string purse, which barely held keys, lipstick, and wallet, on the back of her chair. Then, in reply to Tim, Rannie requested a glass of white wine.

It was a comfortable, old-time-y joint, a step—but not a giant step—above the few remaining Blarney Stones, Dublin Houses, and other Irish watering holes that had managed to avoid being pushed aside by trendier bars and restaurants in the neighborhood. An enormous gilt-framed mirror ran the length of the bar, reflecting a crowd of people, mostly guys, not a single one wearing anything hipper than khakis or a windbreaker. The men glanced up every now and then, between sips of beer, at a baseball game on the TV that hung from the ceiling.

"I'm warning you right now. You'd better not ditch me again," Rannie said as a waiter brought her glass of wine.

"My cell phone's not even on me." Tim was wearing charcoal slacks, a herringbone sportscoat, and a button-down shirt without a tie. Nicely dressed but not too date-y.

Rannie squinted at the chalkboard menu. Corned beef hash. Veal chop. Meatloaf. Shepherd's pie. And skirt steak. He wasn't counting on heavy vegan traffic.

"It's all pretty decent. Have the veal chop. Trust me. It's good. Nice and thick."

Tim smiled. She'd forgotten how one of his front teeth overlapped the other one slightly. Very attractive. Nice crinkly laugh lines around his eyes too.

They both ordered, a veal chop for Rannie, the meatloaf for Tim, and made small talk. He was easy to talk to. A good listener, not one of those "enough about me, now what do *you* think of me" men. And here he was, in exactly the same boat she was, facing the unwelcome prospect of living alone, come fall.

"I've got to get a full-time job," she confessed. "Not only for the money. I'll go nuts if I'm in the apartment all day by myself. I'll have to become a cat lady and that'll be hard since I'm highly allergic."

Tim laughed.

"People say, 'How fabulous to work at home.' I hate it." Rannie paused. Was she blathering? "I like having this whole other 'work world' to go to. I hardly ever use my Metrocard anymore." If she was blathering, Tim didn't seem to mind.

"Yeah, next year scares me too. I can see me spending eighteen, twenty hours a day here, just to avoid an empty apartment. It's an easy trap when you live right over the shop." He pointed to the pressed tin ceiling then finished his club soda. "You know you never said if you're divorced or a widow."

"Divorced. Isn't that what practically all single parents our age are? You're the exception."

"I know, but in the directory, you're the only one listed under Nate's name. So I thought maybe your husband had died."

Rannie followed his reasoning. In divorced families, both parents' addresses and phone numbers usually appeared in the directory. "My husband, my ex-husband, lives in California. So what's the point of having him on mailing lists?"

Tim told Rannie that his wife had died in a car accident when Chris was only three. "She was about your height and dark, too, like you. Mandelbaum was her maiden name. Deborah Mandelbaum." Tim looked at her questioningly.

"Yup. Me, too. A member of the tribe."

"Only my wife, she wasn't as thin as you.... She was a little more—" He held out both hands searching for the word. Strong hands, she noticed, and before she could stop herself, Rannie was imagining Tim leaning across the table and touching her face.

"—*Zaftig.* That's the word. She had more meat on her bones."

Rannie focused on her glass of wine. "Listen to you with the Yiddish." Yiddish with a Boston-Irish accent.

Tim held up his glass of club soda and waited for the bartender to bring over another. "I've been a widower much longer than I was a married man." Tim raised his eyebrows, shaking his head slightly in disbelief.

Tim wasn't handsome, Rannie decided. But he was intensely masculine. And the spiked silver hair paired with the boyish features added up to something better than just another nice-looking Irish guy. Had his wife ever seen him gray? she wondered. Rannie also liked the "guy" way he spoke. Unpretentious and declarative. A person's speech patterns revealed a lot. Her ex-husband spoke with lots of ellipses, pauses, and qualifiers. That should have been a tip-off.

From talk of looming empty nests and living on the Upper West Side, Rannie steered the conversation to Chaps and Mr. Tut. Here was a direct, plainspoken guy; Rannie decided to be direct herself.

"So? What do you hear about the murder?"

"Which? Most of the talk here is about the S.W.A.K. murders."

She chose not to mention how close to home the last victim had been found. "No. I meant Mr. Tut."

"The sergeant on the case won't talk about it. But, yeah, I hear stuff."

"Like what?"

"No trace of drugs in the scotch bottle. And the killer planted false evidence."

The arrival of their food—plates set down with a "*bon appétit*" from the burly waiter—interrupted Tim. Rannie held her glass with an expectant expression that said, "Please, continue."

"There was a glass on Tut's desk, tipped over as if it fell out of Mr. Tut's hand right as he's supposedly having a heart attack. There are whiskey traces in the glass but no GHB. And the fingerprints on it, they're Tut's. But from his right hand. And the man was left-handed."

Yes, as he said it, Rannie remembered Tut referring to his tennis game.

"Also the rim of the glass is clean, no indication he ever put his mouth to it. Strange, no? Was the guy drinking scotch through a straw?"

"Sooooo." Rannie tried envisioning possible tableaux and put forth the one she liked best, one featuring Tut with someone over the legal drinking age. "Tut and the killer are in the office, Tut's having his Dalwhinnie. The killer, too, most probably."

"Look who's up on her single malts."

"The killer manages to slip GHB in Tut's glass. They chat, whatever. Then the killer has to wait for the GHB to do the job." Rannie paused. Unfortunately, it was very hard to picture Tut and David Ross toasting each other's health. "The drug either works quickly and Tut dies right away. Or the killer pretends to leave but hides in the Annex waiting, because he's got to be absolutely sure Tut is dead. Am I right? I'm right, aren't I?"

"You're doing fine, Nancy Drew."

"What was the time of death?"

"What I hear, their best guess is between six and eight."

Not the answer she wanted. In the police's eyes, that still left Nate in the running.... Rannie finished the last sip of wine and continued thinking out loud while Tim motioned to the bartender to bring another glass of wine. "Once Tut is dead, the killer takes his own glass, which has no GHB in it, wipes it off, and puts Tut's fingerprints on it... maybe by wrapping Tut's hand around the glass. The thing is the killer takes Tut's right hand, not realizing he was a lefty." Rannie paused. "But the rim of the glass?"

Tim shrugged. "Who knows? Maybe the murderer forgot about that ... he was thinking ahead, just not far enough ahead."

Rannie smiled thanks for the new glass of wine. "Everybody I talk to keeps saying they think a kid did it. But whoever's on the security tape could be an adult disguised to look like a kid."

"Your veal chop's going to get cold."

The wine had loosened her lips. "Do you know about the nasty letter sent to Tut?"

A forkful of meatloaf was poised near his mouth. "Yeah, I heard about it."

"I heard that more than one might have been sent."

Tim shrugged. "No way to tell. There's no evidence of the first. The cops went through the apartment very thoroughly. All they turned up was a pair of earrings."

"What do they look like?"

"Only a woman would ask that."

"You laugh but women are observant."

"Well, the answer is I don't have a clue."

Rannie was only half-listening to Tim and thinking of Ms. Hollins. "As far as suspects, has anybody's name come up that you know of?"

"Look, is this a date or an interrogation?"

Rannie was brought up short by the sharp edge in his tone. And as soon as she stopped all the mental gymnastics and took a close look at his face, she saw the sea change in his expression. Here she'd just been saying how observant women were . . . well, somewhere along the line, she hadn't been paying attention, because the crinkly laugh lines were gone. So was the smile with the sexy crooked tooth.

Since she suspected Tim could tell if she dissembled, Rannie bit the inside of her cheek and admitted, "A little of both, I guess."

"Fine." He stabbed a French fry with his fork. "You pumped me for all I got. So eat your chop and I'll put you in a cab."

"No! You've got it wrong. Look, I wanted to see you again. I wouldn't have said yes otherwise. It's just my son's been questioned twice. And that was *before* the cops knew for sure it was murder." Rannie saw him taking in her outfit. She'd wanted to look sexy tonight, to feel sexy. Now he thought the "fuck me" shoes and short skirt were bait to get him to spill. Suddenly, she felt ridiculous. Rannie eyed the mammoth veal chop on a bed of spinach. Suddenly, she had no appetite.

"Look. Don't get up. I'll get myself a cab." She stood. Maybe take off the shoes, she counseled herself. Exiting in bare feet was going to look stupid but still beat taking a header right in front of him.

Tim sat back in his chair, put his napkin on the table, and sighed. "No. No. Sit down." He called to the waiter. "Tommy, could you put this back under the broiler for a minute?" As the plate was whisked away, he pushed the breadbasket toward Rannie. "Come on. Take a piece. That way I won't be eating alone."

Rannie sat down. She nibbled halfheartedly on the heel of the loaf, but when her plate returned, her appetite still hadn't. The thick slab of veal looked like too much work. And the wine had left a sour aftertaste.

"Come on. Eat. You're making me feel bad."

"I can't. I think the second glass of wine was a mistake. I feel a little woozy."

"What, you're not a heavy hitter? The Dalwhinnie line was just to impress me? Have some coffee then. Maybe a piece of cheesecake."

Rannie shook her head but when Tim didn't let up, asking if there wasn't *something* she'd eat, Rannie surprised herself by saying, "Peanut butter and jelly on white bread."

"Not down here but upstairs."

As in apartment. Rannie thought about it for a moment and said yes.

Chapter 32

NATE WAS PERCHED ON A DRUM STOOL, WIPING SWEAT OFF HIS FOREHEAD with the back of his sleeve, ready for the next song. There was a decent turnout in the gym, and it felt good not to be thinking about anything except banging out some rock and roll.

Once Ben and the other guys retuned their guitars, Nate knocked his sticks together three times, and they kicked into the opening bars of "I See Red," a Crowded House song that by now Nate could practically play on autopilot. His eyes wandered over the crowd. Ms. Hollins setting out soda and cookies. Elliot making moves on some freshman whose tits were so big, it looked like she could tip over. Then his eyes fell on a cop by the doorway. Shit. Even at a stupid school dance.

Somebody in his class already had a Website—*whowhackedtut.com*—with photos of teachers and kids, each scanned in so it looked like they were wearing a hoodie and Chaps lifer jacket. There was a pool going. Nate had thirty bucks on Elliot, who was the odds-on favorite. Nate first heard about party drugs from Elliot who came to one of the bar mitzvahs with a pocketful of red roofies and thought it'd be a big joke to spike the girls' Cokes.

The minute Nate finished off with a cymbal on their last song, Mr. Marshall came over to the mike and said, "Whoo, hoo. Let's give it up for . . ." He glanced down at a piece of paper in his hand. "For 'Spiteful Muse.'" Then he did a spazzy overhead clap.

Nate's backpack was stashed under the bleachers. He went over and changed into the spare tee shirt he'd brought, mopping his face on the dirty one. Then he sneaked a quick whiff under his arm. Jesus, he reeked.

"Hey. You guys were good."

Nate swung around.

She wearing yellow Asics wrestling shoes, a denim jacket, and a pink frilly ballerina skirt. The TCB lightning bolt hung from the chain around her neck.

"Hey." Please say she hadn't caught him smelling his pit.

Olivia tapped her cup, indicating it was empty, and headed in the direction of the refreshment table. So did that mean, nice talking to you, dude, but conversation over? Nate decided to follow; he could always kind of grab some cookies or something, so that it didn't look like he was stalking her. He was reaching for a Chips Ahoy when Olivia pointed to the mikes where a hip-hop group called Smoove—mostly juniors, all white—were starting their shout outs. "Those guys suck. Want to go sit someplace else?"

"Sure. I just need my backpack." There was Chapstick in it, and his lips felt crusty, like they might crack and start bleeding in front of her. She walked to the bleachers with him.

Nate unzipped his backpack. . . . Shit, could anything look lamer than whipping out a tube of Chapstick? "Um, guess I left my cell home."

"Use mine." Her hand went to her jacket pocket.

"Nah." Nate tossed the backpack under the bleachers. "The call can wait."

They left the gym and walked down a corridor lined with glass cases of old pewter trophies, the zombie fluorescent lighting so harsh it made Nate squint. In the darkened auditorium they settled themselves on the floor against the back wall. The brickwork felt pleasantly cool through his tee shirt.

Olivia was staring out at nothing, chewing her lip, one leg jiggling so hard he could almost feel the vibrations. He was wondering what to say before the peaceful silence turned into an uncomfortable silence when she said, "Nate? Can I tell you something?"

Instant boner hearing her say his name.

"I was over at Lily G.'s before. She made me watch her again on TV."

"Ben and I saw it last night." Lily had come on at the end of "Crime Blotter," for about thirty seconds. The rest of the show was all about the woman murdered right on his block. Ben had said, "Dude, whatever you do, *don't* carry any Duct tape on you."

"Lily said something, something very strange while we were watching." Olivia tilted her head toward him. "All of a sudden, Lily squeezed her eyes shut and goes, 'God, we were *so* dumb. Elliot would jump off the Brooklyn Bridge if we told him to!' And when I asked what she was talking about, right away she started waving her arms around and going, 'Oh nothing nothing.' She said they made Elliot steal some CDs for them at Virgin Megastore."

"So? They always make him do stuff like that."

"Exactly. I'm positive that wasn't it. . . . She looked scared. It was right when the guy from 'Crime Blotter' was talking about roofies and GHB and Ecstasy and showing photos of all these kids who are, you know, like vegetables or else dead."

"Olivia, hold on! You think the Lilys killed Tut? Or got Elliot to do it?"

"What if it was only supposed to be a prank? Like they didn't mean for Tut to *die*, but just get high?"

"You mean like, 'Ha. Ha.What a goof ... we'll make Elliot slip Tut some raver shit.'"

"I don't know. I don't know what I think." She looked upset and swallowed hard. "Swear you won't say anything if I tell you something else?"

He nodded.

"Today I went and saw—" She stopped, started to speak again, and then seemed to change her mind again. "I really need a cigarette," was all she said.

"Want to go outside?"

But just then a shaft of bright, hard light suddenly sliced into the auditorium from the hallway. They both turned at the same time. Mr. Marshall was standing by the door holding Nate's gray backpack, the one with his initials embroidered at the top and under that "CHAPS SUCKS" scrawled in black Sharpie across the zipper compartment.

"Nate, could you come out here for a moment, please ... I need to speak to you."

Nate scrambled to his feet. Olivia stayed sitting, squinting, and shielded her eyes with one hand, like a visor.

"Olivia, this doesn't concern you. So please go back to the gym." Mr. Marshall waited while Olivia stood and started taking slow steps down the corridor, turning around once to see what was going on.

"This is your backpack?"

Nate nodded.

"This was in it." Mr. Marshall was holding a small Ziploc bag in his other hand. A Ziploc bag with two joints and a bunch of red pills. Roofies.

"What! No!" Nate yelped. His voice came out high pitched and hysterical, like some twelve-year-old girl's. Out of the corner of his eye, he caught Olivia, down at the end of the corridor. She raised a hand to her ear with pinky and index finger extended—the universal "I'll call" gesture before ducking inside the gym.

"Sir, that stuff's not mine. I swear it!"

Mr. Marshall cut him short. "I got a call a few minutes ago at the front desk, someone saying to check a backpack, one with the initials NBL on it, and I'd find something interesting. So I looked."

Nate's eyes stayed glued to the baggy in the headmaster's hand. Fuck, fuck, fuck. His heart was bouncing around in his chest like a tennis ball. He sank back against one of the trophy cases, making the glass rattle.

Mr. Marshall seemed to soften a little. "Okay, look, calm down. You need to sit."

Nate slid down to the floor. He rubbed his temples with the palms of his hands. Sweat was breaking out all over him. Mr. Marshall bent down on one knee beside him and calmly told him to take a couple of deep breaths.

Nate did and felt better. "Mr. Marshall, I had my backpack open just a few minutes ago. Olivia was with me. It wasn't in there then. You can ask her." Nate blew mightily through his lips. "I can't believe this is happening. . . . Could you tell who it was on the phone?"

"No, they wouldn't say. The voice was muffled."

"Please, Mr. Marshall. . . . Anyone could have put that stuff in my backpack. It's been there all night, under the bleachers."

"Why would anybody do that?"

Nate stuttered, "Maybe somebody—I don't know—maybe somebody had stuff on them, and they got scared, seeing a cop, so they dumped it in a backpack. . . ." He looked up at Mr. Marshall. "They said *me*? To look in my backpack?"

Mr. Marshall nodded, almost sadly. A little vein was twitching on the side of his forehead.

"Sir, I swear to you. Somebody set me up."

Mr. Marshall was kneeling so close to Nate that he could smell the headmaster's breath. It was fresh and minty.

"I want to believe you, Nate. I do. But I can't get around what I found."

"Did you tell the cop?" Nate winced as if waiting for a punch.

"I came to you first. But the police have to be told."

"Oh, shit," he groaned. The panicky feeling which had started to evaporate came back with a vengeance. It was hard to swallow; tears sprang to his eyes. Mr. Marshall asked for his mother's number and began punching the buttons. At the far end of the corridor, the gym doors opened. Great, now Olivia would catch him blubbering.

But it wasn't Olivia.

Elliot, an ear-to-ear grin plastered across his face, waggled a naughty-naughty finger at Nate as he headed out of the building with the Lilys. It was all Nate could do not to chase after him and jump the ugly motherfucker.

Elliot said he'd get him. Well, he had—he got him back good.

Chapter 33

Saturday night

"IT'S NOT SMUCKER'S RASPBERRY JAM AND I PREFER CHUNK-STYLE TO smooth. But I'm thrilled you had Wonder bread," Rannie told Tim as she polished off a second sandwich.

"Very high maintenance, aren't you?"

Tim came in to the living room with two mugs of coffee and placed them on the glass-topped table in front of them.

"Only smart move I ever made, buying this building," Tim had told her on their way up to the apartment. He and Chris had just moved from Plymouth when he'd spotted a "For Sale" sign and soaped windows on the ground floor. "Dumb luck. I wanted a house. One of my sisters was living with us back then, helping out with Chris while she was finishing up at Marymount. The real estate market was still pretty much in the toilet, and this block was dicey, even with the precinct so near."

"Dumb luck is all you need." Rannie wished she had more of it.

"I've got two renters on the top floor. And I'm refinancing. That's how Chris is going to college."

Rannie sat back against the deep cushions of the sofa, blowing on her coffee. Tim was drinking his, the sleeves of his shirt rolled up.

The living room was attractive enough, although impersonally furnished, as if one day Tim had flipped open a Crate and Barrel catalogue, called an eight hundred number and said, "Page one hundred. I'll take everything on it." On one of the shelves of a pale wood wall unit, she spotted a framed photograph of a young woman laughing and holding a toddler with chocolate smeared all over his face.

Tim caught her looking. "My wife and Chris, it's the last picture I have of Deb."

Rannie nodded but made no reply. She wiped her mouth with a napkin. It touched her that Tim had insisted on serving her sandwich on a china plate with a cloth napkin.

"I'm sorry I blew up before. Irish temper. It was worse when I drank."

So noted, Rannie thought to herself. "Forget it. I *was* pumping you. We're both sorry." Climbing the vestibule stairs had been torture, and all she wanted now was to kick off the killer shoes. So she did. And if that was sending a signal. . . . Well, so be it.

"So where are you from? I'm guessing not the East Coast. Midwest, maybe?"

"Guilty. Cleveland, home of the Browns and flat vowels." After all these years and still her accent was a dead giveaway. "I came to New York right after college."

"Where'd you go?"

"Yale."

Tim raised his eyebrows. "You say it like it embarrasses you."

In a way, it did, she supposed. "People hear Yale and they expect all sorts of other impressive accomplishments in your life."

"I got kicked out of Holy Cross for raising holy hell. Exactly what my parents and everyone else expected of me." Tim leaned forward, his arm extended. "Hold it. You have a little peanut butter in your hair."

Rannie's hand flew to her hair. "You should have brought me a bib instead of a napkin." Then Rannie stopped talking. Tim had caught her hand. He pulled gently at a strand of hair near her ear. He was looking at her. Really looking at her. She returned his gaze and swallowed hard.

He stroked her hair, saying it was as soft as a baby's, and tucked it behind her ear. Then he traced the outline of her ear while his other hand moved to the back of her neck, drawing her closer.

They were kissing. One soft kiss and then another. Rannie closed her eyes. Tim smelled delicious, just his own freshly showered and shaved smell. The pressure of his hand at the back of her neck brought her nearer and before giving herself a chance to think twice, she opened her mouth. His tongue darted in lightly then more insistently. She ran hers over the ridge of his crooked tooth, then deeper inside the roof of his mouth. God, he tasted delicious too. She could feel her pulse throbbing in her throat.

When they pulled back for a moment, his chest was heaving. "You are a very impressive kisser."

Rannie smiled and nodded. "Yes, Yale and kissing." Then she leaned forward, and they kissed again. When he grazed her ear with his lips and she felt the rush of his breath, a little groan escaped from her. She ran her tongue down his throat to the bottom of the vee in his open-necked shirt and kissed him there. As he cupped her cheek with one hand and brought her mouth up to his again, his other hand went to her breast and even under a turtleneck and bra, her nipple stiffened instantly.

Are you nuts? Here you go again! A tiny little part of her brain started screaming, "You're not in high school at some make-out party." But another part urged her to keep on going because it felt so natural. That was the part she chose to listen to. She needed sex, pure and simple, as much as she needed a job. She let Tim push her down on the sofa and the weight of a man's body on top of hers, the hardness of his erection, made her feel fully alive. She put both hands on his ass, a gorgeously tight ass, and pulled him as close as she could. He gasped, murmuring her name.

For a moment she thought that the faint humming sound was also coming from Tim.

No. It was the cell phone in the pocket of her raincoat. The sound of the phone was an instant reality check. Rannie pushed Tim off her and sat up, staring at her moaning raincoat. She was panting. Tim backed away to the other side of the sofa. He had the stunned look of a high-school boy who, a second ago, was sure he was going to get laid and suddenly realizes the night may end without even so much as a hand job.

The noise of the phone stopped, a ridiculous noise that sounded like the lowing of a teeny herd of cattle in the back forty. The whole scene was ridiculous. The two of them—middle-aged and horny. A combustible combination. She couldn't help catching a glimpse of herself in the mirror over the fireplace. Her hair was a wild horror. Tim was rubbing his hand over his jaw. One of his shirttails was out.

A second later the phone began pulsing again. This time Rannie picked it up. The number on the screen was unfamiliar to her. She clicked the talk button. It was Jem Marshall.

"Is Nate okay?" she asked, instantly frantic.

"What's wrong?" Tim asked.

She ignored the question and continued listening to the head-master and when he put Nate on the phone, she said, "I'll be home in a minute. Of course, I believe you."

She sprang up and grabbed her coat, her miniature purse. And the shoes. She picked them up off the floor.

"That was Jem Marshall. Nate just got busted at school. Some-body planted some pot and pills in his backpack."

"Oh shit, no."

"Oh shit yes. And he forgot his keys. He's waiting in our lobby."

She put on her shoes and Tim led her downstairs. He wanted to see her home in a cab. However, Rannie shook her head so vehemently, he relented, saying, "I'll call tomorrow. You be careful getting home."

Rannie swiveled into the back seat of a taxi and, before shutting the door, looked up at him. "You okay?"

"Nothing a cold shower won't cure."

At least he said it with a smile.

While the cab drove northward, taking advantage of the staggered lights on Amsterdam Avenue, Rannie combed her hair and reapplied lipstick. Her cheeks still were flushed. She tried to wrap her brain around what little information Jem Marshall had given her. A Ziploc bag with pot and pills that Nate said looked like roofies. Why would someone do that, plant drugs on him? Now of all times? The answer was plain: Someone was trying to frame him.

The cab made the trip in good time until it tried to turn into her block. A few feet ahead, a heavyset black man and a gypsy cab-driver had jumped out of their cars and were yelling at each other. The cabbie had sideswiped the guy's SUV.

Some men playing canasta at a card table in front of the *bodega* were circling the car and inspecting the damage. One of them was yelling at the gypsy cab too. Rannie felt her heart racing. "Can you get around them?" she asked through the Plexiglas divider.

"Sorry, lady. No room."

The S.W.A.K. killer had already hit her block. Lightning didn't strike twice. "Here." She stuffed a bill in the dish of the window guard.

The entrance to her building was at the end of the block, only a few steps in from Broadway. Hobbled by her shoes, she took nervous little baby steps down the dark street, passing the storefront *eglesia,* the parking garage, its metal grating already pulled down for the night, and the stoops of rundown tenement buildings.

The chilly night air raised goose flesh on her bare arms. She threw her raincoat over her shoulders, walking as briskly as the shoes allowed. Then, halfway down the street, just before she reached the dumpster, there was a slight movement in the shadow between two parked cars. A man darted out. An involuntary squeak leaped from her mouth. A kitchen knife was in his hand.

Oh God! She was going to be tomorrow's headline! Panic ballooned in Rannie's chest. She was about to throw up. Post-divorce, she'd taken self-defense classes although they never told you how fear erased everything you'd learned. "Please!" she whispered, realizing there wasn't enough air in her lungs to scream for help.

He was Hispanic, maybe early twenties with a scraggly mustache, scrawny and jittery and definitely high. It would be easy to pick him out of a line-up, except that she was going to be dead!

He didn't say a word, just pointed to her purse. *For her lipstick!* Terror made Rannie's hand lock around the draw strings as they stood face to face. *Release the fucking bag,* she commanded herself. *Breathe so that you can scream.*

The guy said, "Hurry up. I ain' gon' hurt you. I ain' that S.W.A.K. sicko."

Did he say that to all his victims? As she handed over her bag, he said, "That, too." He was pointing at her father's old Rolex. Her hand was shaking too much to manage the clasp.

"Hurry up, I said!" His eyes darted to both ends of the block. He looked like he wanted to get away. Maybe he really was just a garden variety mugger!

The watch was so loose on her wrist, it hung like a bracelet; finally, squinching together her fingers, Rannie wriggled it off. Sobbing, she thrust the watch at him. Then he made her take off her shoes, which he tossed in the dumpster before taking off toward Broadway.

Shaking and sobbing harder, Rannie ran to her house barefoot, the rough concrete sidewalk biting into the soles of her feet, shredding her pantyhose. She was alive. She was unhurt.

Nate was in the vestibule by the intercom, sitting on a radiator ledge. "Ma!" he jumped up when he saw her. "Hey, don't cry. It'll be okay. Nothing bad's gonna happen to me." Then he stared at her feet. "Where are your shoes?"

"I just got mugged."

"No!" He enveloped her in a hug. Then he pulled back and a look of bafflement came over his face. "Ma? They stole your shoes?"

The ludicrous logic of the question coupled with a surge of relief at being home safe and relatively sound made Rannie stop crying. Sniffling, she told him what happened. It wasn't until she started to fumble for Alice's handbag that was no longer hanging from her shoulder that she realized neither of them had keys.

The super buzzed them into the lobby, but their hall neighbor wasn't home. The only other person with keys to their apartment was her mother-in-law.

First Rannie called 911, thankful her cell had been in her coat pocket. The tiny buttons proved too hard for her still-trembling fingers, so Nate punched in the number. An emergency operator said a patrol car would be right over. Within five minutes one was. The officer rolled down the window, then stared at her feet. "The guy stole your shoes?"

Rannie slid in the back seat.

"A woman walking alone in this neighborhood, you're lucky you're in one piece," he chided.

"I know," she said contritely while watching Nate call Mary. As the patrol car took off, she said, "Tell Grandma you're locked out and you can't get hold of me. Tell her my phone must be turned off or something. Nothing else. Got that?"

When she returned home an hour and a half later, in a pair of oversized Nikes borrowed from a woman cop at the precinct, Nate said, "Any luck?"

"They figure he jumped on a subway. I went and looked at about a million mug shots. No luck." She shrugged. "At least I wasn't carrying any credit cards. . . . But he took Grandpa Nat's watch." Instantaneously and despite every effort not to, tears sprang to her eyes.

"Aw, Ma. I'm sorry."

"I don't know what got into me. Here I'm always screaming at you and Alice to be careful at night." She shut the door behind them and collapsed against it for a moment before heading into the kitchen. "Come. I'll make hot chocolate. Tell me what happened at school."

"Ma, no. *Please.* Come on, can't it wait until tomorrow? I just want to chill. Mr. Marshall believes me. . . . Ben says there's nothing to worry about."

"Oh well, if Ben says that, we can all rest easy."

"Ma! Why be bitchy?"

Rannie's shoulders sagged and she turned to face him. "Look, Nate. I'm in a really pissy mood." Nate was still in the foyer, both hands rammed into the pockets of his jeans. "And if there's a prayer of me getting any sleep tonight, you have to tell me what happened. . . . Okay? *Okay?*"

She could hear Nate's long, irritated sigh exhaling behind her; nevertheless, he followed her into the kitchen where she poured milk into a saucepan and set it on the front burner. While it was heating up, Rannie rummaged around in the cabinets for the can of Hershey's chocolate powder and the bag of mini-marshmallows.

A few minutes later they sat at the dining room table with their mugs of hot chocolate, little blobs of marshmallow dissolving on the steaming surface. "Elliot did it, Ma. I'm sure of it. My backpack's got my initials on it. He'd know which one was mine. And he has it in for me."

Nate told Rannie about stuffing Elliot in the equipment shed, although that incident by itself didn't convince her that Elliot was behind what had just happened. Bringing drugs to school? Especially now. There had to be more at stake for Elliot than merely "getting back" at Nate. Maybe Joan's pissed-off teenager theory was right; even if Elliot was indisputably no genius, he still could have inherited a gene for caginess from his dad. If Elliot had murdered Tut, he could be trying to point the finger at Nate, a kid whom he already had a grudge against. Rannie blew on the hot chocolate that was still too scalding hot to drink.

"Nate, you think Elliot is on steroids?"

He stopped twiddling his spoon and eyed her quizzically. "Yeah, maybe. He bulked up fast. And he's got backne."

Rannie took a tentative sip of cocoa. So? Elliot could have waited until Nate's meeting with Tut was over and then returned to the office, at which point Tut, before closing up shop, was pouring himself a drink. All Elliot would have needed was a narrow window of opportunity—Tut turning to the file cabinets, getting something from his couch—to slip in the GHB.

Nate's cell phone started ringing. He checked caller ID. "Look, Ma, we done?" he asked and before she could answer, he put the phone to his ear, said, "Yo. Yeah, I'm okay," and started toward his room, the mug in his other hand.

A second cup of hot chocolate and one hot bath later, the tension in her body still wasn't ready to call it a night. She lay in bed with the lights out, on her back, staring at the flaking plaster on the ceiling, her shoulders hugging her ears, Ed Sullivan-style, killer cramps in both legs and a headache that reached all the way down to her toes. And, oh yeah, she'd have to remember to get the locks changed tomorrow. The little bastard not only had her keys but her address from her driver's license.

Her big toe locked, seizing Rannie with such pain, she sat bolt upright, gasping. As she sat kneading her foot, her father's face floated before her. He had taught her to tell time on the Rolex. *When the big hand is on the twelve and the little hand is on the five, that's when I leave my office and come home to Mommy, you, Emily, and Betsy.* Okay, it was just a watch. She'd been mugged, not murdered. Still she felt especially sorry for herself and started crying again because there was nobody around to feel sorry for her.

A Chaps phone directory lay in the drawer of her night table.

"Did I wake you?" she asked.

"Nah," Tim said. "Just watching TV. Your son okay?"

"Yeah. I guess. We're supposed to see Jem Marshall first thing Monday morning. It sounds like he believed Nate."

Tim asked her to reconstruct what happened. At one point he made her stop. "When he came and got Nate, Marshall had the bag of pills in his hand?"

"Yeah. I'm pretty sure. Why?"

"If he'd left it where it was, in the backpack, the cops could've checked the prints on it."

"I didn't think of that."

"The whole thing sounds fishy to me. Cops know a set-up when they see one."

"You're not just saying that to make me feel better."

"No. I'm not. Honest."

"This was a pretty horrendous night."

"Would it make you laugh if I said you're not the first date to tell me that?"

"I got mugged coming home."

"Aw, Jesus, no!" It was uttered with such sincerity that Rannie started crying again, tears trickling down her cheeks into her ears as she lay back in bed and recounted what happened.

"I thought at first it was the S.W.A.K. guy." She reached for a Kleenex and blew her nose. "I was an idiot. I should have stayed in the cab."

"You sure should've." He fired off a bunch of questions—all the same ones the cops had asked, in a very similar, cop-style way. Did the assailant have a weapon? Did he assault her? Then Tim asked, "Listen, you want company?"

"No." *Yes.* "I just wanted to talk to somebody. . . . I wanted to talk to you."

Rannie plumped pillows behind her and leaned back. The knots in her shoulders were loosening up a little. She tried to picture Tim in his bedroom. He'd be in a tee shirt and boxers. Or just boxers. Definitely didn't strike her as a blue-pajamas kind of guy. "Look, if I'd slept with you tonight, that would've been it—at the next school meeting, as soon as I spotted you, I'd have to duck and run the other way."

"Why? I don't mind being used."

"I'm serious. What I need is a friend." *Friend?* What was she saying? Joan was a friend. She didn't need more Joans. A fling. That's what she wanted. Right? Yet Tim didn't strike her as "fling" material.

"Fine. We take it slow."

After she hung up and lay back down again, she did feel better, somewhat, until she automatically felt for her wristwatch to place on her night table. Tim was nice. And he was sexy. As Rannie settled back in bed, she told herself that she was not going to behave like some horny teenybopper the next time she saw him. But there was nothing wrong with a little fantasizing, especially since it always helped get her to sleep. All-natural Xanax.

Rannie closed her eyes. She imagined Tim beside her, the clean, guy smell of him, the warmth of his body so that she could almost feel his breath on her neck. Tim's hand/her hand bunched up her nightgown and lazily, lightly began tracing ever narrowing circles around each of her breasts—first the left breast, then the right. A slow hand. Her legs spread involuntarily and the lovely throbbing increased while his hand/her hand moved down her body to the warm wet place between her legs. She drew up her knees and arched her back as his/her finger moved faster and faster. It was all for her. He wanted her to come and wouldn't stop until she did. Rannie swallowed hard and stiffened the muscles in her back, pressing down, so that every bit of concentration was settled in that one spot. No thoughts. No worries, not right now. Just intense feeling that rose and rose; it was like swimming underwater, the pressure building inside her, becoming almost unbearable as she moved toward the surface. And then she burst free.

Five minutes later, she was asleep.

Chapter 34

Sunday afternoon

RANNIE SAT BY THE FLOWER GARDEN IN RIVERSIDE PARK, THREE HUN-dred dollars worth of new keys in her pocket, sections of the Sunday *Times* weighing heavily in her lap.

It was an Indian summer Sunday. Nate had taken off to see Alice at Yale, and whereas a Sunday by herself with no one to answer to was sometimes a treat, this morning being in the apartment alone had been unbearable. The bright sunlight and the sight of other people made Rannie feel safe.

All around her, Upper West Fall Fest was in full swing. Children were getting their faces painted and decorating orange-frosted cupcakes. A little farther off, a horse-drawn wagon, its tiny passengers perched atop bales of hay, circled the grove of crab apple trees that stretched from 91st to 95th Street. Fifteen years ago, she and Peter would have been among the waving parents.... Had they been happy back then? Or was she already assuaging herself with the rationalization that their marriage was no worse than most others?

Right after the divorce, her mother—astute to a fault and never one to mince words—remarked, "Darling, be honest. Peter didn't break your heart; what's upsetting you most is how unhappy the kids are." Absolutely true: Peter had never been essential to her being, not in the way Nate and Alice were.

Watching one mini-melodrama made Rannie so wistful she felt her throat tighten. A little boy, dissatisfied with the leaf collage he'd made, dripping with glue, its few leaves already sliding off, collapsed in his mother's arms, wailing.

"I think it's beautiful," the mother soothed. Rannie envied her. Small children. Small problems.

Her thoughts were an agitated jumble, as if her brain was on spin cycle. She felt disoriented without her watch, jumpy from the mugging, distressed about the incident at the dance, and embarrassed by her behavior at Tim Butler's last night. And yet here she was sitting on the promenade where joggers came loping by, at exactly the same spot where she'd seen him before, more than half-hoping to encounter him.

What was it Tim Butler had said? The only item of interest the police had come across in Tut's apartment was a pair of earrings? Surely they belonged to Ms. Hollins, but what if there were other things that wouldn't necessarily raise suspicions in the minds of the cops but might in hers? Something that might jump out, catching her attention, in much the same way that errors in manuscripts did. Of course, Ms. Hollins had already seen to some housecleaning. Still, if there was a way to gain entry into Mr. Tut's apartment . . . What Rannie wanted, pure and simple, was to discover an overlooked clue.

The thick Real Estate section, at the top of the heap, suddenly started sending signals that were impossible to ignore, and in spite of herself a plan began to take form in her mind.

Sunday in Manhattan—the day desperate New Yorkers searched for apartments. After the divorce, if the kids were busy and she wasn't, Rannie sometimes staved off depression by checking out open houses in the neighborhood. If her mother was in town, the two of them would go together. It was visual eavesdropping, a chance to see the way other people lived—what possessions were dear to them, how they arranged their furniture, all the little ingredients that assembled together made up a home. Rannie still remembered one cramped apartment that was basically storage space for the owner's vast collection of old toasters.

A blue pencil in hand, she began scanning ads for open houses, circling those in the West 90s, Tut's neighborhood. The ruse taking shape in her mind was more than a little Lucy Ricardo-like. Still it might get her in the door.

From the park exit at 95th Street she headed to an apartment building that had advertised an open house at one o'clock. It wasn't long before people emerged from the lobby holding floor plans. Rannie spotted a woman, frowning and shaking her head at a male companion.

"So? What'd you think?" Rannie asked.

"Don't waste your time," the woman advised Rannie. "It's a chopped-up studio." She willingly relinquished the layout advertised as a "convertible two-bedroom apartment."

Now Rannie had her prop. During the short walk to 94th Street, she rehearsed what to say.

In the vestibule of Tut's building, she kept pressing intercom buttons until finally a guy picked up and told her to see Mike in One-B, an identical brownstone, two doors down.

Mike appeared in an undershirt and beltless gray trousers. He had gray hair rippling off his forehead in thinning waves, slick with hair tonic.

"I'm not supposed to show the apartment. It's not for rent."

"Please. I know a friend of Mr. Tutwiler's—"

"Then you know he got murdered." The door to the man's apartment was partially open, a Giants game in progress on a portable TV. He glanced back to catch a play.

"But he didn't die in the apartment. It's not a crime scene, is it? Please. I'm desperate. I'm—I'm moving back to New York. My friend, she told me about the apartment . . ."

"Jeez, I don't know, lady." He was shaking his head but his tone grew a fraction more amenable. "Like I told you. I'm not supposed to let anybody in. If the cops found out . . ." He cleared his throat. "I mean . . . I'd *like* to help you out."

Rannie smiled gratefully. The man made no move. Then suddenly she got it—and almost smacked herself on the forehead. As Homer would say, "Doh!"

"I understand, and for your time and trouble . . ." Rannie cradled the newspaper and floor plan under her chin while fishing for the loose bills in her pocket. She handed over forty dollars, earmarked for grocery shopping.

"I shouldn't be doing this," he said, his palm still outstretched.

Neither should I, Rannie scolded herself. It took six more ten dollar bills, doled out one at a time, before he went and threw on a flannel shirt, then accompanied her to Tut's apartment. Rannie stifled the urge to babble on about the difficulty of finding living space in New York, the outrageous rents, and so on. The man's canny eyes gave her the distinct impression he wasn't falling for the b.s. Why pile on more?

"Pretty," Rannie commented while looking around Mr. Tut's apartment, a comfortably furnished one-bedroom that had access to a small yard carpeted in yellowing leaves from a gingko tree.

It surprised and saddened her to see how much in evidence Tut's illness was. A cane, something Rannie had never once seen Tut use, was propped against an armchair. There was also a hospital bed and an invalid's high-seat toilet with railings in a bathroom stocked like a small infirmary—gauze pads, bandages, heavy-duty painkillers.

The closets were empty; the tabletops already cleared. So what had she learned coming here? Only that this was the home of a very sick man. Rannie was about to leave the bedroom when she paused before two large oval-framed black-and-white photos over a bureau. In one, Mama and Papa Tutwiler—also a man who liked bow ties—posed formally with their two young sons, the taller boy undoubtedly the brother who, according to Ms. Hollins, had drowned. Tut was still young enough to be in knee pants.

The other photo was a seated portrait of his mother, her hair pulled in a bun, a double strand of pearls at her neck. A stately looking woman, the kind of woman you didn't see much anymore, with strong, well-delineated features and a no-nonsense expression, a woman who might be described as "handsome" or "battle-ax" or both.

"You about done?" Mike called to her.

Rannie turned to face him. "I'm afraid it's a little too small."

"Having a yard helps. My place, I got a grill, a picnic table. Nice." A note of regret had crept into his voice. He raked a hand through his oiled hair. "I'm gonna miss that."

"You're moving?"

"Not by choice. I told you before, the apartment's not for rent." He held the keys, pointing one gun-like at Rannie and she followed him. "Take a look on the street," he said, locking up. "You'll see most of the apartments are already vacant. The ones of us still here, the building owner's trying to force out. Cutting off heat, turning off the boiler. There's going to be a big fancy high-rise."

"This whole row of brownstones, it's all going?"

"Yeah, the ones on Ninety-third Street, too. The fronts—the facades—they'll keep them like they are, but there'll be a forty-story building on top. Mr. T. was fighting Ross every step of the way."

"Ross, you said? David Ross?" Suddenly Rannie felt as if one of the slot machines at the Ross Riviera casino in Atlantic City had just paid off, going, "Ding! Ding! Ding!" and spewing forth quarters.

"Mr. T. knew he was dying. So really what'd it matter to him? But he hired a lawyer. He told us, 'I'm gonna stop this bastard.' Legally, Ross can toss me out, but the old folks here, they'll be here 'til they get carted out feet first. And David Ross can't do anything about it."

As he showed her out, Rannie silently congratulated herself on the sleuth-worthy way she'd discovered this latest bit of info. Mr. Tut was double-whammying his long-time enemy, David Ross. Which current offense was more egregious in Ross's mind, Rannie wondered, sticking it to his only son or stymieing a business deal?

"Look, if you find an apartment and need furniture, a lot of stuff in there is gonna be sold. I have the name and number to call. It's a woman from the school. Maybe it's your friend—her name's Augusta Hollins?"

"No! I don't know her! Never heard of her before!" Rannie yelped. "Thanks for your time. I—I have another apartment I have to look at." And she made a rapid getaway.

Chapter 35

"TWO EGG-AND-CHEESE SANDWICHES—CHEESE RUNNY, EGGS DRY . . . and bacon, too, please," Alice told the waitress behind the counter at the Doodle.

For someone who was barely one hundred pounds and claimed, without much justification, to be five-one on her driver's license, Nate's sister had a large, authoritative personality. People who met her after talking to her on the phone were always shocked by how little she was—even shorter than their mother.

"I'm telling you, Al, I'm a suspect. If I wasn't before last night, I am now. Plus I'm like the only kid with no alibi." Ben had been at the orthodontist. Chris was getting extra math help from one of the teachers. Oro was in Brooklyn practicing with his church singing group.

"What about Elliot?"

"In his limo with the Lilys."

He told her about overhearing Elliot and Tut.

"Wait a minute," Alice said. "Elliot said to Tut, 'You know what my father's gonna do.' What's that supposed to mean? Was it said like a threat?"

As the waitress placed their plates before them, Nate said, "I didn't think so, not then."

"Well, think *now!* Was that how it sounded? . . . Like if Tut didn't get Elliot into Harvard, he was gonna wind up in a block of cement and be the cornerstone of some cheesy Ross hotel. . . . Have you told the police?"

When he shook his head, she said, "Do it. But look. Don't worry. The cops can't seriously believe a doofus like you could kill anyone."

"Thanks." He understood the put-down was meant to make him feel better. And it did, sort of. His sister was always so definite about everything, she made you a believer too.

By now the line of Yale kids waiting for counter seats trailed onto the sidewalk, so they scarfed down their breakfasts, Al finishing off the last of his bacon and home fries. Then, patting her tummy, she said, "I've got an appetite like King Kong and the metabolism of a hummingbird—I am blessed."

They played tennis doubles that afternoon. Then Nate walked Alice back to Davenport. He was planning to catch the 4:24 to New York.

At the Davenport gates, Nate blinked, thinking he was seeing things. There was Grant Werner, and for a second Nate thought Grant was waving at *him*. But then Grant came up and kissed his sister . . . and it wasn't any casual "hi, pal" kiss either.

"I was gonna tell you. . . . But you were caught up in your own stuff," Al said, although a caught-in-the-act smile gave her away.

Jesus! Grant Werner of all people! His sister had had major hots for the guy in high school. But Nate figured she was all over that. He hoped Grant was as clean as Olivia claimed.

"Hey, man," Grant said and shook Nate's hand.

Yeah, Nate thought, trying not to scowl . . . on Monday right after his Columbia interview, it was definitely Grant he'd seen coming out of the West End. He was sure of that now.

Al reached up to hug him good-bye and whispered, "Remember, Nate. The Eleventh Commandment."

He nodded—"*Thou Shalt Not Blab to Ma*"—and took off.

Chapter 36

BACK IN HER NEWLY MEDECO LOCKED APARTMENT, RANNIE MARINATED chicken breasts in Peter Luger sauce for dinner and pondered motives. Surely the police must realize by now that Nate didn't have one while plenty of other people did. Danka had said her husband was a staunch believer in the "more is more" philosophy of life; well, Ross had motives for murdering Tut in spades. And Ms. Hollins? Her connections to Tut became ever more tangled and murky. Then, as penance for blowing all that money "investigating," Rannie made herself return to Dr. Mengele.

The chapter she was proofing theorized that Mengele's obsessions with identical twins stemmed from the possibility that Mengele may have been a twin himself, the other fetus having died *in utero*. The scant evidence supporting the theory was Mengele's mother's difficult pregnancy, one that required bed rest, as well as Mengele's fascination with his own reflection, interpreted as "a never-ending search for his missing mirror image." It sounded off-the-wall cuckoo to Rannie. A couple of farfetched "what if" pages ended the chapter: *"There is an intense symbiotic relationship between*

identical twins, where normal sibling rivalries are squared, even cubed.
The stronger, more able of the pair dominates the lesser 'shadow' twin. In
Josef Mengele's case, what if this charismatic, domineering, forceful man
had grown up with a weaker, needy brother to control, to 'torture' in all the
acceptable, if not commendable, ways of siblings? Would it have made a dif-
ference to history?"

A call from Nate made Rannie put down her blue pencil. He
was at Grand Central but planning to meet up with Ben. So now a
difficult question: To broil or not to broil the chicken breasts? The
ringing phone interrupted the decision-making process.

"Change of plans?" she asked Nate.

"What? It's Tim. Tim Butler." He told her he was heading out
to a movie at the 84th Street Loew's. "Want to come? I'll spring for
super-size popcorn."

The movie was a complicated diamond-heist thriller that Nate
had already conned her into seeing. "I'll meet you in an hour," she
told Tim.

With the chicken in the fridge, Rannie raced to Alice's closet
and tried on a cute pair of black pants and a retro beaded cardigan.
Raiding Alice's closet was so much fun—like playing dress-up, only
in reverse. She was all ready to grab her coat when she caught her
reflection in the hall mirror. Nix the sweater! Rannie told herself. It
looked like something out of a fifties B movie. All that was missing
was a torpedoe-cone bra.

Instead, she arrived modestly garbed in a pair of mom jeans and
a long-sleeved striped turtleneck. As they settled into seats, she
managed the bucket of popcorn and sodas while he took off his
jacket, revealing a 2004 Red Sox tee shirt.

The convoluted triple-crossing plot of the movie—was Matt
Damon in cahoots with the diamond thieves? once married to the
gorgeous FBI agent? or both?—proved no more comprehensible on
second viewing, in fact less so. This time there was the consider-

able distraction of Tim to deal with, his intensely physical presence right beside her in the darkened theater, a thigh an inch away from hers, a bare arm on the arm rest. Twice their hands met as they groped for popcorn, and reflexively both their hands pulled back. It rekindled memories of junior high, the embarrassed accidental touching.

After the movie, they went for coffee and dessert. Besides being rivetingly attractive, Tim had an appealing clear-sighted manner that made her yearn to spill everything she now knew or guessed about Tut and the murder. She wanted to display all the bits and pieces she'd picked up, like odds and ends at a tag sale, for his assessment. But in addition to Lieutenant Peratta's strict command to stay mum, she didn't want to anger Tim. Nevertheless, over a mile-high piece of chocolate cake that she ate most of, she couldn't resist asking why he thought Tut had been murdered.

"I had a feeling somehow that subject might come up," he said with wary amusement. He put down his coffee cup, then sat back, thinking, his arms crossed behind him around the back of the chair. *"Who's Your Daddy Now?"* his tee shirt said. She couldn't help smiling—the bleacher-seats taunt was appealing. Ditto the slight downward tilt of his dark eyebrows, the spikiness of his hair. Black Irish must have been an apt description before his hair turned silver.

"Okay. It was premeditated. That we know. The way I see it, killing somebody is a selfish act. The killer does it because he's got something to gain. Or it's solving a problem for him. *Any* murder is about self-interest."

"You sound like a cop." She'd noticed that before.

He frowned and shrugged. "From being around 'em, I guess. Look, this S.W.A.K. nut job, he's killing women because it's the only way he gets off. Other people, they do it for money, revenge. Or it could be wanting to shut somebody up who has dirt on them."

"Come on! You think Mr. Tut was blackmailing somebody?"

"I didn't say that. Maybe he found out something by accident, stumbled on information that somebody else didn't want coming to light."

She hadn't considered that before.

"Here we are, the two of us, talking, having a nice time. Who's to say what I'm holding back from you? Or how angry I'd be if you found out."

The remark didn't seem intended to carry a sting; nevertheless it did ... a little. *We're strangers* was the subtext and whereas a moment ago there had been a bantering easiness between them, now the distance across the table seemed to widen.

"You're asking me about motive," Tim went on, "and maybe that's because the motive is more interesting to you than people's alibis. But the police, right away they start checking out where everybody was and when. If anybody's airtight, then that's it."

He saw she was finished and signaled for the check, shooting Rannie the same "Don't argue!" look he had before when he paid for her on the ticket line.

Walking uptown to her house, Tim kept an arm on her back, his hand under the collar of her jacket. The quasi-proprietary gesture was a turn-on and while he chatted about family—he was one of seven, second-youngest in the family, his eldest brother not all that much younger than Rannie's mother—Rannie couldn't help fixing on his mouth, remembering that only twenty-four hours ago that mouth had been kissing hers. She filled in some Bookman genealogy for him and upon hearing about the UJA mah-jongg cruise her mother was on, he mentioned he played the game online. He also played backgammon twice a week for considerable stakes.

At Dolores Court, she refrained from inviting him up. Nor did he ask. Perhaps he wasn't even interested in a repeat performance of last night's feverish groping.

As the crotchety elevator door closed and clanked its way up six stories, Rannie experienced the underwhelming satisfaction of having acted prudently. "You stay out of trouble, okay?" was all he said. Tim Butler wasn't easy to read, a complicated guy with undercurrents. Black Irish in temperament as well as in looks, she sensed. Yet pulling out her shiny new keys, she realized something startling—and vaguely disconcerting. It wasn't just sex that she wanted.

She wanted Tim Butler.

Sunday night
FROM: alice.lorimer@yale.edu
TO: bookperson43@aol.com

Mom, it was great seeing Nate but didn't get as much reading done for my psych paper as I hoped. I feel bad but no way can I make it down tomorrow for the Tut thing.

xxx

P.S. Stumbled on a poetry book of Tut's I borrowed years ago. It has his name in it, written in fountain pen—I'd forgotten how distinct his handwriting was—very forceful! I'm glad I forgot to return it.

The Cathedral Church of St. John the Divine

A Celebration of the Life of A. Lawrence Tutwiler

Hymn..................................... "Oh, God, Our Help in Ages Past"

Lauren Hood, Tenth Grade...................... Chopin's Piano Sonata

Griffith Handler, former Headmaster .... Old Friends

Augusta Hollins............. "Ozymandias" by Percy Bysshe Shelley

Chapel School Choir...............A Medley from Lerner and Lowe

Hymn.................................... "Oh, Praise Him, Allelujah!"

Chapel School Orchestra.................... Moussorgsky's Promenade
from "Pictures at an Exhibition"

Chapel School Kindergarten .... "Everything Is Beautiful"
and "Here Comes the Sun"

Chapter 37

Monday morning, after the service

SHE WAS IN STANDARD FUNERAL ATTIRE. A KNEE-LENGTH NAVY SUIT AND gold beads, navy stockings and navy pumps with patent leather toes. In the past year, the ensemble had had too many outings. Walter's high-Wasp send-off at St. Thomas's on Fifth Avenue, the scattering of her Aunt Hilda's ashes in Cincinnati, as well as the funeral for her father's oldest friend in the temple of her childhood. The "buffer zone" generation was fast disappearing, and suddenly Rannie found herself wishing that her mother wasn't aboard *The Nordic Princess* so she could pick up the phone and hear her voice.

Rannie stood outside the side portal of the unfinished Gothic cathedral, waiting for Mary. For a city of eight million people, New York was like a tiny hamlet for certain natives. No matter where her mother-in-law went, Mary invariably ran into somebody she knew.

The "celebration," tasteful and dignified, with sun streaming in through stained glass windows, had been conducted before an outpouring of the entire Chaps community—kids, teachers, parents, old alums, two former headmasters. Rannie had found it genuinely moving when the kindergarteners marched to the front of the choir stand and, en masse, began singing in high, earnest voices, wearing uniforms that all looked several sizes too big.

Jem Marshall, sporting a red bowtie, had limited himself to brief remarks. In Rannie's estimation, it was a sweet gesture, but then she was feeling especially charitable towards the headmaster after their earlier meeting in his office at Chaps.

Jem Marshall had started off by saying, "Let me assure you both that I believe Nate about—about the 'incident.' I don't know what else to call it, and I certainly don't know what to make of it, but then this whole past week defies imagination."

Rannie listened, wishing Nate would stop cracking his knuckles and that the tie he was wearing for Tut's service wasn't so horribly stained.

"Yesterday, I reported what happened at the dance, and Sergeant Peratta will be here shortly." Jem Marshall held up a hand like a traffic cop when a frightened gulp issued forth from Nate. "Don't be alarmed. He just wants to know if your backpack was in the same place all evening, how long it was left unattended, that sort of thing."

Indeed, the sergeant's questions had been asked politely—no whiff of the third degree about them. He finished taking down what little information Nate could provide—his backpack had been unattended the whole time except for twice when he needed to get something from it.

Once the sergeant departed, Jem Marshall rose, smiling at the two of them. "Nate, by the way, I hear you're applying to my Alma Mater. Just between us," he said, addressing Rannie and her son, "I think Stanford has it all over the Ivies."

Rannie smiled, pumping his hand, trying her best to ignore the grammatical boo-boo. There were three people here—it was "*among* us" not "*between*."

Now, with an eye out for Mary, she visored her eyes with her program and gazed at the deep central portal of the cathedral. For Rannie, St. John's was a familiar and comforting place. After the divorce, she'd sought solace at some of the Sunday "come one, come all" services. The history of the place fascinated her, its great bronze doors cast by Barbedienne of Paris, who had also cast the Statue of Liberty. She loved the solemn saints on both sides of the portal, the fluted columns with lacy stone decoration, the huge rose window floating above and higher up, to the right, the single tower against the sky. Work had begun in 1892 on what was to be the largest cathedral on the continent, the largest in the world except for St. Peter's. A hundred-plus years later, it remained unfinished, the pace of construction even slower than in medieval times. Funds were always in short supply. Several years ago, there'd been a disastrous fire destroying the north transept. In a strange way, however, St. John's incomplete state appealed to Rannie. Some things were hard to do. Some things still took a long time to accomplish.

Ah, there was Mary, tall and elegant in sunglasses, a black-and-white hound's-tooth coat, her bag and ladylike gloves clutched in one hand. Again, Rannie was struck by how much older, more tentative Mary seemed outside the confines of her apartment.

"I'm famished, dear, are you? I find funerals, or whatever this was, do that to me," Mary remarked. They proceeded slowly toward Broadway, Rannie grasping Mary gently under the elbow. At the corner, a window table was free at a patisserie that served excellent croissants and café au lait.

"Why, what a darling little place!" Mary exclaimed at the sight of the stenciled walls, Provençal pottery, and mosaic tabletops.

Supposedly famished, Mary took exactly two bites of her croissant while filling Rannie in on family news, most of which revolved around Peter's brother's recent trip to Thailand.

"Whit refused to send a single postcard. It's his way of punishing me because I don't do e-mail. But I *like* getting postcards."

All of a sudden, Mary stopped talking and, staring at the window, exclaimed, "My Lord, do you know that woman? The one outside lighting up a cigarette? She certainly is shooting daggers at you!"

Rannie followed Mary's gaze. Ms. Hollins was standing outside. Outfitted in black garb, her usual hippie braid transformed into a thick bun at the nape of her neck, Ms. Hollins presented an altogether more intimidating persona.

Rannie, horrified, watched her toss the cigarette and enter the café. Ms. Hollins marched toward their table.

"I got a phone call. I know what you were doing yesterday!"

One hundred bucks had evidently not bought the guy's silence. Rannie made no reply, her eyes rivetted on the silver brooch pinned schoolmarmishly to the collar of Ms. Hollins's blouse.

"What on earth's wrong with you? This has got to stop!" Then Ms. Hollins turned and strode back out to the street.

"My word!" Mary said, a hand at her throat.

"She's a teacher at Chaps," was all Rannie stammered out. "I'm not one of her favorite people."

"You? How could she not like you? If you ask me, the woman looks unhinged," Mary replied loyally, and if Rannie hadn't been so rattled, she might have laughed. At times Mary sounded almost as much like a Jewish mother as Rannie's own genuinely Jewish one. She touched Mary's hand affectionately and Mary, with her classic Wasp upbringing, didn't press her any further.

While waiting for the check, Rannie mulled over Ms. Hollins's altered appearance. Just now Rannie was reminded of someone, although who it was remained slightly out of reach, floating at the edge of her consciousness. Then it came to her. The photograph in Tut's bedroom, the one of his mother. Ms. Hollins shared quite a remarkable physical kinship with Mama Tutwiler.

As she helped her mother-in-law outside, Rannie mentally ze-roed in on one other detail. The brooch. Rannie had noticed Ms. Hollins wearing it once before, but in the patisserie just now Rannie had taken a much closer look. The silver pin was in the shape of a dragon. Rannie recalled the presents of dragon-motif jewelry Mr. Tut had given Laura Scales. Rannie's hunch, however, was that there'd been only one "Dragon Lady" in his life.

After putting Mary in a cab, Rannie hurried back to her apart-ment, hoping Daisy Satterthwaite was home.

Chapter 38

Monday afternoon

THE LITTLE CHURCH ON 108TH BETWEEN AMSTERDAM AND BROADWAY reminded Olivia of the one Carlotta went to in the Bronx, the same painted plaster crucifix behind the altar, Jesus's eyeballs rolled heavenward, blood dripping from the nails in his hands and feet, a crown of thorns keeping his long wavy hair in place.

The AA meeting in the basement wasn't starting until four; most people were gathered by a table with a coffee urn on it and a tray of Lorna Doone cookies. The snapshot of Grant was in her purse. What she was about to do was exactly the sort of thing everyone at Al-Anon meetings gave her grief about, how she had to stop being Grant's watchdog. Still, she wanted proof that *something* Grant had told her about last Monday was the truth.

"Olivia?" a man filling up a Styrofoam cup of coffee said. His silver hair stuck up in a quasi-punk way.

It was Chris Butler's dad. "Uh, hi, Mr. Butler."

He didn't seemed embarrassed or even all that surprised to see her. She was mortified.

One time last year she'd been over at Chris's, the week of spring finals, Mr. Butler had come home unexpectedly. She and Chris were stark naked. Mad scrambling to get dressed, open textbooks, smooth the bed and appear to be studying when Chris's dad knocked on the door and poked his head in to say, "Hi." It was only after he left, saying, "Glad to see you're both working hard," that they noticed neither of their flies was zipped.

"Your first time at this meeting?"

"Uh, yes."

"It's a good meeting. Very basic." Then he cocked his head. "Can I treat you to a cup of this swill they call coffee?"

She laughed nervously. "No, no. That's okay. Actually—um—I may not be able to stay."

"Look, don't leave 'cause of me. How long are you in the program? . . . You know that whatever's said here stays here."

She wet her lips. "I'm not exactly in AA. I'm not an alcoholic."

"But you didn't wind up here by accident?"

"No. It's kind of complicated."

"Listen, completely up to you, but"—he gestured with both hands out, one holding his Styrofoam coffee cup—"there's still about fifteen minutes before the meeting starts. If you want to talk, I'm happy to listen."

Olivia swallowed. Up to now she'd spoken maybe ten words to Chris's dad in her life. Nevertheless, she found herself saying, "Yeah, maybe I would. It's about my brother."

They sat on two folding chairs by a sign saying, "First things first." She told him all about Grant, everything. "Grant said he came to this AA meeting before going to Chaps. I brought a picture to see if anybody recognized him."

"I'm not sure I follow. If he *was* here, that would prove—what?"

"Grant lies so much, I just want *something* to be the truth."

"You know, we have a saying here. 'Let go and let God.' It works for people like you who care about alcoholics or drug addicts.

It works even if you think God is the greatest hoax ever perpetrated on mankind . . . what your brother does is out of your control." Chris's father frowned for a moment, then stuck out a hand. "Lemme see the photo. I was here last Monday. . . . It's not like I'd be breaking his anonymity."

While Olivia fished for the photo in her bag she explained how Grant had wanted to make amends to Tut.

Mr. Butler glanced at the photo. "Yeah, he was here."

"Did he seem, you know—okay?"

"Are you asking, 'Was he high?' I don't think so. He looked okay to me."

Relief washed over Olivia.

"So where does that leave you?" He handed back the photo and rubbed his chin and mouth. There were tiny flecks of silver stubble on his face. "You know, the point of making amends is to take responsibility for your actions. And I gotta say your brother's not doing that. He should tell the cops what he saw."

Olivia nodded and left before the meeting started. Upstairs, the church was empty, so she sat in a pew with her cell out. Maybe all the millions of prayers people had offered were still floating around and would rub off on her phone call in a good way.

The person who answered at Windward shouted, "Werner, it's your sister."

"Whazzup?"

"Look, Grant. I've been thinking about this a lot. You have to tell the cops what you saw."

"Hold on." There was a pause, then Grant whispered, a frantic undertone in his voice, "That's crazy! And I don't know anything."

"You were there. You heard Tut with somebody."

"And I have no idea who."

"It was probably his killer."

"Olivia, you're the one who said it's me plastered all over the newspapers."

"But you didn't do anything." Right?

"I'm a recovering addict. Tut got me thrown out of Chaps. And I suddenly happen to show up at Chaps right before he gets murdered. You do the math."

"Grant, it's not right—"

"And the first thing they're gonna ask is how come I waited so long to come forward."

"You tell them the truth. You were scared. Listen, you wanted to make amends. So—so, going to the cops is like doing that." She wished Chris's dad were here; it sounded so much more convincing when he said it.

"Going to the cops won't do squat for Tut. He's dead."

Grant was still whispering; even so Olivia could hear his voice turning icy. "What I need is to concentrate on staying clean. Got that? . . . That's what Tut would want."

Grant was great at twisting stuff to make it mean whatever he wanted it to.

"Will you at least think about it?" she asked.

Silence. "Are you gonna go to the cops if I don't?"

"I didn't say that." She'd already lied once about the phone calls. Not telling the police about Grant being at school wasn't lying. It was worse. But she would never rat out her brother. And Grant knew it.

Chapter 39

Monday afternoon

WHEN RANNIE CALLED DAISY, A WOMAN ANSWERED SAYING THAT MRS. Satterthwaite was expected home shortly. Rannie left her number.

The yearbook layouts were still sitting on her coffee table. This time, when she compared the photos of Mr. Tut and Ms. Hollins, the family resemblance seemed startlingly obvious, especially around the eyes. Rannie picked up her blue pencil and, while awaiting Daisy's call, looked over a new layout, the one for Jonathan Edwards Marshall, headmaster. According to Nate, it had taken some coaxing before Mr. Marshall relinquished his senior yearbook from Palo Alto High School.

"He kept saying it was lost, the same b.s. all the teachers give at first. Then when Chris Butler threatened to go on eBay for a copy, Marshall suddenly found it. Ma, nobody—I mean absa-fuckinlootly nobody—gets rid of their high school yearbook."

Yes, Rannie thought, definitely one of life's verities. She found herself wondering what Tim Butler looked like at seventeen, what his yearbook would have revealed about him, pretty certain they wouldn't have hung in the same crowd. Then in one of those little

ESP hiccups, the phone started ringing. Tim. He was working at the bar until nine that night, he told her, but wanted to see her. Rannie suggested a late dinner at Dolores Court.

Returning to the yearbook layout, the mental image of Tim made the head shot of Jem Marshall appear all the more antiseptic; he was a decent-looking man but juiceless, slightly robotic. A never-married man his age always prompted the obvious guess, but Jem Marshall didn't strike her as gay. What he seemed was unconnected.

Next to his imposing I-am-your-leader photo was the smaller one of Jem at eighteen. Rannie stared at it, the same even, unremarkable features, the same thatch of straight hair parted neatly on the side. Except for being a little more than twenty years younger, Jem Marshall had looked no different and yet completely different. At eighteen, there had been an easygoing openness to his smile as opposed to the starchy demeanor he now presented to the world.

Setting aside her blue pencil, Rannie leafed through his Palo Alto yearbook and found him with the Mathletes and debate team, exactly the extracurriculars she would have predicted, but also on the prom committee, the baseball team, and in several candids, goofing with friends, blasting an unsuspecting teacher with a water pistol, and writing something in a notebook, using the back of a cute girl in his lap as a desktop. He seemed popular, friendly.

Rannie was adding the missing "s" to Jem Marshall's middle name on the layout when the phone rang again.

It was Joan, barely able to contain herself. "Rannie! I just came from a board meeting. We learned the general terms of the will. *Tut's* will. Rannie, you're going to plotz! It's an eight-million-dollar estate—more than anybody thought. And Chaps is getting six. . . . But now I come to the juicy part." A dramatic pause at the other end of the line. "The other two million—and all of Tut's personal effects—is an outright bequest to one very lucky teacher. Take a wild guess!"

Only one name popped to mind. "Augusta Hollins."

"Atta girl! I never believed the rumors. But I guess maybe the kids were right. Who woulda thunk, huh? And there's more. It was a new will . . . signed three weeks before he died!"

"No kidding!"

"You cannot—I repeat *cannot*—reveal a word of this," Joan said before they hung up, which made Rannie feel guilty for all that she was withholding from her friend. She held onto the phone, thinking. . . . A new will. And now suddenly Ms. Hollins was an heiress. Children, what does M-O-T-I-V-E spell?

Rannie decided to try Daisy Satterthwaite's number again.

"Lunch was such fun!" Daisy said. "I've been gobbling up all the news of the murder, haven't you?"

"Actually that was why I wanted to speak to you."

"A date rape drug. Imagine," Daisy Satterthwaite said. "We didn't have such things in my time. . . . Fellows didn't need them. There were plenty of girls only too willing."

"I wanted to ask you a question about your friend, Laura Scales. I know you feel honor-bound not to reveal a confidence. But would you mind telling me what year she left New York?"

A pause. "Oh Lord. Darling, I'm lucky I remember what year it is *now*. I do know it was right before my second marriage because poor Laura was so blue at the time, and I remember feeling a teensy bit guilty because I was in love and happy. . . . But the year? That's hard." A longer pause. "Oh I know how I can tell."

Rannie remained on the line while Daisy went searching for a bracelet from her second husband, given to her before their wedding. The year was inscribed on the back.

After Daisy supplied the date—1960—Rannie thanked her and hung up. Forty-seven years ago a pregnant Laura Scales had left

New York. Forty-seven—that was how old Rannie judged Ms. Hollins to be, give or take. And checking the date imprinted in gold leaf on Ms. Hollins's boarding school yearbook bore her out.

Along with the news of Tut's will, suddenly there was a storyline in which all the pieces seemed to fit. If Ms. Hollins was Tut's daughter, as Rannie now suspected, how long had Ms. Hollins known? Since childhood? Or far more recently? When had Tut first become an active presence in her life? The vision of Ms. Hollins at Tut's house with her suitcase in hand made sense now. A concerned daughter, staying overnight to care for her ill father, might misplace earrings, would keep clothes at the apartment. Or at least a daughter who *appeared* concerned. Rannie felt her brain was on information overload. She needed to sort out what she knew and, even more important, decide what to do with it. She needed coffee and some peanut butter and jelly.

Logic was never her strong suit, she reminded herself as she ground up coffee beans and filled the pot with water. Okay, going on the assumption that Ms. Hollins was Mr. Tut's daughter, the question was: Had she pressured him to write her into his will? Guilted him out to do right by her, then murdered him in case he might change his mind and his will? Maybe long-simmering resentment finally boiled over. Ms. Hollins was someone Tut must have invited into his office for drinks many times. Maybe she even convinced herself it was an act of mercy, slipping GHB into a sick old man's drink.

Rannie watched the steady plunk plunk plunk of coffee dripping into the pot. At Chaps, a lost-and-found box was by Mrs. Mac's desk, always filled to overflowing with kids' clothes. Ms. Hollins, taller and bigger than many of the boys, could have disguised herself for the cameras and made a quick exit.

But what about the threatening note to Tut? *Watch out! Your days are numbered!* How did that fit in? It either was totally unrelated to the murder or had never existed. Just something Ms. Hollins had fabricated. But if nonexistent, what had motivated Ms. Hollins to go running to the police, telling them about it? It was Ms. Hollins who indirectly initiated the whole investigation. Rannie pressed her fingertips to either side of her head. Right behind her eyes a headache was threatening. The best and only explanation she could fashion was that from the get-go Ms. Hollins expected an investigation into an unwitnessed death and was attempting to divert suspicion from herself.

On a whim, she dialed Daisy's number again. But although they'd spoken only a minute ago, no one picked up. Rannie had an unsettling image of Daisy at the other end staring at her phone, letting it ring and ring. Daisy had revealed all she wanted to.

Chapter 40

Monday evening

"DUDE, WHAT DO YOU MEAN YOU'RE NOT GOING?"

Nate was stretched out on Ben's bunk bed. "It's too demeaning. The asshole plants drugs on me but I'm so hard up, I show up at his party?"

"Don't give me this 'demeaning' crap. You're a party whore. Live with it."

Half an hour later they got off the subway at Columbus Circle and walked east on Central Park South. At the Ross Maharaja, a doorman wearing a purple Nehru jacket and a turban with a fake jewel asked to see Chaps I.D., then said, "Go past the bronze statue of an elephant—you can't miss it. Take the elevator straight to the penthouse."

Monday night parties were rare, and it looked like half the high school had shown up for this one, a mixed-bag crowd that cut across all lines—jocks, artsy drama kids, prepsters in pink Lacostes with the collars up in back, stoners, a few rah-rah student leaders.

"Hey, over here, you guys!" Katie Spielkopf shouted, holding up a beer bottle and waving it at them. She was standing beside Chris

Butler, whose arm was draped around a life-size statue of Elliot's father that was scarily real looking—the hair, the eyeballs, the teeth, the clothes. Somebody, Chris probably, had stuck a BoSox cap on its head and a joint in its mouth.

"Say hello to our host," Chris said.

"Quel zoo," Katie shouted over the blasting music. She was in one of her early Stevie Nicks get-ups, long flowing skirt, cowboy boots, straw cowboy hat, dangly earrings.

"They have three floors. But get this," Chris said. "No kitchen. They just order room service."

Ben arched a skeptical eyebrow.

"I love when you do that! Teach me how!" Katie tugged at Ben's elbow.

Chris tilted back his beer and drifted off. Nate did too, seeing that Ben was already moving in on Katie, his arm raised and pressed against the wall, hemming her in.

On the terrace a bunch of kids sat circling the rim of a stone fountain, passing around a joint. Fifty-something floors below, the rectangle of Central Park stretched northward, edged all around by tall buildings. From this high up all he could make out were glowing dots from streetlamps and curving roadways lit by moving traffic.

He felt a tap on his shoulder.

"Hey. I was hoping you'd show up."

As always his heart started thrumming wildly. Olivia was wearing a pair of old jeans with a ripped knee, a plain white tee shirt, and a belt that looked like it was made out of a bungee cord. She moved beside him and leaned over the terrace railing, pointing down in the general area of the ice skating rink. "Wollman's is gonna be open soon. I can't wait."

"I hate ice skating. I suck at it."

"I'm really good." She pretend-skated. "You should try it again."

"Nah. They don't make skates with double runners in my size."

Olivia smiled that beautiful off-kilter smile. Then she said, "Nate, lookit. I need to talk. . . . Can I trust you?"

He said sure although a sick feeling slithered in his stomach. Trust and lust, they rhymed, but they sure didn't go together. He bet no woman ever said she trusted Lord Byron.

They moved away from the kids by the fountain. Her voice, always low, dropped to a whisper. "Promise you won't tell any-body. . . . It's about my brother—it's him in the *News* photo." She told him why Grant happened to be at Chaps last Monday evening. "Grant didn't know who was in the office with Tut. But it sounded serious. He heard Tut go something like, 'You have a lot of explaining to do.' "

"Do the cops know?"

"Only me—and now you. I want Grant to go to the cops, but he's scared they won't believe him."

Nate listened, scowling. Why the fuck did Alice have to hook up with Grant? The guy was bad news, end of story.

"Remember what I told you about Lily, how weird she was acting when I was at her house watching TV?"

"You mean when you were watching 'Crime Blotter'?"

"Yeah. I still think the Lilys made Elliot do something, some-thing to Tut. Maybe, maybe if we like go upstairs and look around in Elliot's room, we'll find something."

Snooping around the Rosses' apartment sounded pretty flaky to him, like Olivia wanted to play a real-life game of "Clue." What did she expect to find? A bottle labeled "*Extra GHB from when I killed Tut*"? But upstairs, in Elliot's room, alone with Olivia? Just call him Colonel Mustard.

"Yeah, sure," he said. "Let's go."

Chapter 41

DAISY SATTERTHWAITE LOOKED AS IF SHE'D SHRUNK SINCE LUNCH AT THE Colony Club. Perhaps it was the gargantuan living room where she greeted Rannie that dwarfed her size. Even a Sotheby's showroom worth of furniture didn't begin to fill the space—back-to-back sofas in gloomy green brocade, a grand piano in the corner, laden with silver-framed photos, and fussy upholstered chairs and tables arranged as if in cliques.

"You're very kind to let me come over." Rannie accepted a spindly legged chair Daisy pointed to but murmured "no thanks" to a tumbler of scotch. The room, with its damask-covered walls and heavy draperies tethered in strangleholds of tasseled swags, was all a bit too haute Miss Haversham, poorly lit, musty, pervaded by the smell of stale, cigarette-scented air.

"Kind? I crave company. It's only me, rattling around in this mausoleum. The apartment upstairs went for seven million, can you believe it! But where would I go?" Daisy sat down and dug out a pack of cigarettes from the pocket of her silk dressing gown, the color of Pepto Bismol. She was still wearing jewelry.

"Beatriz! Beatriz, do you hear me? You may go home now," she hollered to the rooms beyond, then turning back to Rannie added with an impatient sigh, "she's fiddling with the TV, trying to tape something for me. She'll just screw it up, I know it, and I won't be able to watch a thing."

Beatriz, Rannie surmised, was the elderly maid, with the same short coarse blond hair as Daisy. She'd shown Rannie into the apartment moments earlier, an apartment on Park Avenue a few blocks south of Mary's.

Daisy picked up a heavy cut-glass lighter which she had to click a few times before the flame appeared and said, cigarette between her lips, "You know you're the first person I've ever star-sixty-nine-ed. My grandson was here and showed me how." Daisy seemed tickled as she puffed away. "I knew it was you calling me back. . . . star sixty-nine, imagine! . . . I thought my grandson was talking about some pornographic movie!" She paused to swirl her drink while Rannie stole a glance at a small blue-enameled carriage clock on the table between them. She had a little over an hour before Tim arrived. Not a lot of time for small talk.

"So, I gather you're trying to piece together more of Laura's sad story," Daisy said slowly. "And I suppose after all this time, who is left to care if I blab?" With pauses to sip and smoke, Daisy confirmed for Rannie that Laura Scales had returned to Asheville, North Carolina, in 1960 about six months before the birth of her daughter.

"Knocked up at Laura's age. Ridiculous, if you ask me. Oh, Laura claimed to be overjoyed. *Please.* Both Laura's parents gone, her brothers and sisters scattered, no friends left in Asheville and living alone in the house she grew up in—and if you're envisioning Tara, you're wrong."

"But you said she'd wanted children—this was her chance."

"She wanted Larry. Truth to tell, she was a somewhat cold mother."

"Did she stay in touch with him?"

"With Larry? Heavens, no. Laura was too bitter. I'm sure she expected Larry to go chasing down to Asheville and beg her to come back. When he didn't, she erased him, like chalk from a blackboard, and invented a father for the child. Told her that Ted Scales—he was Laura's second husband—was her father."

"He was the husband from D.C.? The one in the State Department?"

Daisy answered with a nod. "Ted died smoking in bed, drunk as a skunk. He set himself on fire. Ghastly. It happened while Laura was pregnant. So the timing worked perfectly for her absurd story. The baby grew up with Scales for her last name."

"Mr. Tut—Larry—did he know when the baby was born? Did he know it was a girl?"

"Oh, yes. He found out that much."

"What did she name the baby?"

"Polly was what she was called. Short for Pauline? I'm not sure. I've wondered what became of her."

All of a sudden a little soupçon of suspicion flitted across Rannie's mind. Perhaps Daisy knew exactly what "Polly's" given name was and exactly what had become of her.

"Laura refused to let Larry see the baby. Refused his offer of financial help, at least so she said." Daisy waved absently at her housekeeper who was letting herself out of the apartment. "Good night, Beatriz. See you in the morning."

Rannie recrossed her legs. The chair was impossibly uncomfortable. "From what Mary said, I wouldn't have expected Laura needed any financial help." Rich divorcée had been her mother-in-law's exact words.

Daisy snorted and inhaled so deeply that almost an inch of her cigarette turned to ash. "Mims never gets her facts straight. You should know that by now. Laura got a settlement from Ted Scales after they divorced. That kept her in a cute little apartment near here, over on 63rd Street and Lex, and allowed her to lead a very comfortable life. But she'd just about run through all that money by the time she left New York. As for her family, well, Laura's people were Southern genteel but not a pot to piss in." An impossibly long stream of smoke blew out the side of Daisy's mouth.

"How then Foxcroft? A horse of her own?"

"Darling, I didn't say the family was on *welfare*. Laura spent every nickel she had. Loved clothes. Gave terrific parties. She and Larry traveled like gypsies every summer, places nobody went to. Japan. Australia. And then there was the club and the place she rented on Hilton Head. I told you. She liked to have fun. And fun always costs a bundle."

Daisy tossed back her drink, allowing Rannie a moment to ponder this latest tidbit and the harsh light it cast on Augusta Hollins. Having a rich mother would have crossed out money as a motive for murder. But the twofold news that there'd been no inheritance from Laura Scales along with the sudden windfall from Tut's recently changed will put Ms. Hollins in "most likely suspect" territory.

"Over the years, when he saw you, did Mr. Tut—Larry—ever ask about Laura? Or Polly?"

"No. Never. I was Laura's best friend. He'd see me at the club occasionally, and we'd wave, smile. Nothing more." Daisy sighed. "And I saw less and less of Laura too. It wasn't just because she lived so far away. She didn't want her past intruding, I suppose, and destroying this elaborate fabrication she'd created for her daughter. And of course I couldn't help but remind her of painful times." Daisy killed her cigarette in a matching cut-glass ashtray. "I'd hear from Laura now and then, Christmas cards, that sort of thing. Polly went off to boarding school and college—Wellesley, I think. I remember Laura writing to tell me her daughter had married and was living in Atlanta. That was the last I heard. Laura's been dead now, oh, it must be ten years."

Rannie nodded, piecing together more of the story's missing fragments. So Augusta Hollins apparently went by her married name. She had begun teaching at Chaps at some point after her mother's death. It seemed out of the question to consider coincidence as the cause for her winding up at the same New York private school where her father taught; Mr. Tut *and* Ms. Hollins couldn't both have been unaware of their relationship. Either both of them knew, which was the nicest possibility—a late-in-life reunion between Mr. Tut and his daughter. Or else one of them already knew by then, but the other didn't. . . . "Hello, this is Larry Tutwiler. I'm an old friend of your mother's whom you've never met or heard of, but it suddenly occurred to me that you might be a teacher and might be interested in moving to Manhattan and joining the faculty at Chapel School." No. If only one of them knew about their shared genes, it had to be Ms. Hollins, who must have discovered her mother's cover-up and then tracked down her real father.

"So? What do you make of all this? Obviously you think it has bearing on Larry's murder." Daisy seemed to savor saying the word "murder," as if it were a piece of Swiss chocolate melting slowly on her tongue. "Don't tell me you think Polly suddenly appeared out of nowhere, deciding after all this time to seek revenge on the man who done her mama wrong?"

"No, I don't think that. I honestly don't know what I think." Equally unsure of what Daisy might be keeping close to her vest, Rannie refrained from any mention of a newly minted heiress named Augusta Hollins. And when Daisy pursed her lips and eyed Rannie appraisingly in a way that made Rannie suddenly shift uneasily in the chair, she had the distinct impression Daisy already knew everything Rannie was withholding.

"Well, Laura's daughter didn't find out about her father from me. I met Polly exactly once, when she was thirteen. A large ungainly girl, tripping all over herself. She stayed holed up in her bedroom, reading the whole time. I learned of Laura's death from the Fox-croft alumnae magazine."

Rannie nodded, again not entirely convinced she believed Daisy. So where did that leave her? As Rannie was shown out of the apartment, it crossed her mind that Daisy might have invited her over expressly to find out what *she*, Rannie, knew. And what she'd told Daisy a moment before was the truth: She didn't know what to make of anything. All she had were suspicions that didn't have much more substance than the smoke curling from Daisy's new cigarette.

Chapter 42

IN THE ROSSES' LIVING ROOM ELLIOT WAS HOLDING A FORTY-OUNCER by the neck and weaving in the direction of the Lilys who were sharing a blunt the size of a cigar. Nate and Olivia steered clear of them and found their way to the backstairs. A collapsible wooden gate, like for a dog or a baby, had a warning—DO NOT GO UPSTAIRS— taped to it. Olivia hopped over the gate. Nate followed.

The leopard-print carpeting in the hallway upstairs muffled their footsteps. The door to one room was ajar, and Nate could hear a girl giggling softly. "Ben, shhh . . . I hear somebody."

Katie Spielkopf.

The door shut.

Elliot's room—actually it was more like a little apartment—was on the other side of the hall. In the living room part of it, two gray suede couches were at right angles and a giant flat-screen TV took up most of one wall. In the enormous bedroom, the top sheet on one of the king-size beds was folded back diagonally. Resting on the pillow were chocolate wafers with *Ross Maharaja* printed on the foil. Just like at a fancy hotel . . . but, *duh*, this *was* a fancy hotel. Nate tossed a chocolate to Olivia and opened a cabinet, expecting stereo equipment.

"Man, check this out—there's like the world's largest minibar. Wanna beer? Soda? Champagne? Macadamia nuts?"

Olivia was examining stuff in the medicine cabinet. She came out holding something that looked like a fat black magic marker except it was buzzing. "Yuck. A nose hair clipper. Same kind my dad uses." A minute later she disappeared inside a closet and while he opened a Sam Adams and ripped open a bag of Sun Chips he could hear her pushing clothes hangers around. "And I thought my closet was big," he heard her say.

Nate walked to the closet. "So? Find anything suspicious?" he said, stepping inside.

They were surrounded by racks of Elliot's clothes. Nate held out his bottle of beer to her, but she shook her head. "I don't drink anymore. Don't do any dope either."

"Cause of your brother?"

"Yeah, kind of like moral support." She shrugged as if it was stupid. "I'll take some Sun Chips."

Nate shook a few into her hand. As she nibbled on one, he noticed her nails were bitten way down below the quick. Nate put down his beer and the chips on a closet shelf.

"Don't look at my hands. They're gross!" She balled them into fists but before she could shove them behind her back, Nate took a step closer and grabbed them both.

They stood, not saying a word. Slowly her hands relaxed in his. He wanted to tell her how beautiful she was but he didn't trust his voice.

"I like that scar," she said.

"What scar?"

"Let go of my hands and I'll show you."

When he did, she touched the corner of his upper lip, then continued slowly tracing the entire outline of his mouth with the tip of her finger. He pulled her toward him.

The next second he was kissing her. He wrapped his arms around her. It wasn't a dream. It was real, realer than almost anything he'd ever experienced. She pulled back for a moment and he could feel her warm breath on his cheek when she exhaled, soft as a whisper. As they settled into another kiss, he pushed his mouth against hers harder.

Then suddenly he felt her body tense up all over. She pulled back. "Nate," she whispered. Someone was stumbling around in the bedroom.

Nate felt like he was on ten-second lag time, barely processing what she was telling him. But then he heard someone knocking into furniture. There was a thud on the bed, the sound of mattress springs heaving. A second later, he heard gagging, followed by the thump of feet running to the bathroom, violent retching, and the sound of a toilet flushing. Somebody praying to the porcelain goddess. A faucet turned on, turned off and then the sound of the bed creaking gently again.

Olivia pushed him away and stole a peek into the bedroom. "Shit. It's Elliot."

"Maybe he'll pass out. We should just stay here." That seemed like an excellent plan to him; he couldn't resist coming up behind her and kissing her on the back of her neck.

"Stop," she hissed. "You want to make out with Elliot there?"

Of course he did. He wouldn't care if it was in front of a full house at Madison Square Garden. But Olivia's expression made it plain—for her, the moment was over. Her brow wrinkled and she was biting her thumbnail, thinking. "Come on. Let's just get out of here.... At least we'll give him a good scare."

She kicked open the closet door so hard it banged against a wall.

"Holy shi——!" Elliot sprang to a sitting position on the bed. His eyes took a second to focus and then bugged out. "Olivia?"

"Don't have a heart attack, Elliot," she said. "We were just going."

Elliot's eyes settled on Nate. "You!" His mouth pulled into a crazy grimace. He lurched off the bed and groped for a phone. He turned and blinked. "I'm calling the cops, Lorimer. This is like . . . like breaking and entering."

Nate snorted. "Oh please. What's your fucking problem? Let's go, Olivia. The party sucks anyway."

Elliot dropped the phone. "My problem! My problem?" He took a step toward Nate, his Popeye arms swinging a little, his hands starting to clench. "You're the asshole who brings roofies to school, and you're asking what *my* problem is?"

"That you planted on me, you dumb prick!"

"Me? Get the hell out of here. Go fuck your slut in someone else's closet."

"What'd you say?" Nate yelled and lunged at Elliot.

"Don't!" Olivia shouted.

He felt her grabbing the back of his tee shirt but he was already on top of Elliot, punching him in the face and knocking him back on the bed. Elliot snatched a fistful of Nate's shirt, pulled him closer, and the next thing Nate knew, he was in a headlock and Elliot was punching him in the ribs.

"Stop it!" Olivia was screaming at both of them.

Nate dug his elbow into Elliot's stomach and heard him grunt. As Elliot relaxed his grip, Nate ducked out of the headlock and punched him again, two short chops to the face.

Blood was flowing from Elliot's nose. Nate leaned back, startled by the sight of blood on his fists. The half-second he let up was all the time it took for Elliot to knee him in the balls. Not a direct hit. But bad, bad enough to send him reeling backwards on the bed, doubled over in pain, not even able to gasp.

When Elliot's face floated into view, Nate head-butted him. Elliot disappeared and Nate rolled off the king-size bed, thudding to the floor. He was dimly aware of Elliot moaning and Olivia yelling, but all he could do was keep his knees pinned to his chest and rock from side to side, sandwiched in the small space between the two beds, until finally some air returned to his lungs. He let out a long, low groan. Olivia crouched over him asking if was he okay. No, he was definitely not okay, but he couldn't answer. All he could do was rock from side to side, his eyes squeezed shut, waiting for the nauseating pain to slowly trickle out of him.

He could hear Elliot, muttering and swearing, and when Nate finally cracked open his eyes, Elliot was bent over on his knees, only a couple of feet away, using the edge of a bedspread to wipe blood off his face. Olivia was sitting on the other bed, lighting up a cigarette. Her hand was shaking. When Elliot motioned for one, she threw the pack and lighter at him. He sat back on his heels, and in between puffs kept feeling his nose.

"I think you broke it."

"Tough shit," Nate said, although he wasn't a hundred percent sure the words actually came out or if he only thought them. At last the red-hot pincers squeezing his balls began to loosen their grip, but his head was still ringing.

Olivia was cross-legged on the bed, chewing on the thumbnail of one hand, oblivious to the lengthening ash at the end of her cigarette. Her eyes stayed fixed on Elliot. "Elliot. It wasn't you who put the drugs in Nate's backpack?" she finally asked.

"Of course it was," Nate croaked.

"Get serious. Like I even know which backpack was his?" Elliot pointed his cigarette at Nate. "Look, all I ever did to you was that stuff in the shower room. And that was payback for locking me in the shed."

"You told the cops *I* was the one who said Tut better die soon."

"Okay, yeah. That, too. But nothing else."

"Lookit. I believe you, Elliot."

"Olivia, are you nuts?"

Olivia ignored Nate. "The thing is, we *know*. I'm telling you this for your own good. . . . Lily told me and I told Nate . . . so, like we *know*."

"Know what? What the fuck are you talking about?"

Nate's exact same thought.

"About what you did . . . to Tut," Olivia went on in a calm and reasonable voice, all the while shaking her head as if she felt really sorry for Elliot. "I mean, I can't believe you trusted those girls. Don't tell me you honestly thought they'd keep a secret. Everybody's gonna know soon. . . ."

Nate managed to raise himself to a sitting position. Elliot was watching Olivia with worried eyes. His Adam's apple bobbled as he swallowed nervously, and his face seemed to collapse a little. He switched from the floor to the edge of the other bed, where he sat, his head in his hands. "Those bitches! They *swore* to me." He looked up at Olivia who was standing now, her hands on the hips of her jeans. "It was their idea, all their idea. Just a prank, they said, to, you know, to scare the old bastard."

Elliot stubbed out his cigarette. Then he cupped his head in his hands again and started rocking back and forth. "I am so fucked. My dad'll kill me if this gets out. And Harvard? . . . Oh shit. I am so fucked."

"Tell me how you did it," Olivia demanded.

"It wasn't like *hard*. It took two minutes." He rose and winced. "What the fuck, I'll show you."

Nate forced himself to stand so he could go watch Elliot open up Photo Shop on a laptop and scroll down through the fonts until he reached one called Ransom Note. The sample word featured letters in different sizes with jagged edges, appearing as if they'd been cut from a newspaper.

"That's what we used," Elliot said, shrugging, and clicked into Word, where he retrieved a document named "Tut" dated a little over three weeks earlier. When it opened, the screen displayed two sentences in giant-size Ransom Note letters, saying, *"Watch out. Your days are numbered."*

"You sent this to Tut?" Olivia asked. "Why? Why'd you do that?"

"It was their idea. They just wanted to yank his chain a little."

Nate's voice was hoarse when he spoke. "Wait a minute. Let me get this straight. . . . First you sent that and *then* you go ahead and murder him? So, he'll like be—what?—all prepared?"

"Murder? Are you fucking nuts? Who said anything about murder?"

"You did!" Nate said. "Didn't you?"

"Fuck no!"

"So all you did was send Tut some dumb note because the Lilys thought it'd be a goof?" Olivia dropped her cigarette down the neck of the forty-ouncer.

"You're crazy if you think I murdered Tut. . . . My dad dug up some dirt on him. I don't know what, but it was something Tut didn't want getting out." Elliot pressed his nose and winced. "My dad was there early Monday afternoon. He told Tut he was gonna go public if Tut didn't write me a good recommendation for Harvard."

"So your father was trying to blackmail Tut? And it was all about getting you into *Harvard?*" Nate said. "And after I saw you leave, you went straight home with the Lilys?"

"They wanted to stop at Serendipity so we did."

"Did somebody say our name?"

The Lilys came in and went over to the TV and began fiddling with the remote.

"Get the fuck out of here!" Elliot screamed.

"Excuse me!" Lily G. said.

"You morons told Olivia!"

"Time to go," Olivia said to Nate.

"Told her what?" Lily B. said. "Shit, how do you get this fucking TV to work?"

As he went down the hallway, Nate heard more shouting. About the only thing he could make out was Elliot screaming, "You bitches are never getting another ride with me again!"

Chapter 43

Monday night

THE CAB BECAME HOPELESSLY ENSNARLED IN TRAFFIC ALMOST THE SEC-
ond it entered the 97th Street transverse at Fifth Avenue. Rannie
had allowed a good half hour to get home from Daisy's apartment,
and now she'd be lucky to be there before Tim. Shit. Her head was
whirling; Ms. Hollins did indeed have a motive for murder. Her father had abandoned her mother, whose post-Tut life was lonely and
dreary. And the money. Maybe Augusta Hollins felt it was her turn
to live it up a little, leave New York and—what? Travel? See the
world as her parents had? Daisy was right: Fun did cost a bundle.
Rannie glanced at her wrist, at the wristwatch that wasn't there, and
was horrified to learn from the driver that it was almost nine. She
was going to be late.... Twenty-five minutes late, to be precise.
Tim was waiting in her lobby.

"Nice of you to show up."

"I'm really sorry. My cab was stuck in traffic. I had to pay a
quick visit to a friend of my mother-in-law's." A half-truth ...
what a pseudo-word that was; there was no such thing after all as a
half-lie.

"Mother-in-law? You're divorced."

"We're still close. How'd you get in the lobby?"

"A delivery guy from Whole Foods, he had the door wedged open. Some security system you got." That seemed to tick him off too. "There was a murder the other day on this block. Why don't you just put up a sign—S.W.A.K. KILLER WELCOME BACK!"

Rannie waved him toward the elevator. "Come on upstairs, please. Don't be mad. I'll make dinner."

"Nah, forget it. I had a hamburger at work.... Let me ask you something? You going to do something to piss me off every time we see each other?"

"If you asked my kids, they'd say yes."

Tim stepped in the elevator after her, nodding in a way that suggested he was only partially mollified. And that clinched it.... In the cab from Daisy's Rannie had been debating whether or not to bring up news about Tut's will and what she knew about Ms. Hollins. But uh uh. Save that for the police. Tell Peratta. As for Tim, no mention of murder would pass her lips. Not tonight. He looked tired and edgy. She was too. So why not push all that troubling stuff out of her mind and for a couple of hours simply enjoy the company of a very attractive man.

"This place looks like you." Tim stood in the foyer, taking in the yellow dining room to the left and wall-to-wall books in the living room.

"You mean everything's a mess and nothing matches?"

"It's lived in ... in a nice way."

Rannie took his jacket and led him to the kitchen, where he sat on a stool by the counter while she punched down slices of Wonder bread in the toaster and reached for jars from the cupboard.

"Nah, come on! ... Peanut butter and jelly again?" Tim watched her spreading on the Skippy's. "You know what, make me one too."

They ate their sandwiches in the kitchen then moved into the living room, carrying half-drunk glasses of milk. Rannie showed him photos of Alice and Nate, neither of whom Tim recognized. In a Chaps yearbook, he pointed out Chris on the page with the basketball team, tall and pretty much a ringer for dozens of other boys Rannie saw in the Chaps hallways. Tim told her that Chris was almost finished with his application to Amherst, just had to polish his essay a little more. "It's about his mother. I haven't asked to see it and he hasn't offered." He went on to explain, avoiding Rannie's eyes in the telling, that he'd been at the wheel in the car accident that killed his wife.

There was no correct response to that so Rannie just nodded and said nothing, which he seemed to appreciate. She remembered the photo in his living room. And the man didn't drink alcohol but had intimated that he used to.

When Tim noticed the Chinese scroll with giant brushstrokes hanging in her living room, it was Rannie's turn to fill in a little past history. No, she hadn't been to China; her *ex*-husband had learned calligraphy and then later took up Chinese brush painting. "It means 'follow your dreams.' "

"He's an artist?"

"No. Just someone who gets enthusiasms and then loses interest." She had been one of Peter's longer enthusiasms, Rannie realized. The marriage had lasted twelve years so that meant she came right after tennis. "He writes for a life-style magazine in California and plays a lot of tennis. We've stayed on decent terms, easier I suppose when you live on opposite coasts."

"Remarried?"

"No. A long string of short-term girlfriends."

Oddly Tim seemed cheered upon learning that Peter had gone to Hamilton, not Yale as he had supposed, and was also a college dropout. They talked politics, movies; it turned out Tim liked taking walking tours of New York, something that Rannie always meant to do but never got around to. She folded her legs up under her on the sofa and leaned back, enjoying listening to Tim talk about the Woolworth Building downtown, designed by Cass Gilbert, which used to have a mosaic encrusted swimming pool in the basement. It was his favorite skyscraper. The pleasure of getting to know someone new—it was like starting a really good book by an author you'd never read before, cracking open the pages and becoming instantly absorbed.

Rannie showed him a heavy gift book on Stanford White that she'd copyedited years ago, and leafed through it with him.

He set his empty milk glass down on the coffee table, on top of the business section of the *Times*, rather than on the table, a small gesture certainly, nevertheless one that was endearing, thoughtful.

"If I ever went back to school, it'd be for architecture," he said. "Not to become an architect, too late for that. Just to study it. Late nineteenth, early twentieth-century buildings, that's what I like. Forget Frank Gehry, Rem Koolhaas. Grandstanders in my book. The only other city I'd consider living in is Chicago. Full of beautiful buildings."

"Do you think about moving?" It struck her as the words came out of her mouth that she was hoping the answer was no. And she saw Tim could tell.

At eleven o'clock they watched the local news in the "den," aka Alice's room, which now had a pull-out couch, end tables instead of nightstands, and expensive mocha pin-dot carpeting, initially ordered and ultimately rejected by Mary for her own apartment. There was a long segment on the S.W.A.K. killer—what else?—and what different block associations were doing to ramp up security at night. All during it, Rannie had been debating. Finally, she got up, turned off the TV.

Tim stood. "Yeah, I've got an early day tomorrow."

"Nate's not coming home tonight. He's staying at a friend's."

She'd caught him completely off guard.

"Okay." He stretched out the word. "So that's an invitation." He blew out his lips and shook his head. "You know, you're a tough one to figure."

No, I'm not, she felt like saying. I'm lonesome, unhappy, and horny. You can take care of two out of three.

Tim's hands were on his hips. "A friend, that's what you said you needed."

"Maybe couldn't we be, like the kids say, 'friends with benefits'?" It was said half-jokingly and also in utter seriousness.

Another painful second went by.

"Sorry. Look, Tim, forget I—"

Rannie got no further. Her face was cupped in Tim's hands and he kissed her.

In her bedroom, he lay back on the bed (thank God, it was made, and no dirty underwear in sight) and told her to undress; he wanted to watch. When she was down to her bra and panties he patted the mattress beside him.

"Want a back rub? I'm really good," he said, flexing his fingers playfully.

Rannie lay on her stomach, Tim straddling her. He kneaded her shoulders, neck, then worked his way down her spine.

"You are a man of many talents."

"Shhh. No talking allowed."

Shifting his weight to one knee, he rolled her over on her back, unbuttoned his shirt and pulled off his tee shirt. He was leanly built; the hair on his chest was much darker than she expected.

He didn't need to be told the bra she was wearing fastened in front. He undid it and slid it off her arms. "Beautiful," he murmured and kissed one of her breasts, circling his tongue around her nipple before drawing it into his mouth, sucking, bearing down with more pressure with his lips. Then the other breast. Rannie could barely breathe. "Oh," she gasped and arched her back, holding the back of his head.

The only time he moved off her was to let her wriggle out of her panties. She expected him to undress then. He didn't. Instead he kissed her breasts again, and just as the pleasure became so intense it was almost unbearable, he slid down past her waist, his mouth between her legs, his hands gripping her hips. It was as if he had known her body for years.

A minute later Rannie came with a wallop of a shudder, followed by another less seismic one. While she lay there, little aftershocks of pure sensation rippling through her, all the way down to her fingers and toes, she felt Tim roll beside her. His hand grasped hers and squeezed it.

How long did they stay there, side by side on the bed? Rannie didn't know or care. When she sensed him hoisting himself up on his back, she opened her eyes to watch him take off the rest of his clothes. A lovely body with a whorl of hair around his navel, something she inexplicably found tremendously sexy on men, and a path of hair down to his cock.

She propped herself up on one arm, then leaned over, about to take him in her mouth.

"You—" Tim started to speak.

"No. Now it's your turn to keep quiet."

Later they showered and ate chocolate ice cream with sliced bananas while watching *Duck Soup*, which Nate had rented from Blockbuster and which was already so overdue, one more night wouldn't matter. Sometime around two, they made love the old-fashioned way and again in the morning, Tim first awakening her by snuggling behind her and cupping both her breasts in his hands.

"I gotta get going," he said afterwards.

Rannie nodded, threw on a bathrobe, and while Tim dressed, she made a small pot of coffee, which they shared.

Not once all night had even a prickle of anxiety plagued her. Everything would all work out okay: Tut's murder would be solved, the S.W.A.K. killer caught, Nate would find a fat envelope from Stanford come December, and she would find a better job at a higher salary . . . amazing how endorphins could fool you into thinking this truly was a safe and just world.

Chapter 44

HER PLAN TO SPEND THE GREATER PART OF THE DAY ON MENGELE GOT scotched after a call from Mrs. Mac, who felt a migraine threatening and hoped Rannie could cover for her at school. An hour later, Rannie was stationed at Mrs. Mac's desk, fielding calls, nibbling M&M's from a glass jar, and deciding if she had the nerve to search through personal files in the cabinet behind her. On the corkboard, a cutesy calendar cat for October—a black kitten in a trick-or-treat bag—peered at her solemnly; next to the calendar, on a push pin, the key to the file cabinet dangled temptingly. Before Rannie's superego had a chance to hold her back, she grabbed the key, opened the cabinet and pulled the two files that might either support or contradict information gleaned from Daisy Satterthwaite.

Mr. Tut's file was bulgingly thick and hard to sift through, nothing in chronological order, his class schedules from the 1970s mixed in with citations from the National Council of Teachers of English, changes in his pension plan, a copy of his commencement speech from a few years ago. And a whole separate folder relating to Grant Werner's expulsion. Unfortunately, nothing new in there.

Then suddenly Rannie struck gold. In her hand she held a letter on onion-skin paper that was typed in the blurry ink of manual typewriters. It was from Tut to the then-headmaster notifying
him of *"my need, for personal reasons, to take a short leave of absence in
November."*

Hurriedly checking through Ms. Hollins's folder, Rannie confirmed that Tut's requested leave was for the month following Ms.
Hollins's birth on October 17, 1960, in Asheville, North Carolina.
So, had Tut gone down to Asheville after all? Maybe Daisy was
wrong or had purposely misled Rannie. Perhaps Tut hoped to reconcile with Laura Scales, maybe in the back of his mind he was
even ready to chuck Chaps and raise a family. Or, at the very least,
had he been compelled to lay eyes on his newborn baby? His letter
revealed nothing other than he had taken pains to ensure all his
classes were covered during his absence. Other dated bits of info
Rannie found attested to his return to Chaps less than a month
later.

A fast look at Ms. Hollins's application to Chaps confirmed what
Daisy said: Ms. Hollins was divorced; had taught English at an all-
girls' school in Atlanta; and was a magna graduate of Wellesley. Her
initial inquiry letter stated the caliber of Chapel School and a desire
to live in New York as the reasons for seeking a position. She listed
herself as Augusta S. Hollins on the application. No reference to
Scales as her maiden name. Absolutely nothing acknowledging any
connection whatsoever between Mr. Tut and herself.

But another tidbit. More about Grant Werner. Three years ago,
a month after school began, Ms. Hollins had lodged a formal com-
plaint against Grant. He was behaving "inappropriately in class,"
often showing up "glassy-eyed and lethargic," other times acting
"belligerent." Clipped-together memos attested to meetings with
Grant, his parents, Ms. Hollins, and the headmaster. Grant claimed
Ms. Hollins was "out to get him." Rannie read: *According to Grant,*

Ms. Hollins is spreading rumors about him to other teachers, including the two who are writing his college recommendations. The contretemps had played out over first semester of his senior year; second semester he switched to another English class before getting expelled that spring.

Rannie replaced the files and then, on impulse, swiped one more—Jem Marshall's—though she wasn't sure why except that she was curious. On his résumé: Graduate of Palo Alto High—something she already knew. Ditto the B.S. from Stanford. A year of travel preceded a long stint at a renowned high school in Westchester County, where he first taught chemistry before switching into administration. Ultimately he became principal at the school. Then it was on to City Prep for seven years and next stop, Chaps. A memo dated a week ago—in the same tiny cramped handwriting she'd noticed when he was signing letters—referred to an encounter with two neighborhood drug dealers whose base of operation was Turtle Park. Mr. Marshall had gone over and warned them to stay away from students. He'd also written to the precinct captain.

Just as Rannie was about to replace his folder, the Annex—quiet as a tomb 'til now—became a hive of activity. Several seniors appeared, all wanting appointments with the new college director, the hot-shot private counselor Rannie had glimpsed at the Werners' rooftop party. The woman was moving into Tut's office next week. There were also kids needing bus pass forms, others searching the carton for lost clothes. A middle school teacher came looking for Mr. Marshall and then Mr. Marshall himself came downstairs from his office, Augusta Hollins following behind. Both had the clamp-faced look of people who'd recently exchanged words neither wanted to hear.

Rannie, half-expecting the fates would conspire against her in exactly this manner, managed to keep her cool. Instead of frantically trying to hide Jem's folder in her lap, she remained at Mrs.

Mac's desk, looking efficient and innocent, writing a pretend pink message slip. Neither the headmaster nor Ms. Hollins seemed to take notice of her.

"Augusta, please, one favor—take time and reconsider," he was saying to Ms. Hollins. "We'll talk again."

Ms. Hollins's response was a noncommittal shrug, then, stony-faced, she swept past Rannie without so much as a glance, much less an evil eye.

A moment later, as Jem Marshall returned to his office, Rannie stood, calmly put back his file, and relocked the cabinet.

What needed reconsidering? Rannie wondered. Was Ms. Hollins resigning? Again Rannie remembered Daisy Satterthwaite's words about fun costing a bundle. Well, soon Augusta Hollins would have a bundle. Maybe she'd decided it was time to trade in her Birkenstocks for a pair of Manolos and kick up her heels. Two million dollars could finance a whole lot of fun.

Rannie's cell suddenly sprang to life.

It was Mary. Immediately, Rannie intuited that she was calling with bad news. Peter had had a heart attack. Mary was making arrangements to leave for California.

"Peter assured me it was a mild one, a very mild one," Mary said nervously. "But I'm so worried. I want to be there with him and speak to the doctors, face to face."

"Is Whit going too?" Mary was not up to this kind of trip by herself. Really, Peter's older brother should be going in Mary's stead.

"He refuses. Evidently he and Peter aren't speaking to each other."

Typical of Whit not to come through for Mary—he was a selfish, self-righteous prick.

"I'll go with you," Rannie offered.

At some point in the conversation, an endless discussion of arrangements—who would pick up whom, which flights to choose, where they might stay—it became abundantly clear to Rannie that the far simpler plan was to go to California by herself without the additional responsibility of tending to her mother-in-law. "I'll speak to the doctors, make sure Peter's okay, and then come back. It's no big deal."

Ultimately, Mary conceded, adding, "It *is* a big deal and you're an absolute love."

Chapter 45

Tuesday, 11:00 A.M., before English

NATE WAS IN THE GREAT HALL. HE TOOK HIS CELL FROM HIS BACKPACK, looked at it, put it back, then took it out again. He was about to stash it once more; instead, before he could stop himself, he called Sergeant Peratta. He told the cop all the stuff he'd heard Elliot say about his dad last Monday in Tut's office. And he described the threatening note he and Olivia had seen on Elliot's computer. The one sent to Tut that said, "Watch out! Your days are numbered."

"I don't think those kids killed Mr. Tut, but I thought you should know what they did. And I know I should have said something before about hearing Elliot arguing with Tut. . . . It's still the truth."

Okay, you're a stoolie, Nate told himself after hanging up. But as Ben would say, "Live with it." He'd only squealed about things he'd heard or seen himself. He wished the cops knew about Grant Werner being at Chaps, but that was something Olivia had to deal with herself.

Nate had started for the stairs when his mother came flying from the Annex and spotted him.

"Nate! Wait! I need to speak to you."

Chapter 46

WHILE OLIVIA WAS IN THE CAFETERIA EATING A DANISH, HER BROTHER called. He sounded frantic, hysterical. Grant was at a pay phone near Windward.

"There's a patrol car outside! You promised not to say anything!"

"I didn't!"

"You just couldn't keep your fucking mouth shut!"

"Grant, I swear!" At the next table, kids' heads swiveled. She lowered her voice. "Maybe the police aren't there 'cause of you. But if they are, *please,* just tell the truth—"

The words were wasted. Grant had already hung up.

Her first reaction was to run out of the cafeteria, and—and do what? It suddenly struck Olivia: There was absolutely nothing she could do, not really, except maybe go have a cigarette. The realization unexpectedly had the same effect as nicotine—it calmed her down. She headed to English class.

Chapter 47

"HOW MANY OF YOU BELIEVE, 'WHOEVER DIES WITH THE MOST STUFF wins'?" Ms. Hollins was asking as Nate slid into his seat. He was replaying what his mom had just told him. . . . How could his dad—a total fitness freak, Mr. Organic Foods—have had a heart attack? Nate wanted to go to California with her.

Ms. Hollins cupped an elbow with one hand while her other hand stroked her cheek nervously. "Yesterday at St. John's I read a poem called 'Ozymandias.' It's a harsh, sobering, uncomfortable poem, but Mr. Tut liked what it said about ambition and our capacity to delude ourselves. We were discussing it recently. Mr. Tut thought its message was particularly meaningful for all of you here at Chaps—that's why I chose it. The poem was written by a friend of Byron's who also died young. He drowned swimming off the coast of Greece. His name was Percy Bysshe Shelly."

Chris Butler snorted softly, muttering, "Jesus, what were *his* parents thinking?"

Usually Ms. Hollins indulged wisecracks, especially Chris's. Not today. "Excuse me, Chris?" she said stonily.

"Nothing, sorry . . . just the guy's name."

Ms. Hollins made Chris open his book and read the poem aloud. "Page seventy-three," she ordered.

Chris began reading:

> *"I met a traveller from an antique land,*
> *Who said: 'Two vast and trunkless legs of stone*
> *Stand in the desert. Near them on the sand,*
> *Half sunk, a shatter'd visage lies, whose frown*
> *And wrinkled lip and sneer of cold command*
> *Tell that its sculptor well those passions read . . .' "*

When the poem was over, Ms. Hollins said, "Okay, Chris. Tell us, what's the poem about?"

"Uh . . . I think it's about a statue, a broken statue of a king who used to be very powerful."

"Correct." Then she recited the last lines from memory, her eyes closed, her eyelids twitching slightly. *"And on the pedestal, these words appear: 'My name is Ozymandias, king of kings: Look on my works, ye Mighty and despair!' "* A pause. Her eyes popped open. "Just like Ozymandias, we're all going to die—me, you . . . you . . . you. . . ." She went around the room, stopping to stare at every single kid. "No matter how powerful, how rich, how famous we become, we all wind up the same—dead." A creepy little smile flickered on her lips. "Someone has the largest house in the Hamptons, the most designer shoes, more money than could be spent in ten lifetimes—does it matter? Do the toys mean anything? . . . If all of us are going to die, what's left in the end?" She shrugged and pointed to Lily B. "Tell us."

"Yes, Ms. Hollins, I get it," Lily B. said sullenly. She was examining a short strand of hair in front of her eyes, twirling it and untwirling it. "You're dead, and sooner or later nobody has a clue you were once a big deal."

Ozymandias at one time was feared throughout the world, he—Lily, you have *got* to stop playing with your hair! I've watched you for weeks and it's about to drive me wild!"

Lily's hand froze. Her mouth dropped open.

"Colossal statues and monuments were built to exalt him. As for us," Ms. Hollins continued quite cheerfully, "why we'll be lucky to get a few lines on the obituary page in the newspaper. 'Food for worms,' Shakespeare said. That's how we'll end up."

Thankfully the bell rang. Nate scooped up his books and backpack.

"Nate, could you stay a moment?" Ms. Hollins called after him.

"Uh, I'm kinda in a rush." He wanted to call his father. And Olivia, who'd jumped up the second the class was over, was signaling to him, like she wanted to talk out in the hall.

"Then could you stop by my office later?" Ms. Hollins was putting their papers into her tote. She walked out of the classroom with him and gestured at his backpack. "I heard about what happened to you at the school dance."

Her and the rest of the world. Two sophomores had come up to him this morning asking if he had any weed on him they could buy.

"We need to talk," Ms. Hollins said. "Maybe I can help. Come by before six."

Help how? "Thanks," he said uncertainly.

Mr. Marshall was striding past and overheard the exchange. He stopped, nodded approvingly as if giving a thumbs-up to Nate—*See, kid, we're all in your corner!* Ms. Hollins watched the headmaster resume his march down the hall before saying, "So six? You'll be there?"

Nate nodded. Farther down the hall, Olivia was casting a nervous glance at the stairwell. Nate followed her gaze. Sergeant Peratta was lumbering up the stairs. On the landing, he stopped to catch his breath and looked around, squinting.

Shit, what had the cops found now? A dead body stuffed in his locker?

Chapter 48

Tuesday, right after English class

WHEN SERGEANT PERATTA REACHED THE TOP OF THE STAIRS, HE CALLED Olivia's name and said he had a "few more questions."

"Uh, I think maybe I better call my dad," Olivia told him, her voice shaking. Then realizing neither of her parents was in the city, she called their lawyer instead. Her parents thought Mr. Ledbetter was God—God on a good day. He had kept her brother out of jail more than once.

An hour later, Olivia and Carlotta were waiting in front of the police precinct on West 84th Street when Mr. Ledbetter's limo pulled up. His feet emerged first, and the wingtips he was wearing were so hard and brightly polished, they looked more like weapons than shoes.

As they proceeded to the second floor, Carlotta's tiny hand held hers reassuringly. "Don' be frightened, Livvy. You my girl."

"I wasn't expecting such a crowd," Sergeant Peratta commented and pulled another metal chair over to his desk. He motioned for them to sit.

"Arthur Ledbetter, the Werners' attorney. Ms. Hernandez works for the family."

Carlotta, who kept her coat buttoned up to her chin and her purse clasped in her lap, nodded at the introduction.

"This shouldn't take long." Peratta's chair was pulled away from his desk. His tie was loosened. "Just need to follow up with Olivia on one or two things."

"Olivia's already told the police, twice, everything she knows," Mr. Ledbetter interrupted in a "don't fuck with me" tone of voice. "To go over it again would be traumatic. I've spoken to her psychiatrist who agrees—"

"This isn't about finding Mr. Tutwiler's body." Peratta turned to her. "Olivia, you told me about some calls you made on your cell phone the afternoon before Mr. Tutwiler was murdered. You remember? You told me you tried to reach Mr. Tutwiler a couple of times on Monday."

Olivia nodded and fumbled for Carlotta's hand.

"Sergeant, how are phone calls Olivia made last Monday relevant?"

Peratta didn't reply. He leaned forward and reached into a desk drawer for a wide sheet of paper. "Olivia, I'm interested in calls made Tuesday." He made a little sucking sound with his tongue, as if there was food caught in his teeth. "So okay. The number of your cell phone is 646-555-3010, correct? And your home phone number is 212-555-2828, a land line, if I'm not mistaken."

Peratta didn't seem to expect her to answer so she didn't.

"On Tuesday morning after finding Mr. Tut, you went home."

"Olivia's already told you that."

"A call was made at 11:53 A.M.," the sergeant continued, ignoring the lawyer, "from your home phone to your cell phone. That was you making the call?"

It was the call to Grant in New Haven; she'd made it from her bedroom.

"Yes," she told the sergeant in an unsteady voice.

"Oh, come on, Sergeant. Haven't you ever forgotten where you put your cell phone—"

"And called the cell number from the land line. Absolutely. But, Olivia, about ten minutes later, 12:05 P.M. to be exact, there's a record of another call. This one was made from the cell phone to your home phone."

Suddenly Mr. Ledbetter seemed caught off guard. He turned to Olivia and shot a warning look that said, "Remember: Say nothing."

"Now you're not going to tell me you used your cell to find your home phone."

Grant had been at work when she first called and had to call back a few minutes later from the storeroom. On her cell phone.

"And later, there's a call to a Domino's in New Haven. I know they guarantee delivery in thirty minutes, but I don't think that's playing fair."

Mr. Ledbetter was frowning.

"Your brother's in New Haven. He had your cell phone, didn't he? On Monday, he was the one trying to get in touch with Mr. Tut, not you. . . . Your brother was here in New York, right?" The sergeant got out the security camera photo. "This is him, right?"

Tears sprung to her eyes and rolled down her cheeks. Olivia swiped at them with one hand while Carlotta patted the other, murmuring, "Livvy. Don' be scared. Just tell the truth."

"You don't have to answer anything. We're leaving." Ledbetter stood.

Olivia remained sitting. What did it matter? The cop already knew anyway. She took a deep breath and admitted everything, including lying to him before. Mr. Ledbetter looked disgusted but quickly reminded Peratta that the earlier conversation with Olivia, a minor, should have been in the presence of an adult or "counsel" and could not be used against her.

"Grant never got to see Mr. Tut. He told me somebody was in the office. The door was shut. Grant heard Tut say, 'You have a lot of explaining to do.' But Grant couldn't tell who it was Tut was talking to."

Peratta took it all down then said they could go. As Mr. Ledbetter strode down the hallway, Olivia could hear him on his cell phone, leaving a message for her father.

In the cab home, Carlotta patted Olivia's hand and got out a roll of butter rum Life Savers, something Carlotta always kept in her purse along with jet-black rosary beads, ones blessed by the Pope that Olivia had brought back from Rome years ago.

As the sweet smoothness of the Life Saver rolled over her tongue, Olivia decided that she felt better. There was a strange sense of relief; whatever was going to happen was out of her hands, kind of like when teachers said, "Okay, everybody, pencils down," and you handed in a test.

The second she got home, her cell phone started ringing. She steeled herself and hit the talk button. But it wasn't Grant; it was his counselor, the guy with the spacers. He'd been trying to reach her parents. Nobody at Windward had seen Grant since breakfast.

"A cop was here before," he said. "Olivia, what kind of trouble is he in? Look, you can tell me. Whatever it is, I guarantee you I've heard worse."

"Grant swears he didn't do anything." Once again Olivia found herself repeating Grant's version of events.

The guy softly muttered "shit" a couple of times while listening. "He's been doing real good lately, taking the program much more seriously. No slips lately. He's got well over ninety days this time. I just don't want him to blow it."

Ninety days? So the almost one-year anniversary, that was a lie too.

Phone message from Rannie to Tim Butler
Tuesday, 5:00 P.M.

Tim, it's five o'clock. I'm at Kennedy. Something's come up and I have to leave for California. I'll try to call tomorrow.

I-M's between Lily G. and Lily B.
Tuesday, 5:30 P.M.

God we R so lucky. 3 days suspension. I thought 4 sure
    we'd B kicked out.
Me 2 Elliot's dad saved our asses Marshall is such a
    pussy
Shit. . . . so now we owe Elliot?
Big time.

Chapter 49

NATE WAS IN THE YEARBOOK ROOM, HEADPHONES ON, WORKING PATIENTLY on one of the Macs, arranging a collage of photos from when everybody was in kindergarten. He felt much better now after receiving the call from his dad, whose doctor also got on the phone and assured Nate there was nothing to worry about; no need to travel to California.

He pasted in a photo of him and Ben running around the Annex rooftop playground. They had been playing Butts Up, a made-up game with amazingly complicated rules that had to be renegotiated every day so that by the time they actually started playing, recess would always be ending. Nate shuddered at the image of his younger self. How had his mother let him out in public with that fag haircut and clown glasses?

There was a tap on his shoulder. Nate pulled his headphones down around his neck.

Ben said, "Dude, I'm outta here. You ready?"

"Nah, not yet. What time's dinner?" He was staying at Ben's while his mother was in California.

Ben shrugged. "Seven? Fuck—did you just fart?"

It was the souvlaki that Nate had brought back from the Acropolis.

"Shit, light a match, the place'll explode!" Ben said and left.

At quarter of six, Nate shut down the computer, unkinked his shoulders, and let another one rip. Then he ditched the aluminum foil from the souvlaki and gathered his stuff.

Downstairs in the Great Hall the new security guard was in his overcoat, locking up his set of walkie-talkies. In the Annex the screens were blank on both Mrs. Mac's computer and the one in his mother's cube, their desktops neatly arranged, swivel chairs pushed in. Nate started upstairs to Ms. Hollins's office. Maybe she'd heard somebody at the dance say something . . . maybe she'd seen something.

Between the second and third floors, he became aware that it was growing colder each step of the way. When he reached the landing, the door to her office was open. Some papers on her desk were ruffling around. But no Ms. Hollins. The draft, Nate realized, was coming from the floor above. At the stairwell, peering up at the rooftop, he called out her name. He could see the access door had been hooked back. Ms. Hollins smoked like a fiend; maybe she was having a cigarette.

Nate climbed the last half flight of stairs, calling her name again. In Lower School, before there was a real playground on the turf, recess was on the rooftop, teachers constantly screaming at kids to stay away from the parapet. He stepped outside on the tar paper and waited for his eyes to grow accustomed to the dark. A ladder was near the door, there was a beach chair with a coffee can full of cigarette butts beside it, an old pair of workman's gloves on the ground. Nothing else. Nate farted again. It was creepy out here.

The waist-high parapet ran along three sides of the rooftop, one side overlooking the turf and the equipment shed that he'd stuffed Elliot in, but when he gazed down, all he could make out were the hulking silhouettes of the slides, the swing set, the jungle gym. They looked almost beast-like in the dark.

Although he'd never been scared of heights, sweat was beading in his scalp and Nate felt light-headed, almost as if he had a buzz. To steady himself, he gripped the sooty edge of the parapet. "Ms. Hollins?" he called one last time, like she might actually be down there playing on the monkey bars or swings.

Shit, the souvlaki had been a mistake; it felt like a dead mouse rotting in his stomach. When he belched, sour flecks of chewed meat came spurting up. He swallowed them back down. What he should do was leave and go to Ben's. But something made him move along the parapet to the right, to the side facing the main building.

All of a sudden, his heart started thudding like crazy. There was something down there in the narrow alleyway, something lit by a bare bulb at the bottom of the fire escape. A body. Two legs stuck out of a skirt hiked all the way up to a pair of panties. The legs, splayed out in a wide vee, ended in shoes, one of which was dangling off the right foot of his English teacher. Ms. Hollins's body was twisted, like some rag doll, her head at a crazy angle. There was no duct tape over her mouth but blood ran from both her nostrils down her lips and chin. The last thing he saw before he crumpled to his knees and started throwing up were her eyes. It looked as if she was crying bright red tears.

"Augusta? Are you out here?" someone was calling.

Nate couldn't answer. Someone stepped out onto the rooftop. He retched again, his eyes watering.

"Who's there?" The figure was coming toward him and then suddenly the headmaster was crouching down beside him. "Nate? Jesus! What are you doing out here?"

Nate motioned to the side of the parapet. A second later he heard Mr. Marshall suck in his breath sharply and curse. Then he was on his cell to 911.

Chapter 50

THE FIVE O'CLOCK FLIGHT TO SAN JOSE HIT WHITE-KNUCKLE TURBU-lence for the first hour and then settled into pleasant boredom, al-lowing Rannie to partake in the bounty of business class, which Mary had insisted on.

At Kennedy Airport, Rannie realized her cell phone was not in her purse and suddenly had a mental picture of it lying on her bed back at the apartment. The sense of being out of touch was liberating. She boarded the plane and, whatever her worries, they remained in New York. She was in anxiety-free limbo and enjoying every minute of it; the Mengele manuscript stayed under the seat in front of her for the entire flight. She had a glass of champagne, sampled every hors d'oeuvre that came by, and watched a Cameron Diaz movie during dinner.

Chapter 51

Tuesday, 6:00 P.M.

IT WAS AFTER SIX O'CLOCK BY THE TIME OLIVIA'S SESSION WITH DR. E. was over. She felt like a wrung-out washcloth. Walking home down Lexington Avenue, she stopped at a Circuit City. There, on all the TV screens in the window, was Chaps looking like a lunatic asylum or something out of a horror movie. A reporter with a mike and a purple pashmina scarf slip-knotted around her neck was mouthing words at the camera, police cars were in the background . . . and an ambulance. What now? Olivia went inside and found out.

Chaps Lifers Message Board

Did U hear about Hollins?

YEAH, SHE'S DEAD

I heard the S.W.A.K. psycho got her

Wrong Hollins jumped

No She didn't jump I heard Nate killed her.

!!!!! Y

She gave him an F or something so he tossed her

No shit.

IS HE IN JAIL

No but they're gonna arrest him any second He killed Tut 2

Nate? Nate Lorimer?

U never can tell about kids

word it's always the ones u don't expect

E-mail from Lily Black to Olivia

This message is from Lily and me. Did you know Nate blabbed to the cops about the stupid note to Tut? The cops told Marshall but he only suspended us for three days. BFD. It's not even going on our record. If you had anything to do with this, we will NEVER, EVER speak to you again. Got that?

E-mail from Olivia to Lily Black, cc to Lily Grey

I didn't, but do me a favor anyway and NEVER, EVER speak to me again. Got that?

Chapter 52

Wednesday morning

THE NEXT MORNING AT FIVE O'CLOCK CALIFORNIA TIME, RANNIE TRIED Nate, hoping to catch him before school.

"What! And you didn't call?" she screamed. Ms. Hollins was dead! Nate had found the body!

Rannie never went anywhere. Her mother was the world traveler, the one racking up frequent flier miles. Yet now where was Rannie, the one time she should have been home? Irrational resentment surged through her: It was so typical of Peter to have a heart attack just when Nate needed her.

A minute later, she called Joan.

"Honey, he seems fine," Joan told her. "You know kids. I went to school and took him home. He ate a good dinner, called the hospital to see how your ex was. Then he and Ben played poker for hours. School's closed today."

"Was there a suicide note?"

Rannie got the answer she didn't want but had expected.

"No. But yesterday morning Augusta handed in her resignation. She wanted to leave Chaps immediately."

Rannie nodded to herself, remembering the brief conversation she'd overheard between Jem Marshall and Augusta Hollins.

"Jem said Augusta was highly emotional. And Ben and Nate both said she'd been acting oddly in class—talking about dying and how everybody winds up being food for worms."

"But why would she kill herself?" She wouldn't, that's why. Would she?

"Jem was supposed to meet again with Augusta at the end of the day. He hoped to convince her to stay on at least 'til the end of the semester. She wasn't in her office and when he heard noise on the roof . . . that's where he found Nate."

"Great! So now the police can try to pin a double murder on Nate."

"Rannie, that's not funny."

"Swabs. Nate told me when the police arrived, one of them swabbed under his nails . . . and they took his fingerprints. Were you there?"

"Yes, but I called George first. He spoke to Nate. George said Nate should let them do it."

Yes, Joan's husband was a lawyer . . . a copyright lawyer.

In the hotel coffee shop, decorated in the two most hateful colors—flesh and mint green—Rannie forced down some breakfast and tried to rein in galloping paranoia. Yet one ugly fact kept thwacking her in the face.

The minor role she'd played in Ms. Hollins's life was that of the buttinski, a meddlesome, uncaring fly in the ointment, someone who'd only added irritation and distress to Ms. Hollins's last days. And even so, Ms. Hollins had wanted to help Nate, that's what her son had reported. Something to do with the drugs found at the school dance. But help how?

En route to the hospital in a rental car and with a temporary license, Rannie harkened to Joan's parting words: "There's nothing you can do, so try to put all this out of your mind. Nate is okay. My advice, compartmentalize."

Well, she was doing her best to follow that sensible advice, and the directions to the Stanford Medical Center proved just challenging enough to keep her focused. Poor Ms. Hollins. Heiress for a day . . . horrible but it almost sounded like a pitch for a reality show.

Chapter 53

NATE AWOKE TO HIS CELL PHONE RINGING. HE GROPED FOR IT AND, pressing it to his ear, heard his sister Alice say brightly, "Hi. It's me. I'm at Grand Central."

Nate was lying in the bottom bunk of Ben's bunkbed. His eyelashes were stuck together with crud. At four he'd woken up in that horrible way when your eyes fly open and immediately your brain goes from zero to sixty, picking up exactly where it left off before you fell asleep, crazy, scary thoughts blasting away at you like hard-packed snowballs. He'd already spoken to his sister last night, telling her, "Al, I'm serious. . . . they think I threw Hollins off the roof." When he was leaving school with Ben's mom, Nate had seen Peratta giving him the once-over. The cop's eyes had swept over Nate, sizing him up, as if he was making up his mind whether Nate was big enough, strong enough to push a large woman over the ledge. And the answer on Peratta's face was yes.

"Meet me for lunch. My treat," Alice said.

He was fully awake now. "Wait. Did Ma put you up to this? I can hear her, 'Alice, your poor brother went through something very traumatic.' "

"Jesus. Is it so hard to believe I'm just being nice? I *am* a nice person. I even called Dad to see how he was because I knew it would make Mom happy."

An hour later Nate met her in Grand Central Station at the Oyster Bar. Alice was already seated at a table. She held up the front page of the *Post*. The headline read, IT'S FALL SEMESTER! SECOND BODY FOUND AT HORROR HIGH!

"I don't want to read it. And I don't want to talk about it either." He didn't believe Ms. Hollins jumped, and there was no way she could have fallen, not unless she decided it'd be fun to try her luck tiptoeing along the rim of the parapet.

Al ordered their favorite, huge platters of fried clams with fries and cole slaw. Once the waitress cleared their plates, Al pushed him to have dessert too. It was when she was scooping out the last of her fudge sundae that his sister came clean.

"Uh, so you know Grant Werner bolted from rehab?" she began cautiously.

"Yeah." Olivia had called to tell him last night. "And I also know he was at Chaps last Monday. But he won't tell the cops what he knows. Great boyfriend you picked, Al."

She ignored the comment. "Grant came by yesterday. He was really worked up." Alice bit the inside of her cheek and kept circling her spoon slowly around the inside of the ice cream dish. "He kept going, 'Alice, you've got to let me stay here! The cops are gonna think I killed Tut.' "

"Maybe he did."

"I told him, sorry, there was no way he was hiding out in my room. I mean, what? Did he think he'd hole up in Davenport, and the police would just forget about him? So he stole forty bucks off my dresser and left. He was acting crazy."

There was something about her tone that made him ask, "Crazy how?"

Alice pressed her lips together, then put down her spoon, and took off her sweater.

"That fucking asshole!" There were marks, like purplish fingerprints, on both her upper arms. "Don't you ever see him again!"

"Believe me. I don't plan to. . . . Look, I honestly don't think he meant to hurt me; he just got so worked up—he was practically crying—and he like grabbed me too hard." She pulled on her sweater quickly and glanced around, as if to make sure other customers hadn't seen the bruises.

"Do the cops know?"

"Yeah. I told the Yale cops, and they called the New Haven police. A cop came and I had to go over everything with him." Alice let out a long gusty sigh and shivered. She suddenly looked particularly small; sitting in a chair, her legs barely touched the floor. However, she was always reminding him that she was his big sister and Nate worried that patting her hand might be breaking some rule in their relationship. Instead he muttered, "That prick."

Alice cocked her head, nodding. "Yeah, it shook me up. I didn't want to stay at Davenport so I went and slept at a friend's in Pierson, but this morning when I woke up, I don't know, I kind of wanted to get away from Yale and see you." Al picked up her spoon again, playing with it. "Eleventh Commandment, okay? Don't tell Ma."

"I won't." Nate promised. Grant Werner was a fucked-up, nut-job junkie, and Olivia was a fool to believe a word out of his mouth.

Chapter 54

BY TEN O'CLOCK, SHE PULLED INTO THE PARKING LOT OF THE STANFORD Medical Center where Peter was one of four patients in the ICU. A pair of headphones dangling from his neck, he was cranked up at a thirty-degree angle in a hospital bed, his long, lanky frame taking up nearly the entire length of it. The resemblance between Peter and Nate was startling. An overhead TV was on and he was reading *Sports Illustrated*, the same issue that Rannie had just purchased for him at the gift store in the lobby.

Peter's first words: "I didn't need anybody coming out here. I told Mother that."

"So much for 'thank you, best ex-wife in the world, for traveling three thousands miles.'"

Peter lay down his magazine. "You know that's not how I meant it."

"Listen, you got off easy.... For a while it looked like it was going to be Mary, Nate, *and* me ... a family reunion." Rannie kept her tone light, although as she pulled a chair beside his bed, a non-compartmentalizing "if only" thought managed to slip in and taunt her: If she'd let Nate come, he would have been nowhere near that damn rooftop.

Peter was in string-tie plaid pj bottoms; wires dangled from circular sticky pads taped to his bare chest while machines and monitors hummed and bleeped away. She felt as if she were staring at a "What's wrong with this picture?" puzzle. There wasn't an ounce of flab on him. All the years of their marriage, he'd chided her on her eating habits and aversion to exercise. But beyond that, Peter simply wasn't mature enough for a heart attack.

It had happened while he was playing tennis. Mild chest pains, he told Rannie, who knew that they must have been considerably more severe for doctor-phobic Peter to go to a hospital. A "friend" had driven him; Rannie sure it was a woman. While he talked, mentioning with evident pleasure that Alice had called the night before, Rannie noticed that, although his face was suntanned, there was an ashen pallor to his complexion lurking behind the ruddy cheeks; for the first time that she could remember, Peter looked sick . . . and scared.

"I'm sorry, Ran. What a drag for you." Peter shook his head; it was then that Rannie noticed a small gold hoop threaded through the lobe of his left ear, the sight of which depressed her. "Peter, for God's sake, grow *up*," she felt like saying.

"The cardiologist said it was so mild, it hardly counts as a heart attack." Peter stumbled over the last words and Rannie saw that he was embarrassed. As far as Peter's own self-image was concerned, she bet he almost would have preferred cancer, which had connotations of tragedy and romance, being struck down in one's prime. A heart attack simply equaled middle age.

They chatted in an amiable, emotionally detached way. Twelve years of marriage? The plain fact was: With Peter, there wasn't much "there" there. In a way if she hated him now, wouldn't it mean she'd loved him more deeply then? Still, because of Peter, she had the

two best things in her life. Genetically her children were fifty percent him, although whatever their faults, neither of the kids could
ever be called shallow, unemotional, or detached.

Peter never brought up Tut's murder so neither did Rannie, who
conscientiously abided by Joan's dictum to "compartmentalize."
Peter, after all, had his own mortality on his mind. At one point, he
held out his hand. Rannie accepted it, the feel of his long fingers
clasping hers so familiar, the hair on his arms blond and curly.

She had jumped into bed with him the very first night they met
at a publishing party, Rannie initially sure that it would amount to
no more than a brief romance. Yet Peter had pushed to get married
four months later after Rannie had missed a period. "I love you. Of
course we should have this baby." His response was so immediate,
so sure. She was dazzled. It was years before she understood that
to him she was exotic, not forbidden fruit exactly, nevertheless, the
first Jewish girl he'd ever been involved with. She wondered if, at
the outset, he might have hoped their involvement would cause
strain with his parents—he reveled in his status as family "rebel."
Yet Walter and Mary had liked her right away. "Of course, they like
you. What's not to like?" her own father had said defensively. In his
eyes Rannie could do no wrong. So if she loved Peter, then he must
be worthy. Her shrewder mother, Rannie learned post-divorce, had
harbored vague, never-voiced qualms all along, although not about
the difference in religion. Temple Sharay Tefilah in Shaker saw
her parents exactly twice a year on the high holy days. "I could
never picture the two of you growing old together," her mother
said. Bingo.

Soon a nurse came to prep Peter for an angiogram. The reassuring news that his arteries were clear came by one that afternoon.
No bypass necessary. Rannie called Mary, Nate, and Alice, leaving
messages. Then she made a reservation on the red-eye.

Peter looked flat-out exhausted, most likely from the anxiety of waiting for the test results, so Rannie decided to explore the Stanford campus while he slept.

A postcard-clear sky showed off the rosy-hued stucco of the Mission-style architecture to best advantage; farther to the east and in the distance were the Santa Cruz Mountains. It was, in a word, gorgeous. The kids, in shorts and tee shirts, Stanford sweatshirts tied around their waists, were good-looking, too—definitely a much lower nerd quotient here than at Yale. Rannie crossed Serra Mall and headed to the Main Quad where a girl, a pro at the backwards-walk mastered by all college tour guides, was leading a large group of parents and high school kids.

Rannie tagged along, learning to her surprise that the arcaded courtyard design of the university was the work of Frederic Law Olmstead and that both Hoovers had been Stanford grads, Mrs. H. the first woman to get a degree in geology. Palm trees were everywhere, bougainvillea staining the walls of buildings purple and fuchsia. There was a cactus garden boasting plants so gigantic they could supply enough aloe vera for the entire nation. The names of streets, or malls, were liltingly Spanish. Escondido. Duena. Lagunita. Galvez. Absolutely beautiful. Everything. Absolutely nothing not to love. And yet to Rannie it all seemed a little unreal, a little too healthy. Wasn't grim Gothic architecture more conducive to studying? Wouldn't too much sunshine and fresh air do weird things to your brain?

The tour ended in Old Union, another courtyard complex where the admissions department had offices and where many in the group were going to pick up applications or have an interview.

"I will die if I don't get in," one girl plaintively wailed to her mother.

Could Rannie envision Nate here? No, not really. But that was beside the point. He could. The only question that mattered was whether Stanford Admissions could envision him here. Suddenly, hearing all the freshly toured families muttering ominously about Stanford's insanely high median SATs, Rannie began worrying about Nate's chances, something she chose to interpret as a "normal" neurotic-parent sign as opposed to, say, worrying about murder one charges and orange prison jumpsuits in his immediate future. Which was why Rannie found herself joining the crowd in the admissions offices.

When a smiling middle-aged woman behind a computer asked if she could help, Rannie heard herself inquiring whether her son's application for Early Admissions was in and complete.

Eyes on the computer screen, fingers tapping instructions, the woman kept a steady flow of friendly chatter ... Had she enjoyed the tour? Was this her first time on campus? She certainly had picked a perfect day. Oh, she lived in New York City, right in Manhattan?

The woman blinked at the screen. "Yes, here it is. Nathan B. Lorimer? Let's see ... yes, your son has completed his part; the school has sent his transcript; his board scores are here; recommendations in; yes, it looks like everything's in."

"A Stanford alum is the new headmaster at my son's school," Rannie informed the woman. "He's from Palo Alto."

"You don't say! I wonder if Mr. Richards knows. He's on the East Coast right now, visiting high schools. I'm from Palo Alto, too. What's the headmaster's name?"

"Jonathan Marshall."

She shook her head, not that Rannie had expected the woman's eyes to light up and for her to start shrieking, "Jemmy! Unbelievable! My sister had a crush on him in seventh grade!" The woman clicked more keys, asked for exact spelling of the name and approximately what year he might have graduated, and waited for something on her screen to pop up. Her brow furrowed for a moment. She typed in more information and waited again. "That's funny. He's not showing up."

"It's Jonathan *Edwards* Marshall."

More typing, another pause, and then "Here we go. . . . Jonathan Edwards Marshall. Yes. But the computer has an asterisk by his name, which means deceased or no information available."

"He just moved to a new apartment."

The woman nodded. "That's probably it. Or else a computer glitch—they've been acting up a lot lately."

A pad and pen was placed before Rannie. She felt unsure about supplying any information despite the woman's assurances that Mr. Marshall wouldn't suddenly be inundated with fund-raising calls.

"Mr. Richards will like knowing the Chapel connection to Stanford."

Rannie settled by writing down nothing other than the Chaps general number and Jem's full name.

With the woman wishing "good luck to your son" and holding up two crossed fingers, Rannie retraced her steps across campus.

In the hospital cafeteria, she sat down with a Coke and a surprisingly tasty chicken burrito, thinking about Stanford and college in general. No matter what anyone said, where you went did count. She hadn't left Yale singing "Be True to Your School," nor had she ever returned for a Harvard-Yale game. Still college had molded her. She'd listened to Harold Bloom analyze *Hamlet*, heard Vincent Scully rhapsodize over Le Corbusier's chapel at Ronchamps. She remembered finishing a paper in which she discussed the religious symbolism in Spenser's "The Faerie Queene" and the Unicorn Tapestries at the Cloisters and feeling that writing the analysis had expanded her mind in an upliftingly thrilling way. But it went beyond the education. Applying to college had been the first choice she ever made for herself, deciding to go East, to an Ivy, when her smart friends were picking Northwestern or Michigan's honors program. Consciously she had not said to herself, "I'm never living in the Midwest again," but being at Yale made her see New York, not Chicago, as the next step in her life and from there . . . well, going to Yale had determined so much else.

Returning her tray, Rannie took the elevator to Peter's room. He was awake and on the phone with Mary. As soon as he got off, they hugged good-bye. Peter seemed vastly relieved by the good prognosis, his tone almost jaunty. His parting words to Rannie were, "Remember. Tell Nate, I beat him to it . . . first in the family to get admitted to Stanford."

....

Wednesday night e-mail sent to Chapel School Senior Class
FROM: jemarshall@chapelschool.org

While not everyone had the good fortune to have taken one of Augusta Hollins's classes, I know that all of you are saddened by her sudden passing. Please join the high school faculty and me at an assembly Thursday morning at 11:30 to share memories of Ms. Hollins. There will be a formal memorial service for the entire Chapel School community at a later date.

Chapter 55

IT TOOK A LITTLE FIDDLING BEFORE RANNIE'S NEW MEDECO KEY TURNED in the tumbler. Total darkness greeted her, a sure sign that Nate—Con Ed's dream customer, someone physically incapable of turning off a light switch—was still staying at Joan's. Rannie dropped the mail on the hall table, plunked down her suitcase. Heading for her bedroom, already pulling off her sweater, unzipping her pants, it struck her that her bed remained unmade from the night Tim stayed over, a task neglected in the rush of packing and getting to the airport. It sent a pleasurable shiver through her, the anticipation of seeing tangled bed-clothes, the possibility that traces of Tim—his scent, the indentation of his body—might still be present. In the same instant came another, delayed realization: When Peter had been holding her hand in the hos-pital, no current had passed—she hadn't felt one watt of desire.

Then as she walked past the den, something suddenly caught her eye. An indistinct shape moved inside the room.

She screamed.

An arm was visible; a hand groping toward her. Rannie screamed again.

Then one of the table lamps grew bright.

"Oh Jesus! Alice!" Rannie's hand flew to her heart while she let out a ragged gasp of relief. She sank down on the edge of the pull-out couch.

Alice sat up in bed, blinking. "Ma?" She had on a Davenport College tank tee shirt; a disheveled Pebbles Flintstone ponytail sprouted from the top of her head. She rubbed her eyes. "Nate didn't think you'd be home so soon." Her face was puffy and her voice hoarse from sleep.

"Nate's here?" Rannie asked, kissing her cheek.

Alice shook her head no. She was sitting under the quilt, her arms wrapped around the tent of her legs.

"How come you are? . . . Is everything okay?"

Alice didn't reply, and something about her body language, the slight lowering of her head, started warning signals flashing. Suddenly Rannie zeroed in on the bruise marks on Alice's arms, purple as eggplants.

"Alice, what happened!"

"One sec." Alice swung her legs around from under the quilt. "I gotta pee."

Rannie knew a stall tactic when she saw one; nevertheless, she waited until the toilet flushed and Alice returned before inquiring, in what she hoped passed for calm parental concern, if anything was the matter.

As she listened to daughter, Rannie thought: There had to be—what?—a couple thousand undergrad guys at Yale, all of whom were smart and at least some of whom had to be semi-attractive and unaddicted to drugs. But who did Alice get involved with?

"Wait. You're telling me Grant was at Chaps, outside Tut's office, right before he died? Do the police know?"

Yes. According to Alice, Grant supposedly heard Tut arguing with someone. Rannie was skeptical.

"And since when has he been missing?" He could be in New York right now.

"Tuesday morning."

"So, he's a suspect!" A prime suspect! There'd been bad blood between Grant and Ms. Hollins as well—it was all there in Ms. Hollins's file.

"You don't have to sound so happy about it!"

"He hurt you!"

"He didn't mean to. I knew you'd make a big drama out of this."

But Rannie saw past Alice's bravado and held her tongue. Grant must have frightened her more than she was willing to let on, why else seek the security blanket of home?

"Look. Go back to sleep, honey. I'm glad you're home," was all Rannie said. She enfolded her daughter in a hug, stroking loose wisps of blond hair off her forehead, then trundled off to bed, just as the sky was turning from black to skillet gray. It wasn't right—kids were supposed to take turns causing you worry. That's how it was supposed to work. . . . If Nate was suffering through a rough patch then Alice was usually coasting along problem-free. And vice versa. Once she'd mentioned this to Joan and rather than looking at Rannie as if she was cracked, Joan said, "Oh, absolutely." Her theory was that kids could calibrate their mother's precise breaking point. "So they work in tandem. Otherwise they could really send you right over the edge."

At last Rannie, forcing herself to turn off her mind, collapsed into bed. She inhaled the pillow next to hers, but sadly all traces of Tim Butler had vanished.

Chapter 56

Thursday morning

WHEN RANNIE AWOKE AT NINE AND STUMBLED INTO THE LIVING ROOM, Alice was sprawled on the couch reading a fat textbook, a laptop and several books spread out on the coffee table, a yellow highlighter clenched between her teeth. The sight was so cheering, so welcome, that Rannie couldn't resist covering her daughter's face with kisses.

"Ew, dragon breath," Alice said around the highlighter that she then removed. "They think they caught the S.W.A.K. killer!"

"No kidding!" Rannie scurried to the kitchen, turned on the radio and, over two cups of coffee and a bagel, listened raptly.

At midnight, an undercover cop, young and attractive and one of many acting as "bait" in the neighborhood, had been stopped by a middle-aged man on crutches, asking for directions to Saint Luke's Hospital. As soon as the cop drew close enough, the man lunged at her and attempted to push her into a parked car.

"The minute he spoke to me, I had a feeling," the officer said. "Don't ask me how, but I did." She sounded young to Rannie, an almost teenaged breathlessness in her voice.

The police commissioner was more circumspect, saying only that someone was in custody and being questioned. The suspect's name was Howard Something and he'd worked at a Staples on Broadway. It occurred to Rannie that she might have bought stationery, boxes of blue pencils from the guy. Creepy with a capital C. Still, the news was reassuring, and as she showered, dressed, and went to Zabar's, Rannie felt more lighthearted than she had in days. Both her children would be home for dinner. And no need for Mace anymore.

"Oh, you're supposed to call the headmaster, what's-his-name," Alice shouted into the kitchen after Rannie returned and was unpacking groceries. Alice sauntered in. She was in the same tee shirt but had added Rannie's bathrobe and sheepskin slippers from L.L. Bean. "And there's a message about some job. Ooh! What's in the dessert box?"

"Lemon tarts. Stay away! They're for tonight!"

The call-back was from Croyden and Woolf, the publishing house. Could Rannie come for an interview next week? Yes! Yes! Yes! She would impress everyone with her skills, her experience, her commitment to children's books. After all, she had read the complete works of Judy Blume, every single title in The Babysitters Club series, and could still recite all of Ludwig Bemelmans's *Madeline.* Not to mention being on quite intimate terms with Nancy Drew.

Jem Marshall, it turned out, had merely called to let her know that he'd seen her son earlier and Nate seemed fine. "Rannie, I understand you were in Palo Alto for a family emergency."

He'd never addressed her by her first name before and so, in the spirit of camaderie, she replied, "Yes, Jem, Nate's father had a mild heart attack." Jem. . . . His name sounded so foreign on her tongue. She mentioned taking the Stanford tour and stopping by the Admissions Office.

"I told them you were an alum." She confessed to giving out his school number. "I hope that wasn't presumptuous."

"Not at all. But they absolutely have all my information already—I'm on a reunion committee. Had to be some computer foul-up. Anyway, I got a call yesterday and it's all straightened out."

After their good-byes, Rannie brought coffee over to the computer and went online checking out the title list of Croyden and Woolf Publishers. Lots of award-winners. Several children's classics. "I'd be head of a four-person department. Copyediting and production," she told Alice.

Alice nodded in a distracted way. She was reading from an overweight tome titled *Left-handedness and Learning Disorders*. Another textbook, *The Sinister Hand: A History of Myths and Fables*, lay on the coffee table.

"This for the paper you've been working on?" Rannie asked.

Alice nodded and withdrew the highlighter from her mouth. "Abnormal Psych. We're studying brain anomalies. Being left-handed counts. That's what I'm writing my paper on.... Remind me to check Nate's head. I wanna see if his hair swirls counterclockwise. I never thought about it before, what it's like to be left-handed. But it's a right-handed world."

"At least it pays off in tennis," Rannie remarked. Most of Nate's opponents were righties, and his shots naturally went to their backhand.

"It comes from an Anglo-Saxon word. '*Lyft*,'" Alice read later from her book, "which means broken or deformed. Listen to this. This is so crazy ... In the 1600s you could get burned at the stake for being left-handed."

Rannie fetched the Mengele manuscript from her totebag; she hadn't looked at a page the whole time she was in California. For the next couple of hours, she and Alice worked companionably in the living room, Norah Jones providing background music, Alice pausing every now and then to share other tidbits she came across, the most arcane being that typewriter keyboards were intentionally designed with the most-used letters—a,s,e,d,t,r—on the left-hand side. This slowed down typists, the vast majority right-handed, and thus prevented the fragile mechanisms on the first typewriters from breaking down as frequently.

At some point Rannie remembered there was still unopened mail on the hall table.

She opened the latest cheery missive from her mother, sent from Copenhagen. Was her mother the only person left in the world who still sent letters on thin, pale blue air mail stationery? She tore up junk mail and set aside bills until the only remaining envelope was one with the Chapel School crest. Her name and address were written in purple blocky capital letters instead of the usual preprinted label. And the envelope was hand-stamped, not metered.

Rannie was expecting exactly what she saw; yet that didn't stop a sickening shiver from escaping. The message, spelled out in the same ransom-note letters as before, said: *"Watch out! Your days are numbered!"* It had been mailed Monday. Ms. Hollins had probably sent it after encountering Rannie at the patisserie.

"Ma! You okay?"

"Yes. Just a bill from Chaps, one I wasn't expecting." She put the note back in its envelope and considered calling Lieutenant Peratta; instead she called Tim, explaining the reason for her California trip. "Could I stop by the bar after dinner? Maybe you'll treat me to a Diet Coke?" That was fine, he said. Then she checked in with Mary.

"Rannie darling, you're home! I just spoke to Peter. He's out of Intensive Care and in a private room," Mary informed her, then paused before going on. "Darling, Daisy's here."

Suddenly Rannie discerned the false cheeriness in Mary's tone.

"It turns out she knew the teacher at Chaps, the one who killed herself."

"She didn't kill herself, Mims!" Rannie could hear Daisy saying indignantly.

"Daisy's quite upset," Mary went on.

So in Wasp-ese that translated to something akin to uncontrollable hysteria.

"Is there any chance you could stop by; you're welcome to stay for an early dinner."

"I don't know about dinner, Mary—"

Alice heard and immediately started shaking her head violently, mouthing, "Don't say I'm here! I'm not eating there!"

"—but I'll be right over."

Chapter 57

WHEN EARLA SHOWED RANNIE INTO THE DEN, MARY WAS AT THE BAR, regal and serene, in a raw silk blouse with a bow at the neck and a pale gray skirt. Mary filled a highball glass from a greatly depleted gallon bottle of Dewars and kissed Rannie, who then settled into the striped armchair across from Daisy. The older woman had a sodden handkerchief and cigarette clenched in one hand while the other reached gratefully for the replenished highball.

"You guessed, didn't you? About Augusta? It wasn't my secret to tell, you understand that, don't you?" Daisy was wearing pilled wool slacks and scuffed leather pumps. The heavy gold necklace over her turtleneck looked like an eighteen-karat-gold choke chain. She gazed up at Rannie with bleary, pink-rimmed eyes.

"Guessed what?" Mary sat down on the loveseat with an equally plentiful glass of vodka.

"Poor Augusta! I can't believe it. It's just too too awful!" Daisy let out a loose wheezing cough. Tears spilled down her leathery tan cheeks and a quarter inch of cigarette ash landed on her bosom. Her red lipstick was smeared across her mouth like a wound.

"Dear, try not to upset yourself so." Mary patted Daisy's knee consolingly. "Chaps again, my Lord! I couldn't believe it when I turned on the news the other night—Rannie, help yourself to whatever you'd like, there's wine in the ice bucket.... Did Nate know the poor woman?"

"Ms. Hollins was his English teacher," Rannie said and left it at that.

"I don't believe for one second it was suicide. Augusta wasn't the sort to go leaping off some roof. Since the moment she knew Larry was murdered, she was desperate to leave that school. She was frightened. I spoke to her Sunday; she was planning to resign." Daisy coughed into her handkerchief. "Larry was leaving her considerable money. Not that Augusta cared a fig about that. You saw the way she dressed, like some folksinger." Daisy squashed out her cigarette, then stared at Rannie. "You know you're making me very nervous, sitting there empty-handed.

"Besides, Augusta was Catholic," Daisy went on while Rannie obediently poured herself a glass of wine. "Well, half-Catholic. They all think you burn in hell if you kill yourself, you know."

"When exactly did Ms. Hollins learn she was his daughter?" Rannie asked.

"Oh, ages ago. While she was at Wellesley. She'd always been suspicious that her mother had fed her a cock-and-bull story about her father. So she made it a point to find out the truth. Larry was thrilled when she contacted him. I remember she'd pop down to New York for the weekend to visit him. From the very first time they laid eyes on each other, they connected. She'd stop by to see me, too, sometimes."

"Whose daughter?" Mary asked, patting her silvery pageboy in place with her free hand.

"*Larry Tutwiler's*, Mims. The woman who was found dead at Chaps was Larry's *daughter*. Larry and Laura's daughter."

"No, really, Daisy! And she was teaching at Chaps, too? How extraordinary! I don't think I ever met her. Was she ever at the club?"

Bit by bit, Daisy laid out the entire story in a fairly coherent fashion considering what the alcohol-level in her blood had to be. According to Daisy, Laura and Augusta hadn't enjoyed a close or easy relationship, Laura unable to relate to her bookish, socially clumsy daughter, a girl who was horsey but not a horsewoman. " 'Why isn't she boy crazy?' Laura would ask me."

To Rannie's ear, it sounded as though Mr. Tut was by far the more empathetic parent, although Daisy's unwavering allegiance was to Laura. "She was the one left in the lurch. I would never agree to see Larry socially."

"Are you sure he never tried to reconcile with Laura after the baby was born?" Rannie said, remembering Tut's leave of absence.

"Laura never said so. Neither did Augusta. Wouldn't Larry have told Augusta rather than let her go on thinking he'd abandoned the two of them?"

Not necessarily, Rannie thought but kept silent. Mr. Tut was a gentleman and gallant; if Laura had spurned him, she also had willfully denied her daughter a father. Perhaps Mr. Tut thought it would be too painful for Augusta to know the depth of her mother's selfishness; easier to keep the blame squarely on his shoulders.

"Did Augusta tell her mother?"

"Yes, eventually. Laura said if Augusta planned to see Larry, that was her business. Really, what else could she say? But Laura remained positively *adamant* about never seeing him herself. 'That chapter of my life is over,' she told me." Daisy turned to Mary. "We were all closing in on our sixties by then, and I think the real reason was she didn't want him to see her old."

"Sixty? Old!" Mary scoffed, before thanking Earla, who appeared at the door of the den to announce dinner would be ready in five minutes.

"Oh, I know, Mims! It sounds young to me now too. But Laura was vain. She made Augusta swear never to show Larry any photos."

Ms. Hollins's brief marriage—"some fellow from *Wyoming*" Daisy said in a way that made it seem sheer folly to wed anyone west of the Hudson—broke up not long before her mother's death. "Augusta was teaching English at a girls school in Atlanta; then when a position opened at Chaps, Larry persuaded her to apply and move to New York."

"Did anyone at Chaps know he was her father?" Rannie inquired, remembering David Ross's oblique remarks about skeletons in Mr. Tut's closet. Perhaps this information was David Ross's "bargaining chip."

"I wouldn't imagine either one of them went around broadcasting that," Daisy answered tartly.

"The police? Do they know?"

"Yes. She told the police right away when Larry's body was found. I must say, from Day One, Augusta suspected murder." This time the word sounded bitter on Daisy's tongue. "The last few weeks before he died, she often stayed at Larry's—he suffered terribly, you know; pancreatic cancer is not a pleasant way to go. She was a good daughter. Anyway, Augusta insisted a police officer come to the apartment while she packed up her belongings. I thought she was being ridiculous, paranoid. . . . And now she's dead, too."

Daisy lit another cigarette and composed herself, swiping at tears with her hankie while Rannie again suffered remorse over the memory of tailing Ms. Hollins down West End Avenue. Then, just when Rannie assumed that was it, end of story, time to eat, Daisy delivered more interesting tidbits. The night Mr. Tut died, Augusta Hollins had met Daisy for dinner and a movie. Rannie recalled running into Ms. Hollins on Riverside Drive, stealth smoking. Hadn't she mentioned plans that had kept her out late? Yes, Rannie could hear Ms. Hollins, the regret in her voice over not being with Tut.

"She was upset. She'd seen Larry, oh, not half an hour before I picked her up. Augusta was odd: She knew Larry had money and was very stubborn about never wanting any. Well, he'd just told her he'd changed his will recently and, like it or not, she was getting two million dollars. He said she could give it away, even burn it, for all he cared, but he insisted on providing for her."

Rannie sat, absorbing all of what Daisy was saying. . . . So Daisy was Ms. Hollins's alibi. Tim had said she was investigating assbackwards. Well, there was no way to work in the next question subtly so Rannie simply asked flat out, "Do you remember what time you met Augusta that Monday evening?"

Daisy was not so crocked that she didn't stiffen slightly and peer quizzically at Rannie. "Right before six," she said with certainty. "We had a reservation at Ouest. Dreadful food and hideously expensive. I like to eat early. Mims knows that."

"Earla will be ready for us in just a moment, dear," Mary assured her and she stood and began transferring empty glasses and a plate of untouched Triscuits and Wispride to the bar.

Daisy rose too. The elasticized waistband on her slacks was less than an inch under her bustline. Mary took hold of her friend's arm, Rannie following them in the direction of the dining room, unsure about who was propping up whom.

"Mary, I can't stay; I really should be getting home," Rannie said.

"You're sure? What a shame when Earla's made such a lovely dinner." Mary helped Daisy take her place at the mahogany table. "Now no more talk of anything upsetting," she instructed as Earla appeared, bearing a Wedgewood bowl of what appeared to be a ball of off-white knitting yarn. Accompanying the spaghetti was a gravy boat of watery tomato sauce and a salad of limp iceberg lettuce and carrot curls.

"Good-bye, dear." Mary tilted her face to accept a peck on the cheek.

Rannie gathered her jacket and purse.

"Be sure to save room for dessert," she heard Mary telling Daisy. "It's your favorite."

"No! Earla's Jell-O Surprise!" It sounded as if Daisy's mood had brightened considerably.

Rannie closed the door to the apartment. For years now she'd been trying to determine what exactly the "surprises" were, suspended in the only gray Jell-O she'd ever encountered. Nate said Magic Lucky Charms, and for all she knew he was right.

Chapter 58

Thursday, late afternoon

THE TURNOUT FOR THE ASSEMBLY THAT MORNING HAD BEEN PATHETIC— not even two rows in the auditorium were filled. A couple of teachers talked, and Katie Spielkopf got up and started crying, saying how Ms. Hollins had opened her eyes to the beauty of poetry. But when Mr. Marshall asked if anybody else wanted to say something, everybody just looked at the floor.

School closed at one. No sign of Olivia. Ben was at Columbia for his interview, and Nate's sister, who was still home, was working on a paper and wouldn't go to a movie.

"No, I won't come home so you can see how my hair swirls!" Nate told her. Instead, he ended up going to Central Park with a bunch of kids, walking all the way down to the Bethesda Fountain where stoners always hung out with their skateboards. A couple of kids went over to buy joints from them, but Nate decided to head out of the park. When he reached Strawberry Fields, he called Ben. Dry leaves blew around the candles and bunches of flowers left on the mosaic circle that said "Imagine."

"How'd it go?" Nate asked.

"I just got out. Pretty good, I think."

"Want to meet up? Or you planning to go slobber over Katie somewhere?"

"Meet me at the Beasty Burger."

The place served crap food, but Nate said, "Half an hour," and caught the uptown local at Broadway. When he got out of the subway at 116th Street, he saw someone on the other side of Broadway coming out of a deli with a can of Coke and a Twix. At first Nate thought his eyes were playing tricks on him.

"Grant! Yo!" he shouted, crossing the street.

Grant turned. The instant a flicker of recognition crossed his face, he took off down Broadway.

Nate started running. He had to weave around an old man with a grocery cart and a nanny pushing a stroller, but a truck turning in to 114th Street blocked Grant for a second.

A second was all Nate needed. He caught up and lunged, sending them both sprawling to the sidewalk. "You fucking prick! You come near my sister again, I swear I'll kill you!" They rolled around on the ground, on top of each other, Grant gasping, "Take it easy, man!" while trying to plant a fist in Nate's gut.

Nate's arms were clamped around Grant when he felt someone else yanking them apart. Panting, Nate lay on his back, gazing up at a dark blue uniform.

"Awright, awright, break it up, guys." The cop was young—there were major zits on his forehead. A patrol car was at the curb. Grant scrambled to his knees, ready to make a break for it.

"Uh, uh, buddy. You're not going anywhere. I want to see identification. From both of you."

Grant started to say something, then stopped, dug his wallet out of his back pocket, and handed over his driver's license.

The cop looked at it briefly, then said, "Now you," to Nate.

Nate stood up. Except for a fake license for twenty-six-year-old Alan Mandel from Syosset, all Nate had was Chaps I.D.

The school name registered with the cop instantly. "Chapel School, huh. This is suddenly getting more interesting. So what's going on here? You first." The remark was directed at Grant.

"I wasn't doing anything. I came out of a deli when suddenly he starts running after me and jumps me."

Nate faced the cop. "He's a miserable sack-of-shit junkie. He hurt my sister."

"That true?" the cop said.

Grant said nothing.

"He also stole forty bucks from her."

"You shut the fuck up now," the cop told Nate. "Both of you. Don't move." He handed Grant's license along with Nate's I.D. to the cop in the patrol car who got on his walkie-talkie and said a minute later, "They want us to take the Werner kid home."

"Home!" Grant look scared. "I didn't do anything. He started this."

"Apparently his folks have a friend down at One Police Plaza," the cop in the car told the cop with zits. "There's a bulletin out."

The young cop grabbed Grant's arm and pushed him toward the car. "Get in the backseat. We're taking a ride." His neck twisted toward Nate. "You. Beat it."

Right across the street, Ben was waiting outside the Beasty Burger.

"I saw!" Ben said to Nate. "Man, what is it with you and the cops! You just can't stay away from 'em!"

Chapter 59

"GRANT, OH MY GOD! YOU'RE HERE!" OLIVIA CRIED WHEN SHE GOT HOME.

She had treated herself to a Mental Health Day. Chaps was closing early, so really it was only like cutting half a day. She went to the Costume Institute at the Met to see an exhibit called "Jazz Babies" and then caught a movie starring Clive Owen. All afternoon she tried her best not to think about her brother. And now there he was, sitting in the breakfast nook, eating a melted cheese sandwich.

Carlotta said, "Your parents, they with the lawyer upstairs." Carlotta pointed her spatula at Grant. "A cop brought him home. Livvy, he was high. He thinks I'm too stupid to know. Oh, yes, I know," she muttered, wiping grease off the griddle on the Viking range. "Your brother, he's never gonna learn. Never."

"Olivia, why'd you tell the cops about me seeing Tut—"

"They already knew! They checked all the calls on my cell. They—they saw a call you made to some Domino's in New Haven. How was I supposed to explain that!" Olivia felt like a rope was knotted tightly around her skull. She sank down on the edge of the booth and rubbed her temples.

"Your sister loves you! You want her to get in trouble, too?"

"Why couldn't you just stay at Windward?"

"I—I panicked," Grant stammered. He'd been staying up at Columbia again, at Eric's since Tuesday afternoon. "Okay, I'm sorry. I know I fucked up. I—"

"Don't use that filthy talk in this house!"

Grant ignored Carlotta and extended a triangle of sandwich, which Olivia pushed away. "After Ledbetter finishes with Mom and Dad, I have to go to the precinct.... My luck, they'll say I gave Hollins a push."

"How'd the cops find you?" Olivia asked.

"Nate Lorimer saw me."

"Nate?"

"The next thing, we're on the ground and he's punching me. A cop broke it up."

She took a closer look at her brother. Yeah, Carlotta was right. Grant's eyes were glassy. "You told me you had almost a year, Grant."

He started to give her some b.s., but she shook her head.

He sighed. "All right, yes, I've had a couple of slips. I'm not happy about it either. But it's not the end of the world, and it's not your problem. So let me deal with it, okay."

"Livvy, you supposed to be at the doctor's at five-thirty, don't forget."

Oh shit. Dr. Ehrenburg! She'd forgotten. She could also hear her parents and Mr. Ledbetter coming downstairs from the parlor floor.

Grant put down the crust of his sandwich. "Now the fun begins."

Olivia got her bag, which was hanging on the louvered doors that hid the washer/drier. When he realized she was leaving, Grant jumped up and said frantically, "Where are you going? Come on, don't go!"

Olivia didn't know what to answer so she shrugged. "It's not my problem. You just said so yourself. You deal with it."

As Olivia walked to Dr. Ehrenburg's office, the evening air on her cheeks felt soothing and the pounding in her head grew fainter. And even though she burst into tears almost as soon as she settled into the black leather recliner, using up one Kleenex after another, it wasn't the usual kind of crying that left you feeling hopeless and horrible; she actually felt better.

Olivia found herself telling Dr. E. about a book she'd read over the summer. *The Bell Jar* by Sylvia Plath.

"I got it because I heard it was about a girl working at a fashion magazine," Olivia explained. Her favorite part was when the girl threw all her new clothes off the roof of a hotel. It was supposed to be a sign that the girl, her name was Estelle—no, Esther—was going crazy. Each piece of clothing went sailing off into the night, like a big bird, floating down until it landed on some building. Esther was getting rid of things she didn't want anymore, things that were a burden. And to Olivia, the more she thought about it, that didn't seem crazy at all.

"I agree," Dr. Ehrenburg said. "Sometimes the best thing, the *only* thing, you can do is let go. It doesn't meant you stop hoping. Olivia, your brother has his whole life ahead of him. Letting go isn't the same thing as giving up on him."

Olivia dug into a hangnail. She thought she understood. She also desperately needed a cigarette. You weren't allowed to smoke in the office, but there was a little garden outside that faced the gardens of other brownstones.

"Olivia, come on. You can wait. We only have a few minutes left. And I had a new security system installed. I'm not even sure how to use it." Dr. E. pointed to a panel with numbered keys on the wall. Olivia had never seen it before.

"If anybody opens that door, from inside or outside, a siren goes off that can wake the dead. Then, unless I punch in an eight-digit code in the alarm box, the police come. All very high-tech, all very complicated. Way beyond me."

"So you're never going to open the door again?" The little garden was beautiful, especially in spring.

Olivia managed to forego the cigarette, and soon Dr. E. was glancing at the small travel clock she kept on the table beside her, positioned so that she alone could see its face. "I'm afraid our time's up." Then she smiled, the new unnatural smile where her mouth widened but her cheeks barely moved and not a single laugh line crinkled at the corner of her eyes.

Chapter 60

WHEN RANNIE RETURNED FROM MARY'S, SHE FOUND A NOTE FROM ALICE, saying, "Mom, I decided to take the five o'clock back to New Haven. Call Nate! Big news!"

"I found Grant Werner!" he said excitedly and gave a brief rundown of events. "I'll tell you more later. I'm meeting someone for dinner." And he cut her off before she could get in another word.

All the food she'd bought at Zabar's so they could enjoy a nice meal together, the three of them, like they used to. . . . Rannie remained staring at the phone for a moment, then grabbed her jacket, the box of lemon tarts, and the threatening note.

"Hey bartender!" she said. "I'm early."

Tim was behind the bar, holding down the tap, filling up a frothy glass of beer for a customer. He looked up, wiped his hands on a dishtowel and smiled. "So what'll it be?"

"Diet Coke. Make it a double."

"Tough day?"

"A weird one. You know, I wouldn't mind a cheeseburger too. I brought dessert."

After Tim hosed up two Cokes, he motioned to a waiter to take over at the bar. Flipping up the hatch, he picked up the glasses and ushered Rannie to a back table. As he sat across from her, Rannie recapped the day, omitting only what Daisy confirmed about Mr. Tut and Ms. Hollins. When she got to the Grant part, Tim, surprisingly, already knew from his own son more than Rannie did.

"Yeah, they were trading punches up around 114th Street and Broadway. A patrol car stopped them and ran a check on the Werner kid's license; he's at the precinct now."

A fistfight? Because of Alice in all likelihood. Rannie's cheeseburger arrived while she was telling Tim about the letter. She took out the envelope.

"You think Augusta Hollins sent this to you?"

"Yes. This is the second one. The first one came about a week ago. It said 'Stop Snooping.'" Rannie steeled herself, then without any prelude or justification, out it all spilled, unedited and unvarnished. Tailing Ms. Hollins. Bribing her way into Tut's apartment. Swiping files at school.

He handed back the letter, holding it carefully, just at the edges. "And you're doing this because?" He eyed her in a way that left the distinct impression snooping was not a quality he looked for in a relationship. "It's not just from worrying about your son, is it?"

"No. Not just that. It's more complicated," she admitted as she put away the letter. "My life's kind of a mess right now." Snooping was a distraction, time that could be better spent on any number of other worthier endeavors yet addictively involving, nonetheless. The same way playing computer Solitaire was or doing crosswords for hours. Finding Mr. Tut's murderer, however—well, that would be altogether different, that would validate her in a way that escorting families around Chaps and depositing unemployment checks didn't. It would right a wrong.

"Ms. Hollins didn't kill Tut. I'm positive of that, Tim. Remember what you told me, about the glass on Tut's desk? She knew him well enough to know he was left-handed; she would've made sure to put the correct fingerprints on the glass. I think she was murdered too."

She waited for Tim to concur. Instead, he kept his eyes on her and rubbed his chin.

"You think it's possible Grant Werner murdered them both?" she asked and saw he was teetering on the edge of exasperation.

"Rannie, I don't know. I'm not a cop. I own a bar. You should be showing the police that letter. Not me."

"I will. And okay . . . subject over." *For now,* she added to herself. She poured on ketchup and mustard and dug into her cheeseburger. Then she told Tim all about touring Stanford, described the buildings to him, the kids, even the amazing cactus garden.

He nodded attentively, smiling now and then at things she said. It brought home just how satisfying it was to sit and talk to someone who, unlike her kids, seemed to enjoy listening.

"It's a slow night," he said when she was all done with her dinner. "Chris won't be home for another couple of hours."

Rannie reached for her purse and tarts.

Upstairs, they wasted no time undressing and the sex was as amazing as it had been the other night. Some men instinctively knew what to do in bed. Tim was one. From the moment he began kissing her, it was clear he sensed what she wanted. After Tim was inside her, he leaned back on his knees, holding both her wrists at her sides, looking down at her, moving slowly, purposefully, which made her clench her muscles even more tightly around him. Then he told her to touch herself. For a moment she wasn't sure she'd heard correctly. But he said it again. "I want to watch you, Rannie."

And he let go of one of her hands. So she did, thinking right at this moment she'd do anything, whatever he asked. She shut her eyes, and any embarrassment she first felt quickly became beside the point once pure sensation took over. He let go of her other hand and began caressing her breasts, cupping them while tracing a finger over her nipples, still moving slowly inside her then a little faster. It felt so good, almost *too* good, and at the exact instant when the connection forged between them seemed unbreakable, he dropped down on top of her and they both came.

They kissed and held onto each other, letting their breathing return to normal, Tim stroking her hair. Then she hopped out of bed to get the tarts. Tim's bedroom, she now noticed, had the same impersonal air as the living room—the blond wood furniture could have come straight from the Marriott she'd just stayed in. It saddened her that his home didn't feel more inhabited, more peculiarly his. Then her eye stopped at the diploma on the wall.

"You were a policeman! You never told me that."

The framed certificate, issued by the Plymouth, Massachusetts, Municipal Police Academy, proclaimed that Timothy Edward Butler had completed training successfully.

He'd been lying on his back, the sheet up to his waist, his arms crossed behind his head. Now he sat up, his features suddenly guarded. All he said was, "That was a long time ago." Rannie sat on the edge of the bed, the sight of her clothes and underwear strewn on the floor suddenly making her feel exposed, the "connectedness" of a moment ago gone. The fact was, she hardly knew this man. And wasn't that how she wanted to keep it? Enjoy him. Enjoy the sex. But keep it light. If parts of his life pained him or were best forgotten, there was no reason on earth he should reveal why.

He reached for her, and she allowed him to wrap his arms around her one more time. They each polished off a tart and afterward she reached for her clothes, saying, "I should get going. I haven't seen Nate since Tuesday."

"Rannie, wait. You okay?"

Her chest was a mottled rosy color, and her skin still felt alive from the sex. "Fine!" she said brightly, but Tim was shaking his head.

"You are very hard to figure out, you know that? What do you want? A friend? Somebody to fuck you? A soul mate?" He ran a hand through his hair and exhaled heavily. "Look. I used to be a cop. I'm not now. It's not part of my life anymore." His eyes shifted to the certificate. "I keep it as a reminder. It's not something I talk about much."

"You don't owe me any explanations. Really."

For so long she'd been insisting that she didn't want or need much from men. As she dressed, she remembered confessing to Joan, not long ago, about an S&S rep she'd been seeing, a guy barely over the threshold of thirty. Joan's response was: "Nooners at a midtown hotel? That's enough for you, Rannie?" At the time it had been.

Tim got dressed and put her in a cab. On the way home, holding the box with one remaining tart for Nate, she could almost hear her mother, "You overthink everything, Rannie." Part of Peter's appeal had been that he wasn't a brooder, a worrier; it had taken years for her to admit that, in her husband's case, "uncomplicated" was a synonym for "shallow." Yes, she overthought everything, and yes, she wished she didn't. Yet you were born with complex genetic wiring that was uniquely yours and you tackled everything in life accordingly. There really wasn't a choice.

Chapter 61

AS SOON AS RANNIE FINISHED COPYEDITING THE FINAL PAGES OF THE Mengele manuscript, she placed it in a brown envelope, along with the style sheet she'd assembled, the borrowed books on Mengele, everything ready to deliver. Then she left a message at the precinct for the lieutenant to call.

Nate's poetry book was on the counter near the phone. The sight of it made her sad ... and guilty. Ms. Hollins had been a good daughter and a good teacher. On a past Parents Day, Rannie had listened to Ms. Hollins discussing her classes, so animated, so excited once again to be sharing the work of writers she loved. Augusta Hollins was a person who probably had been happiest, most at ease, in a classroom.

Right now Rannie shut her eyes to block out a dreadful vision of Ms. Hollins plummeting from the Annex rooftop. At the very least, Rannie hoped it all happened fast and that she was dead before ever knowing what hit her.

Rannie's doorbell rang. It was her downstairs neighbor with her toddler astride her hip, a cast encasing one of his arms up to the elbow.

"Lukie! How's the arm?" Rannie asked.

He held out his arm proudly, his hand gripping a sandwich bag of Cheerios. "Boo boo," he announced while keeping a thumb plugged in his mouth.

"Rannie, do you have a sec?"

"Sure. Want coffee?" She beckoned them inside.

"We're withdrawing Noah's application from Chaps."

"I don't blame you. I'd do the same thing."

"The thing is, I'd appreciate it if you didn't say anything to Jem Marshall yet."

"I guess he's ruing the day he ever left City." As Rannie was filling another mug in the kitchen, Luke eyed a Pepperidge Farm box and chirped, "Cookie?" But his mother shook her head and reminded Luke about his Cheerios.

"You liked him? Jem?" Rannie asked once they were back in the living room, Luke sitting cross-legged on the rug, in an undershirt, diaper and cast—a vision in white.

Melinda tilted her head, squinted, and pressing her lips together, thought for a moment. *"Like?"* She shrugged. "I admired his dedication, that's for sure." Melinda took a rattle from the back pocket of her jeans and handed it to Luke. "I mean, the school seemed to be his whole life. Every picnic, every play, every game, he'd be there cheering like it was Super Bowl Sunday. And I told you about all the money he raised."

"But?" Rannie prodded, picking up on the unstated. She watched Luke, who was now plucking Cheerios, one by one, from the sandwich bag with his thumb and index finger and placing them carefully on the rug.

Melinda leaned back on the sofa cushions, exhaling. "A couple of years ago, I ran the Christmas Fair and we spent a considerable amount of time together. Jem and me. But there was never any joking around. I had my role. He had his." Then Melinda caught

Rannie's affectionate gaze and said, "It's amazing how quickly he adjusted to doing things with his left hand. I thought having the cast would be a nightmare—you know the frustration level at this age. Less than zero, right? But our pediatrician said he's still pretty ambidextrous."

"Right from the start, Nate reached for everything with his left hand." And as soon as the words were out of her mouth, Rannie called to mind the specific image of Jem Marshall signing letters, another leftie. She recalled watching him struggle with a pen, the hunched posture, the curled-in hand. Just like Nate. But now suddenly another image of Jem surfaced, overlaying the first, only something was out of register. It hit her, stunning her like a joy buzzer, a jolt that felt almost physical.

"Who's a good boy?" Melinda was cooing while she bent down to swipe away a pendant of drool hanging from Luke's chin. Then her nose wrinkled. "Ooh, fella, you reek!" She turned to Rannie. "Somebody needs to be changed—Hey, are you okay?"

Rannie managed a nod. "Fine. Just remembered something."

Chapter 62

OLIVIA WAS SITTING IN THE BREAKFAST NOOK, DRINKING ORANGE JUICE. James was driving her parents and brother back to Windward.

Last night around ten, after returning from the precinct, Grant had knocked on her door. He was walking oddly because of the ankle bracelet. "This thing hurts like a bitch. But that was the condition. Otherwise the cops wouldn't let me go back to Windward." He sat down on the bed beside her, and after glancing over the top of her pad to see what she was sketching, leaned back against the wall. "They took fingerprints and samples of my hair to see if anything matches stuff they found in Tut's office—or Hollins's. Nothing's gonna. I can swear to that, Olivia. I had zip to do with any of that."

Olivia looked over the top of her sketchpad at him.

"You believe me, don't you?" Grant asked.

"Yeah, Grant. I don't think you killed anybody."

"That's all you're going to say?"

She put down the pad and her grease pencil. She was about to ask how many slips he'd had the past year. But really, whether it was four or five or fifty, what did it matter? "I thought last Thanksgiving was gonna be like a turning point. I thought you'd hit bottom." Dammit, she teared up.

He wrapped his arms around her, and she let him hug her. "I'm sorry," he kept saying over and over. When they pulled apart, she saw he was crying too. "I dunno. I really don't. I try to do what they say at Windward, focus on staying off drugs one day at a time. I've been there over a year. I mean I know I'm an addict; I'm not fooling myself about that anymore. But sometimes I wake up—I may not even be depressed or anything. I wake up feeling pretty good, but it hits me that what I want most in the entire world is to get high that day. And so I will. I'll get hold of some coke and do a line or two and think"—Grant nodded to himself—" 'yeah, this is how you're *supposed* to feel.' "

"I don't get it, why are you that way and not me? I mean, we have the same shitty parents, the same genes."

Grant lifted his shoulders in a "beats me" shrug. "The first time I ever tried pot, right away I knew this was something *major*. And just a toke or two wasn't gonna do it. Right away what I wanted was to get stoned out of my fucking gourd."

They went downstairs to make Jiffy Pop and root beer floats, like they used to. Then they watched a horror movie in the den. Before going to bed, Olivia hugged her brother again.

"Look, don't give up on me, okay?" Grant said. "I don't know what I'd do if you did."

"I won't, Grant. I want so much for you to be all better."

"Me too. All I can do is keep trying."

"I know." Olivia held up her hand, fingers crossed. That was about all she could do—keep hoping.

Now, as she rinsed out the juice glass, all at once Olivia found herself thinking about Dr. E.'s office, the door to the garden, and something Dr. E. had said started ringing in her head. In her mind

Olivia forced herself back to the morning she found Tut, trying to see everything as if it were separate frames in a movie. She was in Tut's office. . . . Mr. Marshall came. . . . They went downstairs. . . . Mr. Marshall got her water. . . . Olivia was sitting on the couch. . . . The other family left—Olivia remembered the little girl's legs wrapped around her father's waist as he walked to the Annex entry-way. . . . Mrs. Mac arrived all upset. . . . Then the two guys got there with a stretcher.

The guys with the stretcher. They'd come right in the Annex front door—that was what she'd forgotten before. It was such a little detail.

She picked up her cell and made a call. She didn't want to go to the precinct alone.

Chapter 63

THE MOMENT HER NEIGHBOR LEFT, RANNIE TIPTOED INTO NATE'S ROOM, where he was still asleep, and which reeked in a distinctly teenaged boy way, a pervasive testosterone-loaded scent of perspiration, greasy hair, dirty clothes. The mountain under the quilt moved. "Ma! I'm sleeping."

"Tell me where the yearbooks are. The ones from teachers."

A groan. "Look on my desk."

They were on the floor *near* his desk. Close enough.

Rannie found the Palo Alto Pennant and returned to the living room where she searched for the picture she remembered, the one of Jem using the back of a girl as a desktop. When she found it, Rannie studied it closely. The girl was glancing over her shoulder, smiling, as if trying to make out what he was writing. From the body language and smile, Rannie suspected the girl was interested in Jem.

Rannie's eyes remained fixed on the page, her field of vision narrowing in on the detail that popped out at her like a broken mattress spring. It didn't compute. He was writing with his right hand. She blinked as if to clear her head and searched for a mistake that would explain away the disconnect. But in the photo, a map of France on the wall made visual sense. The girl's sweatshirt was only partially visible, the letters *"TO"* all that could be seen, the others blocked by her position and the piece of paper Jem was writing on. Reversed, those two letters would still "read" correctly but *"TO"* was the more likely correct sequence—part of Palo Alto High School.

In the sports section another photo showed Jem in the outfield, mitt outstretched with no scoreboard sign or other detail to erase the same disturbing contradiction. The mitt was on his left hand. She flipped to his senior portrait and again was struck by the ineffable difference between the young boy staring out at her, a half-smile on his face, and the buttoned-up man she saw at school. Then she grabbed her barn jacket, barely noticing the tip of one of her lethal blue pencils poking through her pocket. A hole, dammit.

In ten minutes she was at Chaps. Today the new guard made her sign in as well as present her Chaps I.D. The ground floor of the Annex was empty. On an upper floor she could hear the voices of policemen who, she guessed, might be in Ms. Hollins's office. Rannie looked in the boardroom, checked the doors to other offices—all locked and empty. Mrs. Mac's spiral-bound phone log was on her desk; Rannie took it to her own and began leafing back to the messages written on the Monday Tut was murdered, searching for the one from Stanford.

She dialed the Stanford number; the three-hour time difference meant it was just past nine o'clock in California. The admissions office picked up right away.

"May I speak to Byron Richards, please?"

"Whom shall I say is calling?"

"*Who*" not "whom" the grammar cop, never off duty, silently corrected. Rannie gave her name. "I'm from Chapel School in New York City."

"Please hold. I'll see if he's available." A moment later, Rannie was asked to leave her number, he'd get back to her. She jumped when the phone rang barely an instant after she'd hung up.

"Hello, Chapel School," she said.

"Ms. Bookman? This is Byron Richards."

"Thanks for returning my call so quickly."

"I don't take any calls directly anymore. This week alone, two parents called pretending to be high school guidance counselors putting in a good word for their child. We computer check phone numbers now."

Rannie laughed and hoped it didn't sound like nervous laughter crossing three thousand miles of telephone wire. "Can't be too careful, I guess."

"So what may I do for you?"

"You know of course that Mr. Tutwiler is . . . is gone. Our director of college admissions."

"Gone?"

Wonder of wonders, not all New York news was automatically national news. She was surprised, then encouraged—that meant Byron Richards was unaware of the circumstances. "Yes, Mr. Tutwiler died recently."

"Sorry to hear that—I spoke to him only a week or two ago." Byron Richards's appointment as Stanford's Director of Admissions was a recent one. Before that he'd been Associate Director for the West Coast and thus wasn't familiar with all the East Coast schools or people. Still, he had known Tut by reputation before their recent conversations.

"I'm following up on Mr. Tutwiler's last phone calls," Rannie explained, "to make sure there are no loose ends, that everything's up to speed." Rannie mentioned the name of Tut's interim replacement and her start date. "There's a message in the phone log from you to Mr. Tutwiler. Actually on the day he died. We didn't know if he had returned the call."

"Yes, he did. One of your seniors is applying early."

"Nate Lorimer, I believe," and she managed to refrain from adding, "Wonderful boy! Stanford would be lucky to have him!"

"During an earlier conversation Mr. Tutwiler had brought up that your new headmaster is a Stanford grad."

Something in his tone of voice made Rannie swallow hard. Suddenly she felt as though she were in the front car of a rollercoaster, climbing up, up, reaching the top of a steep hill. "Yes, Jonathan Marshall."

"I'm an alum. The name sounded vaguely familiar so later I looked him up in our records." Then he related what Rannie had witnessed herself while in the Admissions Offices at Stanford: Jonathan Marshall's name was followed by an asterisk, meaning "deceased" or "MIA"—whereabouts unknown. A computer glitch had been Byron Richards's initial assumption as well, so he pursued the matter further. "I didn't know him but turns out we graduated the same year. So I got in touch with our class agent who did remember him. She called him John-o Marshall."

"John-o? Everybody calls him Jem now."

There was an uneasy pause. "I'm afraid nobody's calling him anything now. He's dead."

The rollercoaster plunged downward. A chilly sweat broke out on her body, trickling between her breasts. *Dead.* "Jonathan *Edwards* Marshall? Early forties? Grew up in Palo Alto."

"Yes. Mr. Tutwiler's reaction was the same as yours. Look, I'll tell you what I told him. Our twentieth reunion's coming up; plans are in the works for a memorial arboretum, a tree for every person who's died. A list was mailed, which is why the name rang a bell. He was the first to die. The woman who knew him told me it was a plane crash, not even a month after graduation. Both parents were on the plane too. I tell you, it sent a chill through me."

Nothing like the one going through Rannie right now. Was Tim right? Had Tut been murdered for stumbling on this information?

"That's why I called Mr. Tutwiler a week ago Monday. He called me back, early afternoon your time. Look, Chapel School has an excellent reputation so I didn't want to make any accusation unless I was a hundred percent sure. I checked every other Jonathan Marshall who went to Stanford, every Jon and John Marshall. Nobody was even remotely the right age. And nobody had the same middle name. More than that, I can't tell you. . . . I don't know who's running your school, a clone?"

No, not a clone. But close, she suspected. After she hung up, Rannie willed her hands to stop shaking so that she could turn on her computer. The Marshalls were a local family. The newspaper must have run an article at the time. And obituaries. While her Mac booted up, she closed her eyes and mentally envisioned the name of the newspaper left on the hallway carpet outside her hotel room. *The Palo Alto Record.* That was it.

Once connected to the paper's web site, she searched through archives, scrolling back to the year, then combing through issues from May and June, graduation time. A little hunting and she found it. June 29th. Franklin Marshall, age fifty-three, had owned a car dealership; Eloise Marshall (née Edwards), age forty-nine, was a homemaker and part-time bookkeeper for an accounting firm. Their son, Jonathan Edwards Marshall, twenty-two, a graduate of Palo Alto High School, had just received a B.S. in chemistry from Stanford. The plane, a flight from L.A. to San Jose, crashed almost immediately after takeoff, the cause attributed to wind shear during a summer storm.

It was all as Byron Richards had related, but there had to be more. An obituary offered up the missing piece, listing the time and date of the funeral service as well as the one remaining member of the Marshall family. Jonathan's brother, Jeremy Elliot Marshall. Jonathan's twin brother.

Somehow Rannie managed to force her trembling finger to hit the print icon. It felt as if lights—pinpricks of light—were suddenly flashing on and off in the outer corners of her eyes, and she wondered if she was about to experience a full-blown anxiety attack. Her first. Then her stomach decided to get in the act, roiling in a way that sent her running into the nearest bathroom off the Great Hall.

Behind the locked door, she felt safer and stayed in the stall until her heart stopped galloping and her vision cleared. She pressed a wet paper towel to her forehead. There had been no sign of a Jeremy Elliot Marshall anywhere in the Palo Alto yearbook. Photos of girls had flanked the one of Jonathan Edwards Marshall in the alphabetically arranged senior section. Rannie was positive of that. Where was this other twin while his brother was catching baseballs in right field, planning the senior prom, having cute girls flirt with him? Was Ms. Hollins aware of Jem Marshall's concocted persona? Had she, like Mr. Tut, paid dearly for the knowledge?

Rannie dialed Sergeant Peratta's number, leaving her home number and her cell number, asking him to call as soon as possible. A chapter in the Mengele manuscript had focused on the symbiotic relationship between twins, identical twins in particular, and how occasionally it went radically askew. What had gone on between these brothers?

The cops she'd heard earlier in the Annex didn't respond when she called up to them from the stairwell. Far too spooked to remain a moment longer in the building, Rannie grabbed her bag, her jacket, and returned the log to Mrs. Mac's desk.

In the Great Hall, Jem Marshall was at the security desk, hunched over the sign-in sheet, a pen clamped awkwardly in his left—"lyft," "sinister"—hand. He looked up as she came through the entryway.

Rannie stopped cold; her lips twitched into an unnatural smile. Her eyes were open way too wide. "Hi," she said, then erupted in a nervous titter. She tried to stop grinning although it wasn't easy with her upper lip stuck to her gum. Then, as fast as her size five feet could carry her, she scurried outside and starting running, never once breaking stride until she was all the way home.

Phone message on Rannie's machine at home

It's Tim. I'm going up to Amherst with Chris today for his interview. Back tonight. Call. I want to see you. We need to talk.

Chapter 64

Friday, early afternoon

AFTER NATE WOKE UP AND SAW THE MESSAGE FROM OLIVIA ON HIS CELL, it took him less than fifteen minutes to shower, throw on clothes, and meet her at the Acropolis.

When he turned the corner, there she was, waiting out front, smoking; he wondered if there'd ever come a day when the sight of her wouldn't make his heart catch and his body weak.

"You like this place?" she said dubiously, killing the butt with the toe of a scuffed cowboy boot. They settled into his usual booth and waited for coffee. She slid off the Sergeant Pepper's bandleader jacket she was wearing, and her serious, honey-colored eyes fastened on him. "Nate, I keep playing over in my head what I saw that morning I found Tut. The whole time everybody's going on about the cameras and that photo. But what if that has nothing to do with the murder?"

"How do you mean?" Nate willed himself to focus on her words and not her tits.

"The entryway isn't the only way in and out of the Annex. There *is* a front door. We never think about it because nobody ever uses it.

But that morning, the EMS guys came for Tut's body through the Annex *front* door. I watched Marshall punch in the code on an alarm panel so the stretcher could get through. He couldn't remember the code at first. He had to go back up to his office to get it."

"So you're saying that's how the killer could have sneaked out of school?"

"Yeah, exactly. And I think it's Marshall." She told him about running into Arm and Hammer near the Garden. "What they said made no sense then. But maybe that's how Marshall got drugs."

The fucking headmaster buying drugs from Arm and Hammer! "But why would he want to kill Tut?"

Olivia just shook her head. She was playing with a blue packet of Equal.

"What was it your brother heard Tut say? 'You've got a lot of explaining to do.'?"

"Something like that."

"So if it's Marshall, maybe he did something that Tut found out about . . . He was there, the night Tut died, Marshall I mean," Nate said. "I saw him locking his office right before I went in to see Tut. But I never saw him actually leave. Maybe he went and hid out in the boardroom or some place." His mind lasered in on the missing glass in Tut's office. Marshall was someone Tut would have offered a drink to. . . . "Mr. Marshall buying raver drugs from Arm and Hammer!" Nate shook his head. It was almost harder to picture that than believing Marshall was a murderer. "But if he did spike Tut's drink, he must've hung around 'til Tut was dead and then made sure nobody was outside on the street before sneaking out."

Olivia nodded. "And meanwhile I was like having a heart attack over my brother on the stupid camera."

"You're brilliant."

Olivia shrugged dismissively. "None of this hit me 'til this morning."

"Why haven't the cops thought of it?" Nate said, suddenly ravenous from the smell of breakfast grease wafting all around him.

"Maybe they have. How would we know?"

He motioned for the waiter and ordered a short stack and fried eggs with sausage; Olivia wanted an English muffin and more coffee. When their food arrived and he was about to plow into the eggs, Nate considered something else. "The sonofabitch planted the roofies on me, has to be." He balanced a forkful of egg and pancake, running a possible sequence of events in his head. "Marshall calls the main school number asking for himself; someone comes into the gym and gets him; he goes to the front desk and, in front of the security guy, takes the call, acting like he's talking to someone. Then when he comes back, he finds my backpack and slips in a bag with a couple of joints and roofies, saying the stuff was in there already."

"Yeah, that works, I guess ... and right away everyone starts thinking, 'Ooh, party drugs! Just like what killed Tut!' ... What's he got against you?"

Nate shook his head as he shoveled another loaded fork of food into his mouth. "You should've heard him going on to my mom, how he was sure I was innocent. Maybe Ms. Hollins somehow knew what he was up to, too."

Olivia took another bite of English muffin; even the way she chewed got him hot, her lips closed, a speck of butter streaked in the corner, the muscles in her jaws moving slowly back and forth.

"Let's go to the cops now." He folded the last pancake around the one remaining sausage and shmeared it with syrup.

Olivia made a face. "What? That's supposed to be like a wrap sandwich?"

Chapter 65

NO SIGN OF NATE WHEN SHE RETURNED HOME. RANNIE STRAIGHTENED up his room, making the bed, tossing dirty clothes into the hamper. Then she had a peanut butter and jelly sandwich. Odd that there was no message from Peratta on the machine; that meant two calls from her that remained unanswered.

Getting out the Mengele manuscript, Rannie settled herself on the couch, her cell phone and land line both within easy reach on the coffee table. Although the job was done, with a bill enclosed for twenty-seven hours of work, she wanted to reread one chapter. Out of habit she sharpened a blue pencil and kept it poised because the plain fact was she was physically incapable of reading manuscript pages without one.

The chapter was called Paired Lives. It offered anecdotal information on certain twin phenomena such as creating secret languages and experiencing telepathic bonds—one twin was quoted as knowing the instant her twin died even though her sister was a continent away. The chapter cited reports of twins, adopted and raised separately, who upon meeting as adults exhibited remarkable similarities, both large and small—marrying the same year, divorcing within weeks of each other, smoking the same brand of cigarettes, working in the same profession, reading magazines back to front, giving their children the same names and on and on and on.

A couple of pages, the ones most germane to the question of Jem Marshall, were devoted to mirror-image twins, a phenomenon that occurred from a late-term splitting of the egg *in utero*. In extreme cases, the "reflection" twin would not only write with the opposite hand and feature hair whorls going in an opposite direction but would have all internal organs on the wrong side of the body. Interestingly, one father of mirror-image twins was quoted as saying his girls never appeared all that physically alike to him until the day he held one of his daughters in front of a mirror. While he was used to seeing his own face in a mirror, he wasn't used to seeing hers that way. The reflection suddenly reversed all the asymmetries in her features, and her face suddenly turned into an exact copy of her sister's.

The yearbook senior picture of the real Jonathan Edwards Marshall was less than two inches square. The compact mirror that Rannie took from her purse and held to it produced a visage certainly closer to the Jem Marshall she knew although it was the open expression of the boy in the yearbook that still struck her as the most telltale difference.

According to the manuscript, the left-side twin in a mirror-image pair was more likely to be alcoholic, psychotic, epileptic, dyslexic, and to suffer from allergies, all this despite the fact that both twins' genetic makeup was identical.

Rannie startled at the moaning of her cell phone and pounced, but it was the editor of the book, not Peratta.

"The job's done. I'm just rereading some parts now," Rannie told her. "Look, I'm expecting an important call. Okay to drop it off this evening?"

That was no problem; then right before hanging up, Rannie asked her friend whether she'd mind if Rannie spoke to the author of the Mengele book. Copy editors never contacted authors directly; everything was blue-penciled on the manuscript, ready for the editor to accept or discard and then discuss with the writer, but Rannie was quick to assure that her request had nothing to do with the book. "I'd like to ask him about being a twin . . . because of someone I know."

The author, George Pepperdine, taught at a liberal arts college in southern Ohio, although his distinct broad vowels, so like her own, suggested to Rannie that he'd probably grown up, as she had, in the northern part of the state. He was delighted to talk about his area of expertise, predictably imparting a little more information than she needed or wanted.

"Mengele wasn't the only one interested in twins' genetic make-up. The Russians were doing amazing ground-breaking studies of twins in the thirties at the Maxim Gorky Institute. But hardliners stopped it," he said, a note of regret creeping into his voice. "Studies of inherited abilities went against the whole Marxian credo that environment determines everything. . . . The research is probably gathering dust on a shelf somewhere."

"Mmph, a shame," Rannie murmured consolingly then attempted to steer the questioning closer to the issue on her mind.

The author said, "Usually the lefty in mirror-image twins has no deficits and is at no discernible disadvantage, vis à vis the other twin, other than the minor hassles all left-handed people deal with."

Rannie then brought up the instances he'd cited in the manuscript—lefty twins being more prone to psychosis, addiction, and other serious troubles.

"Yes, there's data supporting that. Obviously, I can't give you a percentage."

"What impact might it have on the twins' relationship?"

"All I can say with certainty is that sibling rivalry is always more intense between twins. If one is perceived within the family structure as disabled, inferior—well, then the relationship tilts one of two ways." He posited that the less able twin might distance himself from his twin, withdraw from any arena of competition, pull away from the family. "Or he might become more and more dependent on his twin to carry him along in life, all the while harboring resentment. Or some combination of the two. Is the person you know dyslexic, depressive? Was it a rocky childhood?"

"I have no idea. Outwardly he's a successful, accomplished person . . . his manner is pleasant in a—" Rannie searched for the best way to describe it, "in a *pro forma* way, if you know what I mean. His job requires public speaking and he handles that pretty confidently . . . the most I can say is that he has a removed way of dealing with people, when it's one on one . . . if the situation calls for him to just be himself, he seems uncomfortable. Almost like he needs a script, he can't ad lib with people."

Pepperdine said he knew exactly what Rannie was describing. "At the other extreme are people who are extraordinarily intuitive and perceptive emotionally. Very much at ease in social situations. They have a real knack for decoding intention. Neurobiologists attribute it to a group of neurons, ones connected to the brain's emotional region. They're called 'mirror neurons.'"

So Jem Marshall might be a *mirror*-image twin with faulty *mirror* neurons? This was getting too Escher-like. She said, "If a twin dies, it must be unlike any other loss for the surviving one."

"Absolutely. It's beyond devastating. The twin never again feels complete. It goes way beyond loss, something you can't begin to comprehend unless you're a twin yourself. I've interviewed surviving twins and it's almost as if they died themselves."

Rannie thanked the professor for his time, repeated how much she'd learned from his manuscript. Then she returned to her computer and, in the hope of learning something about Jeremy Elliot Marshall's past, went online again, trying the lost classmate site that popped up all the time with laughable photos of girls in bouffant hairdos. It cost ten bucks to join, but she supplied her Visa account number and registered, entering the year of high school graduation, narrowing the region to Northern California, and typing in his name. Zip came up.

All she really knew was that Jem Marshall hadn't graduated from Palo Alto High School, hadn't gone to Stanford, and at some point after his brother's death had assumed his identity. No, actually, she knew a little more than those few facts. Jem Marshall's résumé had included all his previous jobs. Those all had to be things *he'd* done; his brother was already dead by then. He had taught chemistry. She wondered whether GHB might be something that a chemistry buff could whip up by himself.

Tut had learned about the hoax sometime around noon and had died in the early evening. In that time, Jem had hatched a plan to murder Tut and somehow got his hands on GHB. For all her nosing around, Rannie had never thought to ask about Jem's schedule that day. David Ross had been in Jem Marshall's office that afternoon. Now it crossed her mind to wonder whether David Ross suspected Marshall all along and simply didn't care. But what about Ms. Hollins? Where did she figure in all this?

Mr. Tut was murdered because his killer had lied about where he went to college. On some level it struck Rannie as borderline ludicrous and also crazily appropriate. At Chaps, how could anything not be linked up with college? Rannie was wading knee-deep in all the heavy irony when she stopped cold, the last bite of her sandwich suddenly turning into a glutinous lump jammed in her mouth. She forced herself to swallow. Where was Nate? What if he'd stopped at school for some reason . . . Jem was there. The man meant her son harm.

Rannie's message on Nate's cell: "Call! Whatever you do, don't go anywhere near Chaps. If you're there, leave. Come home!"

Rannie's message on Peratta's cell: "This is urgent. Jem Marshall is the killer! This is the third time I've called!"

She was practically hopping up and down when she dialed the precinct number. "Where is Sergeant Peratta? This is important! It's about a murder . . . two murders!" But either she sounded unhinged or the receptionist was inured to shocking pronouncements, because Rannie was told to please wait, kept on hold for what seemed eons, then told in a calm, no-nonsense tone that she'd take a message. And no, unfortunately Officer Heffernan wasn't available either. "She's busy with clients. If you leave your number, ma'am—"

"I just did!"

"I'm sure the officer will get back to you."

Rannie hung up. She tried Tim Butler even though she knew he was in Massachusetts. She felt an overpowering need to make contact with someone, an urge to blab what she knew to another living human being and not a recording device. For the next half hour, she alternated between staring at the phones, willing one to ring, and pacing around the apartment in case phones were like pots and only an unwatched one would ring. But the only call to come in was from Ellen, the editor.

"Listen, I'm home, Rannie, and I'm going out for dinner. Any chance you could pop by now?"

"Umm, gee, that's a little difficult. What if I drop it off later tonight?"

There was a pause, one that suggested the possibility that Ellen's plans for the evening might *not* include coming home. "I really hate having stuff lie around in the lobby. . . ."

Okay, she was on her way, Rannie told her. One more call to Nate with a repeat of her last message, then she scooped up her jacket, cell phone, bag and was stepping inside the elevator when she realized one other thing she'd neglected to take. The manuscript.

As soon as Rannie had handed the package to her friend, she turned to leave. It was almost five-thirty. "I found out way more about Josef Mengele than I wanted to know . . . not that I'm complaining," she said while waiting for the elevator. "I'm very grateful for the work."

Ellen promised the next job would be lighter fare. "I'm almost done editing a first-time mystery. A double homicide on the Upper West Side. Interested?"

"Sounds right up my alley!" Rannie said and waggled fingers at Ellen as the elevator slid shut. Then her throat went dry. The Marshall family obituary, the one from the newspaper. It was still sitting in the Annex printer. Chances were good—no, great—that Jem Marshall would have seen it.

In the cab home, Rannie tried Nate's cell one last time.

"Yeah?" He sounded disoriented, aggravated.

"I left you a million messages. Where are you?"

"Home."

"Good. Stay there."

As the cab weaved its way up Amsterdam, Rannie gripped onto the pencil in her pocket as if it was a magic wand or talisman imbued with special powers to protect her. All she wanted was to be safe behind her Medeco-locked door, slathering Skippy's finest onto a piece of toast and nuking cold coffee.

Chapter 66

"SHIT. SHE'S ON HER WAY HOME."

Olivia was lying beside him on his bed, in nothing but a pink and black thong, her tits pooled on either side of her chest, so that gazing down at her, as he was now, she looked almost flat-chested.

A police car had driven them back to Dolores Court after the cops had finished questioning them. The cop offered to drop Olivia at her house, but nobody was home, and she said she'd feel safer staying with Nate. In the elevator, she casually asked, "Is your mom home?" and when he said no, she smiled.

She sat up now and suddenly her tits swung back into normal position and became full again, the lightning bolt dangling in between them, just as he had imagined so many times. "You are my fantasy life," he almost told her. He couldn't resist grazing a finger over one of her nipples again. It was just about the same size and pink color of a pencil eraser, and as he gently moved his finger back and forth, he leaned over and kissed her one more time. The softness of her lips, the even softer skin of her nipple, which wrinkled and hardened under his touch, every inch of her was beyond beautiful.

"You're not mad, are you?"

"No."

"You sure?"

"Olivia. I swear I'm not mad."

It all started so naturally. One minute they were in the elevator talking excitedly about the murders and Mr. Marshall and Grant and Arm and Hammer and how everything was going to turn out okay; then what began as a hug turned into a kiss. In his room, when they started making out, she had seemed totally into it. In fact, she had been the one to pull off her tee shirt first and made no move to stop him when he reached over and unhooked her bra. The short little gasp that escaped from her while he was kissing her left tit almost made him come right then and there, and once he pulled off his jeans, she'd been quick to follow. There was a tattoo of a lightning bolt on her ass. He was lying on top of Olivia, both of them practically naked, and the hallucinogenic thought crossed his mind that in the next minute he would actually be fucking Olivia Werner. His hand groped for the waistband of her thong but just as he made contact, he felt her hand on top of his. Her body tensed.

"No. Please don't," she whispered.

"Huh?" He swallowed hard, removed his hand, and rolled off her so they were side by side on his bed, Nate staring up at the dumb glow-in-the-dark constellations stickers on the ceiling instead of down at his boxers and what looked like a pup tent.

"I don't want to do it . . . not so soon." She told him how she always jumped into things too fast; she wanted it to be different with him.

"Look, if I have to wait, I can wait," he replied. "I just want to be with you."

"I heart you, Nate," and making the outline of a heart with her index fingers, smiling in a way that said she knew she was being a dork but also was half-serious, she kissed him again, both her arms wrapped tightly around his waist, their bodies pressed so close together he could feel the TCB lightning bolt digging into his chest. That was when his cell started ringing again. This time Olivia said maybe he'd better pick up. And sure enough, it was exactly who he expected—his mother.

Chapter 67

TRAFFIC WAS HEAVY ON AMSTERDAM, A STALLED CAR THE PROBLEM. Rannie tried calming herself by attempting to figure out more of the puzzle. Perhaps Jem Marshall, not Ms. Hollins, was the mischief maker all along, responsible for the glass of Coke on her desk, the creepy notes. He probably had been told of the one sent to Tut. Rannie could envision Ms. Hollins, in her soft drawl, saying something along the order of, "Jem, Larry's received a threat. He thinks it's nothing. But you should know..." Jem Marshall had heard Augusta light into Rannie for snooping. He'd caught Rannie searching through the school phone log... and perhaps she hadn't been so clever about concealing his personal file.

It took ten endless minutes before the cab finally turned onto her street. However, a "Say It With Flowers" truck was double-parked by her building, and the cars stalled in front of her cab were honking in staccato bursts that became ever more insistent the longer the truck didn't budge. She considered paying now, then cautioned herself to remain right where she was, fidgeting with her trusty blue pencil, until finally a delivery guy exited her building and jumped into the passenger seat of the flower truck. It drove off a moment later, allowing other cars to move and the cab to drop her directly at her doorstep.

Keys already in hand (but no Mace, alas!), she sprinted from the cab and buzzed the intercom, a signal to Nate that she was on her way up. Prudently she checked over her shoulder before unlocking the inner door and entering the empty marble-columned lobby. Her heart was still hammering in her chest. Calm down, she commanded herself, and concentrated on the numbers on the brass plaque above the elevator as they blinked from four to three to two. The elevator creaked to the ground floor, wobbling up and down for a second before it came to full stop. The door opened; Rannie entered and was pushing the sixth-floor button when suddenly she felt herself shoved from behind with enough force to send her sprawling to her knees in the elevator cab. As the door closed, a hand clamped over her mouth, allowing her no time to scream.

The elevator started slowly ascending. Her head was wrenched back so far, it felt as if her neck would snap. She found herself staring upside down at the brim of a baseball cap. Please, please just be another ordinary mugger, she chanted, although her brain had already registered the fact that a knife pointing at her chest was grasped in her attacker's left hand. Right then a primitive terror, cold and liquid, seized hold of her, shuddering up her spine, turning her legs floppy as a rag doll's. Rannie groped wildly for the alarm button, her arms pinwheeling, making contact with empty air. Her teeth bit down on the thick canvas glove over her mouth; her legs kicked uselessly.

"Shhhhh, stop struggling. It won't do any good," Jem Marshall whispered almost soothingly in her ear while he hit the top floor button. At the sixth floor, when the elevator door opened, the sight of her umbrella stand, her front door only feet away, brought tears to her eyes. She made another futile attempt to break free, but the elevator door closed and the next time it opened, it was on ten.

Roughly he pulled her into the hallway towards the back stairs. Her brain was too frozen to remember who lived on the floor, whether anyone was likely to be home. *Go limp,* some atavistic instinct for self-preservation ordered. *Make it harder for him.* But he managed to drag her up half a flight of stairs, under his arm, with no more effort than a parent subduing a tantrum-throwing toddler. He wasn't even breathing heavily when he spotted the door to the rooftop and unlatched it.

"Scream and you're dead," he said quite matter-of-factly before scanning the rooftop space, a rectangular area of about 200 square feet hedged in by a low retaining wall. Satisfied that no one was around, he pushed her outside.

Oh, God! Oh, God! He was going to throw her over the rooftop, just like Ms. Hollins. Rannie's brain didn't seem capable of holding onto any other fact except this single horrifying one. She never came up here although she suspected her kids sometimes did with their friends, to drink or smoke pot late at night. Her eyes darted around, looking for a means of escape, but except for the wood-slatted water tower in front of them, the rooftop was nothing more than an expanse of fake grass. Lights glowed in some of the windows of the two taller apartment buildings to the north, but the sky was growing darker by the minute—already a deep menacing purple, like a bruise mark—and it was doubtful that anyone glancing out a window would take notice of them.

"I don't want to hurt you. I really don't," he said.

A flicker of hope. Maybe he wasn't going to kill her.

"It'll be quick. I promise."

Flicker extinguished. She was outraged at her own stupidity, forgetting the fucking obituary, a careless oversight that was going to leave her kids motherless.

"Sit."

Rannie lowered herself onto the fake grass right beside the dried-out, belly-up carcass of a water bug. He sat facing her, his back pressed against the access door. With the tip of the knife pointed at her, Jem Marshall said, "Remember what I said. Scream and I'll kill you right now."

She nodded. He had changed out of the gabardine trousers and blazer he'd been wearing at Chaps earlier and now, in addition to a Yankees cap, was clad in baggy jeans, an open North Face windbreaker, a Triple Five Soul hoodie underneath it.

"You had to keep poking around, didn't you? You just wouldn't stop." With his right hand, he pushed back the brim of the cap. His face was flushed, his hair damp with sweat. "When I saw the obituary you left in the printer, it hit me that John-o's been dead almost as long as he was alive." He turned his gaze toward Rannie. "He was a *great* brother. He understood me. Mother and Father bought whatever the shrinks said, but John-o knew I wasn't dangerous." He caught Rannie's eyes sliding to the six-inch kitchen knife. "I'm *not* a violent person. This is *your* fault. I warned you. Many times."

"He was your twin," she managed to say, sounding, she hoped, sympathetic. "It must have been a terrible loss."

"I'm not stupid so *don't* patronize me! I was just as smart as John-o," he sputtered vehemently. "When I took the SATs, I got a 790 on math—twenty points higher than John-o. One of the doctors at the hospital timed me, just like it was the real thing."

Life was beyond farcical: This was the ultimate truth, Rannie realized, that she would carry to the grave. Here this man was about to kill her and yet taking the time to brag about his SAT score. He was facing her, his legs sticking straight out in front of him. His choice of footwear, she now noticed, was bizarrely out of whack with the rest of the outfit. A pair of buttery leather Italian driving loafers, the kind with nubbly soles advertised in high-end catalogues. Rannie had always wondered who actually bought them; now she knew—homicidal maniacs.

"How'd you get in my building?"

"Easy. I was across the street waiting. A delivery truck arrived. I went over to your front door, told the delivery guy I forgot my keys and when he got buzzed in, in I went, too." Marshall shrugged and added in a condescending tone, "That's a risk you take living in a non-doorman building, I guess."

His wristwatch, with an expensive alligator band, told her it was now 6:15. If he was going to kill her, what was he waiting for and why was he so eager to chat? To justify himself? To boast? And why the clothes? Did he plan to make it look like a robbery gone bad? Her bag was only a foot away on its side. The tip of her cell phone was protruding. The possibility of distracting Marshall, hitting Nate's number, threw itself out like a lifeline. Had Nate thought to wonder why she wasn't in the apartment already? She'd buzzed him from downstairs.

Chapter 68

The same time

IT WAS MAYBE FIVE—NO, MORE LIKE TEN MINUTES—SINCE HIS MOTHER had buzzed up from the lobby. So where was she? Why had he and Olivia bothered scrambling to get dressed? The floor lamp in his room backlit the downy hair on Olivia's arms as she tucked her tee shirt into her jeans. Already the fact that only a few minutes ago she'd been undressed, in his bed, was becoming harder to believe. She raked a hand through her hair, which looked exactly the same afterwards, messy and choppy, a girl-band look. The Sergeant Pepper coat was lying on the floor beside her socks and high tops. She started dialing her cell.

"James, could you come get me?" A pause. Then Olivia nodded as if the guy could hear her. "On the West Side somewhere. Hold on." She turned to Nate. "What's your address?" He told her and Olivia relayed the information. "Okay, so like half an hour, you figure?"

Once she clicked off, he said, "You don't have to go."

"No, I better. What's taking your mom so long anyway?"

"She probably remembered there's nothing for dinner. The only thing we never run out of is peanut butter and jelly. It drives me crazy."

Chapter 69

A minute later

JEM MARSHALL NOTICED THE CELL PHONE PEEKING OUT OF HER PURSE AT the same instant Rannie did and read her mind. "Uh-uh. No calls." He turned it off before tossing it several feet away.

Play for time, that was all she could do now and hope some-one would miraculously appear to rescue her. The ledge was no more than fifteen feet away; he had close to a hundred pounds on her. Let's guess who'd lose in a struggle. "Look. May I ask you something?" Rannie attempted to keep her voice calm, curious, conversational.

"Why I had to kill them?"

Rannie nodded.

"Augusta overheard me at school, at the dance, asking to speak to myself. So I had no choice." He shrugged as if what happened to Ms. Hollins had been beyond his control—bad luck, fate, the stars, the domino theory, whatever. "When she resigned, I could tell she guessed I planted the roofies on Nate and was putting it together about Tut too."

"Why Nate? What'd he ever do to you!" she cried. No, no! Sounding mad was a bad move. Stifle maternal instinct for now. Think self-preservation.

"I had to make someone look guilty of Tut's murder, didn't I?" He sounded defensive, petulant. "And if Nate wasn't so hell bent on Stanford—well, this would have all turned out different."

"Differently," her inner copy editor ludicrously insisted. Forget about his fucking grammar! It doesn't matter! she told herself, while in the next instant a faint spark of hope suddenly glimmered before her. The pencil in her pocket. It was sharp, but could it inflict significant damage?

A dreamy expression flitted across his face. "Once I took over for John-o, it was almost like he hadn't died. . . . We were *twins*—we practically were the same person."

Rannie kept nodding and managed to inch a little closer to him, placing her hand casually inside her pocket.

"After I was released from the hospital, the only thing I never got used to was answering to his name," he went on. "Somebody'd call out, 'John-o,' and I'd turn, expecting to see him. At City Prep, I went back to Jem—it's short for Jeremy." Suddenly he grew irritated. "But you—*you* know that already. Jonathan Edwards Marshall. Jeremy Elliot Marshall. Who cares? It's not who you say you are, it's what you do! So what if I didn't go to Stanford?

"I tried explaining to Larry. . . . Oh, he was very courteous, as I knew he'd be, and asked if I'd like a drink. I expected he'd do that too, and I had the drugs with me—but that was only if he *made* me use them. At one point, I thought he understood. 'I promise you I'll do great things here at Chaps,' I told him. But no, he said there was no way I could remain at school. If he had just been more reasonable. You understand now?"

"Yes! Completely!"

"Good." There was a note of finality in his voice that made Rannie's heart pick up speed again. She tried not to think about herself plummeting to the ground. At the same time they both heard the sound of a door opening onto the back stairs. There was the heavy thud of magazines and newspapers dropping on the cement floor, something Rannie did herself each and every evening, followed by the door clicking shut.

Jem looked fearful now and turned businesslike. He whipped something out of his pocket. For a split second Rannie thought abject terror had warped her vision because what she saw in his hand couldn't be right. . . . It was a roll of duct tape.

"No!" she howled as he grabbed her, muffling her scream. As he ripped off a piece of tape, smacking it across her mouth, she could feel his chest heaving. Hers was too. And it was hard to breathe. What was going on? Was he some kind of pyscho overachiever—the Chaps murderer *and* the S.W.A.K. killer? Did the police have the wrong guy? Blood thrummed in her ears, she felt clammy, her hands and feet shot with pins and needles. She pointed to the duct tape in entreaty.

He ignored her, and poking around in her purse again, brought out her lipstick, newly purchased in the Marriott hotel shop. He looked at it distastefully, as if it smelled bad. "If you're thinking I'm the S.W.A.K. killer, wrong! I'm not some sicko. That guy is disgusting. He kills for fun."

Suddenly it dawned on her. He'd never had any intention of pushing her off a roof. He wanted to kill her in a way that seemed unrelated to the murders at Chaps. It was smart . . . in an insane, twisted way. It would throw off the police, make them wonder if they had the right guy in custody. Maybe make them think a copycat killer was suddenly on the loose.

He smeared his lips with lipstick. Bile started to rise in her throat and she was hyperventilating—short, choppy breaths huffing out of her nostrils, faster and faster.

"Close your eyes. I look ridiculous! I hate you for making me do this!"

Scrambling to his knees and clasping the back of her head, he drew her face to his and kissed her hard on the mouth, right over the duct tape. S.W.A.K. Sealed with a kiss. He pushed her down on her back and threw a leg over to straddle her.

Please, please, God, whatever happens, don't let Nate see my corpse. A terrible blinding fright threatened to overwhelm her, leave her a puddle of helpless ectoplasm, but Rannie forced herself to focus. The blue pencil. She gripped it in her fist. He was sitting on top of her now. From a distance, it might have looked as if they were fucking. His left arm swung back.

She made herself remember the self-defense class, points of vulnerability.

His face, lips insanely pink, swarmed above hers. There was only a foot between them. The knife in his hand had already begun a descending arc. Rannie willed every ounce of strength she possessed to flow into her right hand, and she thrust upward at his face.

Chapter 70

A second later

NATE HEARD A GLASS-SHATTERING SCREAM AT THE SAME TIME THE doorbell started buzzing furiously. Someone was pounding on the door too.

"Okay! *Okay!* I'm coming!" Nate shouted.

It wasn't his mother—it was a black guy in sweats.

"I'm a cop." His badge was out. "Where's your mother?"

Nate shook his head, frightened suddenly.

His gun pulled, the cop dashed through the back hall door toward the sound of the scream. Nate was right behind him. "Go back!" The cop ordered, but he didn't. At that moment, the universe consisted of his mother, no one else; her face was the only face he wanted to see. He took the stairs two at a time. With a longing he hadn't experienced since he was little, Nate called out to her, tears streaming down his face. "Ma, *please!*" But there was no answer.

He was at the ninth floor now.

"Holy shit!" he heard the cop say.

Fuck. Fuck. Fuck. Fuck. When Nate reached the rooftop, the cop was standing in the doorway, his gun still cocked, blocking his view.

Nate pushed past him and forced himself to look. The body was on its back. It took him a second to realize it was Mr. Marshall, and another second to realize he was dead.

"Ms. Bookman?" The cop shouted.

He heard his mother rasp back that she was okay. She was huddled by the water tower. Nate ran to her.

Chapter 71

The same time

RANNIE HAD SCRABBLED TO THE WATER TOWER ON ALL FOURS, LIKE AN animal, panting. She ripped off the duct tape, more tears pricking her eyes. "Help!" she whispered raggedly. Was he dead? She heard the sound of frantic footfalls thudding up the stairs. Then she heard Nate.

"Don't come up here!" she tried to warn Nate, but the words were barely audible even to herself.

In the next instant, she heard a man shouting her name. Nate reached her and flung himself on her, the funky, familiar smell of him suddenly the best smell in the world, and she was being told by an extremely good-looking black guy with dreadlocks that it was all over, Marshall was dead.

Somehow she found herself in the elevator with Nate—was the other man with them? The next moment she was in her living room. Her sense of time and what people told her was jumpy, out of order. Olivia Werner was there. The black guy was a cop. Peratta was there. Then Olivia wasn't. One detail didn't escape Rannie's notice, however—the vibe between Nate and Olivia. Sexual, teenage lust.

"Ma, *you* killed him!" Nate was shaking his head now in disbelief. The last time she'd heard admiration like this in his voice was when he'd discovered she could burp on command.

A cup of hot tea appeared. Rannie felt her head clearing bit by bit. Had she honestly ended another person's life? Jem Marshall would never draw another breath, eat another morsel, have a sleepless night because of her? It was a park bench cliché, albeit a true one, every mother's declaration of how she would kill for her child, but Rannie had killed for herself. She was horrified. She was glad.

Cupping the tea in both hands, more for its warmth than anything else, Rannie told the cops what had happened on the roof.

"A pencil! You definitely knew where to aim!"

"A self-defense class. But it was mostly luck," Rannie admitted modestly to Peratta.

The cops filled her in too. Or tried to. She was having trouble following. In the afternoon Peratta had brought in Armand Hammer for questioning. The dead billionaire art collector? But, no. It wasn't Armand Hammer but Arm *and* Hammer, evidently a nickname for the two drug dealers who used to hang around Turtle Park. They confessed that Jem Marshall had approached them the day of Tut's murder. "He bought some GHB and roofies," Peratta said, "and paid them a few hundred bucks extra to shut up and relocate."

After their confession, Peratta had gone to Chaps to arrest Marshall, but he wasn't there. Another car was dispatched to the Ross River's End. Meanwhile, a plainclothes cop in a parked car—the good-looking black guy—was keeping watch on Dolores Court, making sure Olivia and Nate stayed put, as they'd been told. The cop said, "I see a man approach the building and enter the same time as a delivery guy with flowers. But I didn't think anything of it. It didn't look like Marshall—the clothes fooled me. I see you go in a minute later. I'm thinking everything's fine until the sergeant calls in saying nobody knows where Marshall is—he's not at school, not at his apartment and I figure I better check things out in your apartment."

"Did he tell you anything?" Sergeant Peratta asked Rannie.

"Plenty. He confessed to killing both Mr. Tut and Ms. Hollins. He kept insisting that he hadn't wanted to murder anyone, that he had no choice." Rannie explained about Marshall's true identity. She produced the piece of duct tape from the pocket of her jacket, the adhesive side now covered with lint and hair, the "kiss" mark on the smooth side still visible. "He was trying to make it look like a S.W.A.K. murder. To throw off the police."

Peratta smirked and lifted his eyebrows. "No chance of that. We nailed the right guy. Confession, evidence, the works."

"He thought he was his twin? I don't get it," Nate said. "And Mr. Tut found out?"

Rannie recounted her phone call with the admissions officer at Stanford.

"Ma, so if Mr. Tut hadn't called to put in a good word for me, maybe he'd still be alive!"

"Nate, Jem Marshall was nuts. He was willing to do anything to keep his crazy charade going."

Then she heard the frustrated wail of an ambulance below in the street.

"That'll be the ME guys," Peratta said.

"I want to see the body." Rannie put down the tea and stood, her legs still wobbly.

"You don't, Ms. Bookman," Peratta said. "Believe me."

"Listen to him, Ma."

But she insisted.

By the time the elevator emerged on ten and she made it to the rooftop she could see all manner of law enforcement people outside. Guys with cameras. Guys maneuvering a stretcher. She watched them carefully lift a body and begin shimmying a black plastic bag up over it. For an instant, she caught Jem Marshall's face. *I did that?*

I had to.

His mouth was stretched open in a wide yowl of surprise, his lips the primrose pink of her lipstick. It was not a becoming color on him. His left eye, at least the little that was left of it, looked like a mush of red jelly. Sticking out of the corner, right by his nose, was the last inch of her blue pencil, capped in a bright yellow eraser "helmet."

Making a mental note to buy new lipstick at the first opportunity, Rannie doubled over and threw up, blowing chunks of half-digested peanut butter sandwich and watery tea all over the fake grass.

PENCIL-PACKIN' MAMA ERASES PREP SCHOOL KILLER

COPY EDITOR DELETES COPYCAT KILLER

PREP SCHOOL MURDERS SOLVED:
OOPS! IT'S THE HEADMASTER

October 24—He had a six-inch kitchen knife. All she had was a six-inch pencil. But last night at six P.M. on the rooftop of a West Side apartment building, a plucky and resourceful copy editor fatally stabbed her attacker, the headmaster of the exclusive Chapel School who, according to sources in the NYPD, is guilty of two recent murders there. Jeremy Marshall, 42, was pronounced dead at the scene.

"He was making it look like some sort of copycat S.W.A.K. murder. So there'd be no connection to the murders at the school. But she got him good, the pencil went in his left eye, straight to his brain," said Sergeant Thomas Peratta, referring to Miranda Bookman, 43, the quick-thinking grammar guru whose son attends Chapel School. Sergeant Peratta would not comment but sources close to the investigation confirm that the deceased murdered both A. Law-rence Tutwiler and Augusta Hollins, two longtime Chapel School teachers.

Headmaster Jeremy Elliot Marshall came with an impressive résumé. The only problem—he wasn't who he said he was. Marshall had been masquerad-ing as his twin since his brother's death in a plane crash in 1986. At that time, Jeremy Marshall was a patient at a psychiatric hospital in Los Angeles, California.

Reached by telephone, a spokeswoman from Car-ruthers Hospital would say only that Marshall was released in September of 1987.

Mary Ellen Chase of Palo Alto, California, attended junior high and high school with the Marshall twins. In a telephone interview, she remembered, "Jem Marshall was always strange—a math whiz but very withdrawn, no friends; the only thing that got him excited were role-playing games, you know, like 'Dun-geons and Dragons.' And the only person he related to was his brother. John-o was a terrific guy, a born leader.

"Right after Christmas sophomore year, Jem didn't return to school. The story, according to the family, was he transferred to a boarding school but word got out—he'd tried to kill himself and was in a nut house."

Dr. Henry Brandt, a psychiatrist and author of *Almost the Death of Me: Grief in Identical Twins* had this to say: "I have no prior knowledge of this particular case. However, a twin with a marginal, unstable personality, someone who depends on his sibling as his guide in the everyday world, would feel defenseless without his brother, utterly abandoned. So, yes, I can imagine an emotionally disturbed twin 'becoming' his dead brother as a way of coping. It's not that different from people with multiple personalities. When being oneself is unbearable, a person may slip into someone else."

Marshall's first victim, A. Lawrence Tutwiler, who died twelve days ago, discovered Marshall's true identity accidentally from an admissions director at Stanford University where Marshall claimed to have gone. When confronted, Jeremy Marshall poisoned the 83-year-old college advisor with GHB, a so-called date rape drug. It is believed that Marshall's second victim, Augusta Hollins, an English teacher who was pushed off the roof of a school building Tuesday night, stumbled on information implicating Marshall in the first murder.

Last night, speaking in front of the West Side apartment house where he and his mother live and where the attack occurred, Nathan Lorimer, 18, told reporters that his mother had independently uncovered Marshall's true identity earlier in the day. "He attacked her in our elevator and took her up to the roof to kill her. He's a big guy and she's like almost a midget. But my mother nailed him!"

Miranda Bookman was taken to St. Luke's Hospital where she was treated for minor bruises and released.

Two days ago, Howard Rechsler, a salesman at a Staples supplies store, was arrested in connection with the three S.W.A.K. homicides. When asked if there was any chance that the wrong man was in custody, Sergeant Peratta responded, "Zero chance. There are DNA matches on Rechsler for each murder. His confession included details kept from the public, and lipsticks belonging to the victims were lined up, like trophies, on a shelf. Jeremy Marshall was trying to throw us off the school murders by staging a copycat killing."

Chapter 72

Saturday morning

TIM ARRIVED WITH NEWSPAPERS UNDER HIS ARM, A BROWN LUNCH BAG, and a bunch of orange and yellow tulips in a cone of wrapping paper. Nate was out with Olivia somewhere—Nate had actually spoken her name instead of the usual "I'm meeting someone." Did that mean it was serious?

Alice, who'd come from New Haven last night, answered the door and after Rannie made introductions, her daughter turned with raised eyebrows, tilted her head to the side and mouthed the word "hot."

Tim was in running clothes. He had on a Red Sox cap and a pair of wire-rimmed sunglasses. "Extra copies for you," he said, depositing newspapers on the hall table. "For the scrapbook." He handed over the flowers and inspected her. "You up for a walk in the park?"

"I'm resourceful and plucky—sure!"

"Ooh, very dangerous to start believing your own press."

Last night he'd called upon returning from Amherst. He'd heard the news on 1010 WINS. His was the first of many calls that Nate and Alice fielded. Joan checked in and broke some interesting news of her own.

"They're appointing me interim head," Joan said.

"Great. A woman heading Chaps. It's about time."

"Rannie, the operative word is interim. I was a public school principal. What qualifications do I have?"

"Well, one—you are who you say you are, and two—you're not going to murder anybody. So right off the bat you've got it all over your predecessor."

Then Joan said, "And my first official act is suspending the Lilys and Elliot for the semester. They sent Tut a threatening note before he died. A nasty prank, can you believe it? Jem was letting them off easy, but I'm suspending them for the semester, and I don't care how loudly David Ross screams."

Mary offered to treat Rannie to a week at the Golden Door spa to recover. When Rannie declined, Mary said, "Then you must rest and really take it easy. My Lord, darling! After what you've been through." Her solution was for Earla to come and cook dinner all next week. "Earla's nodding her head so don't say no. We insist!"

Soon after, a case of liquor was delivered from Morrells, including a bottle of Dalwhinnie. Daisy's note, handwritten in girlish, prep-school print, said, "As soon as you're feeling up to it, I hope we may get together and have a drink in memory of Larry and Augusta. It's all just too sad!"

The only other call Rannie took was from her mother, whose cruise ship had docked in Miami and who was spending a couple of days at a friend's condo before flying back to Cleveland. "Louise and I were watching Bryan Williams and suddenly there's your building! And I see Nate talking to reporters! I'm gone two weeks and look what happens."

Rannie found her green water jug and plumped the tulips in it, then announced to Tim that she was ready for an outing.

"Nope, sorry, she's doing 'Oprah' that day," she could hear Al as they stood waiting for the elevator. "No, that's 'The Today Show.' Look, I'll have to have our people get back to your people."

"My publicist," Rannie tossed her head toward the apartment.

"You fought for your life, Rannie. I respect that, I really do. So now it's your fifteen minutes. I'm with your daughter—go for it."

It was beautiful outside, one of those last gasp of Indian summer days. In Riverside Park, they walked as far as the promenade and occupied a bench facing the late morning sun. Tim asked how she was doing.

"Good, but still achy in places." Last night, after taking one of the horse-sized capsules in the tiny white envelope sent home with her from St. Luke's Hospital, Rannie had curled up in a ball on her bed. The next thing she knew it was eight A.M. "That last moment, on the roof, I thought—okay, I'm going to die. But there wasn't any 'This is your life, Rannie Bookman,' wrap-up. I was just pissed at myself."

Tim pulled out two bottles of Snapple from the brown bag. "Take your pick." There was a lemon-flavored one and a peach. Rannie chose peach, which he opened for her.

"You knew more than you let on, didn't you?" Rannie asked.

"Not that much. I knew David Ross was in Atlantic City by five P.M. the Monday Tut died so he had an alibi that was air-tight, vacuum-sealed. And I knew Augusta Hollins was never a suspect. She was with a friend that evening."

Yes, Daisy Satterthwaite. "But the first date we had, at your bar, you mentioned the police finding a pair of earrings at Tut's apartment, and you intimated the cops didn't believe Tut had ever received a threatening note."

"A pair of earrings *was* found. They belonged to Ms. Hollins. She told the cops that she'd stayed over a few nights, nursing Mr. Tut. And the police never actually did *see* a note. That was true too."

"But they believed one existed. You made it sound like they didn't, that she was a suspect."

"Look, I didn't know you from Adam. And you were pissing me off with all the questions. Rannie, cops tell me stuff, I'm not *supposed* to pass it on." Now Tim took a swig of Snapple. "I told you about the glass with the fingerprints. And the liquor bottle being clean. You got that out of me. And I also tried to tell you to stop worrying so much about your son. Right from the start, the cops didn't think it was a kid. Ross was who they liked at first."

"Tim, do you think David Ross suspected Jem?"

"Maybe. If he did, Ross probably figured Marshall was doing him a favor. And maybe if Ross had the goods on Marshall, he was saving it as—"

"As a bargaining chip."

"Exactly." Tim paused. "You'll see this later today in the papers—Ross was blackmailing Mr. Tut. The police found a notebook at school that Tut kept with dates of phone calls, meetings, even photocopies of certain records Ross made. Ross gave them to Tut as proof of what he knew—Tut had a daughter. Ross was threatening to go public if Tut didn't get the crown prince into Harvard."

Rannie nodded. Rannie remembered Ms. Hollins mentioning how Mr. Tut appeared so troubled in the weeks before his death. Ms. Hollins had assumed more threatening notes had come. Rannie now guessed the likely source of Mr. Tut's anxiety was David Ross's threats of blackmail.

"Will he be indicted?"

"No. The notebook can't be used as evidence, but sometimes just creating a nice big tabloid stink is worth it. D.A.s love rattling the chains of apes like Ross." Then Tim rubbed the back of her neck soothingly and turned slightly to her. "Look, Rannie, I need to talk."

Although she couldn't see his eyes behind the sunglasses, his tone was serious, nervous.

"Fine. Just as long as the word murder doesn't come up."

"I can't promise you that, but it has nothing to do with Chaps."

"So talk."

"It's about what you saw in my room," he turned to her. "The thing from the police academy," he added as if she had needed any elaboration. He paused for another swig of iced tea, then sat for a moment, holding the bottle in both hands between his splayed legs, nodding a couple of times as if encouraging himself to keep going. "Look. I want to explain.... You picked up on me being an alcoholic, right?"

"I'm aware you don't drink."

"I stopped sixteen years ago. I'm in AA. The call I got the first night we met, when we were in that coffee shop.... It was from a friend scared he was going to drink."

"I think it's wonderful you're—"

"No. Let me finish. I was one mean fuck when I was drunk. The whole time I was on the force I drank ... and the car crash, the one that killed my wife, I told you I was at the wheel, didn't I?"

She nodded. "Were you drunk?"

"Shit-faced. We were fighting. We'd been at a party. She wanted to drive but I wouldn't let her. Told her she could get in the car and shut up or walk home. She chose the car, like I knew she would because she didn't want to make a scene. I still can remember slamming my foot down on the gas. I *wanted* to scare her. I didn't even make it two blocks before I plowed into a tree. I got out of the car without a scratch."

Although she had never seen him anything but stone cold sober, Rannie could picture him drunk—drunk and nasty and scary—much more easily than she would have wished. He seemed to intuit that, because he waited and nodded, as if he was satisfied that she understood and saw him for who he was, before going on.

"A couple of my buddies who'd been at the party came running. And when the ambulance arrived, one of them told me, 'You shut the fuck up. We're handling this.' So they did. They flashed their badges and the EMT guys let them take me home while they're dealing with my wife. Putting her in a body bag. I watched them."

The cold glass of the ice tea bottle felt suddenly colder in her hands.

"So I killed somebody, somebody I loved, and I got away with it."

"I don't know what I'm supposed to say."

"What's to say?" He shrugged a shrug of self-contempt. "My buddies, they told me, 'Don't think we're doing this for you. We're doing it for Chris. He's got no mother now. Now all he's got is you, that poor fucking kid.'

"I resigned from the force. A week after the funeral I went into rehab. One of my sisters stayed with Chris. Twenty-eight days later, when I got out, I started trying to become a father and a human being and that's what I've been doing ever since."

"Why are you telling me this?"

"I'm not saying I love you; I don't, and maybe that'll never happen, but meeting you . . . it's the first time since Deborah that I want more than sex from a woman. You get on my nerves but I like that. I *like* feeling annoyed. I want you, Rannie, I want to be with you but I don't want you thinking I'm somebody I'm not."

"Your son? Does he know?"

"Yeah, Chris's known for a couple of years now. One night, we're having dinner and out of nowhere he comes right out and asks. He always half-suspected but didn't want to know for sure. I don't blame him. I'm his father. I'm all he's got and yet it's my fault I'm all he's got."

Rannie nodded. In answer to her question about how Chris reacted, Tim frowned. "For a few months it was rough; Chris talked about moving out, living with Deborah's parents, like he owed it to them. He's never going to forgive me, not completely, and why should he? The truth is I don't want him to."

That Rannie understood. Sometimes forgiveness wasn't an option.

"Is a bar the smartest business to be in?"

He laughed sardonically. "It's like a penance, I guess. It's the Catholic in me—my version of a hair shirt. Keeps what I am smack in my face. I need that temptation right in front of me."

Rannie could almost hear her mother. "You don't have enough problems of your own, Rannie? This man has enough baggage to get to the moon and back!"

"I haven't been serious about any man, not since Peter and I broke up.... And there are lots of times I wonder if even my marriage counts as a serious relationship. I liked it that Peter never seemed all that committed. I knew down deep I wasn't either."

"So with me? Is it just about the sex?" Tim had taken off his glasses now. He was as naked as if he had on no clothes.

His eyes had a depth that scared her. What did they have in common? Nothing. And yet she could not look away from him. "No, it isn't. It's more."

Again the grin that reminded her of a small boy, one who'd just received something he wanted but hadn't expected. "So are you in?"

"Yeah, I'm in."

"Good." He stuck out his hand, half-jokingly. Nevertheless, she extended hers and they shook on it.

"I'll be back—" He looked down at his watch. "Twenty minutes max."

Rannie watched him for a moment as he loped off, his finely

shaped legs pumping up and down with the regularity of pistons. Then she opened the grocery bag which had contained the Snapples. In it were two sandwiches on Wonder bread, cut in neat triangles inside separate baggies. Rannie opened one. The ratio of peanut butter to raspberry jam was just as she liked, a little heavy on the jam. She smiled and took a bite.

© Jim O'Connor

JANE O'CONNOR, an editor at a major New York publishing house, has written more than thirty books for children, including *The New York Times* bestselling Fancy Nancy books. This is her first adult novel.

Jane O'Connor